She pulled off the white bathing cap and shook out her long black hair—the blackest hair I'd ever seen, long and straight and almost blue.

Christoph was talking, but I was looking at the girl, who was stepping up the ramp, wrapping a white towel around her throat. She had brown legs and black eyes and long black eyelashes.

"Hallo, Christophero," she said. "Will you drive the boat for me?"

"My sister Elizabeth," said Bobby. "Mr. Ellis, aus Amerika."

"We call her Lili," said Christoph.

———————————

PLEASE TURN THE PAGE
FOR THE RAVE REVIEWS OF

A PRINCESS IN BERLIN

·A PRINCESS IN· BERLIN·

ARTHUR R·G·SOLMSSEN

BALLANTINE BOOKS • NEW YORK

Library of Congress Catalog Card Number: 80-19250

ISBN 0-345-29807-1

This edition published by arrangement with Little, Brown and Company

Manufactured in the United States of America

First Ballantine Books Edition: October 1981

Cover photograph by Anthony Loew

Denk' ich an Deutschland in der Nacht,
Dann bin ich um den Schlaf gebracht. . . .
——Heinrich Heine, *Nachtgedanken*

PROLOGUE

THURSDAY, JUNE 15, 1922

I woke up when the door opened. At first I didn't know where I was, but then I saw Christoph Keith. The upstairs hall behind him was dark, but there must have been a light on downstairs, because I could see his face and his dripping trench coat.

"Peter? Are you awake?"

"I am now. What's the matter?" I turned on the bedside lamp. He limped heavily into the room, closed the door and leaned against it.

"Did you know there is a car parked in the stable?" he asked. "An Austro-Daimler?"

"Yes, I think Kaspar brought it this evening."

"Kaspar brought it? Kaspar cannot drive a car."

"Well, I guess the other fellow drove it."

"Which other fellow?"

"I forget his name. The older man who was with Kaspar the other day, the one you told to get out of here."

"Tillessen? Tillessen brought that car here?"

"Yes, and there was a third man, but I didn't talk to them, I just saw them from the window . . . Why don't you ask Kaspar?"

"Kaspar isn't home, of course." Christoph emitted a sigh, walked across the room, sat down in the wicker armchair and held his face in his hands. I saw that his trench coat was soaked; he must have walked from the trolley stop. Why hadn't he taken the coat off before he came upstairs?

"What's wrong, Christoph?"

He moved his hand away from his eyes and looked at me for a long moment before he answered.

"Peter, I would give anything in the world not to involve you, but I must ask your help. This may be hard for an American to believe, but a German officer does not necessarily learn how to drive a car. We always had

1

drivers in the army, since the War of course we have no
car . . . I cannot drive, Peter. And I cannot start a car
without a key. Will you help me?"

As we were moving through the huge dark kitchen,
Christoph whispered: "One moment, I must get something
from the cellar," and suddenly the lights went on and
there was Meier, the butler, white as chalk, trousers with
suspenders over a night shirt, pointing an ancient cavalry
carbine: "Was ist los, Herr Oberleutnant?"

A hissed command sent the old man back up the
kitchen stairs, and Christoph descended into the basement.
While he was down there I thought about what I would
need. I found a short sharp paring knife in a drawer, and
took a box of matches from the stove. Christoph came
back up the cellar stairs. He was carrying a sledgehammer.

It was a big, expensive car, and it smelled of leather. I
lay on my back under the steering wheel while Christoph
lighted matches for me. I had never even seen an Austro-
Daimler before, so it took six matches for me to find the
right wires. I cut them.

"All right," I said, and sat up behind the wheel.

"You can start it?"

"I think so."

"Please make as little noise as possible, and don't turn
on the lights until we are out on the street."

Brake off, clutch out, hand throttle, choke . . . I
reached down and twisted the wires together fast. No
shocks, no sparks, the engine —still warm — turned over
and caught. Cautiously I eased in the clutch, and we
rolled out of the dry darkness of the stable into the
streaming darkness of the night. I steered with one hand
and flipped switches with the other, trying to start the
windshield wipers.

Jagdschloss Grunewald said the sign. *Einfahrt Verbo-
ten!*

"Is there a chain across there?" I asked, squinting
through the rain.

"No," said Christoph. "German people obey signs. Drive
into the courtyard and then turn sharp to the right."

Our headlights swept the dark empty hunting lodge as

I turned across the cobbled courtyard into what looked like a bridle path.

"Hey, this isn't paved," I said, shifting down into first gear. "This is just sand. We might get stuck in here."

"Go as far as you can."

A deep forest of Scotch pines. Every time the path twisted to the left I could see the misty surface of the lake reflecting our headlight beams.

"All right, in a few meters the path divides," said Christoph, leaning forward to peer through the wipers. "You take the one to the right, away from the water."

"Christoph, won't you please tell me what we're doing?"

"Better not. . . . There is the fork! Give gas, we must climb now."

I was sure we were going to get stuck. This new path was barely wide enough for the car, which lumbered up the hill between walls of thick shrubbery.

As we reached the top Christoph told me to watch for a barricade; a second later our headlights revealed a pile of logs blocking the path.

"Stop," said Christoph. "Turn the engine off but leave the lights on." He opened the door, stepped out, and walked around the front of the car. I saw that he was carrying the sledgehammer. I reached down and jerked the ignition wires apart. The engine stopped—and the lights went out. Now the only sound was rain splattering through the leaves.

"I'm sorry," I said. "I guess the lights were connected to the ignition. Do you want me to cross the wires again?"

"No, it's not necessary. Bring the matches. They are on the seat."

I got out of the car and saw that he had unfastened the latch and opened the hood.

"Light a match and hold it over here, please."

I lit a match and looked at the huge exposed engine.

"Please move a little to the left," said Christoph, and as I did I heard him step back and grunt, and with one tremendous overhead swing he brought the sledge crashing down on the engine. It crushed the air filter and smashed the carburetor, and suddenly the air reeked of gasoline. I dropped the match and stepped on it.

"Don't light another," said Christoph.

"Don't worry!"

"Stand back, it's not enough." In the darkness, another grunt, another, more resonant, crash echoed through the forest — and this time we heard the hiss of escaping steam.

Water splashed upon the sand. He had cracked the engine block.

I felt him approach me in the darkness. He was breathing heavily.

"You think I'm crazy, don't you? Perhaps I am crazy."

"I think you don't want anybody to use this car."

"Yes, that's correct." He put his hand on my shoulder. His arm trembled. "You are a good friend, Peter. I thank you. And I hope this will not cause trouble for you."

"It might help if you would tell me what's going on."

"I'm afraid you will find out soon enough what's going on. Now see how far into the bushes you can throw this hammer, and get my cane out of the car. We have a long walk in the rain before the sun comes up."

BOOK ONE

HOW I GOT THERE

PARIS
1922

I went to Berlin because it was cheap. The trip really began in Paris, the evening my father's lawyer summoned me.

No, that's not fair. He didn't summon me. He sent me a cheerful pneumatique inviting me to dinner at the Grand-Véfour.

Grand-Véfour, a lovely place: mirrors, paintings on glass, red velvet banquettes, and windows looking right into the gardens of the Palais-Royal. The dinner was magnificent. I could not help wondering if the bill would somehow be charged to my old man — knowing I could live for a month on what this was costing — but it didn't matter, because George Graham had ordered a couple of very dry martinis the moment we sat down.

I was touched. A year ago, in Philadelphia, nobody would have allowed me anywhere near a martini, and that had nothing to do with Prohibition.

George Graham is the nicest partner in Conyers & Dean, the firm that has always handled my family's legal matters. He must have been in his early forties, a success, a leader in his firm, a leader in his profession . . . and what was I? A recovering invalid? A student? An aspiring painter? Or a bum who preferred the sidewalks of Montparnasse to the bond department of Drexel & Co.?

"Cheers," said George Graham, lifting his martini.

"Cheers," said I, lifting mine.

George Graham had kind blue eyes. He was the one they always sent when they wanted to be nice. I knew perfectly well what he had come to tell me.

"Peter, the War's been over four years," he began.

"Been over five for me, Mr. Graham. They shipped me home in April, 'seventeen."

"I know that, Peter. And you were in . . . well, an unhappy condition."

7

"Unhappy condition? I was strapped into my bunk! They kept me so full of morphine that I slept from Brest to Hoboken. Didn't know what day it was. Didn't know what *month* it was!"

"You've made a splendid recovery, boy!"

"Painted the azaleas at Friends Hospital."

"The doctors did a wonderful job. And so did you. You've recovered your equilibrium."

"Well, I can get a glass to my mouth without spilling it. I got so I could get through dinner at home without crying."

"Peter, you're sitting here and having a martini and discussing this painful subject without the slightest loss of control. You've made a complete recovery. All the doctors say so. And your pictures . . . the sketch you made of Walter Smith is so good we're thinking of commissioning a real portrait, for the office —"

"— so they want me to come home and sell bonds."

"Not at all!" He put his drink down and leaned forward. "Peter, your parents want you to complete your education. You left college in your sophomore year, didn't you? You've got no credentials to earn a living. Selling bonds was just an opportunity offered by one of your father's patients, but that's not . . . You *know* what your father really wants."

I know what he really wants. He's the most famous surgeon in Philadelphia, and so was his father, and so was his grandfather. You can see their portraits along the halls of the University Hospital. Maybe not the *best* surgeons, but certainly the best known. People felt better just mentioning their names.

When I dropped out of Harvard to join the American Field Service my parents were delighted. Ambulances, wounded soldiers, obviously a step in the right direction. Of course I didn't do it in a spirit of helping wounded people. It was mob psychology.

It is hard to reconstruct the spirit of those times, but it overwhelmed us: the Hun was raping Belgium and driving toward Paris; babies were having their hands chopped off with bayonets; some Americans living at Neuilly bought ambulances and called for American drivers. The thing caught on, especially in the colleges. At Harvard they drove an ambulance right into Memorial Hall, some fellows who had already been on the Marne made speeches, the band played "La Marseillaise," the College gave us permission to drop out, we had to buy our own uniforms and equipment, my father wrote an enthusiastic letter (enclosing a check for a thousand dollars and the required certificate of non-German parentage!) and next thing we were all on the *Aquitania*, headed for Le Havre. The atmosphere was college outing, a patriotic camping trip complete with sleeping bags and all-night singing ("There's a Long, Long Trail A-Winding, into the Land of My Dreams") in the blacked-out first-class dining hall, and the only hint of the future was in the tired eyes of the *Aquitania*'s officers as they silently observed our antics.

"Well, of course your father wants you in medical school," said George Graham. "But you've got to finish college first."

"A twenty-four-year-old sophomore?"

"Why, sure. You'll get much more out of it, and the others will defer to you —"

I doubted that. I doubted it all through dinner, while we talked about other things. George Graham was leaving on the morning train for Cherbourg, going home. He had been in Paris for several weeks, investigating the facts behind a will contest Conyers & Dean was handling. He told me about it: a rich old lady from Philadelphia had adopted a young Frenchman as her son and left him a couple of million dollars when she died. Had he used undue influence? Had she been told that he had served a jail term for embezzlement? Did that make any difference? Should it make any difference?

Not to me. What mattered to me, as George Graham tried to interest me in the facts of his depressing case, was that he found his message to me so difficult to deliver that he put it off until his last evening.

When the coffee came, he couldn't put it off any longer. My father wanted me home. Now.

"The agreement was a year in Paris, to paint, to complete your recuperation, to find out what you really want to do with yourself. The year's up, isn't it?"

"So he's going to stop my money?"

George Graham nodded. "One more check — a very generous one so that you can finish your semester at the Beaux Arts, get out of your lease, buy passage home — but then that's all, Peter. You can't expect them to support you here indefinitely."

"But I've really been working, I could show you what I've done —"

"I'd like very much to see what you've done, but have you sold anything?"

"I sold Mr. Smith that sketch of Walter, and I sold Miss Boatwright a little portrait of Joanne. . . . She was in the hospital with me."

"Have you sold anything over here?"

"That's awfully difficult, Mr. Graham. I don't know anybody —"

"Of course it's difficult, we all know that, and that's why you've got to settle down and learn something that will provide a living. You're twenty-four years old, Peter, and you've got to learn a trade."

"Isn't painting a trade?"

"Not if there's no market for your pictures."

"Mr. Graham, can I ask you a question: Do you agree with them?"

He looked out the window for a moment before he turned back to answer.

"The Friendly Persuasion, Peter. Your people believe in honest labor. Maybe even more than Presbyterians. Certainly more than us Episcopalians. You know that."

"A Quake can't be an artist?"

"I didn't say that. But I'm not sure that a Friend will support an artist indefinitely. He would expect the artist — if he's good enough — to pay his way. If we think of patrons of the arts, who do we think of? Byzantine emperors? Medici popes? Henry Tudor and Charles Stuart? We don't think so much of George Fox and William Penn, do we?"

I had to smile. "You're a good lawyer, Mr. Graham. But it still hurts."

After dinner we strolled through the cool April evening, straight down the Rue St.-Honoré to the Place Vendôme. George Graham was staying at the Ritz, where he was to meet with a French lawyer who was helping with the will contest.

"This lawyer had to take a couple of German bankers out to dinner, so they may still be with him, but he promised to get rid of them as soon as possible. I don't suppose you'd like to show the town to a couple of German bankers, would you?" George Graham's eyes twinkled.

Remember this was 1922. The war was less than four years behind us. Most Frenchmen and many Americans hated the Germans — all Germans — with a passionate, personal kind of hatred.

I never did. I hated the Kaiser, I hated what little I had read about Bismarck and Prussian militarism, and of course the invasion of Belgium inspired me to join the Field Service, but when I got to France I soon saw that the ordinary German soldier was just as much a victim of the system as any other soldier. That wasn't all, though. Underneath my consciousness was the influence of Else Westerich.

In my grandfather's time, and in my father's time, American medical students who could afford it went to German universities, especially for advanced training, and doctors who had done this tour looked down their noses at doctors who hadn't. My father went beyond that: I wouldn't get as much out of the experience unless I spoke fluent German, and the only way to learn fluent German was to learn it as a child, so Fräulein Else Westerich came to live with us in 1906, when I was eight. She taught me German, slowly and gently. She played the piano and taught me German songs. She taught me "Hamburg ist ein schönes Städtchen." and she taught me "Nun ade, du mein lieb' Heimatland" and later she taught me other things too, and she left us when I was fourteen in circumstances I have taught myself not to remember, although one doctor at Friends Hospital got me to talk about her while I was full of morphine. Maybe it helped. Maybe it didn't.

The Ritz Bar was dimly lighted and smelled pleasantly of Scotch and cigarette smoke and perfume. At first I thought it was filled entirely with Americans.

"No, there they are," said George Graham, his hand on my arm, guiding me toward a corner table, where three men turned around, saw us, and stood up. I don't remember the French lawyer at all, but I remember that he made the introductions in English. Baron von Something was as short as I but handsome in a slicked-down, doe-eyed, almost Latin way. Herr Keith needed a cane to get out of his chair. Then he towered above me, gaunt

and skinny; teeth gleamed below his rather British cavalry moustache as he shook my hand, grinning.

"I think Mr. Ellis and I have met before," he said.
Quite overwhelmed, I was pumping his hand and grinning too.

2.

VERDUN
1916

It happened on the road from Verdun to Bras, a demol-
ished village on the left bank of the Meuse, just as dawn
was breaking that April morning in 1916. It happened
so fast that I've never been able to reconstruct it very
clearly.

I was driving back empty. Since this particular road
was sometimes under fire we preferred to drive at night,
but at night you couldn't see the craters and for a while
we were losing more cars to accidents than to German
artillery, so they told us to wait for dawn.

I had brought the last load down at sunset. I was
counting on a whole night's sleep but I didn't get it because they had crammed in one with a terrible wound in
his bowels and they didn't bandage it right or something,
and the whole back of the ambulance was awash in
blood and excrement—the man was dead when they un-
loaded anyway — and after I waited in line to tank up I
had to wait in line again to have them hose down the inside of the car. I finally got an hour's sleep in the dormi-
tory, a roll and a cup of coffee, and then I started off
again. For once there was hardly any traffic going up, so I
was making good time, concentrating mainly on staying
awake and avoiding the craters, when all of a sudden an
airplane appeared — not up in the sky but right in front
of me, not ten feet above the road, floating down above
my head, the angel of death throwing the shadow of his
wings over me, moving so slowly that I could hear the
creaking of the wires as he struggled to control his flaps,

obviously trying to land in the road because it was the only clear stretch in that devastated forest.

He veered to the right, veered to the left, came down with his wheels on the pavé, bounced way up into the air then came down again with a crash that broke his landing gear and whirled him around so that he came to rest across the road, tipped over with his wings sticking up. Only then did I see the Maltese Crosses, black and silver on his wings, and by that time the thing was on fire and I had put on my brakes and was running. . . .

He claims I pulled him out. I don't know. He was hanging in there sideways, had got his belt off but his legs were caught and one of them looked broken and I guess I just pulled hard enough or he pulled against me, smelling the gasoline, both of us pulling with our combined weight until he just fell out, and then stumbling together along the road and underneath the car just as the whole thing went up with a sort of *phoof* — immense blast of heat but not as bad as the big howitzer shells — and then everything came raining down on the car and all around us.

When it was quiet I had a chance to look at him for the first time, lying there beside me. His helmet and goggles were off now. He had short brown hair and a rather old-fashioned cavalry moustache, everything singed. He wore brown leather overalls and a piece of his shinbone was sticking right through his trouser leg. He was obviously in great pain and trying not to show it, looking into my eyes and trying to see why I had done it.

"Merci beaucoup," he said, after a moment, and smiled. His face was black from the fire, and his teeth gleamed.

"Ich bin Amerikaner," said I carefully. I started to roll out from under the ambulance, but he reached for me with his left arm.

"Better not yet," he said in English, indicating the watch on his wrist, and at that moment I heard the first shell clattering across the Meuse like a freight train. The forest exploded, the pavement on which we were lying heaved and buckled beneath us, and the ambulance above us rocked in its springs. The next shell hit farther away, but they kept coming. I had only been at the front a few weeks, but I knew that this was no casual artillery duel; this was the beginning of an attack.

"I would like to thank you for saving my life," said the German, still lying on his side. "My name is Lieutenant Kite."

"Kite?"

"K-e-i-t-h. You say Keith. It is Scottish, eh? My ancestor was a soldier for the King of Prussia. For money, you know."

"My name is Peter Ellis. American Field Service."

Awkwardly lying beneath my ambulance, we shook hands. A slow but steady series of shells came thundering across and crashed into the forest. A rain of steel. Two tires blew out, the car dropped several inches and I jerked away from the hot exhaust pipe, watching him watching me.

"Your first bombardment?"

"Yes."

"Not in such a good place in the middle of the road, but we have no choice now. Try to forget about it. Tell me, why are you here?"

"You mean in France?"

"In France, yes."

"We believe in the Allied cause. We want to help the French."

"Why?"

"Well . . . You started the War, you invaded Belgium . . ."

"But what has that to do with America? You think we want to invade America? No, I'm sorry, you must forgive me! You save my life and I present you with political arguments! It is only that I'm curious why a young man — you are a student? — comes to this crazy place, maybe to be blown up and killed or hurt, when he can be at home to enjoy life — What did you do at home?"

"Not much. Went to school."

"To school? How old are you?"

"Well, to college, university. But I dropped out to come over here."

"And what did you study?"

The shelling went on. I can't remember ever being really frightened before, but I was beginning to tremble now, beginning to fear that in a few seconds I would lose control of my clenched sphincter, and I sensed that his quiet questions were intended to distract me from the skull-rattling explosions.

"What sort of thing did you study?" he asked again.

"I would like . . ." I was still embarrassed to admit it. "I would like to be a painter but my father is a doctor, and he wants me to be one too."

"Oh yes, I see. My father is a general, and I want to be a lawyer."

"Are you a professional officer?"

"I have been one. My brother is one. I have been an officer of cavalry, but the life in peacetime, it's not so interesting, so I have begun to study, juristics, you know, to become a lawyer or a judge. My mother's brother is a judge, and I thought I might like that better than horses all the time. I studied one year at the University, and then the War began, and there was not much use for horses, so I transferred to the aeroplanes. You don't have a cigarette?"

I rolled over on my back, extracting a crushed pack and some matches. I sniffed for gasoline, but didn't smell any.

"The firing seems to have stopped," I said as I lighted his cigarette and mine. I was furious to see how my hand trembled.

"Let us wait a few moments," he said.

Suddenly there was machine-gun fire, very close.

"Not a sound!" muttered Keith, the cigarette clamped in his lips.

More machine-gun fire, then shouts. Then silence. Then the sound of people running, boots on the pavement, the creaking of equipment, and a line of men dashed across the road from east to west, mud-streaked figures running crouched down — helmets, rifles, hand grenades —

"They're yours!" I whispered.

"Much too far over. They are lost."

An instant later they were gone again. I had never seen German soldiers except as prisoners.

"Why didn't you call out?" I asked.

"What could they have done for me? I can't walk, and most of them will be dead before this day is over."

For a long while nothing happened. We heard occasional bursts of rifle and machine-gun fire, and Keith could tell by the sound which side was shooting. A plane flew overhead.

"Nieuport Eleven," said Keith. "Cylinder missing. Trying to get home."

We talked. He told me about his father, the retired general, his brother with the Death's Head Hussars in Rumania, his other brother still in school. I told him about Germantown and Harvard.

By this time we had crawled out from under the ambulance. We sat in the cool sunshine, leaning against the running board. The lower part of his flying suit was drenched with blood and I didn't like the way his face looked now. With some difficulty I cut off one trouser leg, although he didn't want me to ("You think I want to spend the War in prison half naked?") and when I got it off I saw the blood was welling from a bullet hole in the fleshy part of his thigh.

"Well, your father wants you to be a doctor," he said, as I tried to rig a tourniquet and bandage the wound. I'd seen it done, but I'd never done it myself. His face contorted as he clenched his teeth, but he didn't make a sound.

"I have some morphine in the car . . ."

"No, thank you."

"Most people beg for it."

"Yes, but I have seen the side effects. Why don't you draw my picture? You have a notebook or something?"

I did have a little sketchbook in the car, so I climbed in and got it. The ambulance was a shambles — windshield smashed, dashboard splintered, the frame punctured with shell fragments.

I sat down on the road and sketched Lieutenant Christoph Keith, lying up against the front wheel of an ambulance purchased by Mrs. Andrew Carnegie, and that is what I was doing when the first camions packed with French assault infantry came roaring up. They stopped long enough to pull the wreckage off the road, then disappeared in clouds of choking dust. I made Keith lie down in the ditch. When the military police arrived, they would not wait for an ambulance. They insisted on taking him away, sitting up in the back seat of their open sedan. I tore the sketch out of my notebook and gave it to him.

Later, I looked for him in the hospitals of Verdun, but I couldn't find him.

3.

IT'S STEALING MONEY, ISN'T IT?

The whole thing was Keith's idea. It came to him about one o'clock in the morning, at a table on the sidewalk in front of the blazing lights of the Café du Dôme in Montparnasse.

The meeting at the Ritz Bar only lasted one round; it was destroyed by centrifugal force. George Graham and the French lawyer and Robert von Waldstein all seemed embarrassed by the reunion scene and by Christoph Keith's account of how I had pulled him out of his burning airplane. George Graham and the lawyer wanted to discuss their case; I was staring at Keith, still finding it hard to believe that this was coincidence; and Robert von Waldstein apparently had a late date somewhere. He explained that while Germans could not afford to stay at the Ritz in these times, he just wanted to see the place because his father had never used any other hotel in Paris. George Graham asked if there was a connection with Waldstein & Co., the private bank in Berlin. Smiles: of course there was a connection. Waldstein's ancestor founded the bank, both he and Keith were here on the Bank's business.

I had never heard the name, but I could see that George Graham was impressed.

"Doesn't your bank go back to the eighteenth century?" he asked.

"Seventeen-ninety, I believe, is the official date."

"Always in your family? That's really something to be proud of," said George Graham. "And now you are carrying on the tradition, Baron?"

Another smile — a somewhat enigmatic smile, I thought. "I try to carry on, Mr. Graham, but some people believe I will need a lot of help."

"I think you may be late for your appointment," said Christoph Keith, looking at his watch and standing up.

"Maître Delage, we thank you for your hospitality and will report to your chambers at ten tomorrow. Mr. Graham, a pleasure, sir . . . If you visit Berlin . . ."

I stood up with them. "Looks like I will show one German banker the town after all," I said to George Graham as we shook hands. "Give my love to Mother and Dad."

"I'll do that, Peter. And put this in your pocket." He handed me a crisp white envelope.

Keith limped, but he didn't want to take a taxi. As we walked slowly through the summer night, we told each other our stories. I told him about my crack-up and how my family put me into Friends Hospital and how the doctors had gradually got me so I could function again.

He told me about his years in French hospitals and prison camps, his return to Berlin in the midst of a revolution, how he began to study law — and how he stopped.

"There was no money anymore. My parents are living on a pension, one brother was killed in Rumania, my youngest brother has no job because he is not trained for anything except a soldier — we simply had no money, and the Waldsteins gave me a job with their bank."

"Do you know anything about banking?"

"No, but I am learning, trying to learn what I can. They have what you call an apprentice system: you work with older men, you are sort of an assistant, carry papers around, attend meetings, listen to what is said —"

"Are you Robert von Waldstein's assistant?"

Keith laughed. "No, not quite! That is a different problem — and really the reason they gave me this job. Bobby is a wonderful fellow. Generous, polite, loves music and good wine and beautiful women — but banking? Well, he is not so much interested in banking. You have really never heard of the Waldsteins? It is quite a story — a long story. Tell you some other time. The problem now is who will continue in the bank when the old men die, the father and the uncle. Bobby had two brothers. Alfred is the oldest. You have not heard of him? He was in my regiment, he was in Poland and Rumania with the horses, he wrote stories about it, they were published, then he wrote a novel, *Licht Aus!* It was about the end of the war and the German revolution, it made a big success, so now he has become a famous writer, he is writing another book, he is married to a most beautiful girl — and of

course he does not go to the Gendarmenmarkt, to Waldstein and Co. There was another brother, Max, he did
what I did, transferred to the aeroplanes, only he was not
so lucky. Shot down by the Canadians, I think in 'seventeen. That leaves only Bobby, who was too young for the
war. So my job — a part of my job — is to look after
Bobby, try to make him learn the business, anyway try to
keep him out of trouble. They know me, they know my
family, they think I am a good influence. Shall we sit
down here and have a drink?"

We were on the Left Bank now, walking up one of the
streets from the river to the lights and the traffic on the
Boulevard St.-Germain. Despite the hour, a lot of people
were still sitting in the sidewalk cafés. We settled down in
the wicker chairs by a marble table and ordered Calvados. The streetlights shone through the leaves above us.

Keith seemed to think it was my turn again. He lighted
a cigarette and sat back to listen, so I told what had just
happened to me.

I finished my story just as he finished his drink.

"Shall we look at Montparnasse now?"

"That's another long walk," I said. "Let's take a taxi."

"No, it's good for me. We will walk slowly, and drink a
glass at every corner."

That's what we did. We drank our way from St.-
Germain-des-Prés to Montparnasse and got talked to by
lots of women — some very pretty, all very polite.

"Pas d'argent, mam'selle," said Keith to each and every
one of them, smiling and tipping his hat, and by the time
we settled down in front of the Café du Dôme he was
moved to exclaim, "My God, some of them look tempting,
don't they? I can see why you don't want to leave."

"No, that's not the reason I don't want to leave."

"An American in Paris and you don't have a girl?"

"No girl."

He started to ask why, but checked himself and
squashed his cigarette with great deliberation into the
Cinzano ashtray. He continued to stare at the ashtray for
a moment, and then he looked into my face. "I would like
to ask a question, but it is not a question one asks here in
Europe. . . . Still, I will ask it: How much money did Mr.
Graham give you to settle your affairs and go home?"

"Well, let's take a look." I drew the envelope out of my
inside pocket, tore it open, removed a pink check drawn

on The Provident Trust Company and slid it across the table. Christoph Keith twirled it around without picking it up, looked at it, looked up again.

"You owe a lot of money here?"

"No, I think just the rent for next month."

"All the rest of this is clear?"

I nodded.

"Come to Germany," said Keith.

"To Germany?"

"My friend, in Germany we have an inflation. You know what that means? The money is worth less and less, I mean our German mark, it buys less and less every day. You know what an American dollar was worth today — I mean this afternoon when the banks closed? About two hundred marks — so one of our marks is one-half of an American penny! And it is getting worse, they still have not decided how much Germany is to pay in reparations to the Allies, every day the mark drops more, and for this check you can live in Germany — well, very comfortably."

"How long?"

He shrugged. "Depends. How well do you want to live? How bad does the inflation get? Do you speculate in foreign currencies? Do you speculate in the stock market? Some men have become millionaires with fewer dollars than are in this check."

"I just want to learn to be a painter."

"We have very good painters in Germany, and most of them are hungry, I can tell you that. If you live quietly, take private lessons . . ." He drank some Calvados, apparently doing numbers in his head. "On this check you can stay in Germany a year." He paused again and gazed across the Boulevard Raspail. There was much less traffic now, and most of the tables around us were empty. "It's quite strange, isn't it? We sit here and I give you personal advice like an old friend, when we really have only known each other — how long, perhaps two hours — five years ago!"

I felt the same way. Was I drunk? I should have been, but I wasn't. Who is Christoph Keith, this stranger, this German officer, to set me against my old man? My old man, who is so disappointed in me already. I thought about the house on Washington Lane and I thought about the faces of my mother and my father when they first came to see me in the hospital. (I never did get to paint the faces of my parents. Years later Grant Wood — who never laid eyes on them — did a picture he called *American Gothic* and there were my parents, dressed as an Iowa farm couple, with my father holding a pitchfork!)

I didn't want to go back to Philadelphia; I didn't want to go back to college; I didn't want to go back to Drexel & Co. Here was the solution. Do you live life for yourself or for your parents? And is Christoph Keith a stranger? I saved his life. No, you didn't. Yes, I did, he'd never have gotten out by himself, he'd be underground five years by now. But it's stealing money, isn't it? They sent the money to get you home and now you're going to use it to live in Germany. They're going to be furious; well, anyway the old man. Ma will be "disappointed." What they'll really think is that I've cracked again. Might they send somebody after me? No, they'll do nothing and say nothing. What do I do when the money is spent?

"You don't have to decide tonight," said Keith, after he finished his Calvados. "I'm afraid our inflation will not go away so soon."

"I have decided, Christoph. I think it's a good idea, a chance worth taking. Now how do I go about it?"

"Fabelhaft!" Keith slammed his hand on the table so hard that the saucers jumped. "We are going home on Friday. Is that too soon for you? It's much better you come with us, we will find you the right place to stay. And don't leave your dollars here in Paris, we don't know what the French are going to do, they are being very difficult about everything, you transfer your dollars to Amsterdam, we have an affiliate there and it will work much better. If you have any difficulty with your concierge, I will ask Maître Delage to take care of it. We will get you a ticket in the same compartment. And now I must go back to the hotel because we have a meeting in the morning — No, no, I'll pay the bill, you are the client, I have just acquired my first dollar account for Waldstein and Co.!"

On Saturday morning I arrived at the Bahnhof Friedrichstrasse in Berlin, with Christoph Keith and Bobby von Waldstein.

4.

WHERE WERE YOU IN 1919?

Maybe it was the weather, but after Paris Berlin felt damp and gray and dirty. The huge station and the square outside were crowded with gray people, some of them rushing from the trains, others just standing around. Beggars were everywhere: men with only one leg supported by crutches, men with no legs sitting on blankets, blind men with black glasses — most of them wearing pieces of their gray uniforms, all of them wearing medals. The streets seemed crowded with cars. Paris had smelled of coffee and strong cigarettes; Berlin smelled of gasoline.

Christoph Keith and Bobby von Waldstein were both rather quiet this morning. We had consumed a bottle of Cognac in our compartment the previous evening, but I didn't think they were hung over. Looking out of the taxi windows, they showed me a few sights — the Landwehr Canal, the Tiergarten . . . but they seemed depressed to be home, and my thoughts were elsewhere, because the German voices, suddenly and for the first time all around me, brought back the first German voice I ever heard, brought it back so vividly that her lips might have been beside my ear. . . .

We dropped Bobby in front of an elegant old apartment house, promised that Christoph would bring me out to the Waldsteins' country place on Sunday, and drove into the suburbs, old villas along tree-lined streets.

The taxi stopped in front of a dignified house — ivy over faded yellowish stucco — that looked much like the others on this street. The driver carried our luggage to the door, which was opened by an old man in a green apron.

"Herzlich willkommen, Herr Oberleutnant!"

This was Meier, the General's batman since the General had been a lieutenant himself. I had heard of Meier before. He bowed politely to me and took charge of the luggage. Christoph led me through a dark paneled hall-

22

way, hung with antlers and sabers and rifles and old flags and old photographs of groups of men on horseback.

The retired *Generalmajor* and his wife were having coffee and rolls in the dining room. They were of course expecting us, and again I heard myself introduced in what became Christoph's standard explanation of who I was: ". . . hat mich bei Verdun aus der brennenden Maschine gezogen!"

I had not been warned about the General. He had a fine head of snow-white hair and a handsome moustache of the same color and he wore a navy-blue suit with a wing collar, but he sat in a wheelchair and nodded his head without stopping and his wife had just removed a large white napkin from around his neck. I could see the crumbs and coffee stains as she quickly folded it, and stood up to shake hands with me.

She looked younger — tall and bony, with pale freckled skin and the same features as Christoph. Her chestnut hair was pulled back into a severe bun. She seemed pleased to meet me, but her English was not as good as Christoph's. Haltingly, I tried a few words of German. We joined them at the table.

What do you say to a guest who has pulled your son out of a burning airplane? Frau Keith asked polite questions about my parents. Did I have any brothers or sisters? My father was a doctor? What kind of doctor? Nobody could think of the German word for surgeon. I demonstrated, using a silver butter knife to slice open my stomach. Ach, ein Chirurg. And so it went.

Frau Keith then began to talk rapidly to Christoph. I understood most of it, but she told him to translate: Herr General and she wished me to be a guest in their house, for as long as I wanted to stay. She knew I would be more comfortable at a hotel, but on the other hand there were advantages to life in a private home. It was not a large house, but they had an extra room, because they had lost a son in Rumania.

The General nodded emphatically and got out a few words: "Rumänien . . . gefallen!"

I was ready for the invitation. On the trip from Paris, Bobby von Waldstein and I were alone for a few minutes while Christoph went to the toilet. I was trying to sketch Bobby's movie star face in my notebook, we were talking about Goya, but the moment Christoph was gone, Bobby changed the subject:

"Peter, the Keiths will ask you to live with them. They have an extra room because their middle son was killed. Now listen carefully: You will have plenty of money in Berlin because you have dollars, so you can stay at the best hotels, do whatever you like. But if you decide to stay at the Keiths', I must tell you that they have very little money. He is a retired general, living from a pension, and with the inflation that pension gets less every day. The mother also has some income, her father's estate or something, but it's not so very much. They still keep servants, the General's old batman and the batman's wife. Their name is Meier. I have no idea what they are paid, if anything, but they have meals and a roof over their head."

I had stopped sketching, amazed. Bobby the smiling, carefree playboy suddenly sounded like a different person.

"If you stay with the Keiths and give them just a few dollars a week, it will make all the difference in the world to them. A few dollars in Berlin is like a few hundred dollars in America. But of course they won't take it. They won't take it from a guest. So what you do —" Bobby grasped my knee and leaned forward intently. "You put a few dollars in an envelope each week and you give it to Meier. When you are alone with him."

"Will he take it?" I asked.

"Yes. He will take it, and he will buy food and wine and things for the house."

"How much should I give him?"

"Can you give him five dollars?"

"Five dollars a *week?*"

"You can do that?"

"Certainly."

"All right, you do that the first week — and I will tell you if you should give more or less."

I wanted to ask him if the Keiths wouldn't find out I was paying their butler, but the door slid open and Christoph stepped back into the compartment.

Now, in the sunny dining room, I told Christoph's mother that I would be delighted to stay in their house until I could come to know the city and to find my own place. I told her I had lived alone in Paris, and had not liked it . . . and then I heard somebody else come in.

I turned, and rose to be introduced to a blonder, thinner, shorter, much younger version of Christoph, wearing a military-looking trench coat that was too big for him.

"This is my little brother Kaspar . . . Mr. Peter Ellis aus Amerika."

Kaspar Keith grabbed my hand firmly, bowed, clicked his heels. He didn't smile.

"B-B-B-Bild," said the General, quite clearly. *"Bild!"*

Kaspar left the dining room and came back a moment later, still wearing the creaking trench coat, holding in his hands a small framed picture, which he handed me: my sketch of Christoph, face blackened by fire, one leg tied with a bloody tourniquet, leaning his head against the left front wheel of my ambulance — *Verdun 1916* — I had scribbled in the corner before I tore the sheet out of my notebook.

They were all watching me. I didn't know what to say. I handed the picture back to Kaspar. "Thank you very much. That was a long time ago."

Christoph announced that he would have to go to the office but he wanted to show me my room. The General continued to nod, watching. Frau Keith again shook hands. Kaspar apparently wanted to talk to his brother; he followed us up the carpeted stairs.

When they opened the door to the bedroom at the end of the hall, I sensed that it had just been aired and dusted — a comfortable room with a narrow bed, leather sofa, Persian carpet, writing desk and heavy oak armoire. On the walls were more of the decorations I had seen downstairs — framed photographs, groups of smiling officers on foot and on horseback, in gray battle costume, in black-and-silver parade dress, moustaches, tall fur tschakos faced with enormous white death's heads — the *Totenkopfhusaren.*

"Were you in the War too?" I asked Kaspar.

The boy shook his head. "Too young. I was a cadet in 1918."

"But our Kasparle did plenty of fighting just the same," said Christoph. "Marinebrigade Ehrhardt."

That meant nothing to me.

"Freikorps," said Kaspar, raising his chin. "Best one."

"Oho, I'm not so sure," said his brother, smiling. "Remember the Kapp Putsch!"

Kaspar's face turned red, "That was not *our* fault! That was —"

"What's a Freikorps?" I asked.

Kaspar's anger turned against me. "What is a Freikorps? May I ask, where were you in 1919?"

"In 1919 I was in a mental hospital."

"A what?" He didn't understand but Christoph told him in German, adding, "Halt gefälligst die Schnauze!"

"I beg your pardon, sir!" snapped Kaspar, his face still red. He turned and stomped out of the room.

"Peter, I must apologize!" Christoph sat down on the sofa. "You understand he is still very young, and he has had a pretty terrible adolescence." He glanced at his watch. "Will you sit down a moment and let me explain? I have to appear at the office, but I want you to understand about my brother."

5.

RELIABLE TROOPS

"Of course I was not here myself when the War ended," said Christoph Keith, "so all of this I have heard from others. It must have been just indescribable . . . the uproar, the confusion . . . It began with the sailors, the fleet had been sitting in ports, Kiel and Wilhelmshaven, doing nothing for years, the food was terrible, the discipline was harsh, then they heard they were to steam out for one last battle against the British, so this day in November they revolted, put out the fires under the boilers and marched into the towns. It was like a match in dry grass, you know, the people were so exhausted, so tired of the War. The revolt spread to the workers, to the army, in every city there were mobs in the streets, sailors with rifles and red armbands, shrieking women from the tenement houses . . . it was really a revolt of the working people against the established order. And of course, the symbols of the Kaiser's rule were who? The officers. And the people chased officers down the streets and tore their epaulets off!

"Well, to an American I think that is not so important. To a German officer those straps on his shoulder stand for . . . I cannot explain it to you . . . they stand for *everything:* his country, his honor, his rank in the world . . . the epaulets have, what shall I say? A mystic importance. Everybody salutes the man with the higher epaulets. I remember as a little boy, walking along Unter den Linden with my father, every man in uniform saluted. . . .

"All right, now imagine my little brother, sixteen years old, a cadet at military school, he is walking along the street with another cadet, and suddenly they are surrounded by a mob of people, deserting soldiers and sailors and women from the factories, and they grab those boys and knock them down and kick them and tear the epaulets off their uniforms and stand around screaming at them.

"Can you imagine how those boys feel? How they detest everything to do with workers and red flags and bolshevism or socialism?

"Now, in the meantime, what is going on? The country is in chaos. The Kaiser runs away to Holland. Karl Liebknecht proclaims a German soviet. The Social Democrats proclaim a republic. People are shooting at each other from barricades. Nobody knows what's happening. Liebknecht's Spartacus bands — the real Communists — are marching in the street, taking over public buildings — it was revolution, and I tell you, German people, even Socialists, they don't *like* revolution, they don't like workers breaking into stores and shooting in the streets — and so what did the Socialist government do? They called in the army.

"All right, now the army was coming home from France, coming home in good order, marching behind their officers, but they were touched by the revolution too. The ranks were full of Soldatenräte — I don't know what you call that, sort of soldier commissars — and they tried to remove the authority of the officers, hold elections . . . Can you imagine elections in the German army? Well, the government wanted *reliable* troops, in other words troops that would shoot at other Germans, at their former comrades, at Soldatenräte, at the sailors. . . . Where are they going to find reliable troops? Most of the men coming back from France didn't want to shoot anybody, least of all other Germans. They wanted to go home, and that's what most of them did do, the moment they were back across the Rhine.

"Most of them. Not all of them. You have a saying in English, 'He found a home in the army'? Some people had been soldiers so long, they didn't want to do anything else. Some of them tried to go home, could not find jobs, could not stand the quiet life, perhaps they need the marching and the guns and the other men and the excitement . . . and others, like my little brother — furious that the War was over, the War was lost, they wanted a chance to fight for their country, perhaps their epaulets had been ripped off. . . .

"Well, what happened was they raised a lot of little private corps of soldiers. Free corps. Freikorps. An old expression, comes from the wars against Napoleon. Anybody who could find some money and some men to follow him. Generals, colonels, a captain in the navy, lieutenants, even a few sergeants did it. And the High Command let them have uniforms and rifles and ammunition, machine guns, some cannons and some armored cars. General Maercker's Landesjägerkorps was the first, they were sent down to Weimar to protect the professors and the politicians who were writing a new constitution. Here in Berlin there was heavy fighting, Guards Cavalry Division people killed Liebknecht, killed Rosa Luxemburg, they split her skull with rifle butts and threw her into the canal . . . they broke the Spartacus."

Christoph stopped talking and extracted a silver case from his jacket pocket, offered me a French Gauloise, and lighted both of our cigarettes.

"I take it Kaspar joined one of these corps?"

Christoph nodded. "Marinebrigade Ehrhardt. I don't know how he got into that one, because it was mostly navy officers. They recruited among the cadets, and I think someone just persuaded him. Those boys saw terrible things. No trenches. Fighting in the streets, breaking into the workers' tenements, shooting from the rooftops, firing squads in courtyards . . . They didn't take prisoners, they just shot them. The boy was seventeen by then. Fighting here in Berlin, fighting in Munich, fighting in Silesia, and then they came back here to Berlin and

tried to make a revolution of their own — the so-called
Kapp Putsch — to overthrow the Weimar Republic. It
didn't work. They occupied Berlin, but all the workers
went out on a general strike. Everything stopped. No
trains, no omnibuses, no electricity — nothing. The High
Command backed down, Dr. Kapp and the generals behind him flew off in aeroplanes to Sweden, and the
Marinebrigade Ehrhardt marched out again.

"Captain Ehrhardt fled to Hungary, the Brigade was
dissolved, *all* the korps were dissolved, the government
did not need these people anymore. Kaspar just put on
civilian clothes, got on a train, and came home. He's been
home ever since, but he cannot seem to make a new life.
He is supposed to attend the University, and sometimes
he does go to the lectures, but he sleeps a lot in the daytime and spends his evenings drinking with other fellows
from the Freikorps. They detest the government, they talk
politics, and I think they do other things, too."

"What kind of things?" I asked.

Christoph looked at his watch and stood up. "I think I
would rather not know what other things," he said. "Now
I really must go to the Bank. I will be home for dinner,
and then we'll walk about the town a little. All right?"

6.

AN ISLAND

I don't know why I assumed that the Keiths would have
a car, but they didn't have one. To visit the Waldsteins on
Sunday afternoon, Christoph and I had to take the trolley
up to Grunewald station and then the train, through miles
of hilly, sandy forests of Scotch pine, to the village of
Nikolassee. When we stepped out of the little suburban
station into the sunshine, Christoph greeted an old coachman who held the door of an ancient, beautifully polished
open landau.

"Nachmittag, Schmitz."

"Guten Nachmittag, Herr Oberleutnant." Salute. We

climbed in and settled into the green leather seats, the door slammed, the coachman climbed up onto his bench, picked up the reins and made a clicking sound with his tongue. The two glistening brown geldings broke into a trot. On rubber tires we rolled out of the station, through the village and up into the wooded hills.

"Don't the Waldsteins have a car?" I asked.

"Yes, of course. Bobby has a Bugatti racer and the Baron has a big old Horch, but they want to keep the horses and they want to keep Schmitz, so they still have this carriage. It was useful in the War, when there was no gasoline."

The wind blew in our faces. Automobiles roared past as we clip-clopped steadily up a long straight road through the woods. Finally we reached the summit — and a breathtaking view across the wide blue Havel River, glistening in the May sunshine, dotted with white sails, bulging out into the bay of the Wannsee to our left. Directly below us was a small peninsula, really an island connected to the mainland by a narrow bridge.

Christoph pointed. "That's it."

The coachman pulled his brakes. The horses wanted to run now, but he reined back hard, forcing them to hold the coach in a fast controlled walk as we descended the steep slope toward the water. When the hoofs pounded on the wooden planking of the bridge he gave them their head and we shot up into a dark lane bordered on both sides by walls and lilac hedges and huge old oaks and copper beeches. The lane seemed to be circling the core of the island. Occasionally there was a break in the greenery and I caught a glimpse of bright blue water.

We came to the end of a long stucco wall. The horses, now slowed to a walk, turned to draw us between two gateposts into a broad pebbled driveway. I had the impression of some white-washed gatehouses, a large lawn and, in front of us, partly concealed by massive horse chestnuts and copper beeches, a very large and very old white manor house.

Half a dozen shiny, expensive cars were parked down one side of the driveway, and in a shady garden beside one of the gatehouses, a group of chauffeurs were sitting around a table, their caps off and their jackets unbuttoned, drinking beer.

"Was ist den heute los?" inquired Christoph, as Schmitz

opened the door for us, but I didn't understand the reply, which caused Christoph to grumble something indicating mild displeasure.

"Grosse Tiere," he said, leading me across the driveway and toward the gardens at the left of the big house. "How do you say that? Big animals? Important people?"

"We say Big Shots."

"Oh yes. We have some Big Shots here this afternoon. Minister Rathenau and Professor Liebermann."

Neither name meant anything to me.

"They are all down at the lake in the Tea House," said Christoph. "I think we go down the back way and come along the lake front, we don't make such a grand entrance then, we come in quietly, all right?"

He led me across another lawn, then through a charming maze of yew hedges, past two greenhouses and a meticulously cultivated vegetable garden, then down another pebble-covered path descending steeply through a thick forest. Below us the water glistened through the trees.

"Who are these Big Shots?" I asked him.

"You have not heard of Walter Rathenau? He is our foreign minister. A very brilliant man. A very rich man. His family owns electric companies. He has written books about — well, about politics, economics, the future — very complicated things, but most important, he wants to . . . he thinks we have to pay the debts the Allies have imposed upon us at Versailles, he thinks we must do something to . . . accommodate the French and the English before our economy can recover — and many people hate him. He has just made a treaty with the Russians, with the Bolsheviks, with Chicherin at Rapallo, some people believe it was a master stroke to make the French take us more seriously, but many hate him. He is a brilliant man but not an easy man to like."

"And who's the other one? The professor."

"Ach, Professor Liebermann, Max Liebermann, you will *like* to meet him, he is one of our best painters, a wonderful old man, and very funny sometimes."

"And why are they all here?" I asked. We were coming down toward the water now. I could see a tiny beach, a rowboat pulled half out of the water, and tall, swaying reeds.

"Well, they come here for tea, to see their friends — they are old friends of the Waldsteins, I don't think there is any special reason today. . . . Oh, now we have a happy surprise!"

As we came down to the water and turned into another path, we saw a young woman sitting on a bench, reading a book and gently rocking a baby carriage. She was sitting under one of the enormous weeping willows that lined the waterfront, arching their branches far out over the stone seawall and trailing into the lake.

She looked up as she heard us, frowning first, then smiling a dazzling smile as she rose. "Christoph!"

We advanced, they shook hands, we were introduced: "Sigrid von Waldstein . . . and this is her daughter, Marie."

Marie was asleep in the baby carriage, a tangle of blue-black curls.

They spoke in German, but I could understand them. Why wasn't she with the others?

A shrug and still the dazzling smile. Langweilig! Boring. How was Paris? Did Bobby behave himself? How is Kaspar?

She turned to me. "My English is not good, I'm sorry. My husband, his English is *very* good."

She asked if we would stay for dinner, with her and Alfred. It was explained that they had their own house, a cottage above the stables on the other side of the road.

Christoph said we would be happy to have dinner with them.

"Now you go shake hands with Dr. Rathenau," she said.

We walked along the waterfront, under the weeping willows. The screen of reeds disappeared, and through the willow branches we could see the lake and the sailboats and the sandy beaches on the opposite shore.

"That's a lovely girl," I said.

"Yes, isn't she. Her father was a general."

"Like yours."

"Younger than mine. But he is dead, an auto accident in France."

"She looked — a little strange when she asked about Kaspar —"

"She was Kaspar's girl."

"His fiancée?"

"Not officially. They were too young. But he loved her

very much. He still does. Thát is another reason he is so angry."

"What happened?"

"What happened? Another man came along . . . older, stronger, famous, *rich* — our poor Kasparle did not look so attractive anymore — and what could he offer? Her mother is a widow, the older brothers also killed, the younger brother still in school, they have a big estate out in the Mark and not enough money even to pay the mortgage or to feed their horses. . . . No, she did the only thing she could do."

We were coming up to the Tea House now, really more of a pavilion on a flagstone terrace over the water, a thatched roof supported by heavy wooden pillars. Maybe twenty people were sitting on wicker chairs in several circles, the women in flowered dresses and summer hats, the men mostly in dark business suits. Two uniformed maids were passing trays with cakes and pastries.

Below the terrace was a small floating dock. A glistening motorboat swayed gently beside the dock, and Bobby von Waldstein, in white duck trousers and a white shirt, was helping a young girl put what looked like some kind of an aquaplane into the boat. The girl wore a black wool cardigan over a black bathing suit. On the ramp connecting the dock with the terrace stood an old woman, who was dressed in an extraordinary costume — black embroidered blouse, black skirt that touched the ground and an enormous white bonnet that stretched a foot above and behind her head. The woman was shouting at Bobby and the girl, but they were paying no attention to her. She put her red hands on her hips and turned toward the terrace shouting, "Frau Baronin! Frau Baronin!" until one of the ladies in flowered dresses rose and walked toward the railing, and at that moment Bobby looked up and saw Christoph and me.

He smiled, and waved and put on the blue blazer that was draped over one of the pier supports and came bounding up the ramp, right past the old woman in the bonnet. Behind him the girl in the bathing suit turned around to see where he had gone. She looked up and our eyes met.

7.

BISMARCK FOUND THEM USEFUL

The evening before, Christoph had taken me for a long walk along the Kurfürstendamm, Berlin's busiest street.

It was Saturday night, and the sidewalks were crammed with people — all kinds of people: fat businessmen from the provinces, with shaved necks bulging over their celluloid collars; high school boys and university students wearing colored caps; army officers with riding boots and dress swords; people speaking English; people speaking Polish or Russian; prostitutes of all shapes and sizes, walking in pairs, walking alone, stopping to adjust their garters, standing in groups in the doorways. . . . New Orleans jazz came tootling out of a nightclub ablaze with blinking lights and huge posters showing naked girls. Crippled beggars were everywhere.

Christoph limped along beside me. "What do you think?"

"Well, it's interesting — and certainly different from Paris."

He shook his head. "You should have seen it before the war. We have a beautiful city, you will see. But this? Eine Schweinerei!"

We walked on, past the gigantic imitation Romanesque cathedral, a gray stone island in the middle of the traffic. Christoph pointed to an even uglier building just across the street. "Romanisches Café" according to the sign.

"This is where the writers and the newspaper people sit and talk and do their work," said Christoph.

We entered a glassed-in terrace and sat down at a table with a view of the sidewalk. The people at the other tables were talking with great animation or quietly reading newspapers attached to wooden holders, or drinking coffee. I didn't see anybody working.

A waiter came.

"Will you try a Berliner Weisse? It is a special white beer, with a little raspberry syrup."

I nodded.

"Zwei Weisse, *mit*."

"Jawohl, Herr Oberleutnant."

"Do you come here all the time?" I asked.

Christoph shook his head. "He's never seen me before, but they can always tell. Cigarette?" He settled back. "Peter, tomorrow we go out to the island. I want to tell you something about the Waldsteins, because you will be meeting them and everybody knows these things, so they will expect you know them too.

"In the first place, you know of course that they are Jews . . . or perhaps it is more accurate to say they *were* Jews, because they became converted to the Evangelical Church at the time of Napoleon. So they do not think of themselves as Jews, you see, although everybody else does, and one does not talk about it in their presence.

"Why did they become Christians? Because this was a time of liberation, the French army brought the ideas of the French revolution into all these old German states, the idea that all men are equal, and with that came the idea that Jews should not be shut off into the ghetto, speaking a different language, consorting only with each other. . . . There was a feeling among the Jews themselves, some of them, that maybe they were *not* the Chosen People after all, maybe they were just like the other people in the towns they lived in, and they wanted to come out of the ghetto and take part in the life of the world.

"Well, in Berlin we never had a ghetto anyway, it was a new town, but the princes who became the kings of Prussia did not like Jews much and permitted very few families to live here. One of them was Mendelssohn. You have heard of Moses Mendelssohn?"

"Was that the composer?" I asked.

"No, it was his grandfather. He was a philosopher and a writer. He translated parts of the Old Testament from Hebrew into German, so the Jews could learn German. He remained a Jew, but he wanted to bring the other Jews into the German life. He was quite a famous man, although not so rich as his descendants became. Well, he had a lot of children and one of them married David Waldstein, a banker who was *very* rich, maybe the richest

man in Berlin. Why were so many Jews bankers? Because
in the first place it was one of the few things they *were*
allowed to do — moneylending — and it was not against
their religion to charge — I don't know what you call
that, *zinsen* we say, when you charge somebody money to
lend him money?"

"Interest?"

"Yes, interest. I think somewhere in the Bible it forbids
that, you remember about Jesus and the moneychangers
in the Temple? I don't understand it exactly, but all over
Europe, not just in Germany, it was the Jews who did
most of the moneylending, that is, banking, even in the
Middle Ages."

The beer came, foaming in big balloon glasses. We
lifted them ceremoniously, we drank. It tasted just about
the way you would expect beer with raspberry syrup to
taste.

Christoph drained half his glass in one series of tremendous gulps, put it down, wiped his moustache with
his napkin, and continued the story.

"All right, this David Waldstein decided to become
baptized, become a Christian, and he had his children
baptized as they were born. I suppose he wanted them to
be part of the German life and you had to be a Christian.
As I say, this was the time of Napoleon, Napoleon had
beaten the Prussians and occupied Berlin, forced the
Prussians to join his Russian campaign and then, after the
retreat from Moscow, one of the Prussian generals took
his corps out of Napoleon's army and joined the Allies.
One of my ancestors was an officer in that corps and one
of the Waldstein sons was a rider, too — though not an
officer, of course. This same son — his name was Jacob
Waldstein — became famous, he wrote poems and songs,
he wrote several plays, he was a friend of Heine, he was
a friend of Felix Mendelssohn, and he began a literary
magazine with money that his brothers gave him. His
brothers ran the Bank, and had many children and then
their sons ran the Bank — and their daughters married
into our aristocracy. Because now this family, and others
like them, were becoming terribly rich.

"This was the industrial revolution now, it came late to
Germany, it was railroads and coal mines and steel mills,
and to build railroads, to build steel mills, you must raise
money. And who knows how to raise money? Not our

Junkers, our old landholders, descended from Teutonic Knights. Not the king's army officers. Not the king's ministers and privy councillors. No, they don't know anything about money, because that is nothing for gentlemen, that is what the English call being in trade, absolutely forbidden to the gentlemen who run the country. Who knows how to raise money, lots of money, public issues of stocks and bonds, here and in Paris, in London, in New York? Who knows are Mendelssohns and Waldsteins, and Oppenheims and the others, of course, the Rothschilds in Frankfurt and Vienna and London are the most famous, then Bleichröder, Fürstenberg, lots of others . . . not all Jewish, you understand, the whole upper bourgeoisie suddenly bloomed, the money poured in, they built themselves palaces here in Berlin and out in the country, and their daughters married people who already *had* palaces but could not pay to keep them. People with old titles. And then, the next thing, they wanted titles themselves. They paid for hospitals, they gave art collections to museums, the Waldsteins had their journal, the government liked to have the support of such people, they were in fact *extremely* loyal subjects of the king — who was by now also an emperor, the Kaiser. And Bismarck, the man who made his king a Kaiser . . . Bismarck found these families useful. And he gave them — some of them — the titles they wanted. Waldsteins were the first."

"Christoph," I said, "for a hussar officer and an airplane pilot, you know a lot of history."

That seemed to please him. He nodded and paused to sip some beer. "I have told you, I don't want to be an officer, I like books, I like books much more than horses — or aeroplanes — and I would like to go back to the University, but just now it is not possible."

"Well, go on with the Waldsteins. How did you get involved with them?"

"It was not really me, it was my father. In Germany, you know, before the War everybody must do military service, one or two years in the army, and then they stay in the reserve. You do your service in some regiment, and then all your life you go to summer maneuvers with that regiment. For German men, this is — I should say *was* — one of the most important things. Your regiment, your reserve rank . . . it is hard to explain to an American, but in those years, after we beat the French in 1870, before

1914, this thing about the army was . . . well, it was just very important.

"So now the Waldsteins — two of them in the bank, not old Jacob the poet — they were the Freiherrn von Waldstein — Barons von Waldstein — and they had sons. To what regiment would the sons be sent for their service? Very ticklish problem. Everybody wants to be in the cavalry, but cavalry people need lots of horses and a man to care for them, in other words you can't be in the cavalry if you don't have money. Well, the Waldsteins had plenty of money. Then everybody wants to be in the Guard regiments. Guard Grenadiers, although infantry, is better than line cavalry, more cachet, the French say. . . . You think this is all nonsense, don't you?"

"It's a different world, but it's interesting."

"It is a vanished world, I only tell you to explain the Waldsteins. One of the aunts — that is, a sister of the bankers and niece of the poet — was married to Lieutenant General Count Wachenfels, member of the General Staff, commander of light cavalry. He spoke to my father. My father then was adjutant of the Black Hussars."

"That's the hussars with the skull and . . ."

"Yes. This must have been in the 1880s, I don't know exactly when, but the Waldsteins served with the regiment, I think maybe my father saw to it that they were not so badly treated as they might have been. And my father and mother accepted invitations, to the big houses — Pariser Platz, Schloss Havelblick . . . and as my brothers and I grew up we were sent to the same Gymnasium, the same high school, as the youngest Waldstein boys, that is Alfred and Max and Bobby. That is how we came to know them — Oh my God, look who is coming now — in the Romanisches Café, of all places!"

I had also noticed the group just coming in, well-dressed men and women, shouting and laughing, sounding as if they had already had a few drinks; they might have come from one of the nightclubs. They were just settling around a large table at the other side of the room when one of the men, still standing, glanced across at us. He looked surprised, said something to one of the women, and strode toward our table.

Christoph Keith immediately stood up, so I stood up too. The man approaching was tall, as tall as Keith but heavier, a swollen chest, strange melancholy blue eyes in a pale fleshy face, and dark blond hair slicked back from his broad forehead. He wore a double-breasted blue business suit with some kind of military decoration in his lapel. He seemed to be a little older — perhaps in his thirties.

They shook hands, grinning. I was introduced . . . Mr. Ellis, aus Amerika . . . Hauptmann Somebody-Ring, I thought . . . famous flier, squadron commander . . . and again the story about the burning plane at Verdun.

"Will you join us for a drink? I am introducing Ellis to Berliner Weisse."

"Thank you, I will just sit with you for a moment. I am with all these Swedish friends of my wife. . . ." They were talking German, but I could understand most of what was said. They apparently had not seen each other for years, but had heard stories. No, Hauptmann Ring wasn't flying for the Swedes anymore, if he was going to fly at all it would be for Germany, in German airplanes. The waiter came and Ring ordered Cognac. And these swine who signed the Versailles Treaty have agreed that we'll never have airplanes again. What do you think of that?

He was leaning forward, a burly form leaning forward in the spindly iron chair, his elbows on the table, talking rapidly, working himself up so that his face was becoming flushed.

War criminals! Turning German officers over to the courts for trial as criminals. *Criminals!* U-boat watch officers who did nothing but their duty, sitting in prison because these old women who claim to represent the German people are scared of the Allies.

The Cognac came. He drank it with one gulp and slammed the glass down on the marble. You realize if our Rittmeister had lived, he would be in jail now? The face was getting redder.

(I didn't want to ask which Rittmeister, because I didn't want to show that I understood him.)

And now this Rathenau, this Jew with his Rapallo Treaty! Can you imagine a treaty with the Bolsheviks?

Christoph Keith interrupted him: Rapallo might not be such a bad idea. It set the French back on their tails.

The other only snorted.

Christoph lighted another cigarette. "I thought you wanted to fly airplanes — German airplanes."

"We're not allowed to *have* airplanes! They blew ours

up with dynamite! Aschaffenburg. Saw it with my own eyes, a line of beautiful new D-IV's, hardly been flown, I *cried* —"

Christoph interrupted again. "Ever been in Russia? I have, with the horses. A *very* big country, thousands and thousands of kilometers, empty steppes, few roads, fewer railroads . . . and *no* Allied Control Commissions!"

Hauptmann Ring stared at him with hooded eyes.

"I hear this Rapallo Treaty was a fluke," said Christoph. "Not Rathenau's idea at all. Rathenau wants to work with France and England. I hear it was all arranged by Ago von Maltzan. Remember him? He's in the Russian bureau at the Foreign Ministry. Maltzan working with Chicherin, Maltzan persuading Rathenau . . . and the idea didn't start in the Wilhelmstrasse; it came from the Bendlerstrasse."

"Von Seeckt?"

Christoph blew a smoke ring toward the distant ceiling. "Thousand of kilometers, old boy. The steppes look like the ocean. Von Seeckt has seen them. He understands. Who's going to know what a few German civilians are doing with some old tanks and some old airplanes, far away beyond the horizon?"

"You think for one minute that Lenin and Trotsky —"

"Why not? We brought Lenin back from Switzerland, didn't we? It was the *Allies* who invaded him. It was the *Allies* who cut him off from the world. Lenin needs tractors. We make excellent tractors. Yes, I think they'll let us do some training."

The other looked at him quietly. "That's very interesting. I will see if our people agree with you. In any case, our Israelite banking fraternity remains as well informed as always."

"I think you know this doesn't come from banking sources."

"But it has reached them now, has it not?"

"I work for them, yes." Christoph's tone had changed.

"One hears your job is to keep Bobby Waldstein from catching a social disease."

"Maybe I have some other duties too."

"If your predictions are correct, would you come across the steppes with us?"

Christoph stuck out his leg, and tapped it with his

cane: "Can't kick the pedals anymore, Herr Komman-
dant. Sorry."

"Yes, I'm sure you're sorry." He scraped his chair back
and stood up. We did too.

"*Also*," he said, shaking hands with Christoph. "One
always watches with interest what happens to the old
comrades. I never imagined Keith as a banker, but better
an employed banker than an unemployed pilot, I would
say!"

He gave me a huge moist paw, said in English, "Good
evening, sir, a very great pleasure!" and walked back to
his table, where the conversation stopped and the faces
turned to inspect us.

"What have you got there?" asked Christoph as we sat
down again. He reached across and grabbed the round
cardboard coaster which had an advertisement for Spatenbräu Beer on one side, and my pencil sketch of Hauptmann Ring on the other.

"Why, Peter, that's *excellent!* I didn't notice you were
doing that, it looks exactly like him."

"He has an interesting face — a bit like a Roman emperor."

"Better not let him hear you describe him as a Roman,
he thinks of himself as the typical Germanic warrior. . . .
But why do you write 'Hauptmann Ring' down here?"

"Isn't that his name?"

Christoph stared at me and then began to laugh. He
leaned back in his chair and roared with laughter, so hard
that the other patrons — especially those at the big table
— turned to look at us.

"Hauptmann Ring! That's very good! The name is
Hauptmann *Göring*, last commander of Richthofen's Jagd-
staffel, holder of the Order *pour le mérite*, one of our famous aces — and, as you heard, one of the noisiest, most
bitter enemies of Versailles, of the German government
that signed at Versailles."

"Was he in a Freikorps, too?"

"No. He's been up in Sweden, earning his living flying
mail and supplies and perhaps a few passengers to isolated fishing towns, logging towns . . . what do you call
that?"

"A bush pilot?"

"Exactly so, a bush pilot, but then he took a Swedish
countess away from her husband and her children — that

must be the lady there beside him — and I suppose they had to get out. I understand he's living from her money, but he'll have to find work here."

"I guess he can't fly airplanes here," I said.

"No," said Christoph, looking across the crowded, smoky room. "Today he can't fly airplanes here. But I'll tell you something: he'll never rest until he can. And there are hundreds like him. *Thousands!*"

8.

INTRODUCTIONS

She pulled off the white bathing cap and shook out her long black hair — the blackest hair I'd ever seen, long and straight and almost blue. I had to stop looking at her, because Bobby was shaking my hand, smiling, at the same time guiding Christoph Keith and me around the old woman who was still shouting at the girl on the dock. He spoke sharply. "Will you stop that noise, Ma, you're disturbing the guests!"

"Es ist zu kalt! . . ." The rest was in some dialect; I couldn't understand a word.

"She's *not* going in, Ma. Go find Frau Alfred and help her with the baby. Go along now!" and quietly he moved her away from the ramp in the direction we had just come. "My God, what a nuisance. Have you seen a Spreewald-Amme before?" he asked me. "Before the War everybody had them as wet nurses, peasant girls from the forests on the Spree, they always wear these costumes, this one came to us thirty years ago to care for Alfred. . . ."

"And nobody ever leaves the Waldsteins' employ," said Christoph, but I was looking at the girl, who was stepping up the ramp, wrapping a white towel around her throat. She had brown legs and black eyes and long black eyelashes.

"Hallee-Hallo, Christophero," she said. "Will *you* drive the boat for me?"

"My sister Elizabeth," said Bobby. "Mr. Ellis, aus Amerika."

"We call her Lili," said Christoph.

She gave me a cold slim hand. "Good afternoon, Mr. Ellis. I am so pleased to meet you," she said in perfect English. "Do you know how to drive a motorboat?"

"Bobby!" called a lady from the pavilion. "Bring Christoph and his friend up here."

Christoph advanced, bent over the lady's hand.

"Frau Baronin, may I present Mr. Peter Ellis. . . ."

From then on it was a kaleidoscope of faces and names as Christoph and Bobby took turns introducing me. A few faces stood out: Bobby's father, a tall thin old man with white hair, a white moustache, a white flannel suit and the same eyes I had seen on his daughter; Bobby's older brother Alfred: black hair and a trim black moustache and a blue English blazer — every inch the retired cavalry officer, the successful novelist.

"That's Minister Rathenau, over there," said Christoph.

The foreign minister stood beside the wrought-iron railing, gazing out across the water. Tall and bald; gray moustache; gray goatee. Two people were competing for his attention: an exceptionally beautiful woman in a black dress and a black straw hat that did not quite conceal her platinum hair, and a short stout man with short blond hair and a short blond moustache.

"Want to meet him?" asked Christoph.

"Well, I don't know why he would want to meet me . . ." but I was already being propelled forward.

The lady turned first, and I realized she had been watching us the whole time. "Hallo," she said; "how was Paris?" and smiled and extended her hand and Christoph kissed it, and I noticed that the only other hand he had kissed was that of Bobby's mother.

"Prinzessin Hohenstein-Rofrano," said Christoph, after introducing me.

"How very formal we are today! My name is Helena."

"Die Schöne Helena, we call her," said Walther Rathenau, who had also turned. "Nachmittag, Keith," and for the first time I heard Christoph click his heels.

"Exzellenz! Darf ich vorstellen . . ."

Rathenau shook hands and looked down at me with

dark intelligent eyes. "Good afternoon, sir," he said.
"From what part of the States do you come?"

I told him, and then the other man had to be introduced: Geheimrat Dr. Strassburger, a partner in Waldstein & Co., who immediately inquired if I knew Mr.
Mitchell Morris of Drexel & Co.

"Yes, sir, I worked for him — for a while."

"Ist das wahr? Is that really so?" Dr. Strassburger
seemed delighted, took a deep breath, and launched into
a story about a meeting he had had with Mitchell Morris
at Baring's in London in 1913, but his English was not
very good, the story was not very interesting, Walther
Rathenau began to look across the water again, Christoph Keith stared fixedly at the Princess, and the Princess
examined her fingernails as if she had never seen them
before. Then Rathenau produced a heavy gold watch,
opened it, snapped it shut again and put it back into his
vest pocket. "Helena, I believe —"

"The Minister has an appointment in town."

He shook hands politely. She did not, but simply
turned to move into the crowd. He followed her.

Dr. Strassburger said: "I understand that you have
opened a dollar account in Amsterdam —"

Christoph Keith cut in: "Dr. Strassburger is *managing*
partner of the Bank."

Leaning closer to me, Dr. Strassburger said, "I think it
may be possible for us to recommend some interesting investments for you. Perhaps you will allow Leutnant Keith
to bring you in to see me when it is convenient?"

"Dr. Strassburger, it's a *very* small account —"

"I know the size of the account, Mr. Ellis. You see, it
is in dollars, and dollars increase in value here every
day, so a person with access to even a small dollar account has . . . unusual opportunity."

He didn't look over forty, but he wore a pince-nez.
Frosty magnified eyes. Blue eyes. I said I would be
happy to have his advice on investments, and he said he
would be much interested in reestablishing contact with
Drexel & Co. Recently they had been working mostly
with New York firms, but . . . He stopped abruptly, his
expression changed, he bowed. "Fräulein Elizabeth!"

I turned to find that Lili von Waldstein had joined us
— in a short white summer dress, black silk sash, white
stockings and flat black patent-leather shoes, with straps.

She was transformed: in the bathing suit she had been a grown-up woman; now she was a child — even her black hair was braided into pigtails, tied with black silk bows.

"Good afternoon, Dr. Strassburger. Bobby has told me that Mr. Ellis is a painter, so we want him to meet Professor Liebermann. Will you excuse us?" and she simply took my elbow and moved me away.

A moment later Christoph Keith was beside her.

"Lili, what are you *doing*? You can't just walk away from Dr. Strassburger!"

"Dr. Scheissburger, I call him."

"Lili, for God's sake —"

"You know what he did? He asked Mama if he could take me to the theatre . . . and he didn't even ask *me!*"

"Well, I think that's quite correct, he *should* ask your mother first!"

"Are you absolutely crazy? You think I would go *anywhere* with . . ."

"Is that why you've put on this costume?"

"What costume?"

"This . . . er . . . costume, to make yourself look twelve years old. I mean it hardly fits anymore. . . ."

"You wish to advise me how to dress, Leutnant Keith?"

"All right, let us stop this. . . . How are we going to get the Professor away from those people?"

Another circled of wicker armchairs had been assembled on the lawn just outside the pavilion, in the shade of an enromous horse chestnut. In the center of the group, the Baron von Waldstein and another man were drinking tea and swapping remarks, and while the other people were talking among themselves, it seemed to me that they were mostly listening to the Baron and his friend, another old man, quite bald, thin, with a prominent nose, a strong, clipped moustache, and a mischievous look about his face.

Lili marched right into the circle and dropped on the grass between her father and the other man, who stopped talking and leaned down toward her. She said something into his ear. He looked up at Christoph and at me. His expression changed twice: for an instant his eyebrows rose: Oh my God, another one? but then he smiled and gestured with his arm. We were to come over.

Again Christoph led the way, shook hands. "Herr Professor, darf ich vorstellen?"

Professor Leibermann gave me a firm handshake and said, "Good afternoon, sir," and that turned out to be all the English he wanted to attempt. Christoph began to explain about Verdun, and that I had come to Berlin to study painting, and might it be possible to find a student who would be willing to give lessons . . .

Professor Leibermann nodded, looking even more dubious. Was I interested in any particular kind of painting?

I said I liked to paint faces.

"Ja, ja," he said, nodding and looking into the grass. "Hmmm . . ."

Suddenly Christoph reached into the side pocket of his jacket, pulled something out and handed it to Professor Liebermann: the cardboard beer coaster with the advertisement for Spatenbräu on one side.

The old man held the thing at arm's length, handed it to Lili, put on his spectacles, took it back, studied it, then looked at me over the tops of his glasses: "Lieutenant Ring, eh? He's made some nice friends in Berlin!" and then he began to roar with laughter, while Christoph launched into the explanation: Romanisches Café . . . alter Kriegskamerad . . . came over and sat down . . . Ellis never heard of him . . . but the old man was still laughing, and Lili and her father were looking at the sketch.

"Tell him it is quite good," said Professor Liebermann as he took off his glasses. "Really quite good! Know why? Because with just a few strokes it captures the inner man, the inner man inside the flesh and the bones of the face. The inner man — in this case the essential Schweinehund!" and he began to laugh again.

Everybody was looking at us now. I had scored a success. The cardboard disk was being passed from one wicker chair to another.

"He wants to take lessons?"

Both of us nodded eagerly.

"And of course he will pay in dollars?"

"Of course, Herr Professor," said Christoph.

"Hmm . . . Ja . . ." Professor Liebermann rubbed his moustache and stared into the manicured grass. "I will think about it, perhaps I have a young man . . ." Again, a long pause, a cigar was taken out, the cigar end was snipped with an ivory cutter, the cigar was lighted, a blue cloud surrounded the thoughtful face. "I will speak with him, see if he is interested."

"Herr Professor, that's very kind of you," said Christoph, taking a visiting card from a slim leather case. "Ellis is living with me for the moment. . . ."

The old man took the card, put it into his vest pocket, nodded. "It has been a pleasure." He reached out his hand, I shook it, Lili was instantly on her feet, Christoph shook hands, we were dismissed.

The tea party was ending. One couple departed in a large beautifully polished motor launch, manned by sailors in white uniforms. People shook hands with each other and with their host and hostess, moved slowly up the steep graveled path. I examined the house for the first time; it was not really white, but more of an eggshell off-white, built along classic lines in a deceptively simple style, a cool uncluttered style; straight lines, square corners, and many tall windows overlooking the sweeping lawns, the horse chestnuts, the willows dipping into the water, the broad expanse of the Havel River and the dim blue hills on the distant shores.

"Quite a place, isn't it?" asked Christoph, following my gaze.

"Did they build it? It's beautiful."

"Oh my God, no. It is called Schloss Havelblick. Schinkel built it, one of our greatest architects, for one of the Brühls, I think about a hundred years ago, but Alfred will know. . . . Hallo, see who has returned!"

The Princess was coming down the gravel path, walking slowly and carefully in her high heels, shaking hands with people passing her on the way up. I watched Christoph watching her until she stood in front of us.

"Gentlemen . . . who will give me a cigarette?"

Christoph produced one in an instant, lighted it, and asked: "What happened to His Excellency?"

"Dinner and reception at Frau Deutsch. I am not invited. What are your plans, if I may ask?"

"We are to have supper with Alfred and Sigrid."

"In the Schloss?"

"Oh no, im Kleinen Haus."

"Just you two? No other ladies?"

"I don't know, my dear."

"Well, I think I shall find out about this." She turned and walked through the pavilion, where Lili von Waldstein and her brothers were still talking to groups of departing guests. She calmly detached Lili from the others and they disappeared, arm in arm, along one of the paths.

"That's the first princess I've ever met," I said to Christoph, who was still staring at the place where the girls had been. "Is she really a princess?"

"Oh, unquestionably. She is the widow of a prince, Austrian, the youngest son of a very ancient house. Very ancient but not very prosperous. They had land, but the land is all in Bohemia and Galicia, in other words it is gone, and he was the youngest son anyway, and he is gone too. They married in September 1914 and he was killed before Christmas, somewhere in Poland."

"And what's she got to do with the Waldsteins?"

"She is one."

"She *is* one?"

"Yes. You don't believe it?"

"Well sure, but —"

"But she doesn't look the part, eh?" Christoph grinned in a rather nasty way. "My friend, you had better forget some of your . . . I'm sorry, I don't know the word —"

"The word is 'stereotypes,' and I'm sorry."

"It is all right, I should not have said that, I am sorry too."

"Well, anyway," I said to make the moment pass, "what is she doing now?"

"What is she doing now? I think she is trying to be invited —"

"No, damn it, what is she doing with her life? She's been a widow for eight years? A girl like that?"

"Oh, she has done different things. In the main, she has tried to be an actress. She has had a few roles, perhaps it helped that her uncles give money for the productions, but on the other hand it's not so easy for a princess to become an actress. She calls herself Helena Waldstein and at the moment, as you see, I think she tries to become Frau Aussenminister Rathenau."

"What? You must be joking."

"No, not at all. Such a handsome man, such a successful, intelligent, famous man, such a rich man . . . and he has never married. Can you imagine how the ladies pursue him?"

"I don't see it."

"What does that mean, you don't see it?"

"That was not the impression I got."

"Oh no? What impression did you get, Mr. Ellis?"

Should I tell him? "I got the impression she likes being seen with the Foreign Minister, but that she was very happy that you're back from Paris. And that you were very happy to meet her, although you knew she'd be here."

Christoph had been looking over my shoulder at the sailboats. He took out a cigarette, lighted it, and let his eyes return to the sailboats.

Finally he said: "You watch people carefully." He still wouldn't look at me. "As a matter of fact, I did *not* know she would be here, I understood she was still in Vienna trying for a part. But the rest of it . . . You are quite right. A princess and a penniless bank trainee? It was different during the War. I had my black Husaren uniform, then I was a flying officer, I think we looked good together, but as you know — better than anyone else — the War was over for me on the eleventh day of April, nineteen hundred and sixteen. I told you when the French let me come back: first day of March, nineteen hundred and *twenty*. Four years gone. What was she to do, knit socks?"

We had wandered up to the iron railing of the pavilion now. The water was lapping at the seawall beneath our feet. An excursion steamer, loaded with Sunday trippers, had just passed the island; the floating dock and the Waldstein motorboat rode gently up and down as the steamer's wake reached the shore.

I didn't say a word and Christoph smoked his cigarette.

"Are you gentlemen ready for cocktails?" Bobby had changed into tails.

"You look as if you are going to serve them," said Christoph.

"I *am* going to serve them, because my brother does not understand the American martini. But then I must leave you, I am expected back in town. Shall we go up to the Kleine Haus now? I think Lili and Helena are going to have dinner with you."

I followed them out of the pavilion where two maids

were collecting cups and saucers and plates, across the lawn and up the winding path.

"Where's Strassburger?" asked Christoph.

"We finally got rid of him."

"He wasn't intending to take her out tonight, was he?"

"No, next week. But if he discovered that you and Peter are invited to Alfred's . . . The whole idea is *impossible!* She has never been allowed out alone with a man, here is somebody old enough to be her *father* —"

"How old is your sister, Bobby?"

He looked at me. "She is seventeen. So you wonder, how old is my father? He is sixty-four. The answer is my mother, Lili's mother, is his second wife. Alfred and Max had a different mother. She died when Max was born."

"I told him Max was killed in France," said Christoph.

"Yes, another airplane pilot. Had nobody to pull him out."

"I'm terribly sorry."

"Thank you. But why are we talking about such subjects?"

"I was wondering about Dr. Strassburger."

"Oh God, yes, Strassburger. Geheimrat Dr. Erich Strassburger. What shall we tell you?"

By this time we had reached the top of the hill and were walking around the front of the Schloss — broad flagstone terraces and tall french doors.

"Strassburger came to the Bank as a young lawyer. My father and my uncle, they thought it would be good to have a lawyer in the house. Extremely clever. Works very, very hard. He has not married. He has made himself an expert in foreign trade transactions. Also in selling German securities in England and America. For example, before the War, he managed a syndicate to sell the bonds for Rathenau's electric companies, for the AEG, in London. That sort of thing . . . complicated big things, and a great deal of money for our Bank. In the War he was not in the army, he was in the Ministry of Finance for a while, he spent much time working with the Dutch, I think. And then he came back to the Bank, most of the younger men had been in the War, my father and my uncle and the other partners were getting older —"

"Dr. Strassburger is a very important partner," said Christoph.

"He is the most important partner," said Bobby.

"Oh, I would not go that far," said Christoph.

"I would go that far," said Bobby. We were entering the maze of yew hedges as we rounded the northern end of the Schloss. "We are always a little careful what we *say* in here, because you don't know who else might *be* in here."

And then he was gone. He had turned right into an opening between two hedges and I followed him, and when I was in the narrow tunnel, he was gone.

"Hey," I said, walking along the tunnel.

"Dr. Strassburger has decided it is time for him to marry," said Bobby, very quietly, his voice just inches from my ear.

The tunnel was coming to an end. There was a gap in the hedges to my right and another to my left. I stopped, waiting to hear his voice, but he didn't say anything. I turned left and found myself looking down another, shorter passage.

"When you learn German better, you will notice Dr. Strassburger's accent," said Bobby. His voice seemed farther away. "He comes from Dresden, and he was what we call a Saxon accent. We don't think it is very elegant."

I looked up and tried to figure out which way the sun was setting. I had a feeling that the Tea House had been in the shadow of the hill and the Schloss, so I should be headed toward the sun, to the west. When I came to the next opening, I turned left, because the sky looked a little brighter up ahead.

"Strassburger comes from a nice Jewish family in Dresden." Bobby's voice was right beside me again. "They own a jewelry store. The father's dead, the old mother is *so* proud of her successful son, Geheimrat Doctor Strassburger — but it's time for him to find a wife! And who would be a suitable wife for Geheimrat Doctor Strassburger, the most important partner of the second-oldest bank in Berlin?"

I reached another dead end, and this time there was no exit. I had to turn around and retrace my steps, but then I saw an opening to the left. Had I just come through that? No, I didn't think I'd made a turn here. Maybe I didn't see this hole as I went by. I stepped through and found myself face to face with Lili. She put her finger to her lips. Her black eyes sparkled.

"How about a direct descendant of the founder?" Bobby's voice was off to the right somewhere. "Rich, pretty, seventeen years old, presumably a virgin — and a baroness as well!"

Lili took my hand and led me along the passage. We turned right into another one, a wider straighter one. Beams of sunlight slanted through the tall hedges. We came to an opening at the left but she pulled me past. We came to a second opening, she pulled me through that one, then dashed about ten steps to the right, let go of my hand and shoved me through another opening. I was outside, at the edge of a field of strawberries, and on the other side of the strawberries Christoph Keith was leaning against the wall of a greenhouse, hands in his pockets, grinning.

I put my head back into the maze, but there was no trace of her.

9.

THE LITTLE HOUSE

"Alfred," said the Princess, "Mr. Ellis wants to know how we are related, and I've told him it's much too complicated for *me*."

"Please call me Peter," I said.

"It's not a bit complicated," said Alfred von Waldstein, putting his martini on the little iron table and stretching back in his chair. "Your grandfather and my grandfather — No, one minute, sorry. Your *great*-grandfather —"

"That was Jacob?"

"That was Jacob, the hussar against Napoleon, the poet who put our name into schoolbooks . . . he was the brother, one of the brothers of *my* great-grandfather —"

"That was David?"

"No, Helena, you really should look at the Stammbaum once in your life —"

"I *have*, my dear, I just can't understand it."

"My great-grandfather was Joseph, the second brother.

David was the father, the one who started the Bank and married a daughter of Moses Mendelssohn. Their sons were Jacob and Joseph and Lessing and Benjamin, and they also had three girls, I think."

"But you don't remember their names," she laughed.

"Well, I will go and look them up!"

"Oh, don't be ridiculous —" but Alfred was already on his feet, stalking into the Little House.

We were all sitting under an arbor of grape leaves that formed a kind of terrace outside the open french doors of the dining room, and this was the second commotion caused by the Princess von Hohenstein-Rofrano within the hour.

The first involved Bobby von Waldstein, or rather his Bugatti racing car.

When Bobby finally emerged from the maze of yew hedges to see Christoph and me laughing at him across the strawberry field, he just smiled and brushed off his tails and came over to join us.

"You have a brilliant sense of direction, Peter. Shall we go up to the Kleine Haus now?"

We walked around the greenhouses, across another lawn, passed through a wall of giant hedges and emerged on the broad pebbled entrance court in front of the Schloss. We walked down the driveway, through the open gates, crossed the shady island road and entered a complex of stables and garages on the other side of the road. We came through an arch in a big yellow stucco building and entered a wide cobbled courtyard. I smelled manure. The doors to the stables were open, and I could see some of the horses sticking their heads out of their stalls. The coachman who had driven us from the station came across the courtyard in his shirtsleeves, wearing rubber boots and carrying two buckets of water.

"Abend, die Herrschaften."

"Guten Abend, Schmitz," said Christoph and Bobby in unison.

Two small boys were chasing each other around a gleaming sky-blue racing car that was parked at one side of the court. It had an open cockpit with two seats. The slotted hood was strapped down with leather belts.

"Are you going to drive that in your tails?" I asked Bobby.

"Oh, most certainly, but I am well prepared." He tipped one of the leather bucket seats forward, extracted a dispatch case, opened it, and produced a long white overcoat. When he put it on, it covered all of his head except his face. He put one foot on the front right tire and posed for us with his hands folded across his chest.

"I wish I could take your picture," I said. "At home nobody would believe this."

"It may look funny, but it's very practical, I assure you." He peeled off the coat and the cap and tossed them into the car. Then he led us out of the courtyard through an apple orchard. I sensed that we were approaching the highest point on the island, and when we came out of the trees into the open hayfield, I turned around to see a breathtaking view: miles of open water in all directions, hundreds of sails, the sun sinking toward the western suburbs . . .

Christoph was pointing out sights: "That's the Grunewald to the north, beyond it you see the smoke of the city. Where the sun is going down is Kladow there on the other side, then the Pfaueninsel and behind that is Potsdam. . . ."

"Gentlemen, we are waiting for our martinis!"

The Princess was walking across the field, stepping carefully in high heels. She had taken off her hat, and the wind was blowing a few loose strands of her hair, which was pinned into a bun at the back of her head. As if it was the most natural thing in the world, she took Christoph's arm with one hand and my arm with the other and walked between us across the field — all the time talking to Bobby:

"Everybody is sitting on the terrace waiting for the American martinis that only Bobby can mix. Now that we have an American, perhaps we will find out if they are the genuine thing. But after you have mixed them, you may only drink one, and then I will take you to Nikolassee or you will be late for your appointment."

"What are you talking about, Helena? I am driving into town —"

"If you are driving into town, how do you imagine these gentlemen will get home? How will I get home?"

"Well . . . ah, I imagine on the train —"

"What time is the last train? And how are we to get to the station?"

"Well . . . in the Horch."

"Lili says your mother sent the Horch into town with your Aunt Emma and Cousin Lore and it is not coming back until tomorrow morning, with some guests for Professor Liebermann. . . ."

While the argument was going on we arrived at a clump of trees, a stone water tower, a cottage made of dark wooden shingles. We opened the garden gate, followed a corridor of lilac bushes, and found Sigrid and Lili and Alfred von Waldstein sitting in a grape arbor that extended like a porch from the house.

"Die Schöne Helena," said Alfred. "Always with two men."

They all stood up. Lili was completely transformed again, in a red dress and silk stockings and her black hair parted in the middle and combed back over her shoulders. How could she have changed that fast and beaten us up here?

Sigrid grasped my hand, smiled beautifully and said, very carefully: "It is an honor . . . to welcome you . . ."

"You don't need to speak English with him," said Bobby. "He understands every word."

"Bobby, we are all awaiting your martinis," said his brother.

"Oh yes, I will go into the kitchen," he said, and disappeared. There was a lull.

"This is a lovely house," I said. "Is it very old?"

"I think it was built about 1820," said Alfred. "We have always called it Das Kleine Haus, but when it was built it was the *only* house on the island."

"Did your family build it?"

"Oh, no. Not at all. This island belonged to the Counts von Brühl, same name as my wife's family, different branch. They owned all of that land you see across the water there, across the Wannsee over there, but there was no bridge and the island was quite wild, only fishermen would land their boats. Then I think the Brühls decided to cut some of the trees, to keep livestock over here in the summer, so they built this little house for a family to watch the island for them. Well, then in I think about 1830 one of the Counts Brühl, a younger son, wanted to live out here, to build himself a country place down near the water, and nothing would do but to employ the most famous architect in Berlin — perhaps in Germany —

and that was Karl Friedrich Schinkel. You have seen his
work?"

"Alfred," said Helena, "he has only just arrived in Berlin."

"Oh yes, I'm sorry, you see, Schinkel has built some of
our most famous buildings. He built in what we call the
Prussian Style — very cool, very simple, just the opposite
of the rococo complicated things they did in France and
Austria in the eighteenth century — and also just the opposite of the terrible pompous things they did here in Berlin in the last fifty years. Well, in any event, Schinkel
designed the place and it was called Schloss Havelblick
— a view of the Havel, you see — and the reason the
young Count Brühl had the money for such a project was
that he had married a daughter of David Waldstein, the
banker. The Brühls had land, but David Waldstein had
money."

"Has not changed in a hundred years," said Sigrid von
Waldstein. "The Brühls still have land, the Waldsteins still
have money. *And* land!"

Alfred flushed. "My dear, you know I'm talking about
the *Wasser*brühls!" He turned to me. "The family I'm telling you about, we call them Water Brühls because they
live here on the water, and *her* family — Brühl zu
Zeydlitz — are the *Kartoffel*brühls, because they grow potatoes. They had the same ancestor in the sixteenth century but today they hardly know each other."

"Same ancestor and same financial problems," said
Sigrid, and fortunately Bobby returned with a tray, some
glasses, and a silver cocktail shaker.

He put the tray on the table, poured the martinis, and
handed each of us a glass. Alfred raised his, looking me
in the eye. "To your good health, sir. We are happy to
have you with us."

"Thank you, sir. I'm happy to be here."

We drank . . . and Lili exploded, coughing and choking and turning red. Roaring with laughter, her brothers
pulled her out of the chair, took the glass out of her hand,
pounded her back . . .

"Oh . . . Oh . . . I thought . . . it is vermouth . . ."

"Our baby sister," said Alfred, his arm around her, his
handkerchief now in her hands.

"The English and Americans put gin into everything,"

said Helena. "It is two parts gin and one vermouth, isn't it?"

"We've been putting in a little more than that," I said. "These are excellent."

"Four to one," said Bobby proudly.

"Oh, I think it is *terrible*," said Lili, who had regained her breath.

"Let's get you a glass of wine," said Sigrid. They went into the house.

I turned to Alfred. "You were telling me about how your family came here."

"Oh yes. Well, after the Brühls built the Schloss, one of the Countess's brothers, that is my great-grandfather, Joseph Waldstein, began to rent this house for his family in the summer. They lived in Berlin, but they took this house every summer for years."

"Didn't Brühl get into difficulties?" asked Christoph.

"Yes, not clever about business. He borrowed money to invest in things — for example, in American railroads. This was when the first railroads were being built. It was suggested to him that America was far away, perhaps it would be wiser to invest in railroads a little closer. But no, Count Brühl and his brother had visited America, America was the land of the future, America was the place to invest in railroads. So they mortgaged their land, including the island, and they invested their money in one American railroad — I don't know which one — and before 1845 all the money was gone. Count Brühl must have been one of the first to lose all his money on railroad investments. They did not build one kilometer of track with his money "

"And it wasn't even his money," said Bobby.

"Legally it was his money, but of course it had come with Fräulein Waldstein. Her dowry."

"That must have made things unpleasant," I said.

"Very unpleasant. Especially when the lenders — I think it was the Rothschilds in Frankfurt — wanted to take the island away."

"Who wanted to take the island away?" asked Sigrid, as she and Lili came back out into the arbor with a tray and more glasses and a bottle of wine.

"I am telling the story of my family on this island. Well, the lenders would have sold the island to pay Count Brühl's debts, so of course Joseph Waldstein had to come

to the rescue. He bought the mortgage from the Rothschilds and he gave it to his sister as a birthday present."

"And the Brühls stayed in the Schloss?"

Alfred nodded. "The Count died first, his wife lived
there alone, they had no children, and when she died the
property went to another Count Brühl, another brother's
son. But in the next generation things were just the same,
this next Count Brühl always needed money, he was a
major in the Garde-du-Corps, very expensive regiment,
he did not it seems marry a lady with money, and in
1866, just before he went off to the war against Austria,
he sold the island to Joseph Waldstein the second, that is
my grandfather — who had of course spent all his summers here and who loved the place very much."

"So your family in effect bought the island twice?" I
asked.

Alfred smiled. "The island twice and the Schloss three
times, really, since it was David Waldstein's money that
paid for Schinkel's work in the first place. But I tell you
something: this second Joseph, our grandfather, he was a
smart fellow. By this time the railroad was built out here
to Nikolassee, you could get out here from the city in one
hour, Wannsee over there became a summer resort, people began to use sailboats for amusement, people wanted
houses out here — my grandfather built the bridge, he
had the road built in a circle, and then he sold off one
piece of the island after another, like slices from a cake,
at fantastic prices — mostly to other bankers from the
city, his friends, his competitors —"

"— His brother," said Helena, and everybody laughed.

"Correct, his brother bought the place next door, everybody wanted to have a place as nice as Schloss Havelblick."

"Only Schinkel was dead," said Sigrid.

"Schinkel was dead many years. We are now in the
time of Bismarck, when everybody made enormous
amounts of money and built enormously pretentious
houses — especially my grandfather's new neighbors. Of
course he kept enough land to protect his view, but if we
take you in the motorboat on your next visit, we can show
you amazing sights."

"Unbelievable," said Sigrid. "We have a copy of the
Villa d'Este, but without the waterworks."

"We have two castles from the Middle Ages," said Lili.

"And two Spanish haciendas," said Sigrid.

"Please forget the haciendas," said Alfred. "My cousins built one of them!" Everybody laughed.

Helena suddenly stood up. "Robert, dear boy, it is time for our trip to the station."

So the argument began again: Bobby didn't want to ride into town on the train. Helena insisted; he had done it before, plenty of times. In town, he could use taxis. . . . But who would drive the Bugatti? . . . She, Helena, would drive the Bugatti, as she had only last week, remember? . . . But she couldn't drive Peter and Christoph into town because there are only two seats. . . . Three people have been fitted into the Bugatti. . . . But Christoph can't drive, so will he sit on Peter's lap? Or will Peter sit on Christoph's lap . . .

"Nonsense, my dear. *I* will sit on Christoph's lap and Peter will drive. Americans can drive anything!"

Bobby rose and made a bow. "Ladies and gentlemen, I surrender. Die Schöne Helena has her way — as always. I wish you a pleasant evening."

Helena kissed his cheek, took his arm and walked him away through the lilacs.

I turned to Lili, mumbling: "Couldn't Christoph and I sleep in the garden? It's a warm night —"

She touched her lips, the same gesture she had made in the yew hedges, and rose to her feet. "Alfred, may I show Peter your studio?"

Inside, the Little House was dark and elegantly simple: a stove made of Dutch tiles; dark red Biedermeier furniture — what I later learned was Biedermeier furniture — Turkish carpets; dark yellow wallpaper; a few dark portraits; and the comfortable smell of a very old house combined with the smell of fresh flowers on every table.

Lili said: "Of course you and Christoph could have slept here — there is a guest room. But Helena does not want Christoph to sleep *here*. You understand?"

It was getting dark outside. It was darker in the living room, but even so I could see that she was blushing. She turned away and opened a door. "This is where my brother writes his books."

Another Turkish carpet, a big table piled with books and papers, a lamp, a wooden armchair, a worn leather

sofa, two walls solid with books, and large french doors
through which we could see the hayfield sloping down into
the apple orchard, the roofs of the stables, the tops of the
oaks and beeches and horse chestnuts around the Schloss,
and beyond this solid blanket of treetops, the flat smooth
expanse of darkening water and lights coming on in the
distance.

I stopped looking at the view and looked at Lili, to find
she was looking at me.

"I don't know the customs of your country," I said.

"Pardon? I don't know what —"

"At home I would ask if you would like to go out with
me."

"Go out? You mean into the garden?"

She knew I didn't mean that.

"I mean go out with me to dinner, and to the theatre
. . . or something. Like with Dr. Strassburger."

She smiled. "Oh, I see. Like Dr. Strassburger."

"You said he should have asked you first. So I'm asking
you first."

"And then you will ask my mother?" She was grinning.

"I said I don't know the customs. What should I do?
Would you like to go out with me?" I was very close to
her now.

"Yes. I would like that very much, but they will not allow it."

"Your parents? Why not?"

She shrugged. "With a man alone, no chaperone? I'm
still in school, it's not allowed."

"What about Dr. Strassburger? He must know what the
rules are."

"Yes, perhaps that would be different, because he is
much older, my father's partner. . . . I don't know what
they would say but it does not matter, because I am not
going 'out' with Dr. Strassburger. I don't like Dr. Strassburger."

"Well . . . ah . . . how can we see each other?"

She looked down at her folded hands, then up again at
me. She had the longest eyelashes I had ever seen. "You
don't worry about that," she said. "If you want to see me,
we will see each other."

The round mahogany table was just big enough to accommodate the six of us. The french doors to the grape

arbor were still open. Hurricane glasses protected the candles from the slight breeze that brought the smell of cut grass into the dining room. A young maid, dressed in a black uniform and a white apron, served plates of pea soup. Helena was insisting that she made it back from the station in five minutes flat; Alfred and Christoph refused to believe her. Sigrid and Lili showed that this debate didn't interest them. Alfred caught their looks.

"Peter," he said, "we have been talking all evening about ourselves. Why don't you tell us something about your home and your family?"

Well, what could I tell them? Certainly nothing as interesting as what I had been hearing. Germantown is a suburb of Philadelphia. My father is a surgeon. My grandfather was a surgeon. I went to school —

"What sort of a school?" asked Alfred. "A boarding school, like the English?"

"No, this was a Friends' School, Germantown Friends."

"What does that mean, 'Friends'? Does that not mean Quakers?"

"Yes."

"And you are a Quaker?" The room was suddenly absolutely still. Every eye was upon me. What could these people have against Quakers?

"Well, yes, I guess I was born one, my parents go to Meeting but I haven't been for quite a while —"

Alfred von Waldstein slammed his hand upon the table and fairly shouted: "But that is *wonderful*," and then they were all talking at once.

"We were so hungry," said Lili, "and they brought chocolate pudding to our school."

"They did remarkable things," said Alfred. "In the worker districts the children were actually starving. Just as soon as the War was over, the American Quakers came with powdered milk and chocolate and fruit juice in cans —"

Helena said: "If children like Lili were hungry, you can imagine what it was like for poor people, for the children of the factory workers, for children whose fathers had been killed —"

"When was all this?" I asked.

"Just after the War ended," said Alfred. "Our supply systems broke down, most of the supplies were gone anyway, the British kept up the blockade, we had a famine in the spring of 1919 . . . and suddenly these people arrived, very quiet simple Americans, they made no fuss at all, they made contact with the churches and the schools and they distributed food to the children. . . . I don't even know how they got the food through the blockade."

"Miss Boatwright told me the first shipments came from Switzerland," said Helena.

"Miss Boatwright? Miss Susan Boatwright?"

"You know her?"

"Oh yes. She's a friend of my family. But I haven't seen her . . . for several years."

I had not seen her since the spring of 1919, when I was locked up in Friends Hospital with her niece. Miss Boatwright would sit and talk to me and tell me how much she liked the picture I was doing of Joanne — and come to think she said she was off to Germany.

"Miss Boatwright was out here last Saturday," said Lili.

"Do you know if she's still in Berlin?" I asked. "I would really like to see her."

"I'm sure she is," said Alfred. "She is writing a report on the relief operations in Germany, and she is living somewhere in the city. We will find her address for you."

"Peter, we cannot tell you how much the people here appreciate what the Quakers did," said Sigrid quietly. "I was in boarding school — and I was *really* hungry!"

This embarrassed me. I wanted to change the subject. "Why did the British keep up the blockade when the War was over?"

"To make us sign the Versailles Treaty," said Alfred. "They didn't finally wait until the treaty was signed, but they waited long enough!"

"And you feel it was a bad treaty?"

"*A bad treaty?*" Christoph sounded incredulous.

"I'm sorry," I said, seeing their astonished faces, feeling I had stubbed my toe this time. "I don't know much about it."

They looked at each other. Finally Alfred said: "I think it's too complicated to discuss the whole treaty tonight. But if you ask us — yes, it is a *very* bad treaty, a *terrible* treaty — not only for the land that was taken away from us, not only for the hundreds of thousands of German people who are forced to become citizens of France and Poland and Czechoslovakia — but it is a bad treaty because it does not permit Germany to survive as a nation. I mean, we have a government, a republican form of government now, but this government cannot perform the obligations of that treaty!"

"You mean the reparation payments?"

"That's right. Do you realize exactly how much the Allies expect us to pay? The last number I read was 132 *billion* gold marks! Well, it is simply *impossible* for us to pay, we will never pay — we cannot do it! And the pressure to make these payments is causing this incredible inflation, the prices go up every day, the people don't know what to do, and they are getting desperate. How can any government survive under such pressure?"

I said: "Christoph told me your foreign minister, the man I met this afternoon —"

"— Walther Rathenau."

"Yes, that he wants to comply with the treaty. Isn't that right?"

"He wants to move in that direction," said Christoph. "He knows we can't pay everything they ask, but he wants to work with them."

Alfred nodded. "He does. He thinks it is the only way we can restore our economy, to reason with the Allies, to demonstrate that we will try to pay them as much as we can — perhaps in goods instead of money. . . . I tell you something: Walther Rathenau is one of the most brilliant men we have and he loves his country, and he believes the only way to save this situation is to work with the Allies, to gain time, to build up German trade and industry, to put the unemployed to work —"

Helena interrupted: "And you know what the German people are going to do for Walther Rathenau? They are going to kill him!"

"*Aber Helena!*" Sigrid gasped.

"No, it's true! A priest went to the police, he heard something in confession, the police went straight to Chancellor Wirth, and Wirth has asked Rathenau to have a police escort. But he refuses to have any protection, will not permit it."

"He told you this?" asked Christoph.

"Of course not. His mother told me."

"His mother?"

"You know she *begged* him not to take this position —"

"But why do they want to kill him?" I asked.

"Because he is a Jew!"

I didn't know where to look. I looked at Christoph.

"It's a little more complicated than that," said Alfred.

"It's not at all more complicated," said Helena. "It's very simple."

"They shot Matthias Erzberger last summer," said Alfred. "A Catholic politician, leader of the Center Party. He signed the Armistice in 1918, he led the campaign to have the German government sign the Versailles Treaty. His theory was it doesn't matter what you sign if somebody puts a gun to your head, so the treaty doesn't bind *us*. But that's too sophisticated for them. They killed him anyway."

"And now it's Rapallo," said Christoph. "They just can't understand how Rathenau could sign a treaty with the Bolsheviks. They remember Liebknecht and the Spartacus, they remember when we had a Soviet of Bavaria down in Munich, and now we sign a treaty with the Russians."

"Who are 'they'?" I asked.

"Nationalists," said Alfred. "The extreme Right — General Ludendorff, Karl Helfferich — everybody who hates the Republic."

"— Because the Republic signed at Versailles," Christoph said.

"The people who were army officers, the people who think we were not beaten in the field, we were betrayed by Communists and Socialists in the rear," Alfred said.

"The Freikorps types," said Helena.

I looked at Sigrid and at Christoph. Their expressions did not change, but Sigrid was looking down at her plate.

"There were some good people in the Freikorps," she said.

"I haven't met one," said Helena.

"I have," said Sigrid.

Dead silence for a moment. Then Alfred said: "I'll tell you something: in 1919 there would have been no Republic without the Freikorps. They saved the government, and it would surprise you who gave money — a lot of money — to pay those troops. Walther Rathenau, for example."

"Alfred, you are talking nonsense!"

"Ask him."

"I will ask him!"

"I'll tell you another source of money."

"Oh no!"

"Oh yes!"

Christoph, Lili, Sigrid and I were all silently watching them.

"Remember this was Christmas 1918. Revolution. Chaos. Mobs in the streets. Thousands of people marching — marching with red flags. Singing. You are sitting in your bank. You listen to them singing. What do you think you need? You need soldiers. But the army is falling apart, the army is full of commissars with red armbands, the army can't do a thing. What do the generals do? The generals set up little private armies — volunteer corps, people who still want to fight, people who only follow their own leaders. But they have to pay them. Where do they get the money?" Alfred paused. "They got it."

Heavy silence.

Helena began again: "Your father and Uncle Fritz never —"

"I'm not sure they knew about it."

"Strassburger?"

Alfred nodded.

The soup bowls were removed and the girl was passing the main course in silver serving dishes: thin slices of cold smoked ham, boiled potatoes, steaming mounds of white asparagus covered with melting butter — the best asparagus I had ever eaten. Alfred himself moved around the table pouring the white wine, and when he sat down again he lifted his glass.

"Meine Damen und Herren, I offer a toast: No more politics — at least tonight!"

"Thank God!" said his wife. We all drank. The wine was a little sweeter than anything I'd had in Paris. I asked about it.

"Just a light Mosel — I mean Moselle, of course — a favorite German wine when it was bottled, but now a French wine."

"Alfred!"

"I'm sorry, my dear. Helena, what were you doing in Vienna?"

"I was trying to get a part — or rather *five* parts."

"Five parts in one play?" asked Christoph.

"Five parts."

"I think I can guess the play," said Alfred. "But I did not believe even Die Schöne Helena was *that* ambitious."

Helena shrugged. "It never hurts to try. The director is a friend of mine."

"But what is the play?" asked Lili.

"Ask Alfred."

"Reigen?" asked Alfred.

Helena nodded.

The others looked blank.

"It's by Arthur Schnitzler," said Alfred. "A fascinating play, hardly ever performed. It was privately printed around 1900, but during the Empire they did not dare perform it. After the War they put on one production, but it caused such an uproar that the police closed it."

"It caused an uproar in Vienna?" asked Christoph. "What is it about?"

"It's about love," said Helena.

"Well . . ." Alfred was carefully cutting his ham into small pieces. "You think it is about love? I would say there is very little love. It is about sexual intercourse."

"Alfred!"

"My dear, have you read it?"

"Certainly not! I've never heard of it."

"Well, perhaps you would like to see it. Helena, will they bring it to Berlin?"

"Yes, that's their whole idea, and I thought they might like a nice north German voice —"

"You wanted to play all the women?" Alfred began to laugh, and rose to refill our glasses. "My dear, I don't think Schnitzler would approve. After all, the setting is Vienna. And with so many actors unemployed, I think they should engage five men and five women."

"That's what they did — and I got no part at all! They wanted Vienna dialects."

Lili said, "I think it is not polite that you two discuss this play without telling the rest of us the story!"

"No, that would spoil it," said Helena. "We'll take you to see it."

"Her mother will not let her go," said Alfred. "And the ushers will not let her in!"

"Her mother has never heard of the play," said Helena. "And we will dress her to look at least thirty. With a veil!"

"We will all go together," said Sigrid.

"Now just one moment," said Alfred. "This is my baby sister. You want me to take part in a complot to bring my baby sister to a naughty play?"

"It's not a naughty play," said Helena. "You just said it is not about love, it is about sexual intercourse. I think it is about the way people behave, the way men behave, the way women behave, before sexual intercourse — and afterwards. Do you really think 'naughty' is the word?"

Alfred sipped his wine thoughtfully. Then he said: "No, I agree. 'Naughty' is the wrong word for *Reigen*."

"What is the right word?" I asked.

Alfred looked into the candlelight. "The right word is *triste*."

10.

INDIAN CROSSES

|| **Swastika** (swæ•stika). 1871. [Skr. *svastika*, f. *svasti* well-being, luck, f. *su* good + *asti* being (f. *as* to be).] A primitive symbol or ornament of the form of a cross with equal arms with a limb of the same length projecting at right angles from the end of each arm, all in the same direction and (usu.) clockwise.

—*The Shorter Oxford English Dictionary on Historical Principles*

"*Hackendreuz am Stahlhelm,*
Schwarz-weiss-rotes Band,
Die Brigade Ehrhardt
Werden wir genannt!"

I should have gone directly to bed. Light showed under the door of Kaspar's room, and as I passed I heard the faint sound of men singing, a band playing a marching song. The door opened, and there was Kaspar — red-faced, tousled, in shirtsleeves and suspenders.

"Good evening, Kaspar." I whispered, because the music was louder now, coming from a portable gramophone on his bureau. His parents were sleeping at the other end of the house.

He lifted the needle and stopped the record.

"Do you have American cigarettes?"

I wanted to give him the whole pack, but as I stepped into the room he closed the door behind me. The place stank of cigarette smoke and beer. The bed and the table and the carpet were strewn with open photograph albums, unfolded maps and piles of hand-written letters. Green beer bottles with white porcelain caps were piled into a laundry basket.

"Please sit down," said Kaspar, indicating a wicker armchair, the kind I had in my room. "I can offer you a little schnapps and plenty of beer."

"Well thank you very much, but I've had quite a bit. . . ."

Kaspar wasn't listening. He was already pouring clear liquid from a stone bottle into two small wineglasses, spilling some of it on the table. Shakily he passed one of them to me and raised the other: "Prosit!"

There was nothing to do but drink the stuff. It burned my throat.

Kaspar accepted one of my cigarettes, lighted it, and began to pour foaming beer into another empty glass. "And how are things on the island?" he asked, through the cigarette in his mouth.

"Very nice. It's a beautiful place."

"Not beer but plenty of good wine?"

"That's right."

"And you liked my brother's rich friends?"

"Yes. I liked them."

"And you met Frau Baronin Alfred von Waldstein?"

"Yes. I had dinner at her house."

"Oh, you had dinner at her house." His red face was getting redder. Wanting desperately to change the subject, I pointed to the open notebook on his desk. "Are you writing something?"

He nodded. "Beginning my memoirs. I'm twenty years old, it is time to begin my memoirs, don't you agree?"

I couldn't tell if he was teasing me. "Well, I'm older and I haven't begun mine, but I suppose it's never too soon." I moved the wicker chair close to the table. "May I look at your photographs?"

He came over and stood beside me, talking about the

pictures as I turned the heavy black pages of one album.
"This is my company in cadet school. This is me with my
brothers when they were both home from the Front. . . .
This one was killed —"

"Christoph told me, I'm terribly sorry. . . ."

"This is my friend Brühl, shooting out of the window
when the sailors attacked our school. . . . Frau Baronin
Alfred von Waldstein is his sister. . . . I took this picture."

"Why were the sailors attacking your school?"

"Why? Ask them why! Because they were mutinous Red
swine, they walked off their ships and made a revolution
and made us lose the War!"

"Who is this fellow?"

"That's Lieutenant Kern, a navy officer. He invited
some of us to join the Second Marine Brigade, Captain
Ehrhardt's Brigade, and he took us with him to Wilhelmshaven, where the Brigade was formed. Here we are drill-
ing with our helmets and rifles. I don't know who took
this picture. . . . I'm this fellow here, with the flag. . . "

Now Kaspar was turning the pages as he explained
the shiny photographs, and it was like watching a film:
helmeted men sitting in the door of a freight car; blurred
figures running crouched along the storefronts of some
German city; marksmen firing from rooftops; dead
bodies on the sidewalk. . . . "This is Munich. See the
towers of the Frauenkirche? They had set up a Soviet of
Bavaria down there, a bunch of filthy Russian Jews with
beards were actually running the place, we went down
there and *really* cleaned up. . . ." A brick courtyard, a
pile of women in what looked like white uniforms, splat-
tered with black blood.

"Are these nurses? Look at this one's cap, these are
nurses!"

"We didn't do that," said Kaspar, trying to turn the
page. "Freikorps Lützow did that, these bitches were hiding wounded Reds, they had pistols —"

I held on to the page. "Who said they had pistols?
Nurses with pistols? How do you know?"

"That's what the Lützows said. We only came along
afterwards —"

"Did they have a trial of some kind?"

Kaspar snorted. "A trial? Nobody had a trial, there
wasn't time for trials, we were putting down a revolution!"

I couldn't stop looking at the picture. "Did you take this?"

"Yes."

"Ever show it to your father?"

Kaspar shook his head.

"Not proud of it, are you?"

Kaspar shrugged. "It's war."

"I've been in a war. I saw some bad things, some *very* bad things, but I never saw anybody shoot down two-four-six-nine nurses! And neither did Christoph. And neither did your father."

Kaspar poured himself another schnapps and drank it. "This was a different kind of war, a civil war inside our country —"

"Which means you had German soldiers shooting German nurses."

"They were hiding Reds."

"They were taking care of wounded men — also German, presumably."

"Bolshevik swine who stabbed our soldiers in the back. We don't call them Germans!"

I should have gone to bed and left him to his memoirs, but I couldn't stop turning pages. "What's going on here?"

"That's the parade ground at Döberitz, right outside Berlin here. In the winter from 1919 to 1920, the government brought us from Silesia to clean up Berlin. Döberitz was our base. We cleaned up Berlin. You know what the government was going to do then? Disband us! Send us home. Why? Because your Control Commission told them to. The treaty those bastards signed made Germany reduce the army down to one hundred thousand men by March of 1920, and the Control Commission said we counted as army. Now in this picture General Freiherr von Lüttwitz is reviewing the Ehrhardt Brigade and the Baltikum Brigade at Döberitz. I don't know who took this picture. I am in here somewhere. My God, it was a splendid parade, with the music and the flags, just like before 1918. And von Lüttwitz, the senior general of the Reichswehr in Berlin — that is, regular army — he made a speech to us and he told us he would absolutely not allow the government to disband us.

"And the next thing that happened was the government tried to have us transferred out from under Lüttwitz to the Marineleitung — that is, the navy. That meant they *were* going to disband us. So that was the end. Lüttwitz and Captain Ehrhardt decided to take over the government.

"Here we are, this picture was taken at night, March twelve, 1920, the march to Berlin. Here we are the next morning, arriving at the Brandenburg Gate. These are imperial battle flags. Here is General Ludendorff welcoming us."

"Is this what they call the Kapp Putsch?"

"Yes, but Kapp was a fool, a civilian, a politician who had no ideas, no program. . . . We controlled the whole city and he didn't *do* anything, we all just sat around —"

"What are these white crosses on your helmets? Why does everybody have these white crosses painted on their helmets?"

"Those are Hakenkreuze."

"I think we call them swastikas."

"They are Indian or something. . . ."

"Well, why have you all got Indian crosses painted on your helmets?"

Kaspar shook his head. "I will tell you truly, I don't know. I think it means something about the purity of the German race —"

"Indian crosses?"

"I agree with you, and I don't know who started with those things, it was not Captain Ehrhardt, it was just something . . . everybody was doing it, painting these crosses —"

"Well, here's a symbol I recognize." A group of helmeted men, Kaspar among them, perched atop an armored car that was painted with a huge white skull-and-crossbones — the same hollow eye sockets that stared from every photograph on the walls of the Villa Keith.

"I think it is a better symbol for soldiers," said Kaspar.

"What happened to your Putsch?"

"The Ebert government ran away. I think they went to Dresden. And they called a general strike. The workers just went home. Everybody. The whole city stopped running — no trains, no buses, no electricity, no water, all the stores closed, no food. . . . The banks were closed so we couldn't pay the men. Dr. Kapp told Captain Ehrhardt to break open the Reichsbank, but the captain said he was not a bank robber. . . . What we should have done was shoot a few of the strike leaders as an example . . . but nobody told us what to do, we just sat there guarding this dead city."

More pictures, all much the same: soldiers standing guard, soldiers manning machine guns, bareheaded officers sitting around café tables with sluttish-looking women, everybody grinning and self-consciously puffing on cigarettes. . . .

"Weren't the cafés closed too?"

"They were closed, but we opened them. With rifle butts. And the girls came in. . . . They were the only Berliners not on strike."

Kaspar walked across the room and sank back into the leather sofa.

"I tell you something, it was a very strange time. Just a few days. We didn't know what was happening. When we weren't on guard we sat around and drank and talked about what would happen. . . . You know, there was a song then, they played in all these Dielen, these dance halls where people came to dance in the afternoon. . . ."

Kaspar got up again, wavered across the room, poured a little schnapps for me, another for himself, knocked back his own, approached the gramophone, fumbled in a stack of records, found the one he wanted, put it on the gramophone, cranked the handle viciously, and then sang along with the music, piano and saxophone and a girl's voice:

> *Warum denn weinen, wenn man auseinandergeht,*
> *Wenn an der nächsten Ecke schon ein Andrer*
> *steht —*

"Can you understand that?"

Oh, I could understand it:

> *Why should we cry, when we part,*
> *When on the next corner . . . and so forth.*

Kaspar said: "We sat around and waited and waited for orders, so we made up new words to this song." He picked up the tone arm of the gramophone, moved it back to the beginning, and sang along with the music:

> *Why should we cry if the Putsch goes wrong,*
> *There will be another one before very long!*

*So say goodbye, but remember, men,
It won't be long 'til we do it again!*

He stopped the record and rubbed his hand across his eyes.

"And the Putsch did go wrong?"

He nodded. "Everybody betrayed us. In Dresden, General Maercker was supposed to arrest the cabinet officers, but he didn't do it, he just sent them on to Stuttgart. The British had promised to support us; they denied they ever promised such a thing. The Prussian security police told Kapp he would have to resign, and he did. He simply ran away. He got into a taxi and drove to the airport. Then the people at the General Staff, the Bendlerstrasse, they saw we would not win, so they sent a colonel over and told General von Lüttwitz he must resign. So he resigned, turned over his command to General von Seeckt . . . and there we were, in complete control of the capital city, with no leaders, no orders, nothing. *Nothing!*"

Kaspar was sitting on the sofa again, his face in his hands. I just let him sit that way for a minute, and when he looked up again his eyes were wet.

"But they let us march out. Von Seeckt gave Captain Ehrhardt permission to march the Brigade out, with our music and our flags, and as we did that, you know what happened? All these bastards, these workers and busdrivers and shopkeepers who were on strike, they came pouring out into the streets and they shouted and whistled and threw beer bottles at us, so we had to stop and shoot at them. My God, you should see them run, the swine! I wish we could have shot them all! We marched out across Pariser Platz, through the Brandenburg Gate, with our band playing and everybody singing."

"Where did you go?"

"Back to our base. Döberitz."

"And did the government punish you?"

Kaspar shook his head. "On the contrary, they still wanted to use us against the Communists. They paid a bonus that Kapp had promised us. Then they ordered us to Münster. I knew they were going to disband us, so I just went home. And I was right. In May of 1920 they disbanded the Brigade, sent the men out on the streets to

look after themselves." Kaspar emitted a sigh and sat back
in the sofa, his eyes closed.

"What was the point of it all?" I asked.

"The point? What does that mean?" His eyes were still
closed.

"What did you want when you made your Putsch? Did
you want to bring the Kaiser back?"

"God, no! Nobody wanted the Kaiser back."

"But you carried the Kaiser's flags. You wore black-
white-red armbands. If you didn't want the Kaiser, what
did you want?"

"We wanted to get rid of those bastards, those Socialists and Jews who signed the Versailles Treaty, who ruined
our country, who humiliated our country —"

"But who did you want instead? You apparently didn't
like Kapp —"

"Kapp was nothing."

"And General von — what's his name? Lüttwitz? Did
you want him to run the country?"

"No, he gave up too easily."

"Your Captain Ehrhardt?"

"No, the Captain isn't interested in politics."

"He isn't interested in politics? Here he was trying to
take over the government!"

"Only as a soldier. He wanted to sweep out these
traitors who want to give everything to the Allies —"

"But who did he want to put in their place? If you
don't want a monarchy and you don't want the Republic,
what *do* you want?"

Kaspar finally opened his eyes, and his eyes were blazing. *"We want a strong proud Germany!"* he shouted.

"You're going to wake the house."

"I wish I could wake the country! Look what they've
done now. They've made a Jew our foreign minister, a
Jew who wants to crawl on his knees to the Allies, pay
them 'reparations' of 132 *billion* gold marks. . . . Reparations for that? I mean, it would be a joke if it were not a
tragedy. And now he signs a peace treaty with Moscow!
We spent sixteen months marching back and forth across
Germany shooting Communists, getting shot *by* Communists — Herr Rathenau signs a peace treaty with them!"

"Christoph thinks it was a good idea. He thinks your
army will be able to train in Russia —"

Kaspar belched. "Is that what they tell him at Waldstein's? You know what my brother's former comrades call him now? Der Judenknecht — the Jews' servant."

I finally had enough of Kaspar. "He's hardly a servant. He's a bank trainee. And as I understand it, his salary is supporting you and everybody else in this house." I stood up. "I'm pretty tired, Kaspar, it's been a long day —"

"You're quite correct, Christoph is supporting this house. The pension of a major general who served his country from the age of fourteen will not support him and his wife today, and there are no jobs for twenty-year-old infantry officers. But you found no shortage of money on the island, did you? The Tea House and the motorboats and the Schloss and the stables and the Little House on the hill . . . servants everywhere, and all the Moselle you can drink. And that's only their *summer* place, my friend. Wait until you see the town house on the Pariser Platz. The rest of Germany may have suffered from the World War, but the Baron von Waldstein and his tribe —"

"I believe they lost a son in France."

Kaspar's eyes were closed again. He wasn't listening to me, he was listening to his own voice. Or maybe to his own heart. "And I'm sure you met Her Highness the Princess von Hohenstein-Rofrano. Such a beautiful widow. Such a *merry* widow. Such a good friend of my brother. Such a good friend of Minister Rathenau. Such a good friend — while my brother was a prisoner — of half the General Staff Corps. But nothing less then full colonel, you understand. Unless it was a cabinet minister" — Kaspar's head suddenly slumped forward and his eyes closed — "or a theatre director. . . ." The empty glass fell out of his hand and rolled across the rug.

I turned the light off.

II.

ANOTHER PART OF TOWN

I was having breakfast alone. The General and Frau Keith always took coffee and rolls in their apartment, Christoph had gone to work, and Kaspar was presumably asleep.

Meier had obviously not made up his mind about me. Meier was confused by people without titles that fixed their status: Herr General, Frau General, Herr Oberleutnant, Herr Fähnrich — that was Kaspar, although I now suspected that Kaspar never actually received the ensign's commission before his world collapsed — but how was Meier supposed to behave toward plain Mister Ellis, as he had been told to call me?

As he poured the coffee I decided this might be the moment to follow Bobby's instructions, but I needed an envelope and couldn't think of the German word. The mail was on a silver tray. I pointed and tried to explain.

Meier shook his head. Leider keine Post für Mister Ellis.

No, not mail for me. I want *this* . . . an envelope.

"Ein *couvert?*"

Right, couvert. A French word, after all.

Meier disappeared and returned a moment later with a stiff white envelope engraved with the Keith family crest. I took a five-dollar bill from my wallet, slipped it into the envelope and handed the envelope to Meier. "For the household." I waved vaguely in the direction of the pantry.

Meier understood immediately, but he wasn't sure if he should take it.

"This is between you and me, Meier. A secret. Not for the family. The times are hard, and I eat a lot. You can take it."

Meier looked at me again, nodded, took the envelope,

stuffed it into his inside pocket — and bowed, just a quick little bow. No change of expression.

The doorbell rang. Meier frowned and left the room. I drank my coffee and listened to voices in the hall.

Meier reappeared.

A man to see Mister Ellis. Not "ein Herr," a gentleman, but "ein Mann." He had a letter. Meier handed me me another stiff white envelope. No family crest. No. 7, Pariser Platz, Berlin N.W., addressed by hand to Herr Ellis, bei Herrn Generalmajor a.D. Keith, Knausstrasse 10, Berlin-Grunewald.

I could read the address, but when I opened the envelope I saw that the whole letter was written with a pen in German script; I had to ask Meier to read it. Apparently nobody had done that before, and it seemed to please him. He produced a pince-nez, polished it with a handkerchief, put it on, took the letter, cleared his throat, and read with surprising vivacity:

Very honored Herr Ellis,

I must write in German but hope that Lieutenant Keith will translate. This letter introduces my pupil Herr Fritz Falke. Although Herr Falke's subjects and style of work differ greatly from my own, I believe him to be one of the most gifted young artists in Berlin. I would highly recommend him as an instructor.

With best wishes for a fruitful relationship I am

Sincerely yours,
Max Liebermann

Max Liebermann?" repeated Meier, visibly impressed. "That is one of our greatest painters!"

"Well, you'd better ask Herr Falke to come in."

Meier cleared his throat again.

"What's the matter, Meier?"

"The man is to be received in the dining room?"

"Something wrong with that?"

Meier examined his gloves. "Visitors are received in the salon, Mister Ellis."

"All right, we'll receive him in the salon." I got up and followed Meier out of the dining room, down the dark

hall and into what Americans would have called the par-
lor.

"Mister Ellis," announced Meier, as he opened the door
and then shut it behind my back.

At the other end of the room a stocky blond man was
examining the photographs of Death's Head Hussars. He
wore a leather jacket over a shiny blue suit, and a white
shirt with a necktie, he had placed his workman's cap and
a large brown folder on the sofa.

"Good day, Herr Falke," I said in German. "I have
read your letter from Professor Liebermann."

"Oh, you speak German?" A friendly gold-toothed grin
and a strong, calloused handshake. A round red face.
Broad shoulders. He seemed uncomfortable in the Sunday
suit and the necktie. He was sweating a little.

Did I want to see examples of his work? He began to
open the folder. I was embarrassed: why should a professional artist show me samples of his work? But I looked at
them as he spread them across the couch — and I was
amazed.

You must remember this was 1922; nobody outside
Germany had heard of Fritz Falke. I may have been the
first American to see those savage caricatures in charcoal
and in pencil: the fat cigar-smoking profiteers, the ugly
naked whores on their laps, the starving, begging children
. . . and I didn't see the worst ones that morning, because
Falke knew perfectly well what sort of household he was
visiting, so he only bought a few samples, comparatively
mild ones. He didn't bring the pig-faced army officers
with their Iron Crosses, he didn't bring the killers with
jackboots and machine guns and swastikas painted on
their helmets — but I saw them later. That morning he
showed me mostly portrait studies, grim and realistic faces
of factory workers, bartenders, circus performers, and he
showed me a few luscious almost pornographic half-
undressed girls, done in oil and in watercolor.

He was clearly a skillful and original craftsman, and of
course I asked how we could arrange lessons. How much
would he charge?

He shrugged. "I must tell you I have never given lessons. Let us see how it goes."

Where would we work?

"Have you a studio here?"

No, I said. And I didn't see any way to work with

Falke in the Villa Keith. Should I rent a studio somewhere?

He shook his head. "Come to my place. It is small and
crowded and in another part of town, but we will begin
there and see how it goes. You can always rent a studio
later."

The district of Neukölln was in the southwest of the
city, on the other side of Tempelhof, the old parade
grounds being turned into an airport. The district of
Neukölln was a maze of six-story tenement houses.

We got off the trolley and walked through dark narrow streets. By American standards these buildings were
not high, but they looked as gray and grim as fortresses;
people called them Mietskasernen — rental barracks.

We entered the first courtyard of one of these buildings: overflowing garbage containers, a coal pile, ragged
little boys kicking a soccer ball around, laundry dangling
from dozens of lines that crisscrossed from the windows
above our heads. The cement stairwell reeked of urine
and cooking cabbages. As we climbed, the sounds of hu-
man life climbed with us: people shouting at each other,
doors slamming, children crying, dogs barking . . . we
climbed and we climbed. "Only three more flights," Falke
assured me. "We have better light at the top."

He hadn't said much during the trip. Had I been in the
War? I told him I had. He nodded. He had been, also.
No further discussion. Had I had painting lessons? I told
him about my year at the Beaux Arts. He nodded again.
"I envy you."

I asked about his studies with Max Liebermann.

"A wonderful old man. A giant. Oh, how he dislikes
my pictures! He comes from the upper bourgeoisie, he
does not like to look at the things I see, the things I paint,
he finds them disgusting . . . but just the same, he believes
I have talent, he knows my life is difficult, he tries to
help. . . . A wonderful man."

Panting, we arrived at the sixth-floor landing and he
produced a bunch of keys, but as he began to insert one
into the keyhole of the first door, the door opened from
the inside: a plump, handsome, smiling woman of forty or
so dressed only in a loose bathrobe, and a very small boy,
dressed in shorts and a sweater. "Well, that didn't take
long —" she began in German, but Falke hastily made

introductions: "Frau Bauer — our Mutti Bauer, my little son Ferdinand, we call him Ferdi — Mr. Ellis the American painter, *Mr. Ellis speaks fluent German!"*

I shook hands with the woman, tried to shake hands with the little boy who grabbed for the woman's leg . . . Mutti Bauer? This wasn't his wife? I was shown into what looked like a combined kitchen bathroom — a coal stove, a sink and a laundry tub, a wooden table with wooden chairs, cooking utensils, towels. . . .

"I think we will go directly into the studio — which is also my bedroom," said Falke, opening the door to another, rather dark, room that seemed to have nothing but beds in it, but Frau Bauer lunged forward to stop him. "Shh, Fritz, the girls are still asleep!"

"Well, for God's sake, it is high noon," said Falke, but he lowered his voice. "We have to get into the studio to work."

"Just go through quietly, then, and shut the door."

I followed Falke into the darkness. Cigarette smoke and perfume. The curtain was closed, but in the light from the open door I saw two beds and a small cot. One of the beds contained two young women, sleeping with their backs toward each other. I only caught a glimpse, because Falke opened another door and waved me into a third room, a bright and sunlit corner room, smelling of paint and turpentine. He closed the door behind us.

"I'm sorry, it is inconvenient," he murmured. "It would be better to have the bedroom at the back, but the light is so much better with these two windows. . . ."

He had arranged a small but comfortable studio: a wooden work table, a couple of chairs, an easel, bookshelves and a supply cupboard, a small coal stove, a bed (with a chamber pot underneath). . . . The walls were covered with so many charcoal sketches that the sheets overlapped; the floor was stacked with canvases. One window looked directly into another tenement, but the other one provided a view down a long straight street toward the open fields of Tempelhof.

Fritz Falke sat down in one of the chairs and folded his arms across his chest and smiled at me. "All right, my friend, where do we begin?"

I found a clean white pad and a box of charcoal sticks, sat down on the other side of the room and began to sketch a preliminary study for a portrait. For a long time neither of us said a word. It felt good to be doing this again, I was absorbed and at peace, I forgot where I was. I sat there and fixed my thoughts upon this man, this perfect stranger, and tried to get myself inside him. To do that right, I think you have to talk to the subject, but for a long time neither of us seemed to want to break the silence. I worked.

Noises from the bedroom. Voices. The door opened, two girls dressed only in very short slips; sisters, with reddish chestnut hair and creamy skin. The older one had more generous proportions than were fashionable that year but her hair was bobbed short as a boy's; the younger one was slim as a boy — a boy with shoulder-length hair. I recognized the models for Fritz Falke's more appetizing paintings.

They stared at me and giggled.

Fritz Falke turned around. "Put something on, you shameless trollops!"

The door closed. I couldn't contain my curiosity. "Who are they?"

"The one with the shape is my wife. Her name is Barbara. We call her Bärbel. The little one's her sister, Brigitte. We call her Baby."

"And Frau Bauer?"

"Is their mother. A widow. The man was killed in Flanders."

"But why were they both sleeping in —"

"They work all night. A club in the Friedrichstrasse. They come home at daybreak sometimes, and I'm asleep in here, the mother and the boy are asleep in there, so they just share the other bed. Not convenient, but there's nothing else to do."

The girls came in again, both wrapped in what looked like genuine kimonos. Bärbel's was black, with red flowers; Baby's was red, with black flowers.

Falke introduced us. They both wanted to try their English.

"Leave the man alone," said Falke. "He is doing his work."

Frau Bauer appeared, still wrapped in her bathrobe. "Is anybody hungry? We only have potatoes."

"Get some herrings," said Falke.

"Herrings?" cried Baby. "It isn't Sunday!"

"Potatoes will be fine for me —" I began.

"Baby, go down to the corner and get two nice herrings. And an onion," said Frau Bauer.

"Why do *I* have to go? It's her turn to go — AUU-AHH!"

Her mother had snatched a long steel ruler from the table, and with one vicious whirring curve smacked it full force across the girl's rump. Baby ran out of the room, her mother behind her, and although the door was closed we could hear the shouting as Baby dressed.

For a few minutes everything was quiet. Bärbel took a pack of cigarettes from the jacket of her husband's pocket, lighted one, and padded softly around the room, looking at me, looking at my drawing, looking out the windows, stretching her legs out of the kimono, stretching her neck, presenting her profile — consciously, possibly unconsciously — striking various paintable attitudes. Falke watched her, with the barest suggestion of a smile, the way one would watch a performing cat. I tried to keep my eyes on Falke's face, to catch something of this new expression.

Suddenly a bell began to ring; not a church bell, not an electric alarm bell, but a small bell that somebody was ringing by hand, something like the dinner bell our cook at home uses to call the family to the table.

Falke and Bärbel looked at each other. Frau Bauer burst into the room: "Police in the house!" She wrenched one of the windows open and leaned out. "No *Grüne Minna*? Then it can't be a raid." She ran out of the room again, and Bärbel after her. Falke sat motionless in his chair, so I just continued to work.

"What's a *Grüne Minna*?" I asked.

"Big police van. To carry people to prison."

"Do you have police here often?"

"Often enough. The tenants warn each other. But it was worse in the revolution, I can tell you. It wasn't the police then, it was the Freikorps. Wonderful fellows. I could tell you some stories!"

"Were you here then?"

Falke's expression changed. "Yes and no," he said, but before I could ask him what that meant, a rhythmic metallic tapping sound began to come from the empty coal

stove in the corner. *Tap-tap-tap.* Pause. *Tap-tap-tap.*
Pause.

"What's that?"

"That's the neighbors downstairs, banging on the chimney. Means the police are in our stairwell —" and Bärbel
ran back into the studio: "They're coming up! Mutti's on
the landing watching them."

We heard the apartment door slam, and then Frau
Bauer returned, wildly brushing her hair with a long
wooden hairbrush. "God damn it," she said through the
bobby pins in her mouth; "I *knew* I should have gotten
dressed —" Her face was pink with anger and excitement.

"Mutti, you think they're coming here?"

Frau Bauer nodded, glancing into Falke's mirror, pinning her thick hair away from her face, pulling the bathrobe into a less revealing arrangement. "It's only that pest
from the School Administration again, that dried-up spinster making trouble. Bärbel, get back into bed and be
asleep!"

"Why should I?"

Frau Bauer reached for the long ruler, and Bärbel
dashed into the bedroom. At that moment another hard
instrument was rapped against the apartment door.

"Polizei! Sofort aufmachen!"

I assumed that Falke would take over now, but I was
wrong. Falke sat motionless in his chair. Frau Bauer
cursed softly and went to open the door. Loud voices from
the kitchen, and then a large policeman came stomping
through the bedroom into the studio. He wore black boots,
a long greatcoat with silver buttons, a black leather belt
with a black automatic in a black holster, a nightstick,
and the high shiny black leather tschako of the regular
Berlin Schutzpolizei; a calm-looking, middle-aged man,
probably a sergeant during the War. He looked at us carefully from the doorway.

Falke sat still in his chair and I continued to draw his
portrait, thinking all this was quite different from the
Beaux Arts.

"Guten Nachmittag," said the policeman, and I realized
for the first time that it was afternoon.

"Nachmittag, Herr Wachtmeister," said Falke, barely
turning his head.

The policeman unbuttoned the top buttons of his greatcoat and produced a notebook, which he now consulted.

"Kaiser Friedrichstrasse No. 101, First Courtyard, Apartment 6-A, Bauer, K. . . . You are Bauer?"

"No, Herr Wachtmeister, I am Falke, Fritz, son-in-law in residence. This gentleman is an American citizen, Mr. Ellis. He does not speak German. He is receiving painting lessons from me, as you see."

"Good afternoon, officer," I said in English.

The policeman checked his list, apparently located Falke, Fritz, and walked heavily into the studio to inspect my work.

In the meantime, Frau Bauer was in the bedroom, engaged in a loud discussion with a formidable lady in a black cape, hornrimmed glasses, and a severe black hat. The lady was looking for Brigitte Bauer, and had opened the curtains to make sure that the indignant girl now getting out of bed was not Brigitte Bauer.

"Where is Brigitte?" The lady's voice was shrill.

"I have just *told* you, Fräulein Opitz. I sent her to the library to get a copy of *Faust* —"

"Frau Bauer, I will not be trifled with! The Prussian School Administration will not be trifled with! The girl was not in school *again* today, after all of our warnings . . . and you tell me stories about *Faust*. How many copies of *Faust* do you think there are in the school?"

Frau Bauer sat down on her bed. "Fräulein Opitz, what am I to do? The girl is sixteen —"

"Frau Bauer, I have here in my purse a copy of Brigitte's birth certificate from the Standesamt Berlin-Neukölln, which clearly shows the girl is *fifteen*, as you very well know, and this fifteen-year-old girl is seen every night in the worst places on the Friedrichstrasse, we have *written reports*, Frau Bauer, and this will not continue!"

Frau Bauer had put her head in her hands and was sobbing now. "Fräulein Opitz, what can I do? This new world since the War, the young people today, they do what they want, they pay no attention to their mother, the father fell in Flanders, I'm all alone in the world, I have no position, I must live on the miserable pension —"

"Frau Bauer, please control yourself!"

Instead of controlling herself, Frau Bauer began to howl, and her voice must have been audible in the innermost courtyard of Friedrichstrasse No. 101.

"Oh God in heaven, what am I to do? I'm all alone in

the world with my girls, the rent isn't paid, we have four potatoes in the cupboard —"

"This is absolutely the last warning, Frau Bauer!" Fräulein Opitz parried Frau Bauer's screams with low-pitched, sibilant tones. "If Brigitte is not in school tomorrow, if there are any more unexcused absences, I will bring you before the magistrate. And you know very well what that means: he can fine you, he can put you in jail — and he can put Brigitte into an institution where they will keep her in the classroom — and out of cabarets!"

Grimacing as if in pain, Fräulein Opitz came into the studio. Her spectacles glittered.

"Herr Falke, as the man of the house, it seems to me that you have some responsibility in this matter."

Falke finally stood up and I did too.

"Fräulein, with respect, you know the girl's not mine, I'm only permitted to live and work here through the generosity of my esteemed mother-in-law —"

"As the man of the house, you stand *in loco parentis* —"

"Oh, with greatest respect, Fräulein, I do not stand *in loco parentis*, I have made careful inquiry about the matter."

"I refuse to quibble with you about legal technicalities, Herr Falke!" Now Fräulein Opitz was shouting too. Frau Bauer had appeared at the door, her face streaked with tears, and Bärbel holding the little boy in her arms. The studio was suddenly crowded and Fräulein Opitz obviously felt it.

"Who is this man?" she demanded, as if she wanted to change the subject.

Again, Falke explained that I was an American, I didn't speak German, I was taking lessons. . . .

Fräulein Opitz stepped around the policeman and looked at the drawing I was working on. The others moved in behind her.

She looked at my drawing for a long moment, and then she glanced at the pictures on the walls — Fritz Falke's blazing, phantasmagoric shrieks of protest. "This gentleman is taking lessons from *you*, Herr Falke? I think it should be the other way around!"

Silence, and then Frau Bauer began to laugh.

12.

A VIEW OF THE GENDARMENMARKT

At J. P. Morgan and at Drexel and at Brown Brothers — at all the American private banks that I have seen — everything is done right out in the open. At least they try very hard to give that impression: large opulent rooms, a "floor" where all the partners — J. P. Morgan himself — sit at rolltop desks, working over their papers or talking with their visitors in full view of the world. If you give us your money to invest, you should be free to watch us doing it, they seem to be saying.

In Berlin's financial district around the Gendarmenmarkt — the Jägerstrasse, the Französischestrasse, the Markgrafenstrasse — the atmosphere was different. Not so much as a brass name plate identified the Venetian palazzo at No. 4, Gendarmenmarkt — actually at the corner of Französischestrasse and Markgrafenstrasse. If you didn't know which house this was, you had no business there.

I walked up the steps and rang the bell, and a tail-coated butler admitted me into a gloomy reception hall. No telephones, no stock tickers, no rolltop desks, and no partners — at least no live partners. Oriental carpets, a crystal chandelier, dimly lighted portraits, and a large bronze bust of David Waldstein (1770–1848).

This was not a waiting room, and the butler did not ask who I was or what I wanted. He led me up a few more steps, through a swinging wooden gate and into a corridor lined with closed doors, numbered like hotel rooms. He unlocked one of these and opened it — to reveal another closed door. He opened this second door and ushered me into a small conference chamber containing a beautiful mahogany table and two comfortable wing chairs covered in green leather. The venetian blinds were closed, but sunlight entered the room through the cracks — enough sunlight to illuminate the objects on the table:

a writing tablet, an inkstand, a pair of scissors, a tray with three crystal decanters and two glasses.

"Herr Oberleutnant Keith is on the telephone, sir, but Herr Baron Robert is on his way. Will you have sherry? Madeira? Mosel wine?"

I chose sherry. Just as I finished the little glass Bobby appeared, immaculate in a double-breasted gray suit and a stiff white collar, a fresh white rose in his lapel. We shook hands.

"Welcome to our Bank, old fellow. We have a few minutes before lunch, so let me show you around."

"What are the double doors for?" I asked him. "And the locks."

Bobby smiled. "To assure privacy, of course. When a client speaks with his banker, he wants to be sure that nobody is listening at the keyhole."

"But where do you do your work? Don't you have offices?"

"Oh yes, but we only let very special friends see them. Come along and I will show you."

The butler took my glass and locked the room again. I walked along the corridor with Bobby, wondering what was going on behind all the closed doors we passed. At the end of the corridor Bobby led me up a flight of polished marble stairs. On the second floor, we entered a more conventional reception area, a huge refectory table holding a bronze Chinese goat, some comfortable chairs, more portraits. Through open portals I saw dignified older secretaries typing, and behind them more closed doors leading to what Bobby told me were the partners' offices.

"If you want to see where the real work is done, you must climb still another staircase," said Bobby, so I followed him up another flight. We emerged in a big bright noisy room that looked much more familiar to me: row after row of desks, men working over documents or talking on telephones, girls pounding typewriters, several stock tickers, young boys writing trade prices and currency quotations on a huge blackboard at the end of the room. . . . I didn't see anybody in his shirtsleeves, though. All the men had their coats and ties on. Nobody had his feet on the table, either.

Christoph Keith sat behind one of the desks in a glass cubicle he apparently shared with Bobby. He rose to shake hands.

"You have come to see where the peons work?"

"It looks very much like the place I used to work."

I sat with them while they tried to explain in general what they did: finance exports and imports, represent clients in foreign currency operations, participate in underwriting syndicates, lend money to businessmen. They didn't accept checking accounts, they didn't deal with the general public at all; they dealt with corporations and with governments. Much of their work had always been with clients in Paris and London and New York and South America. This network was being laboriously restrung after the War, and now the devaluation of the mark was making the task enormously difficult. While they talked to me, Christoph and Bobby kept glancing over my shoulder toward the blackboard where the boys erased the changing values of the dollar and the guilder and the pound sterling in relation to the mark, and chalked up new ones.

A girl came in and said something to Bobby. He stood up. "We are summoned to the partners' dining room."

"I think in America very few men go home for lunch," said Dr. Strassburger, as the waiter was removing the soup plates.

"Yes, sir, that's correct. At least in the big cities."

"They all eat in clubs, like the English," said Baron Eduard von Waldstein. "Here many people still go home."

"In Italy they all go home for lunch," said Bobby. "Then they take a siesta."

"They don't necessarily take a siesta," said another partner, whose name I hadn't caught.

"They don't necessarily go home," said Baron Eduard, and everybody laughed. Even Dr. Strassburger.

New plates were in front of us. One waiter passed steaming silver platters with veal cutlets, fried potatoes, peas; the other waiter offered a choice of white and red wines, carefully displaying the labels.

I sat at the long table by the window, between Christoph and Bobby. Half a dozen other men, to whom I had been introduced, sat around us. Baron Eduard, Bobby's father, sat at the head. Dr. Strassburger sat across from me. Through the big window I could see the Gendarmenmarkt — two eighteenth-century churches, a huge nineteenth-century theatre, and a statue of Schiller. Behind me, at smaller tables, other partners were dining with their own guests.

As we ate and talked I watched the faces and tried to imagine what was really going on here. Bobby's father sat at the head of the table — a charming, witty, cultivated man, but a man who looked older than his middle sixties, a man who did not seem entirely fascinated by talk about the Allied Reparations Commission or the possible effect of the Rapallo Treaty. Bobby was even less fascinated by these subjects. (Somebody made a remark about his white rose. Christoph asserted that it brought the spirit of the Champ Élysées to the Bank, but Dr. Strasburger announced, "This is not the Champs Élysées, this is the Gendarmenmarkt, and the damned French are the cause of all our troubles!" Baron Eduard compressed his lips, cut himself a small piece of veal, and said nothing.)

Dr. Strassburger was obviously the one who had issued the invitation. He was full of questions: Philadelphia's role as a financial center, as compared to New York; the present management of Drexel & Company; he understood my people were Quakers — how long had they lived in Philadelphia? What did my father do? And I really wanted to be an artist? Was I taking lessons in Berlin? Oh, excellent, a pupil of Professor Liebermann, had I seen Liebermann's picture of the Baron's father, out in the reception room? . . . At first the name didn't mean anything, but then: Falke? *Falke?* That Bolshevik, with his filthy swinish Red propaganda drawings? The fellow had been with Liebknecht's Spartacists, should have been shot in 1919. . . . Dr. Strassburger's face paled; he drank half a glass of Moselle to compose himself . . . and meanwhile attention shifted, people turned to look at two men entering the dining room.

I recognized the taller one immediately: pointed bald head, graying Van Dyke beard, coal-black eyes, heavy eyebrows now frowning with annoyance. Walther Rathenau obviously thought he was going to lunch alone with his host, a short round smiling man with unmistakable Waldstein features, and here was a whole room full of men, rising to shake hands with His Excellency the Foreign Minister.

He handled it quite well. The host, who turned out to be Baron Eduard's younger brother, Baron Fritz, quickly steered his guest around the long table. Rathenau recom-

posed his features into something that might be described
as a smile, shaking each extended hand. The only awkward moment came when it was my turn. Baron Fritz
looked puzzled, Rathenau clearly didn't remember me,
then Baron Eduard, Bobby, Christoph, and Dr. Strassburger each began to explain who I was, in slightly different words. But that was over in an instant. Baron Fritz
said something to Baron Eduard, who nodded and accompanied his brother and Rathenau to an empty table
in the most distant corner of the room, where two waiters
were already drawing back the chairs.

I tried to watch Dr. Strassburger without turning my
head. The others were watching him too. I wish I could
have sketched him at that moment. I wish I could have il-
lustrated the emotions reflected in the glittering pince-nez,
in the compressed lips. . . . Anyway, he masked it all in
the fraction of a second and made his decision.

"Keith, when Mr. Ellis has finished his coffee, will you
bring him to my office and wait for me." It was not a
question, it was an order. "I have an urgent matter to discuss with Minister Rathenau." He pushed his chair back
and walked across the room.

I wished I had eyes at the back of my head. So apparently did Christoph, who steadfastly ate his strawberry
tart. Some of the men on the other side of the table pretended to be eating; others didn't. Bobby von Waldstein
simply turned around in his chair and stared.

Dr. Strassburger collected Chinese figures of bronze
and jade; his office was full of them. Little horses and
goats and Buddhas stood about on the tables and bookshelves. There was also a Chinese carpet, and a gloomy
Böcklin landscape above the little fireplace, and behind
the enormous desk a big window with velvet drapes and a
fine view of the domed French Church in the Gendarmenmarkt.

"Does the Foreign Minister often eat here?" I asked
Christoph as we sat in the leather club chairs in front of
the empty desk.

He shook his head. "Perhaps once or twice since he has
been in office. More often before that. His company is a
client, of course. He is close to the Barons, especially
Fritz, and he desperately needs the support of all these
bankers for his program. They still have good connections

abroad, in London, in New York — they could be helpful in making the Allies take a more reasonable position."

"You mean about reparations?"

"Yes, of course. The people in the City and in Wall Street, they *must* realize we cannot pay these sums, we simply cannot do it, and if they continue to press . . . well, this government, this form of republican government . . . it cannot survive."

"And Rathenau wants the Waldsteins to carry this message abroad?"

Christoph nodded. "Something like that, I think."

"Will they do it?"

"Well, they are patriotic Germans, they will certainly do what the government asks, but how much sympathy they have for this particular government, this constant parliamentary infighting, this instability . . . uncertainty . . . this policy of trying to reason with the Allies . . . That's another matter. You heard what Alfred said the other night. Who helped finance the Freikorps?"

"But that was to fight the Communists."

"Yes. And they still are more afraid of the Left. Remember they are bankers. Capitalists by profession. Capitalists by definition." Christoph suddenly grinned. "Listen to me talking about *them!* What am I?"

"I don't know, Keith, what *are* you?" asked Dr. Strassburger as he opened the door and marched in. We both stood up. "Sit down, sit down, gentlemen, I'm sorry, I had a difficult situation in Holland to bring to His Excellency's attention, and my partners were grateful that I reminded them. Now Mr. Ellis, I did want to discuss a matter of business with you, and since Lieutenant Keith will handle the details I wanted him to be here too." He settled into the leather swivel chair behind his desk. "You have, I believe, a dollar account with our affiliated bank in Amsterdam."

"Yes, sir. A very small one."

"Mr. Ellis, in Germany today, even a small amount of hard currency, especially located outside of Germany, presents the opportunity" — Dr. Strassburger paused to rephrase — "presents the *possibility* of making extremely profitable investments. Over a short period of time."

I assumed he was talking about currency speculation. He was.

I didn't really understand these things when I was supposed to be working for Drexel, and I didn't understand
them any better as Dr. Strassburger explained them now,
leaning back in his chair, his fingertips pressed together.

It was all perfectly legal, of course. There would be no
transfer of funds abroad because my money had never
been in Germany. The German mark had fallen so
sharply that the Reichsbank, the central bank, might have
to support the price in foreign markets. If they did that,
the value of the German mark would rise — at least for a
little while. If I understood him correctly, he wanted me
to use my dollars to *buy* some German marks, while
everybody else was selling them. When — and if — the
Reichsbank starts to buy and runs the price up, I would
sell.

Why is Christoph Keith staring down at the Chinese
carpet?

Does any of this make sense?

"Dr. Strassburger, the money I have in Amsterdam is
all I have to live on. If this operation goes wrong — for
example if the Reichsbank doesn't stabilize — I'd lose
my money, wouldnt' I?"

Dr. Strassburger smiled bleakly. "Yes, you would, Mr.
Ellis. There is no investment without risk."

"But some investments are riskier than others."

"Absolutely."

What's the point of all this? He knows how little
money I have. Is the second oldest bank in Berlin trying
to bilk Peter Ellis out of a thousand dollars? Of course
not. He's trying to prove something to me. Can I hedge
a little?

"Dr. Strassburger, could I start with just a small bite? I
could put up five hundred dollars. Would that be worth
it?"

Christoph Keith's eyes left the carpet. Was that a twin-
kle of amusement? But Dr. Strassburger was not amused.

"No, Mr. Ellis, I think to make this sort of thing worth
one's time, a somewhat larger investment would be required." He paused, tapped his fingertips together,
turned his chair so that he could gaze out at the French
Church for a moment, turned back to face me.

"I tell you what we will do: you put up a thousand dollars, and our Amsterdam bank will lend you another four

thousand dollars at their normal rate. You give them a note, payable let us say in one year. Then you have five thousand dollars to buy German marks. If you make money on the transaction, you pay them back. If you lose your money on the basis of our advice . . . well, perhaps they will just tear up the note. How does that sound?"

How does that sound? Why is Christoph staring at the carpet again?

"That sounds like a very nice deal for me, Dr. Strassburger. May I ask why you're being so generous, and for such small sums?"

He nodded. "Yes, you make ask. And I will tell you. This is a very old bank, as you know, but it is still a private bank. We have sufficient capital for our needs, but our capital is small compared to the banks with public depositors and public shareholders — the Deutsche Bank, the Disconto Gesellschaft, the Dresdner Bank. Our *real* capital is not in shares, not in money; our real capital is up here." He tapped his index finger against the side of his head. "Our real capital is our professional skill, and hundreds of influential people all over the world who know us and trust in our skill. You understand what I am saying?"

"Yes, sir."

"So I don't like to miss the opportunity to make a new friend, to show a visitor from another land how good we are at our profession."

"But Dr. Strassburger, I'm going to be a painter!"

He nodded again. "Yes. Perhaps you are going to be a painter. And perhaps you are not going to be a painter. You know what I was going to be, when I was a boy in Dresden? I was going to be a writer and a poet. Like Heinrich Heine. I published poems in the newspaper. Did you know that, Keith?"

"No, Herr Geheimrat, I didn't know that."

"Yes, it's quite true. Several poems, and an article about a trip to China. My father sent me to China to buy jade for his store. . . ." Dr. Strassburger suddenly slammed both palms on the top of his desk, stood up, and extended his hand. *"Also!* Do I understand we have made what you Americans call 'a deal'?"

"Yes, sir." I stood up too and shook his hand.

"Very good. Lieutenant Keith will take you upstairs

and have you sign the necessary papers, powers of attorney and so forth. I'm afraid I have another meeting now. Good afternoon, gentlemen."

13.

TWO FOR TEA

The Kaiser Friedrich Museum was a massive triangular structure of imitation baroque, built on the tip of an island in the river Spree, right in the middle of Berlin.

I didn't particularly want to go there that afternoon; I wanted to go down to Neukölln and do my own work in Fritz Falke's studio, but Christoph Keith was quite insistent: "You absolutely must see it. . . . One of the finest collections in the world . . ." Not only that, but it was most important for me to be in the second floor Picture Gallery, Early Netherlands Section, Cabinet 68, at four o'clock. "Because of the sunlight on the pictures. You will find it a very pleasant place, Peter. Please be there."

So I went. I stopped in a bookstore, bought Baedeker's Guide to Berlin like any other tourist, and using the excellent maps, I made my way from the Gendarmenmarkt right through the center of the city, down Unter den Linden and across the wide bridge to the island occupied by the Kaiser's Palace, the Cathedral, and one museum after another.

The sun was glistening on the water, the horse chestnuts were in bloom, and despite the coffee and the strawberry tart, my nerves were still glowing a little from the Moselle. Watching a long black canal boat chugging along beside me, I suddenly realized that I felt almost at home in this strange and complicated city — a feeling I never had in Paris.

Herr Baedeker obviously agreed with Christoph Keith's opinion of the Kaiser Friedrich Museum: he devoted 26 pages of solid type and diagrams to its contents, and 18 of those pages dealt with the collections in the Picture Gallery.

I've heard it said that novelists don't enjoy reading novels because they automatically try to solve the other writer's problems, so reading a novel is work instead of relaxation. The same thing applies to painters. Of course I still spend hours and hours at the Fogg Museum and Fenway Court and our museums in Philadelphia and the Louvre and the Jeu de Paume, but it takes me a long time to look at pictures. That afternoon in the spring of 1922 I made slow progress through eighteen pages of Baedeker's.

As a matter of fact, I forgot all about Cabinet 68: I was still in Cabinet 67, examining *Albrecht Dürer ** 557e. Hieronymus Holzschuher, patrician and senator of Nuremberg, the finest of Dürer portraits, painted in 1526 (purchased in 1884 for 17,500 l.)* when a voice beside me murmured, "Such a *serious* student of German portraiture!" and breathing a cloud of perfume I turned to face Helena . . . and Lili von Waldstein, both giggling.

"Don't you have tea dancing in America?" asked Helena in the taxi.

"Yes, I think we have it, but somehow I've never done it."

"I have never done it either," said Lili. She wore a simple blue dress that might have been a school uniform — which is what it turned out to be — and a gray toque with a black veil. The hat and the veil had been provided by Helena, whose idea this operation seemed to be. Helena had called Lili's mother to ask if Lili could go to the museum with her, and had received permission to pick up Lili at her school. Did the Baroness question Helena's sudden interest in the Kaiser Friedrich Museum? I didn't ask. I just felt their silken legs pressed against me and listened to the chatter about whether Christoph and Helena had selected the best of the "Dielen" for my introduction to the Berlin dancing craze. Although Lili had never been allowed to visit these places, some of her classmates apparently spent their evenings in them, so she had all the latest information. We were not going to the best one. We should be going to the Adlon, or the roof garden of the Eden.

"But those are luxury hotels, Lili. Christoph wants to show Peter the real thing."

Even "the real thing" was going to be expensive for

Christoph, I had a feeling, and began to wonder how I could pick up the check without embarrassing him. And then I thought of something else.

"Christoph can't dance! Why are we going to a dance hall if —"

"Because he enjoys it anyway." Helena put a warm hand on my knee. "In the first place, he wants to show it to you. In the second place, he wants — we both want — Lili to go out into the town a little. And in the third place, *I* like to dance, and he does not mind if other people dance with me. All right?"

Tonndorf? Imperator? Traube? I forget which one they showed me that first time. I think it was right on Unter den Linden. Perfume, cigarette smoke, potted palms, marble-topped tables, an American-style bar, and a black American band in tuxedos tootling "After You've Gone" (and Left Me Crying . . .) on saxophones, trumpets and drums. People were already dancing. The rouged and plucked and mascaraed women at the bar stroked their shingled hair and stared coldly as Helena marched us past, toward a center table where the captain and another waiter were already pulling back wicker chairs, bowing.

Helena ordered sherry for herself and for Lili — "But you must have whiskey," so I asked for a highball.

"And now you must dance with Lili."

Like obedient children we stood up, walked to the dance floor and faced each other. I took her right hand in my left hand, she put her left hand on my shoulder, we stepped off . . .

When was the last time I danced with anybody? On the *Mauretania,* coming over, a year ago. Girls from Vassar and Bryn Mawr, off for their year in Paris, being aggressively nice to an "older man who had been in the War." Many were too tall for me. Most had loud voices. I never saw any of them again.

Lili was the kind of dancer who follows so instinctively that she knows what you're going to do before you do it. Behind the veil her eyes waited politely for me to start the conversation. The well-brought-up European girl on her first date. Certainly not her first date. Why am I so awkward?

"You've really never been here before?"

"No, never."

"You've done a lot of dancing somewhere."

"Oh yes, we all were sent to dancing school, and there are many parties, you know."

"You go to many parties?"

"Oh yes, many."

"Somebody is asking Helena to dance," I said.

Her veil touched my cheek as she turned. "Oh yes, she is a famous beauty. The gentlemen know her."

"Do you know him?"

"No, but he's an officer."

"He's not in uniform. How can you tell?"

"Oh, you can always tell. In Germany."

I'm the Sheik of Araby, played the band, Your Heart Belongs to Me. A tango? I learned the tango in Paris, that first time in Paris. 1916. I still remembered vaguely how to do it and watched the other dancers. If you listen to the beat it's not so hard.

Sliding against me Lili asked: "You were injured in the War?"

I didn't know what to say, because I didn't know how much Christoph had told her. So I said Yes. She nodded and said nothing for a few bars; then suddenly she reached up and threw the silly veil back over her hat.

And looked at me with her coal-black eyes: "You are all right now?"

It hurt. It really hurt.

"No? You are not?"

Nobody had gotten this close to me since I was fourteen. Mortified, I felt my face and my hands begin to sweat.

"Do I look wounded?" I asked.

"Not in the same way as Christoph."

"What way, then?" I felt that Christoph had told her nothing.

"Inside?"

"Are you really only seventeen?"

"Only seventeen!" She rolled her eyes dramatically. "You were wounded in the soul?"

In the soul? I must have looked puzzled.

"We say, you know, Seelenkrank, a sickness of the soul."

"You say that when a person has a nervous collapse? Shell shock?"

She nodded. "Shell shock. That is an interesting word.

Yes, we have *many* cases of that." She was perfectly matter-of-fact, as if it was something like a piece of shrapnel in your shoulder.

"Well, you're quite right," I said. "That's what happened to me."

"Will you talk to me about it?" Lili asked. "Not here, of course."

"Can you read my mind?"

She smiled. "Yes, I think maybe."

The band broke into a Charleston, and I saw Christoph Keith limping past the bar, his eyes on Helena dancing with the other fellow. I took Lili's hand and moved back toward our table. We sat down with Christoph, who also ordered "a whiskey."

"Peter cannot dance the Charleston," announced Lili.

"But I can tell you the name of the one they're playing. It's called 'Would You Rather Be a Colonel with an Eagle on Your Shoulder or a Private with a Chicken on Your Knee?' "

"It is called *what?*"

They laughed as I explained, but I was thinking about how we had played that record over and over on the Victrola in the common room at Friends Hospital. Ziegfeld Follies of 1918.

The Charleston ended and the other man brought Helena back to the table. Christoph knew him. I rose to be introduced. Rittmeister Graf von Something. He wore a monocle. He clearly wanted to join us. I saw Helena cast a questioning glance at Christoph — and get her answer. I did not believe that Christoph really liked to watch her dancing with other men.

"Thank you *so* much, Rudi, and adieu. I must dance with our guest now." He bent over her hand and disappeared. The band was playing "Avalon."

"Oh, aren't they *black!*" said Helena, pressing her breasts against me. She danced differently from Lili; while her feet moved exactly in response to my feet and the music, her body hung in my arms so that I could feel her weight and smell her golden hair. "We have almost never seen Negroes in Germany. The French have African soldiers on the Rhine." She began to whistle the music softly in my ear.

"You don't like me dancing with other men, do you?"

"Why do you say that?"

"Because it shows in your eyes. You think I'm a *very* bad woman."

"No!"

"Yes. But you will learn. I am not. And it is *so* good for Christoph that you are here. A man needs a friend. He always had friends. But you know, they're all dead. All of them." She threw back her head over my arm and looked into my face. "All his friends are dead."

Now they were playing a German song I didn't know. I was dancing with Lili again.

"I had lunch at your father's table today. At the Bank."

"Yes, I heard you would be there. I have never been there, in the dining room. They do not permit women."

"Dr. Strassburger was there."

"I'm sure."

"Why don't you like him?"

"Why is it necessary that I like him? He is a very intelligent man."

"I invested some money on his advice."

"I'm sure about money his advice will be very good." She looked at me. "We will have to leave in a few minutes. Helena promised to bring me home for dinner, so we must take the train to Nikolassee."

"I thought we were all going to have dinner together."

"No. This was all we could manage, and Helena had to tell a lie to arrange it. Can you come out on Sunday? There is a big lunch, but if you come early, we can ride in the motorboat, or something. Would you like that?"

We took a short taxi ride up to the big Friedrichstrasse Station, Lili made a telephone call to the island so that the coach would be sent to meet them at Nikolassee, and then we got on the Stadtbahn together. People were going home from work and the train was crowded. Helena and Lili looked luminously beautiful in contrast to the tired gray faces around us. None of us had much to say as the train swayed and clattered through the city. Lili and I pretended not to stare at each other. Christoph looked out of the window and Helena put her arm through his. When the train reached Grunewald Station, we shook hands with the girls and got off.

I was pleased to see how the cuisine at Villa Keith had improved in the last few days. When Meier let us in, he said something to Christoph about "English high tea" and about Herr Fähnrich's guest, and when we came into the living room we saw that Christoph's mother was indeed pouring tea and Frau Meier had just brought a tray with buttered rolls, sliced ham, sliced hard-boiled eggs and glass jars containing honey and jam. The General sat in his wheelchair, covered by what looked like a horse blanket, trying hard to keep his cup from clattering in its saucer.

Kaspar and the other man stood up for introductions.

"May I present . . . my brother . . . his guest Mr. Ellis, from America . . . Lieutenant Tillessen . . ."

Handshaking. Bowing. The faint sound of heels coming together.

"Tillessen?" asked Christoph, pronouncing the name very carefully.

"Jawohl, Herr Oberleutnant." He was a tall blond man with a smooth handsome face, close-cropped hair, pale blue eyes. He wore a shiny blue suit, white shirt, black tie, some kind of a military ribbon in his lapel.

The General was trying to say something. He pointed to Tillessen with one hand, while the teacup clattered in the other. The words came out with terrific effort: "Leutnant . . . *zur See!*" A naval lieutenant.

Christoph nodded.

Frau Keith told us to sit down and join in the meal. We did. As I ate my roll I saw Christoph's mood had changed. Kaspar talked and Christoph regarded Tillessen in silence.

Tillessen brought news of old comrades, Kaspar explained. Two were coming to Berlin for political conferences, they had very little money, the question was whether beds could be found for them here. . . .

"Oh, I'll just go to a hotel," I said.

"Certainly not, Mr. Ellis," said Frau Keith. "We have another room on the third floor, it's only a question —"

"Mother, we can get another bed from —"

"Just a minute, please," said Christoph, and he said it in a tone of voice that silenced the rest of us. Everybody looked at him.

"Lieutenant, are you related to Henrich Tillessen, presently reported to be in Budapest?"

"I have the honor to be his brother, Herr Ober-leutnant."

"I see. And these old comrades who are to stay in our house, may we assume they are old comrades from the Ehrhardt Brigade?"

Tillessen looked over at Kaspar.

"Of course they are," said Kaspar defiantly.

"And now members of the O.C.?"

Tillessen stood up. "Herr Oberleutnant, you forget yourself!" he said, very quietly. The pale blue eyes looked dangerous now.

The Keith brothers were up too.

"Christoph, have you gone completely crazy?" Kaspar's face was flushed. "You are speaking in front of . . . a foreigner!"

"Lieutenant Tillessen," said Christoph, also very qui-etly, "I must ask you to leave this house immediately."

"This isn't your house!" shouted Kaspar. "Who are you to ask my guest to leave our father's house."

In the excitement we had not heard the General's cup fall to the carpet. Now he was leaning forward, clutching his wife's sleeve, drooling slightly, asking "What's the matter? What are they saying? Tell me what they're say-ing!" and she was white-faced, gasping, "Christoph! Kas-par! What's the matter with you?" and Christoph was limping to the doorway, shouting "Meier! Meier!" and Meier appeared instantly and Christoph told him to take the General to his apartment. "Please go with them, Mother, I think this exictement is bad for him."

"Mother, are you going to let him give the orders here?"

Apparently she was. She turned to Tillessen and ex-tended her hand. "Herr Leutnant, you will forgive me, I must look after my husband. It was a great pleasure."

He bowed over her hand. "Frau General!" He tried to shake hands with the General as Meier wheeled him out, but the old man was too confused by what was happen-ing and kept turning around to look at his wife.

Tillessen was already out in the hall when Frau Keith turned back: "I wish you boys would not quarrel over politics. You were brought up to be officers, and officers should not be interested in politics. Leave that dirty busi-ness to the politicians." Then she was gone.

"We're not quarreling about politics," said Christoph,

to no one in particular. "We're quarreling about murder."

"Traitor!" shouted Kaspar.

"Be quiet! You're acting like a spoiled child."

"You're a traitor to our country, and you're a traitor to our class, which has always put service to the nation first above all other things."

Christoph sat down in one of the leather club chairs and put his fingertips together and said nothing.

"You've gone over to the Jews," said Kaspar, more quietly now. *"Of course* they want to carry out the terms of Versailles. It's good for *business,* for making money, and that's all they're interested in."

"If you think the terms of Versailles are good for business . . . all I can say is you know very little about business."

"They're making money out of Germany's humiliation!"

".Was Matthias Erzberger a Jew?"

"What's that got to do with anything?"

"Ask your old comrade," said Christoph, motioning with his head. Tillessen's shadow was visible in the hall. "Leutnant zur See."

"What are you talking about?"

"You don't know? His brother and another man killed Erzberger last summer. In the Black Forest. On his holiday, in August. He was taking a walk in the woods and they shot him down like a dog!"

Did Kaspar know? I couldn't tell. "Erzberger deserved to die. Erzberger signed the Armistice at Compiègne. Erzberger campaigned in the Reichstag for acceptance of the Versailles Treaty. Erzberger is as responsible as anybody for what's happened to us!"

"So therefore we shoot him? That's your answer to everything, isn't it? What do you think the choices were, in 'eighteen, in 'nineteen? The sailors in revolt, the children starving . . . *What the hell were they supposed to do?* We didn't have any ammunition left, we didn't have have any men left, the Americans were pouring in fresh troops . . . ask anybody who was in France! Hindenburg and Ludendorff calmly announced they couldn't hold the line any longer. The Allies would be right here in Berlin if *somebody* didn't sign. Would Hindenburg sign? Would Ludendorff sign? Certainly not! That's politics. You heard what Mother just said. Officers leave politics to the dirty politicians. Like Erzberger!"

Christoph and I sat amid the remnants of the High Tea. He was still slumped back into the leather club chair.

I thought it wiser to keep quiet.

The argument with Kaspar had continued until Lieutenant Tillessen, presumably tired of waiting, had appeared in the doorway again.

"Herr Oberleutnant . . . I find it hard to address you by that title —"

"Then don't! I was released in the spring of 1920."

"He's a banker now," said Kaspar.

"You were not released from your duty to the German people," said Tillessen.

"Correct," said Christoph. "And I don't require a former navy lieutenant to show me how to perform that duty!"

Tillessen pursed his lips. "I am not alone," he said, very quietly.

"I'm well aware of that," said Christoph, even more quietly.

Tillessen turned to Kaspar. "I must go. Are you coming?"

Without another word, Kaspar followed him into the hall, and then we heard Meier letting them out the front door.

We sat in silence for what seemed a long time. One of the windows was open, and a cool breeze from the darkening garden stirred the heavy drapes. Swallows flew across the patch of sky I could see from my chair. I smoked a cigarette and waited.

When Christoph began to talk, I didn't at first understand what he was talking about.

"I told you the French kept me a prisoner until the spring of 1920. I arrived in Berlin just before the Kapp Putsch began. I was home in my own bed for the first time in four years. A good deal lighter, one leg a little shorter than the other, but lucky to be alive — thanks to you.

"That was before my father had his stroke, he could still get around, he could telephone with his friends and hear the generals gossip, he came into my room one morning and told me, 'Your brother's Korps has captured Berlin, they have made a revolution!' But nobody really knew anything, no newspapers, the general strike began, there was shooting in parts of the city, and I was curious, so I put on some old clothes, a suit and an overcoat and a hat, the first time in civilian clothes, and I walked — rather slowly — up toward the center of the city, feeling strange in the loose old clothes that were now too big for me, walking through empty streets I had not seen for a long time. I walked all the way up to the Hubertusallee to the Kurfürstendamm and there I met a patrol of Schutzpolizei, city police. They wanted my papers and when they saw I was an officer just back from France they were very nice and they said the Putsch is over, they're moving out this afternoon, von Seeckt has taken over the army and has allowed the Ehrhardt Brigade to march out with their banners. So I told them about my little brother, I had not seen my brother since 1916, and they let me in their car and drove me around the Tiergarten, right into the Pariser Platz, in front of the Brandenburg Gate. But now the streets began to fill with people, the police had their hands full keeping the crowds under control, and then I saw troops coming down Unter den Linden, trucks and armored cars with skulls painted on them and soldiers marching. I pressed through the crowds to see if I could find my brother, but they all wore helmets, they all looked alike, and they all looked furious. Because of course they had lost, and everybody knew they had lost. The crowd was very quiet. You could only hear the sound of boots.

"You know what happened then? A little boy — he was quite near me, right in the first rank of the crowd — this little boy shouted something. I didn't even hear what he said — but they heard it! The men in the ranks heard it, and two of them stepped out of the column and they grabbed this little boy — not more than six years old, a little boy in short pants — and they hit him with their rifle butts and knocked him to the pavement and kept on hitting him . . . he screamed . . . his blood was all over the curbstone . . . they hit him and hit him and they kept on hitting him until he stopped screaming and lay still. And everybody watched, nobody did a *thing* — until somebody began to hiss. And then we all hissed. And you should see the eyes under those helmets! The eyes, when they heard the hissing. And then a captain came running along the rank, he was pulling his pistol out and shouting, 'Strasse frei!' Clear the street! and one of their armored cars with the skull and crossbones began to back up, and the machine gun turned. I dropped to the ground. People ran over me, people fell over me, it was a panic, and then the *tak-tak-tak-tak-tak* . . . well, you know the sound. They only fired a few seconds, but they hit some people who didn't drop fast enough, and there was screaming, people calling for help, the whole side of the Platz was black with men and women lying on the pavement, people crawled behind trees and streetlights and advertising columns — anything to get a little protection.

"And I thought here I am back from the War in one piece — Cossacks and airplane crashes and prison hospitals — and now I'm going to get shot by my own brother right in front of the Brandenburg Gate! And then I thought if he is with these murderous swine I don't even want to see him — because that's what they were — and still are. They are murderers, not soldiers!

"You know, it really hurt. Lying on my face in the Pariser Platz! Pariser Platz — we used to fill it with our horses and our music and our flags, people cheering — and here are German soldiers clubbing a German boy to death, firing a machine gun into the crowd, firing a machine gun at their brothers. I wanted to cry for my country."

Christoph stopped to catch his breath. He looked terrible.

"Kaspar told me this story," I said. "It sounded different the way he told it."

"I'm sure. Well, the armored car drove away. The Brigade formed ranks again and marched out through the Gate. The Putsch was over, and later that year the government managed to disband the Freikorps. Including Ehrhardt's. Some of the men were taken into the army, but very few. Most of them went into the streets."

"Kaspar came home."

"Kaspar came home, but he's found nothing to do either. Nothing to do but get into trouble with these 'old comrades.' Lots of them have congregated in Munich. The Bavarians hate the Republic, they hate Berlin — and they help these fellows. Tillessen's brother, the one who shot Erzberger, he fled to Munich and the *police president*, for God's sake, got him a visa to Hungary.

That's where he's hiding now. So Munich has become the white Capital, the contra-capital, the place where all kinds of Nationalist groups are trying to organize themselves — students, landowners, shopkeepers, unemployed officers, and of course these Freikorps people."

"What is it they want?" I asked. "I had a talk with Kaspar about all this, and he didn't seem to know *what* he wanted. They don't want the Kaiser back?"

"Oh my God, what do they want? Who knows? Maybe a few of them do want the Kaiser back. The Bavarians, some of them, want their own king back. But most of them really don't know what they want — as you say. They just know what they *don't* want: they hate the Republic because the Republic agreed to the Versailles Treaty, they want to destroy the Republic and break the treaty; they are deathly afraid of communism, they would gladly shoot every Communist in Germany; and of course they hate the Jews, they blame the Jews for everything that's gone wrong. On one hand they say that Marx was a Jew and most of the Communist leaders are Jews. On the other hand they complain that so many bankers and stockbrokers and lawyers are Jews, and the Jews own so many newspapers, they own the theatres and the department stores . . . in other worlds, there are not so many Jews, but they have done very well in the things they were allowed to do, and so they have become powerful, and they have become *conspicuous* — and people simply envy them.

"What do the Nationalists really want? What would they do if they got control? Look at the Kapp Putsch. What did they do? Nothing. They did nothing. They sat there until they lost the initiative. The Nationalist movement is purely negative, purely destructive. The Nationalists are looking for a program — and a leader."

"What about this O.C.?" I asked him. "You said something about Tillessen's friends being members of the O.C. and he nearly had an attack. Kaspar called you a traitor. What's the O.C.?"

He didn't answer immediately. He got up, walked to the window and looked into the garden.

Finally he turned around. "You did not come here to be mixed up in our problems."

"But I'm interested, I want to understand what's going on."

He nodded. "Yes, you are interested, you are here in our family, and you have heard and seen . . ." He paused. ". . . some things that might endanger you, I don't believe they will touch an American . . . but still, I think maybe it is best if you try to forget what you heard this evening. It's not your problem, and I don't want you involved. You understand?"

"You still claim I saved your life?"

"Of course you saved my life."

"Then I'm responsible for it."

"You are responsible for my life?"

"That's an ancient Chinese law. I heard about it in France, from a captain who'd been stationed in Indochina. If you save a person's life, you owe that life to the Gods, and you've got to guarantee it — with your own life. Forever. So I want you to know that if you're in some kind of trouble now, some kind of danger, then I want to know about it, I want to help you, because I'm responsible for you. To the Gods."

Christoph smiled. "I never thought of you as a philosopher. Especially not a Chinese philosopher. But I do thank you for saying that. And if I need your help, I will call you." He looked at his watch. "It's too early for bed. Shall we go back into town and have a beer?"

"Christoph, Fritz Falke asked me to come to a party . . ." I had written the address on the back of an envelope, and I pulled it out of my pocket. "I think it's a big party — mostly artists — and everybody is supposed to bring a bottle, so I'm sure it would be all right —"

Christoph smiled again. "Different milieu, old boy. This is not America. Your artists won't want me. Herr Falke hates officers. I have seen his pictures."

"No," I said. "You've got him wrong. Those officers in his pictures are the very people you've been telling me about, the people who made the Kapp Putsch, the Freikorps people, Kaspar's friends —"

Christoph shook his head. "They don't make such fine distinctions —"

"Oh, come along and see. You're not afraid of them, are you?" I looked at the envelope. "The man who's giving the party is called Kowalski, he's a sculptor —"

"A sculptor called Kowalski? I don't believe it. May I see that address?"

14.

ON THE TOWN

It turned out to be a gloomy cold apartment house in a street off the Nollendorf Platz. Bicycles chained to the banister, dim light bulbs, a smell of cooking gas, and the faint sound of dance music. We climbed to the fourth floor. The dance music was louder. We knocked.

Fritz Falke opened the door. Behind him, we saw the party in progress.

"I've brought a bottle of Scotch and my friend —" I began, but another man interrupted, shouting "*Keith!* Can it be? The Limping Eagle of La Rochelle?" and he was shaking hands with Christoph, they were grinning, explaining that they had spent years together in a prison camp, had come back across the Rhine in the same freight car. . . . I was introduced to Hans Kowalski, our host: iron-gray hair and horn-rimmed glasses, the torso of a weight lifter, calloused hands. . . . His apartment consisted of two large rooms containing little furniture but lots of people. In one corner a Victrola was playing and a few couples were doing the tango. The air was thick with cigarette smoke, and the only light came from a few candles that flickered in front of the mantelpiece mirror.

"Come along," said Falke, taking my arm. "First we pour ourselves some of your expensive whisky, then we hide the bottle or it will disappear in two minutes, then I will introduce you to some nice girls. . . ."

I was leaning against the wall when I heard the guitar. I made a circuit of the rooms, sipping my Scotch, looking at the dim figures dancing and talking and arguing and kissing and wandering lost like me. One corner of the second room was Hans Kowalski's studio. A strong wooden work table covered with newspapers, some sketches tacked on the wall, a block of yellow stone that

was beginning to look like a woman's face . . . I heard the
guitar. I turned and saw that the player was sitting on the
high table, his legs crossed, the guitar in his lap. I could
barely see him by the light of the candle. He was about
my age, thin short black hair and small black eyes and a
long pointy nose and steel-rimmed spectacles. He wore a
leather windbreaker over a turtleneck sweater. His head
was too small. His ears stuck out. He needed a shave.

He began to sing in a high, hoarse voice, and he had
an accent that made it hard for me to understand his German, but the effect was overwhelming just the same.
Somebody turned off the Victrola, people from the front
room came crowding into the studio, and then there
wasn't a sound except the strumming guitar and the rasping voice of the singer and his song.

He sang, and I could barely understand what he was
singing about (Baal? Who is Baal?).

> *Nicht so faul, sonst gibt es nicht Genuss!*
> *Was man will, sagt Baal, ist was man muss.*
> *Wenn ihr Kot macht, ist's, sagt Baal, geb' acht!*
> *Besser noch, als wenn ihr garnichts macht!*

Magic. He cast a magic spell into the room, and I did
the only thing I could: I put my glass down, took out my
notebook and began to sketch his face.

He sang and sang, and I kept staring and sketching,
and when he finished the place exploded with applause.

"Who is that?" I asked whoever stood jammed beside
me.

"I think his name is Becht."

"Brecht," said Fritz Falke, pushing through. "Bertolt
Brrrecht. Look, you've drawn his picture, come and meet
him," and he pulled me toward the singer, who was surrounded by admirers. He had put the guitar on the table
and was trying to light a cigar stub. We were introduced.
He studied my sketch carefully, puffing smoke.

"I think you've made me prettier than I am."

"That's his problem," said Falke. "He flatters his subjects. I'm trying to cure him."

Hans Kowalski appeared with a glass of Scotch for
Brecht. "This gentleman brought something special."

Brecht raised the glass to me: "Zum Wohl." I raised
mine too.

"Would you write down the words to that song?" I asked.

"Write them down? They are written down, next fall they will be published as a book. It's called *Baal*. It's a play." He looked at me as he drank another slug of whisky. "You know Chicago?"

"Chicago? Well, I've been there, but only between trains. You have to change trains . . ."

He asked questions about Chicago. He asked if I'd been in the American army. I told him no, I'd driven an ambulance. For the French. Brecht started to laugh. "You were what we call a *Sanitäter?* That's what I was." Then he leaned back and addressed the crowd around us:

"In honor of our American guest, I want to sing 'The Cavaliers of Station D,' written Anno Eighteen in the Augsburg Military Hospital, Department of Venereal Diseases." And he sang:

> *Oh wie brannten euch der Lieben Flammen*
> *Als ihr jung und voller Feuer ward.*
> *Ach der Mensch haut halt das Mensch zusammen*
> *Das ist nun einmal so seine Art.*
>   *Oh diese Weiber, Himmelherrgottsackerment!*
>   *Arg schon die Liebe, aber ärger noch der*
>   *Tripper brennt!*

The crowd roared and yelled with laughter, and Brecht and Falke and Christoph Keith, all drinking my Scotch, spent the next half hour writing it down in German, trying to help me translate — loosely — into English, so that Brecht could sign and trade it for my sketch:

> *Oh, how the flames of love burned in your gut*
> *When you were young, when you were full of fire.*
> *Now if it comes to beating up the slut*
> *That doesn't interfere with your desire.*
>   *Oh these damn women, many a lover sings,*
>   *Love's hard enough, love's painful —*
>   *When the pecker stings!*

Brecht said: "Do you want to go to another party? Big house in the Tiergartenstrasse, lots of food, lots of alcohol. I'm afraid we have finished your whisky here."

Christoph Keith declined: "I'm an office slave and have to work tomorrow." Then he drew me aside. "You know these people are Communists?"

They are? I had never met a Communist.

Fritz Falke and Brecht and I took a taxi across town to a mansion in the Tiergartenstrasse. I paid. The block was lined with glistening limousines, each containing a sleeping chauffeur.

"Whose party is this?" I said.

"A Jew from Galicia. Made millions in the stock market," said Brecht.

The butler who let us into an enormous marble foyer took Brecht's guitar without changing his expression.

Blazing lights, crowds of people in evening dress, a small orchestra playing tangos, a long dining room table displaying platters of caviar sandwiches, smoked salmon sandwiches and silver ice buckets containing bottles of French champagne and Polish vodka.

Brecht and Falke made directly for the food.

"Shouldn't we say good evening to the host?" I asked.

"Yes, if we see him," said Brecht.

"You'll see him," said Falke. "He'll want you to sing."

A waiter appeared with three glasses of champagne on a tray. We took them.

"Prosit Bacchus," said Brecht, raising his glass.

"Prosit the stock market," said Falke. We drank.

They pointed out some famous people: a lovely film star; a fat theatre director; the most influential drama critic in Berlin.

"Achtung," said Falke, glancing over my shoulder. "Here comes our host."

He was about as tall as I am, which is not very tall, but he was broad-shouldered and fat, quite bald, with a round flat face and features like a boxer or a football player. It was hard to judge how old he was — maybe forty-five. He wore a tuxedo, and after I shook hands my hand smelled of perfume or shaving lotion.

"Herr Brecht, Herr Falke . . . I'm honored that you could come." He spoke German with a Russian accent. Introductions: My new American student . . .

He tried out his English on me. He offered us cigars from an alligator case. A waiter came with another tray of champagne. While looking over the rim of my glass I suddenly realized why all this looked so familiar: it was a scene from Falke's cartoons. Our host was Falke's creation. I felt dizzy. The champagne was foaming in my skull, and I wondered if I was asleep somewhere and dreaming.

"Herr Brecht, I hope you didn't leave your guitar at home!"

Brecht went to get his guitar and Falke went to get caviar. For an instant our host was undecided whether to leave me or to attempt more conversation.

I tried to help him. "I understand you are in the stock market."

He brightened. Yes! Was I interested in the stock market? I told him of my days at Drexel, trying to make it sound funny. "I'm afraid that stocks and bonds are not my dish of tea."

Conversation: How long had I been in Berlin? What had I done? What had I seen? Whom had I met?

The dizziness had passed and I chatted along, happily primed with my Scotch and his champagne . . . and suddenly I noticed that a curtain had come down. His face looked completely different.

"You arrived here last week, and today you had lunch at Waldstein and Co. That's extremely interesting." He took out a silver instrument and used it to snip a tiny hole into the end of his cigar. "I have been here since the spring of 1919, I am one of the most successful traders on the Berlin stock market, I am received by Hugo Stinnes, I am consulted by Walther Rathenau, all of the interesting and important people come to my house — but I have *never* been invited to lunch at the Gendarmenmarkt!" He put a cigar into his mouth and struck a match, and his hand was shaking. "You will excuse me, please. I must arrange a place for Brecht to sing for us."

We left Brecht at the party, surrounded by adoring women. Falke said it was time to pick up Bärbel and Baby. We had eaten all the hors d'oeuvres we could hold, and I watched Falke wrap three caviar sandwiches into linen napkins and distribute them among his pockets.

I offered to pay for a taxi, but Falke thought we should walk. I fell down twice between the Tiergartenstrasse and the Landwehr Canal, which is only a couple of blocks.

"I'd better go home," I said as he helped me up the second time.

"Is your stomach all right?" asked Falke.

"Yes. It's my head. I'm dizzy."

"Dizzy? That's nothing. You need fresh air and exercise. We will march over to the Friedrichstrasse."

"I'm really not used to doing this all night long," I said, stumbling along unsteadily beside him.

Falke laughed. "We have a saying: 'Man muss die Feste feiern wie sie fallen.' You understand? You celebrate when you get the chance. In Germany today, we don't get many chances."

We were walking through an expensive residential district: big houses, big chestnut trees, immaculate empty sidewalks, an occasional car purring by, streetlights reflected in the black water of the canal. Our footsteps rang in the silence.

"See that bridge?" asked Falke. "That's where the boys from the Guards Cavalry Division dumped Rosa Luxemburg. She wasn't found for weeks. People thought she'd escaped. Then she floated into one of the locks. They made up a song: *'A Rosa Is Swimming in the Landwehr Canal.'* "

"Did you know her?"

"Certainly I knew her."

"She was the leader of the Spartacists?"

"She and Liebknecht. They shot him the same night, back there in the Tiergarten."

I still had to concentrate on walking, but the cool night air was clearing my head.

"What was she like?"

"Well, I can show you a sketch I did. Plump little Jewess from Russian Poland. Not pretty. Passion and brains, bravest of the brave, but sensible too. She knew the people wouldn't rise to a Communist revolution. Tried to talk Liebknecht out of it, but Liebknecht wanted to fight. So we had our little Spartacus Week. January 1919. Didn't amount to much, I can tell you, but it scared the shit out of the middle class. Germans don't like mobs in the streets and red flags and disorder. And Jewish girls from Poland taking over Das Deutsche Reich! So the government brought in the Freikorps. And you know what happened."

"Did you fight with the Spartacists?" I asked.

"No. I'm a coward. I learned that in France. But the soldiers didn't like my pictures. In a way, I fought with pictures, and they came to get me."

"And what did you do?"

"I hid. They shot five men in our courtyard. They threw an eighteen-year-old boy off the roof. But they didn't find me."

"Where were you?"

"In Mutti Bauer's bed!"

The Friedrichstrasse at night was even more brightly lighted and more garish than the Kurfürstendamm, but it was late now and business seemed to be slowing down. The nightclub barkers stood about with their hands in their pockets, chatting with each other. A few tired-looking girls strolled slowly along the sidewalk, sometimes running out to speak with men in the cruising cars.

A tall thin blonde stopped in front of us: "Hallo, Fritz. May I show your friend something interesting?" She began to unbutton her raincoat.

"Thank you, not tonight, dear," said Falke, closing the raincoat and gently turning her around. "We've just come to pick up the girls."

"You won't find Bärbel — and I think there's been some trouble about Baby."

"What do you mean? What kind of trouble?"

"I don't know, the bulls were in there earlier this evening, but I don't think they caught her."

Falke let go of the girl's arm and strode up the Friedrichstrasse. I kept up with him.

"Could this be something with the woman from the School Administration?" I asked.

Falke nodded.

We swept past the uniformed doorman of a big glittering place called Adam und Eva: a foyer of red velvet and gilded mirrors, beyond that a large dim smoky room full of tables and chairs, beyond that an empty stage.

Somebody was playing "I'm Always Chasing Rainbows" on a piano. The last show was over and there were not many customers left, but before I could see much of the big room the headwaiter and a fat young man in a double-breasted blue pinstriped suit appeared.

"Herr Falke!" They tried to draw him aside.

"No, it's all right, he's my friend. American. Where's Baby?"

"She's in there, Herr Falke, but this must be her last night," said the blue pinstripe, apparently the manager.

"The police were here this evening with some woman from the School Administration — of course we were warned and had Baby out the back in plenty of time — but the woman made an unbelievable scene, right here in front of customers, showed me a birth certificate, told me she would close me down. . . . I mean it's just not worth my job to me, Herr Falke, she's a good girl and the customers like her, but I'm not interested in trouble with the police, I can get a dozen girls for every place —"

"Basta," said Falke. "No speech necessary. I understand. Where's the money?"

The manager tugged a bulging envelope from inside his jacket. "Here, I've got it all ready, do you want to count it?"

Falke looked at the envelope but didn't touch it. "We said dollars."

The manager shook his head. "Can't do it. Slow night, we just don't have them tonight."

"You want to see Bärbel here tomorrow night?"

"This has nothing to do with Bärbel, Herr Falke. She isn't even in the house at the moment. . . ."

"You want to see Bärbel here tomorrow night?"

"Herr Falke, believe me —"

"No dollars for Baby, no Bärbel for Adam und Eva," said Falke evenly. "Peter, you go in and sit down and order a bottle of champagne. But don't pay for it! My friend and I will have a little business discussion in his office."

The manager shrugged and disappeared behind a curtain. Falke followed him. The headwaiter, who had watched all this in silence, bowed to me and said in English: "If you please, sir."

I thought I would never make it up all those stairs. Falke supported me on one side and Baby on the other. They did it three steps at a time: "Eins, zwei, drei, *hoppla!*" Pause. Rest. "All right? Aufwärts marsch! Eins, zwei, drei, *hoppla!*"

It was nearly daylight. Workmen wearing cloth caps came tramping down the steps, staring at us, staring mostly at Baby, looking away in disgust.

Falke had let me pay for the taxi, but he wouldn't let me keep it to go back to Grunewald. "We can't send you home like this," he had said, pushing me right out of the car. "You come upstairs with us and sleep it off."

"You don't have room for me." I tried to lie down on the cold gritty sidewalk.

"Plenty of room, plenty of room." Falke pulled me to my feet. "Get under his other shoulder, Baby."

Baby's hair smelled of cigarette smoke. In the taxi she had cried a little. "What are we going to do if I can't work?"

"We'll make it," Falke had assured her. "It won't hurt you to go to school a little."

"I can't stand that stinking school. I'll run away!"

"No you won't," said Falke. "I have other plans for you," but we never heard what they were, because the taxi stopped at Kaiser Friedrichstrasse 101, the tenement in Neukölln.

"All right, you've made it, Peter, we're here, just one . . . more . . . push: . . . zwei, drei, *hoppla!*" and while I held on to Falke, Baby unlocked the door.

Dim, gray silent kitchen. Snores from the bedroom. I sat down at the table and put my head in my arms. Baby and Falke whispered. Falke went into the bedroom. The snores stopped. Baby went back out into the hall. What were they doing? I think I fell asleep. Then they were both in the kitchen again, moving around. Falke's hand was on my shoulder.

"Come on, old boy. One more thing before we sleep."

"No, I'm all right. Sleep here."

"Come on, old boy." He wrapped his thick arms around my chest and pulled me to my feet. "Just a short call at the watering station." I held on to him as we stumbled out into the hallway, passed the doors of other apartments, opened the door to what looked like a closet but turned out to be a reeking toilet.

"Can you stand up by yourself?" asked Falke, right behind me.

"Yes." I held on to the wall, tried not to breathe, unbuttoned my pants and emptied my bladder. As I buttoned up again and moved out to make room for Falke, a toothless old woman appeared, carrying two brimming chamber pots.

"Guten Morgen, die Herren," she said politely and stood there waiting her turn until Falke came out.

I made it back to the apartment, but now the hallway felt like the pitching promenade deck of the *Mauretania*

during an Atlantic gale. When I reached the kitchen I
tried to lie down on the table.

"No, no," Falke whispered, grabbing my arm. "We
have a bed for you." He guided me into the next room. I
could just make out the boy asleep on his little cot by the
door, and Baby already in the big bed which must have
been her mother's. Her eyes were shut. What had they
done with Mutti Bauer? Where was Bärbel? Falke eased
me onto the empty bed, pulled off my shoes, went into
the studio, and closed the door. The last thing I heard
was the creaking of bedsprings.

I was dreaming. I think I was dreaming about a storm
on the *Mauretania* and I was cold, but then I was awake
because a small hand was opening my shirt, pulling my
pants off, rolling me over to pull my arms out of my shirtsleeves . . .

"Baby?"

"Shh! Don't wake the boy. Can't sleep in your
clothes. . . . Move over a bit, will you?"

She slid in beside me, naked, soft, terribly thin. She
wrapped herself around me. I could feel her ribs. I could
feel every bone in her body.

"Listen, Baby —"

She put a hand over my mouth and her lips to my ear.
"Don't talk." She put her tongue in my ear. Her hands
moved.

"It doesn't matter. You've had too much to drink."

It wasn't anything I had to drink. It was my mother's
face — the expression on my mother's face in the doorway, as our eyes met over Else Westerich's broad milky
shoulder. . . .

I fell asleep with Baby's soft hand holding me.

But then I was awake again — I think I was awake
again but maybe I was dreaming — and I was hard as a
rock, inside her, and she was on top of me, all over and
around me, squirming like a snake, hot sticky skin and
perfume and sweat and her tongue in my ear, and I
thought my God you can go to jail for this, this is absolute
jailbait, but I didn't stop and she didn't stop until we were
finished, gasping for breath, and then, after just a minute
or two, I felt her muscles clenching again and she was out

of bed, her feet thumping on the floor and into the studio hissing *"Raus! Raus!"* and in there the bedsprings creaked again, Mutti Bauer appeared naked under an open bathrobe. Stumbling, half asleep, she let Baby shove her into the other bed, let Baby roll in beside her, let Baby draw the heavy quilt over them just as the kitchen door opened and Bärbel walked into the darkness.

Bärbel emitted a tired sigh, sat down on my bed, immediately jumped up, went over to the window, lifted the shade to let more light in and inspected the scene. I thought of a room full of children pretending to be asleep when their parents come in.

Bärbel dropped the shade and walked into the studio. Voices, but low voices; apparently not an argument. A moment later Bärbel came out, dressed only in her kimono, and went into the kitchen. Water splashing from the pitcher, sounds of washing. She padded through the bedroom again, returned to the studio, said "God, am I tired!" and shut the door.

Sinking away now . . . A damp little hand reached out of the darkness, grasped my index finger, let go. . . . Sinking away to the sound of Mutti Bauer's slow and steady breathing, I suddenly realized that I had forgotten to remember my mother's face in the doorway.

15.
_____

A VIEW OF THE HAVEL

The wind shifted slightly to the south, and all along the front, as far as the eye could see, people began to adjust their boats and their sails. I spent my summers at Northeast Harbor where there are certainly plenty of boats, but I had never seen anything like the wide part of the Havel River on a Sunday morning in June. I managed to find some open water just north of the island, but on the other side, toward the Wannsee public beaches and the distant wooded hills of the Grunewald, you could hardly see the shoreline. I wondered how they could all keep out of each other's way. (They didn't, I learned later. We saw several collisions: dull thumps, angry shouts, fluttering sails dragged down. . . .)

The little sloop handled nicely, considering everything; the fittings had been carefully greased, but they were grimy, the woodwork was sticky, and the sail was stained and mildewed. As we tacked hard against the breeze, Lili sat beside me on the gunwhale and held the sheet, her bare brown legs braced against the centerboard housing, her black hair blowing, her black eyes shining.

"Oh this is so *wonderful*, Peter. Can we make it tip more? Can we go faster?"

I smiled at her. "Aren't you the motorboat queen of the Wannsee?"

"That's because Bobby taught me. Nobody ever taught me this. Will you?"

It happened by chance. I had come out on an early train, grateful that I had an invitation and didn't have to hang around Christoph Keith, who was apparently going somewhere with Helena. When I arrived at the Nikolassee station, Lili was on the platform, and the coachman Schmitz had his landau at the door.

"Oh, you have such a nice suit," Lili said. "You did not bring a bathing suit?"

"I thought we were having lunch with your family."

"Oh yes, but first we will go on the water."

When the landau deposited us in front of the Schloss, she led me around the outside and down through the woods to the Tea House, where, after some minutes of rummaging through cluttered dressing rooms, she produced an old-fashioned man's bathing suit. I regarded it without enthusiasm.

"You go in there and put it on. I will go into the other room to change."

"Do we really need bathing suits? I thought we're just going for a ride."

"Too cold for you?"

"No, I'm used to cold water."

She reappeared in the same costume I had seen the first time: tight black bathing suit, black cardigan. She looked splendid. I looked like a clown in a knitted garment of broad horizontal stripes that covered me from my elbows to my knees.

She giggled when she saw me. "The very height of fashion, 1914. Here is a nice warm swimming robe to wrap around you," and she led me across the flagstone terrace to the boathouse.

It was dark inside and cool, greenish water clunking against cement walls, the dim shape of the launch moving gently against padded mooring posts . . .

"Do you see that thing there, that handle? Will you turn that handle, please, to open the door?"

The hand crank wasn't easy to turn. It operated a series of gears connected to a chain mechanism. With a tremendous clanking clatter, I gradually rolled the big metal garage door into the ceiling, and now the sunshine on the water made shimmering patterns on the damp green walls of the boathouse and the white hull of the launch.

Lili skampered down the stone steps, jumped barefoot into the cockpit and began to fasten the aquaplane ropes, but my eyes were attracted by something else.

A wooden shelf, or platform, had been attached to the opposite wall of the boathouse, just a few feet above the water, and this supported what looked to me like the hull of a sailboat — completely wrapped in brown tarpaulin. Then I saw that the mast was there too. It had been taken down and wrapped right in with the hull; the masthead stuck out through the tarpaulin over the stern.

I reached the platform by stepping carefully along a narrow ledge that crossed the back wall of the boathouse. Lili looked up and stopped what she was doing.

"Whose boat is this?" My voice echoed.

"Nobody uses it." Her voice echoed too, and it sounded so different that I turned around. She was looking down again, occupied with the rope.

"Why not? Why doesn't anybody use it?"

"Nobody knows how to sail." She didn't look up.

"Well, why have you got a sailboat if nobody knows how to sail?"

Now she looked up. "That was Max's boat. He was the only one who sailed."

Max? I had to think for a second. "Oh, your brother . . . ?"

She nodded. "I was twelve years old and Alfred was at the Front and Bobby wasn't interested, so they took it out of the water and wrapped it in those cloths and it has been there ever since."

I was examining the thing more closely, unlacing the dusty mildewed cover just a bit, to see if I could get a look at the wood and at the fittings . . . it seemed to be a racing sloop, maybe sixteen or eighteen feet, unusually narrow beam. The brass pulley at the masthead was discolored but well greased, and it turned all right. . . .

I felt the platform move and Lili stood beside me. "You know how to sail?"

"Sure," I said. "I knew how to sail when I was six. Got my first boat when I was twelve."

She took a deep breath. "Would you like to sail this boat?"

"Sure."

"You think you know how to . . . put it back together?"

"Sure, if all the parts are here. I might need a hand to get it into the water without scratching the paint —"

Lili was gone, running like a deer across the ledge and then out of the boathouse.

It was easy enough to unwrap the hull, which must have been painted and caulked after they had taken it out of the water. The centerboard and the rudder assembly were lying on the floor planks. The removable fittings were gone, and so of course were the sails and the sail sheets and the stays for the mast — all put away indoors, presumably.

By the time I had the tarpaulins off Lili was back, accompanied by Schmitz the coachman, an old gardener with a white walrus moustache, and a younger man I took to be an undergardener. They all greeted me politely, but they were dubious about doing what Lili was telling them to do. There was a lot of worried headshaking, a lot of muttering about "Herr Baron," and I began to feel that maybe there was more to this than just putting a sloop into the water.

There was.

The men were reluctant but Lili, clearly used to getting her own way, began to talk with a certain ring in her voice. It was a different voice. She was not polite now, she was issuing orders — and the orders were obeyed.

I saw that the water was only up to my shoulders here, so I jumped in, stood barefoot on cold slimy gravel, and took the weight of the bow as the others carefully slid the hull off the platform. When it was floating free, I sort of walked and swam it out of the boathouse, across the

front of the Tea House terrace and up against the floating
dock, where Lili was waiting to tie it fast. She had already
found the sailbag and another bag containing a lot of
carefully oiled brass fittings.

The sun was high now, warming the planks of the dock,
warming the varnished deck of the sloop, warming my
back as I worked. I needed help in mounting the mast, but
I managed everything else myself. It was like putting together a new jigsaw puzzle: you know the general idea
but you've got to find the right piece for each place, and
some of the German pieces didn't look like ours.

I guess it took me over an hour. I was completely absorbed in what I was doing, so it was only when I had the
mainsail properly fastened and was ready to raise it that
I looked around and saw all the people.

The gravel path leading from the Tea House up to the
Schloss was filled with people watching me. It looked as
if the entire staff had collected there: kitchen help in
white; waitresses and parlormaids in blue dresses, white
aprons and white caps; a table boy; the butler in his
striped vest standing above and behind the others; the
three men who had helped me standing in a tight group
by the ramp to the floating dock — and the old nurse
from the Spreewald, dressed in her long black peasant
costume and her enormous white lace bonnet, standing all
alone on the terrace of the Tea House, her face buried in
her handkerchief.

Up at the Schloss, something glittered, catching the sun.
One of the french doors was opening. Lili's father stepped
onto the terrace, put his hands on the balustrade, and
looked down at us. I could not see his expression; he was
too far away.

I turned to Lili, who was biting her lips.

"We shouldn't have done this, should we?"

"Yes, we should have done it. This is a boat and not a
gravestone! But now are we ready?"

"We're ready. You sit over there, hold the tiller in *that*
direction until I tell you to move it."

When she was in place I released the painter, stepped
into the boat, kicked us clear of the dock, and hauled up
the fluttering mainsail just as fast as I could do it. The
wind grabbed us, the boom ran out and we swept past the
weeping willows. I held the main sheet in one hand and
reached out the other for the tiller. My hand was over

Lili's. I saw the reeds in front of us now, the little beach, shallow water. I moved the tiller, pointing us away from the beach, but as we passed I saw Lili wave so I turned around and looked over my shoulder.

Behind the reeds, Alfred von Waldstein and Sigrid were sitting on black horses, sitting still and gravely watching us. As Lili waved, Alfred took off his scarf, a pale blue scarf, and held it high above his head, letting it stream in the wind.

"I think we are late," said Lili.

As we rounded the point we could see the floating dock, and it was full of people — not servants now, but lunch guests: cloche hats, silk dresses fluttering in the wind, white flannel suits, blazers, everybody was watching us, and I didn't like that. I passed the dock and came about against the wind and told Lili exactly what I wanted her to do. Somehow everything worked. I was afraid the mainsail would stick, but I got it down in time to lose our headway just yards below the dock, and that allowed me to slide in close enough for Lili to jump off the bow and tie us up. I began to fasten the boom and wrap the sail but Lili said: "Please, Peter, we can do all that later, you must be introduced and then we must dress for lunch," so I stepped out of the boat in my idiotic striped bathing suit and there was the Baroness von Waldstein, Lili's mother, who had barely been conscious of me before — just an American friend of Christoph Keith's — and she walked across the planks in her high heels, a short stout handsome woman with pearls and no hat but a net to protect her gray hair from the wind, and she took my arm and turned me away from the people, toward the water, and she said: "Mr. Ellis, when my husband saw that sail go up, when he saw that little boat move out beyond the willows . . . Mr. Ellis, I think he cried."

"Baroness, I didn't understand —"

She pressed my elbow. "No, it's all right, it's time we all got over it, and Lili knew it, and we all hope you will come back often and teach her to sail. That is what I wanted to tell you. Now please come over here and meet someone who has been asking for you."

We turned around and walked toward the people surrounding Lili and the boat, and the next face I saw was the face of Miss Susan Boatwright.

She smiled. "Good afternoon, Peter Ellis. One does find thee in interesting places!"

How can I describe Miss Susan Boatwright?

I guess she's over forty. She never married. Her family owns the Locomotive Works in Philadelphia. She has lots of money. She spends it to help other people. She supports a magazine that publishes the poems of unknown poets; she established a nursery to care for Negro children in the slums of Philadelphia while their mothers are at work; and she spent most of the War years with a Quaker mission in France, trying to help the people whose towns had been destroyed.

I don't think she is actually related to me, but she grew up in the same neighborhood and comes from the same background as my mother and my father so she has known me all my life. However, I came to know *her* in the Hospital. Her niece, Joanne, was in the Hospital too. Joanne is skeletally thin, about my age, a girl with long blonde hair she never washes, a girl who had terrible problems with her father, a girl who had withdrawn, a girl who would sit and look out the window for hours at a time, a girl who took a liking to me, asked me to tell her stories, allowed me to paint her picture.

Miss Boatwright was the only person who ever came to see Joanne, but Joanne would hardly talk to her, and somehow I began telling Miss Boatwright *my* problems — to the extent I could understand what they were — while painting Joanne's portrait. We would sit in the azalea gardens and Joanne would dream into the distance, and Miss Boatwright would question me — not the way the doctors did, but in a cheerful rather bluff manner. We didn't talk about the War. We didn't talk about that last evacuation on the Chemin des Dames where a shell hit Douglas Pratt's ambulance a hundred feet in front of mine and buried me under an avalanche of bleeding corpses. We talked about painting, about pictures we had both seen in Paris, about famous painters she had met.

Why are some perfectly good draftsmen not really *painters?* Why would anybody wish to become an artist? Is it — or isn't it — a frivolous occupation?

We talked about all sorts of things, twice a week for over a year, until she told me that she was going to Ger-

many for the American Friends Service Committee because conditions were desperate, the War was over but
the British blockade was still in force, and children were
starving.

By the time she returned from that trip I had been released from the Hospital, had served out my banking
year at Drexel, and had escaped to Paris.

Joanne was still gazing out of the windows.

A long table was set in the sparkling white dining room
of the Schloss. Linen and silver and crystal glasses, enormous vases filled with clouds of yellow tulips, sunshine
glazing through the open french doors, a view of water
and sails and sky.

Except for some bankers and their wives, most of the
guests seemed to be relatives. I was introduced to a be-
wildering collection of Lili's aunts and cousins and the
people they had married, but fortunately I was seated
beside Miss Boatwright — or rather Lili's mother advised me, when I reported to her, fully dressed, that I
was taking Miss Boatwright in.

"These people like thee," said Miss Boatwright, as she
began her soup. "The Baroness has told me about the
man thee pulled out of an airplane. I never heard that
story."

"Miss Boatwright, they *worship* you! They told me
about the feeding of the children, after the War —"

She nodded. "It was a successful Mission, but of course
it wasn't *me,* it's just that I'm the person they met, by
chance. And the Mission is by no means over, Peter.
Sitting in this . . . this palace, you can't imagine the misery of the working people —"

"I've seen a little bit of it." I told her about Fritz
Falke's tenement in Neukölln.

"Yes, I've been with people in those neighborhoods all
along," said Miss Boatwright. She leaned closer. "I confess that I feel . . . somewhat awkward amidst all this
grandeur, but the von Waldsteins have been of enormous
help to our Mission — in many ways. You see, they were
the first . . . what shall I say? magnates? capitalists? that
I met when I came to Berlin."

"How did you meet them?"

"A strange story," said Miss Boatwright. She covered
her glass with her hand as the butler leaned forward with

the wine. "When we first came to Germany, we began
our work in a modest way. During the War, in France,
we had German prisoners working for us. They did most
of the physical labor at our feeding depots, they loaded
trucks, did all the dirty work . . . and the French army
would not permit us to pay them. So we put their wages
aside. We took their names and their home addresses
and we simply credited them with whatever sums we felt
they had earned by their work. And we took their photographs.

"In the summer of 1919, when we were finally allowed to enter Germany, we made a special effort to locate the families of these men — wherever they might
be. We traveled to the most remote places — in Saxony
and Thuringia and Bavaria . . . and we usually found old
parents or wives and children in the most pathetic circumstances."

The waitress removed the soup bowls and new plates
arrived. Miss Boatwright asked for a glass of water. The
water was brought on a silver tray. Miss Boatwright took
a sip and continued her story.

"After we established our administrative office here in
Berlin, I was asked to go on a similar trip to a village in
the Spreewald, the headwaters of the river Spree, east of
Berlin: dark gloomy swamps, dark gloomy forests, im-
penetrable mazes of little rivers and canals, immaculate
villages, storks on the rooftops, Kassubian peasants still
wearing their traditional costumes. . . . Well, I took a
train to this little town, made inquiries, wound up at the
home of the Bürgermeister, where my presence caused
the usual excitement. Of course the Bürgermeister knew
all about the family, but in this case the nearest relative
was the soldier's mother, and the mother wasn't here, the
mother was in Berlin, employed in the house of the
Baron von Waldstein. As if of course I knew who *that*
was. Well, of course I didn't.

"The Bürgermeister had a telephone — the only one
in the village. He called Berlin, the townhouse on the
Pariser Platz. Tremendous shouting and excitement. A
woman came on the line and of course I couldn't understand a word she said and she couldn't understand a
word I said. More shouting and excitement. Finally a
man came on and said in perfect English: 'Hallo, here is
Baron Waldstein, will you kindly explain your business?'

and I did, and he said, 'Madam, will you be good enough
to remain *exactly* where you are until my car arrives?'
and about an hour later — maybe more than that — an
enormous limousine drove up, the chauffeur opened the
door and out sprang the lady you have seen here, the old
children's nurse they've kept since their first son was born,
and she was absolutely frantic with excitement, her son
had been reported missing, she'd had no news of him,
she'd lost her other son in Russia. . . . Well, she insisted
that I drive back to the Pariser Platz to meet the Herr
Baron, the Frau Baronin and the children, as she
called them . . . and that's how I met the Waldsteins.

"They were not only overwhelmingly hospitable to me;
they were amazed to hear about the work of our Mission,
asked lots of questions, pitched right in to help us. For
instance, the Baron called somebody high up on the railroad service, who expedited our first shipment of powdered milk from Hamburg. . . I can't begin to tell you all
the other things they've done for us . . ."

The waitresses were passing platters of veal cutlets.
The table turned.

"Do you remember that play they were talking
about?" asked Lili. "That play by Arthur Schnitzler?"

"Sure, I even remember the name. It's called *Reigen*."

"Yes, and Helena has got us cards for the opening.
Next Wednesday evening. Would you be free to go?"

"Of course."

"Oh good! Just the six of us: Helena and Christoph,
Sigrid and Alfred."

"How about Bobby?"

She looked surprised, then shook her head. "Bobby
makes his own plans."

"I thought he said he wanted to see it."

"Perhaps. But not with us."

I didn't understand. "Why doesn't Bobby want to come
with us?"

A flash of irritation. "Does it matter so much to you?"
Chastened, I shut up and ate my lunch.

Across the table, Geheimrat Dr. Strassburger caught my
eye. He smiled and leaned forward. "Mr. Ellis, you are
pleased with the operation, I hope?"

"The operation?" I must have looked puzzled.

Dr. Strassburger stopped smiling. "Keith has not reported to you?"

"Sir, I haven't seen him for a couple of days. Bankers and art students keep different hours, you know. He's gone to the office by the time I get up. . . ."

Dr. Strassburger's expression indicated that he did not find that explanation convincing. "Perhaps we have a little talk after lunch."

"Yes, sir."

Fresh strawberries, right out of the garden.

"Who is that gentlemen across the table?" asked Miss Boatwright. "We were introduced but I didn't quite understand who he is."

I explained who Dr. Strassburger was.

"He questioned me most thoroughly about the Locomotive Works, so he clearly knows who *I* am, but I disgraced myself, I fear. I've always left those matters to Cousin Francis and I don't know a thing about his plans for selling locomotives in Turkey."

"Selling locomotives in Turkey?"

"That's what he wanted to discuss. I told him to write to Cousin Francis. Peter, when may I see some new paintings?"

"Well, anytime, of course, Miss Boatwright, but they are . . . ah, the place where I work is down in Neukölln —"

"Oh, I've been there often, most dreadful conditions in the city . . ."

I couldn't visualize Miss Boatwright in Falke's establishment, but she had already opened her purse and produced a pencil and a small address book. I tried to change the subject.

"Miss Boatwright, have you seen my parents?"

"Peter Ellis, of course I've seen them, don't toy with *me!*" so I gave her Falke's address and we agreed that she would come on Thursday afternoon. Then she told me about my parents, and about Joanne.

Although the ladies and gentlemen did not separate the formal way they would have at home, when the coffee was served on the terrace all of the men seemed to drift over to one side. Clouds of cigar smoke and earnest political conversations.

Dr. Strassburger was at my elbow. "I regret that Keith

has not informed you, but your investment in Holland has been quite successful."

"Oh, I'm glad to hear that, Dr. Strassburger."

"Yes, I thought you would be interested." He moved me away from the others, and I thought again of the double doors at Waldstein & Co. "The Reichsbank did enter the market, they made heavy purchases of marks — perhaps a little too heavy, in my opinion — so the mark went up and we sold out your position Friday afternoon. We have also repaid the loan from our Dutch affiliate and restored the balance to your dollar account. I will see that you receive a statement in the morning." He stopped and looked at me.

"Well . . . that's very nice, Dr. Strassburger. Do you recall about how much —"

"We doubled your money!"

"You doubled my money?"

He nodded, fairly bursting with pleasure. "Of course, you understand it was an unusual situation, and in such a short time, I could not expect these results for every transaction. But we are happy to have been of service."

"You seem to have the magic touch, Dr. Strassburger. Should I invest what I won?"

An enigmatic smile. "I did not take you for a gambler, Mr. Ellis. No, I think we wait a little now, and then I am very much afraid we will have to invest the other way. The pressure on the mark is too great, we don't believe the Reichsbank alone can support it, we will need assistance from the Allies, some relief from the demands for reparations in gold, and if we do not get that —"

Dr. Strassburger shrugged.

When we rejoined the others, they were talking about Walther Rathenau. More specifically, they were arguing about him. They settled in a comfortable group, sitting on wicker furniture, smoking cigars, drinking coffee, debating.

"You don't need to explain Walther Rathenau to *me*," said a handsome old man with a white beard. "I've known him all my life. I went to school with him. All this is simply *arrogance!*"

Lili's father was clearly shocked. "Really, Paul, that's an incredible thing to say! He refuses police protection because he's arrogant?"

"What other reason would he have? My God, he's been warned over and over again. . . . A man came to see me from New York last week; in *Wall Street* people are saying the Nationalists are going to kill Rathenau. All his life he's wanted public attention, it wasn't enough to run the AEG his father built, it wasn't enough to sit on fifty or a hundred company boards — no, he's got to write books on philosophy, books on how the future is going to work — and pretty damned dull books, if you ask me —"

"Uncle Paul!"

I turned to Bobby. "Who is that gentleman?"

"That's Uncle Paul. He's Helena's father."

"Helena's father? But she worships Rathenau!"

Bobby smiled his charming smile. "Well, we are a complicated family, you see."

In the meantime, Alfred had walked into the house, and he now returned with a book, leafing around in the book, looking for something.

"Uncle Paul, with respect, here is one of those books he wrote that you find dull, *To the Youth of Germany*. May I just read you one short passage, which *I* believe explains his present behavior a little better than your diagnosis of arrogance?"

Alfred sat down in one of the wicker chairs and read us Rathenau's words:

> I am a German of the Jewish Race. My people is the German people, my home is Germany, my faith is the German faith which stands above all creeds. Yet nature, in mocking perversity and arbitrary liberality has brought the two springs of my ancient blood into tempestuous opposition: the urge to actuality and the yearning for the spiritual. My youth was passed in doubt and strife, for I was conscious of the contradictory character of my gifts. My action was fruitless and my thinking false and I often wished, when the horses bolted with the bit between their teeth, that the cart might dash itself to pieces.

For a moment there was silence. Then Helena's father said: "You don't find that arrogant?"

"I find it sad," said Alfred.

"In other words, he wants to die?" asked another man, a man I hadn't met.

"He accepts that he may have to die," said Alfred. "For Germany."

"What drama!" exclaimed Helena's father, clapping his hands together. "Who asked him to die for Germany? In fact, who asked him to speak for Germany? Who asked him to make a treaty of friendship with the Bolsheviks? Why must a German of the Jewish race — as he choses to describe himself — step forward as leader of the policy to accommodate the Allies and their outrageous demands?"

Alfred said quietly: "In the first place, Uncle Paul, I believe it was Chancellor Wirth who asked him to speak for Germany in these matters, by inviting him to become foreign minister. And in the second place, he believes that we *have* to accommodate the Allies —at least for a while — because if we don't, they will simply occupy the Ruhr, if not all of Germany."

"It's true, Wirth offered him the post. Did he have to take it?"

"There was no one else to take it."

The old man snorted. "Yes, that's what he told his mother. In all of Germany, there was no one else qualified to serve as foreign minister."

"No one else qualified was *willing*, Uncle Paul. I think that was the problem." Alfred was getting angry.

The old man leaned back in his chair and blew out a cloud of cigar smoke. "No one else was willing, so Walther offered himself as a sacrifice. For the German people. 'My people is the German people.' Is that what you just read us? And are *his* German people grateful for Walther's sacrifice? Have you been reading the speeches in the Reichstag? Helfferich's, for example? Have you heard the songs they're singing in the streets?"

"Yes, he's obviously being made a scapegoat."

"But why did he let himself be made a scapegoat?" That's what I'm trying to explain. He did it for the same reason he wrote all those boring, pretentious books. Here is a man who inherited everything he has, advocating that we eliminate the right of inheritance. Here is a man who lives in the greatest luxury, advocating that we do away with private property above a minimum level. . . . Have you heard Ernie's story about Genoa? . . . Ernst von Simson, he was on Rathenau's staff at the Genoa Conference, and they had to go out to dinner and Ernie went up to Rathenau's suite and Rathenau wasn't dressed, and

why wasn't he dressed? Because his valet had disappeared or was late or something, and Rathenau couldn't get the studs into his dress shirt! So Ernie had to help him. This is the Foreign Minister of the Republic. Wants to abolish inherited wealth, wants to abolish private property, can't get dressed without —"

Alfred interrupted. "Uncle Paul, may one ask what your point is?"

"Dear boy, the point is that Rathenau does what he does, takes the positions he takes, just to make people pay attention to him!"

"Walther Rathenau needs attention? The chairman of the largest electric combine —"

"I mean attention as a thinker, a philospher, a statesman! Of course everybody recognizes him as a business leader in Germany, all over Europe. . . ."

Now Baron Fritz von Waldstein leaned forward: "Paul, he did very important work for the country. You must admit it. Just as the Way began, he persuaded the General Staff to stockpike raw materials. Nobody had thought of it! For example we would have been out of nitrates by 1916, and you can't make explosives without nitrates. He thought of the problem, he convinced the army . . . and then he administered the program and kept us fighting years longer!!"

Helena's father raised his hand. "Agreed! Absolutely agreed! He is a brilliant industrialist, a brilliant organizer. *But that's not enough for him!* Aflred just read it in his own words, from one of those expensive printed volumes nobody paid any attention to —"

"Uncle Paul, do you know how many copies of *To the Youth of Germany* sold?"

"Alfred, my dear boy, I don't know and I don't care how many were sold. My point is that the people running this country didn't pay any attention to them. Kaiser didn't, General Staff didn't, universities didn't, financial community didn't — am I right, Eduard? Fritz? Am I right, Strassburger? Considered him a dilettante. Remember what they called him? *Christus im Frack!*" The old man leaned toward me and winked. "Christ in tails."

"Uncle Paul!" Alfred was outraged.

"I didn't invent the name, did I? But then we had the collapse, the revolution, the Republic; new men, new ideas . . . and his chance comes. He gives speeches. He writes a constant stream of newspaper articles, a constant stream of good advice. Unsolicited good advice, so far as I am aware. The Republic is shaky, the Right tries a Putsch, the Left shuts down the country with strikes, governments fall and new ones are formed, and here is Dr. Rathenau, industrial genius, millionaire, philosopher of the future, willing to serve the German people, willing to speak for *his* German people to the rest of the world. Wonderful. Finally everybody pays attention!"

The men were looking up. I turned around. Lili was standing behind my chair.

"Excuse me please, Uncle Paul . . . Father, the sailboat will not fit into the boathouse when the mast is up, we must arrange for some kind of buoy so the boat can float free —"

"Well, we always had one, didn't we? The men will find it —"

"They don't know how to do it, Father. I need Peter to help, before the evening wind —"

Baron von Waldstein smiled at me. "You see who gives the orders here. You are excused, Mr. Ellis. And now you know more about Walther Rathenau than you care to know!"

I didn't get back to the Villa Keith until late Tuesday night.

The house was dark and silent, but there was a light showing under Christoph's door. I knocked and he shouted to come in. He was dressed in striped pajamas, smoking a cigarette and reading a book.

"You have a nice suntan," he said. "Will you join me — what do you call it? Drink a nightcap with me?" He indicated some beer bottles and glasses on a tray.

"Is the house empty?" I asked. "Where is everybody?"

"The Meiers are asleep, I suppose, and Kaspar is out as usual, and my parents have gone to the seashore for a few weeks. My aunt — my mother's sister — is married to a big landowner up in Kolberg on the Pomeranian coast, and my parents usually go there in August but this year there is some problem about August — well, it doesn't matter, my parents could just as well go now. . . . I'm happy they have a place to go that doesn't cost anything. . . ."

"I hear you doubled my money in Holland."

He nodded, but he didn't smile and he didn't congratulate me. I poured myself a glass of beer and sat down in the chair.

"Strassburger was surprised I hadn't heard about it."

Christoph nodded again. "Yes. I have been reprimanded. I should have left a statement on the table for you. I apologize." But he didn't sound apologetic.

"Christoph, wasn't that unusual, to double one's money so quickly?"

"It happens."

"But not often?"

"It happens."

"Christoph, was there something illegal about this transaction? I just did what you and Strassburger advised —"

"There was nothing illegal about the transaction, but it was not *I* who advised it."

"Well, your boss."

"Yes. My boss."

"Well then, what's the matter?"

"You are complaining that we doubled your money?"

"I am complaining that you obviously don't like what happened, but you won't tell me why. If there was some law against it —"

"We have the best lawyers in Berlin. There is no law against it. But there should be."

"Why?"

Christoph Keith finished his beer, put the glass down and lit another cigarette, all the time looking past me at the wall, but he had made up his mind.

"You understand why the price of the German mark suddenly went up, when it had been going down steadily? I mean in the Amsterdam market?"

"Yes, because the Reichsbank began to buy, to stabilize —"

"Yes, they tried to stabilize. They spent a lot of gold in Amsterdam to buy marks, so the mark went up, then it cost them too much, they had to stop, and the mark began to fall again. But for a few days people who had bought marks cheap — like you — were able to sell them at a good profit."

"Yes, I understand that."

"All right, then how do you suppose some people — such as Geheimrat Dr. Strassburger — know exactly when the Reichsbank is coming in to stabilize the price, exactly to what extent they will stabilize, and exactly at what point they will stop stabilizing?"

I just looked at Christoph. "He knew that ahead of time?"

A chilly smile. "Since our Amsterdam affiliate bank is the Reichsbank's *agent* in the Netherlands, actually carries out the Reichsbank's stabilization operations in Amsterdam, a cynical observer might suspect that somebody at the Gendarmenmarkt hears about the Reichsbank's instructions before they are carried out."

"And you mean to tell me that's not illegal?"

"According to the most expensive advice in Berlin *and* Amsterdam, there are no laws or regulations forbidding it."

"But . . . why aren't there?"

Christoph drank some beer before he answered. "Apparently the partners of Waldstein and Co. don't consider it their business to suggest regulations to the Reichsbank or the Ministry of Finance."

"Well, if it's that easy, why doesn't everybody do it?"

"Because it isn't really that easy. In the first place, not everybody has a dollar account that's always been outside of Germany. You have such an account. In the second place, if Strassburger and the others like him — there are a few others like him — made their inside information available to everybody, it would become useless, wouldn't it? You are benefiting from the fact that Strassburger thinks you have important connections in America, and he wants to impress you. He told you that in his office."

"But you don't like it, do you?"

"It's business."

"But not business that appeals to cavalry officers. Or to fighter pilots."

Another smile. "I think quite a few cavalry officers and fighter pilots would be glad to have my job today. There is not much demand for their skills." He opened another bottle of beer and poured it slowly into his glass. "I apologize for my behavior, Peter. I must not bite the hand that feeds me. The Waldsteins have been good to me. And I think they will be good to you." He took a long drink and wiped his moustache with his fingers.

"What have you been doing on the island all this time?"

16.

REIGEN

When Meier served my coffee and rolls, he asked if I wanted a taxi.

"A taxi all the way to Neukölln? Certainly not. But I want your advice, Meier."

"My advice, Mister Ellis?"

"Herr Oberleutnant and I are going to the theatre tonight, with friends. Kleines Schauspielhaus in the High School for Music, Fasanenstrasse 1."

"Yes, sir. I am aware of the arrangements. Her Highness has —"

"There will be six of us, and I want to make reservations for dinner. Where should we go?"

"But Mister Ellis, Her Highness has made the arrangements —"

"That's for the tickets. I want to give the dinner afterwards."

"With respect, sir. I am certain that everything has been arranged, you are the guest —"

"Meier, I'm tired of always being the guest! What's the best place to take a table?"

"The best? There are so many places —"

"Recommend one."

The old man lifted his shoulders. "It all depends. . . . You will wish to dance?"

"Yes. Eat dinner — an excellent dinner — and dance. And not in a Diele! What's the best place?"

"The best place . . ." Meier considered. "Ach, from what one hears, perhaps the Hotel Adlon? *Very* expensive, Mister Ellis."

"Unter den Linden?"

"Yes, sir. No. 1, right on the Pariser Platz."

"All right. I want you to call and reserve a table for six. For what time? After the theatre."

"They will know the time, but I must repeat, sir, Her Highness will have made all the arrangements."

"The Princess Hohenstein has a maid?"

"Certainly, sir."

"And a telephone?"

"Of course."

"You call the Princess's maid, and you tell her that Mister Ellis has taken a table at the Hotel Adlon." I stood up. "Take care of it, Meier."

The old man actually clicked his heels. "Wird gemacht, Mister Ellis!" He was smiling a little. Meier liked direct orders, and I was learning to give them.

The painting went badly that day.

The little boy let me into the apartment. Mutti was out somewhere, Baby was in school, and Falke had left me a note saying that he had to meet a dealer who was interested in one of his large oils. Bärbel was asleep.

Rain beat against the windows. A leak in the sagging ceiling plunked with maddening regularity into a pot they had placed in the middle of the floor. I was supposed to be finishing a still life, an oil painting of a glass of water and a blue plate with dried herring bones. I hate painting inanimate objects, but Falke had developed some notion that he should teach me "painting" in academic style, that I needed the "discipline" to create a photographic reproduction of a glass of water and some fishbones.

I worked as long as I could. I was bored and listless. The boy came in, sat on a stool, and watched me in silence. He had been trained to keep quiet. I was thinking about Lili — or rather I thought I was thinking about Lili, but I was really thinking about Bärbel asleep in the next room, and her sleeping presence distracted me. I still didn't know if she suspected something about me and Baby; or if she cared. I still didn't know if she knew about Falke and her mother. But how could she not know, living in such close quarters for years? Maybe she didn't care about that either. Yes, she cared: I remembered the way Baby had hurtled out of bed. . . .

The water dripped into the pot. The boy sat on his stool and stared at me. My hands grew cold. I knew that pretty soon Bärbel would wake up and saunter into the studio, probably wearing the slip that stuck to her body. . . . I

didn't want to see Bärbel in her slip. I stood up, put my
paints away, and cleaned my brushes with turpentine.

"Tell your father I just remembered an appointment,"
I told the boy. "I hope to see him on Friday at the regular time." I fled through the bedroom. Bärbel sighed,
turned over heavily, and rearranged her naked arms. I
put on my hat and my raincoat and walked down the five
flights, walked through the rain-streaked tenement streets,
walked past a line of grim-faced women in front of a
shabby grocery, walked through the streaming rain to the
Hermann Platz, climbed into a crowded sweat-smelling
trolley that slowly trundled me all the way up to the
Bahnhof Friedrichstrasse, and from there I found my way
back to the pointed island in the river Spree and the Kaiser Friedrich Museum.

For the rest of the afternoon I just wandered around
that magnificent portrait gallery, hypnotized by the beauty
of work I knew I could never come close to, actually for-
getting everything else. They had to wake me at closing
time.

Darkness. A few dim lights in the orchestra pit, a few
musicians playing softly, playing a Viennese ballad. The
little theatre is packed full and smells of bodies and perfume and wet clothing.

Then just one violin, playing at such a high pitch that it
sounds like someone whistling, and the curtain rises. A
soldier ambles across the stage, and as the violin stops we
hear he is whistling the same song. The stage is dark, a
dim streetlight, in the background the impression of a
river, a bridge looming overhead.

A heavily painted young woman — pretty but hard —
is leaning against the lamppost. "Come along, my beautiful angel."

The soldier doesn't want to. He has to get back to the
barracks. He teases her a little. "Am I such a beautiful
angel?"

"Can you understand their dialect?" asked Helena.
"This one's not from Vienna at all, but he's trying."

As a matter of fact, I was having trouble with the dialect, but I understood the idea. She wants him to come to
her room, but he hasn't got time and he hasn't got money.

"Ich brauch kein Geld," she says.

"What did she say?" I whispered into Lili's ear.

"She doesn't need money."

"She doesn't want money?"

"That's what she said."

The soldier doesn't believe it either. Only civilians have to pay, she tells him.

Oh! Now he's heard of her, now he wants to do it, but it's too late, he's due back at the barracks. More talk about a date tomorrow, I couldn't quite understand, she says he won't show up anyway, she wants it now, she points to the river: "It's nice and quiet, there isn't a soul down there now."

"Oh, that's not right!" He's shocked.

"With me it's always right," she says. "Stay with me now. Who knows if we'll be alive tomorrow."

They disappear into the darkness. We hear their voices. Lili's arm brushed mine as she leaned forward in her seat. Not seeing the actors, I had more trouble understanding.

"Watch out," the girl says. "If you slip, you're lying in the Danube." Then I can't understand, she seems to be protesting. "What did she say?"

Lili put her hands in front of her face.

"I can't understand them!" I whispered.

Helena's mouth was at my ear. "He makes her do it standing, right at the edge, she's afraid they'll fall in, she begs him to hold on to the wall. . . ."

Darkness. Absolute silence. Stunned silence.

They reappear in the circle of light.

"It would have been better on the bench," she says.

He wants to go. He won't tell her his name, but she tells him hers: Leocadia. She touches his arm: "What's the rush?"

"I told you. I'm late. What do you want now?"

"Oh, how about some change for the house porter?"

"What do you take me for? A sucker? Servus, Leocadia!" He disappears.

She shouts curses. The curtain falls. Silence.

A cheerful polka fills the air, and in the distance we see the huge Ferris wheel of the Vienna Prater. Offstage people are dancing. The same soldier appears, walking arm-in-arm with a different girl, a carefully dressed girl, a chambermaid on her evening out.

This actress was really from Vienna and I had some trouble understanding her, but again the story was clear enough: she wants to dance but he has other plans. She teases him about the other girls he's danced with, he grabs her, she protests — not very hard. He pulls her into the bushes, but we can hear their voices. . . .

When we see them again he is standing up and lighting a cigar. She is still lying on the grass. She asks him to take her home, but he wants to go back to the dance. She doesn't want to walk home alone. He doesn't care anymore. If she will come back to the dance and wait, then he'll walk her home. She says she'll wait, they go back in, we hear him order a beer — and ask another girl to dance. Curtain. Darkness.

"Oh!" Lili exclaimed. "What a terrible man!"

"That's the way they are," said Helena.

"Well, *I've* never met a man like that, "said Sigrid.

"That's because you've restricted yourself to the officer class," said Alfred.

"You think they're any better?" asked Helena.

"I don't like this play," said Lili in the darkness.

If Helena had objections to my change in her arrangements, I didn't hear about them. Her maid and Meier had negotiated a compromise: Mister Ellis would be the host for dinner at the Adlon if the Princess Hohenstein could invite everyone to meet for tea at Café Kranzler. Christoph and I would pick her up at the apartment. Alfred would bring in Sigrid and Lili on the train.

"The Café Kranzler?" Christoph was amused to hear about it when he came into my room in his dinner jacket. "That used to be the hangout for Guards officers. The talk was all thoroughbred horses, thoroughbred dogs, thoroughbred ballet dancers — more or less in that order. Rather sentimental that Helena still wants to be seen there."

I was still in my shirt, tying my tie. "Christoph, why isn't Bobby going to the play with us?"

"Bobby? Why should he go with us?"

"Well . . . I mean, he's their brother, he's your friend, you work with him . . . I mean, aren't we sort of leaving him out? I asked Lili why he wasn't going with us, and she — it seemed somehow to make her angry."

Christoph leaned back in the wicker armchair, watching me struggle with my bow tie. He didn't say anything for a moment. I glanced at him in the mirror. "Am I prying into something that's none of my business?"

He rubbed his chin. "No. It is a natural question. I should have explained before. As you know, Bobby likes girls. Bobby has lots of girls. Unfortunately, most of them — and one of them in particular — are not girls that his family approves of. In other words, he can't bring them home. Lili would not be allowed to meet them. Isn't it the same in America?"

Is it? I thought about that.

It happened in the fourth scene.

At the beginning, the orchestra is playing the first ballad. A young man, alone, is fussing around in a furnished bedroom apartment. He closes the curtains, he sets up a bottle of Cognac and two small glasses, he sprays the air with perfume, he checks the drawer of the bedside table and discovers a tortoiseshell barrette which he slips into his pocket. . . . The music stops, there is a faint knock at the door, he opens it, the woman who sweeps in is so heavily veiled that we can't see her face at all, but behind the veils she chatters: she is frightened, somebody might have seen her, she can only stay five minutes, her sister is expecting her, she's kept her promise and now she has to go — but as she talks she gradually removes the veils, and then her coat, and then she pulls out her hatpins and removes her hat, looks around the apartment. . . . He's never had anyone else in here, has he? She accepts a glass of Cognac, she bites into a pear and presents it in her mouth . . . and not long after that they are in the bedroom, in wild excitement as he helps her to undress and discovers that she doesn't wear a corset. . . .

Darkness, but we hear their voices.

Again, I had trouble with the dialect when I couldn't see their faces, but clearly something is wrong.

His voice: "I think I love you too much."

Silence.

"All these days I've been crazy with anticipation. I knew this would happen!"

Her voice: "Oh, don't worry about it."

"Of course not. It's perfectly natural. . . ."

"Don't, dear. Don't do that, just relax, you're nervous —" and then he tells her a long story by Stendhal, about a group of cavalry officers discussing their love affairs, who all confess that they have been impotent at times —

— and I turned to Helena because she was laughing softly into her hand and I really couldn't understand what they were saying in the darkness.

"He can't . . . you know —"

"I know, but what are they *saying?*"

"Oh, she is teasing him a little, and he is getting angry, it is *very* well done! He is telling her a story about a couple who went to bed for six nights and did nothing but cry, because they were so happy, you see, and she —" Helena giggled. "— and she says, 'But there must be many who *don't* cry' . . . and he says, 'Of course! That's an exceptional case,' and she says, 'Oh, I thought Stendhal means that *all* cavalry officers cry on these occisions.' She is really teasing the poor fellow —"

And suddenly a man's voice from the audience. *"Schweinerei!"* and then immediately another voice, from the same direction, down in front of us and to the right: "This is a Jewish insult to German womanhood!" and on my other side I felt Lili gasp and jerk back in her seat as if she had received an electric shock. Then she leaned across me:

"Helena, are these people *Jewish?*"

"No," said Helena, "but the author is," and then she shouted, "Quiet! Get out!" so loud that people turned to look at us.

A lot of people were shouting in the darkness now, and some were whistling. Down in front, a group that included women was chanting in unison: "Schweinerei! Schweinerei! Schweinerei!" Other voices from all over the auditorium: "Quiet!" "Shut up!" "Throw them out."

Then there was a loud popping sound, a small explosion, in the right aisle, and a sulfurous rotten-egg smell filled the air. A woman screamed. As the lights went on, we saw that the curtain was down and all over the theatre people were standing up and looking around, trying to decide what to do.

The people shouting "Schweinerei" seemed to be clustered in two groups: one in front of us, to the right; the other in the balcony. The ones in front of us looked young. They were not in evening dress.

"Students," said Helena. *"Call the police! Throw them out!"* Her voice carried.

"For heaven's sake, Helena!" Both Christoph and Alfred leaned toward her, Sigrid sat frozen in embarrassment, and in front of us everybody turned again. One of the shouting students stepped into the aisle and moved toward us. Blond crewcut, chalky pimpled beardless face, faintly bulging blue eyes magnified by heavy spectacles. He may have been twenty. As he neared us Alfred, who was on the aisle, suddenly stood up, so Christoph and I stood up too.

"You find this a suitable play for ladies?" the student asked Alfred in a quiet voice. Behind him, his companions were still yelling "Schweinerei!" toward the curtain. Up on the balcony there was a crash of breaking chairs as somebody fell. Another scream.

"I don't believe our ladies are your responsibility," said Alfred icily. "And I don't believe we know each other."

"Müller," announced the student. "Candidate in Jurisprudence!"

Alfred looked down at him. "Waldstein," he said. "Writer."

An insolent smile appeared on the student's face. He let his glasses slide down a bit and looked over them. "Oh, I *see*. Baron von Waldstein, one of our great new literary figures. No doubt you have a highly developed taste for this type of entertainment. Perhaps the author is a relative?"

— and Christoph was squeezing past Sigrid's knees to stand beside Alfred, who began to say: "Doctor Schnitzler is not a relative, but it would be an honor —" as Christoph emitted an ear-splitting parade-ground bellow: "KANDIDAT MÜLLER, DISAPPEAR!" and the student literally jumped. Every face turned. Müller's companions stopped shouting and began to crowd into the aisle, but they could not reach us because the aisle was packed with people trying to get out. Christoph brought his walking stick into sight and Müller tried to retreat a few steps, but the crowd were pressing from behind.

More noise from the balcony: more crashing and shouting, everybody standing to watch a fistfight in progress . . . then the doors at the back of the hall flew open, we heard a piercing whistle, and the place was filling with policemen — gleaming black leather tschakos, green uniforms with silver buttons, gleaming leather boots: Berlin Schutzpolizei, masses of them, pushing slowly and efficiently into the crowd . . .

Another whistle and a loud police voice: "Everybody will be seated!"

Christoph moved so fast that I only saw the lunge out of the corner of my eye, saw him push past Alfred into the aisle, saw the reversed cane flashing through the air, heard Alfred shout: "Herr Wachtmeister! Over here!" and then I saw the student Müller grasping at his own neck as Christoph pulled him forward with the handle of the cane.

Two policemen were instantly between them, and as Alfred explained that this was one of the demonstrators, they handcuffed Müller and hustled him up the aisle. He looked at us as they passed. His glasses had been knocked off and he couldn't see us very well, but the hatred in his face burned with such intensity that I turned instinctively toward Lili. She had closed her eyes and was biting her lips. I didn't know what to do, so I didn't do anything. I just sat there.

The whole thing only lasted a few minutes. Ushers and people in the audience pointed out the demonstrators, the police dragged them out, the noise subsided, and only the smell of rotten eggs remained.

"You're pretty handy with that walking stick," I said to Christoph as we settled into our seats, but nobody smiled.

"The management was expecting trouble," said Christoph, still out of breath. "The police got here fast."

Alfred shook his head. He looked pale. "I think we'd better get the girls out of here," he said to Christoph.

"Absolutely not!" said Helena. "If the audience runs away, those swine have won the battle," and just then the theatre manager appeared on the stage. The talking stopped. He was small and completely bald. He looked unutterably sad.

"Meine Damen und Herren . . ." The management regretted the incident, a reflection of the instability of the times, the intolerance of certain elements in our society. If the spectators will permit, the actors will continue. He held out his hands: What shall it be?

Helena began to applaud, some people in the balcony began to applaud, and then the entire house was applauding.

"I only hope they don't try to start at the place they stopped," said Helena, loudly clapping her hands.

They didn't. They started with the next scene: the young woman who had been teasing her lover is now with her husband. Again, a bedroom and a bedroom conversation, a very different one. The husband boasts about his experience with other women, other women of a type his wife couldn't even imagine; he makes her promise that if she ever hears that one of her girlfriends has had an affair, she'll drop her — but let's not talk about such things or such people, my child . . . I love one person, and that's you. One can only love where there is purity and truth! He gets into bed, the lights go out, and when they go on again, this husband is just finishing a sumptuous dinner in the chambre séparée of an elegant restaurant — and he is not alone, he is sitting on the couch beside a girl he has picked up on the street. She likes the food, she tells him about her widowed mother, about the little brothers and sisters she takes care of at home — and about the boy who jilted her. He tells her that he loves her, he fills her with wine . . . now only one candle is burning. . . .

"Oh, but what if a waiter should come in?"

"No waiter would come in here now if his life depended on it!"

When the lights go on again he emphasizes that he lives in Graz, he only comes to Vienna occasionally —

Oh, then you must be married! announces the girl.

He is shocked. What an idea! Wouldn't she be ashamed to lead a married man astray?

Come off it, says the girl. Your wife is certainly doing the same thing.

He explodes.

She laughs. I thought you weren't married!

He blusters, but she is a nice girl, she's been around, she didn't expect anything better — and they agree that they'll find a more private place the next time.

Curtain.

"He's really the worst of the lot," said Helena.

"Typical middle class *Spiesser*," said Sigrid. Lili said nothing.

I don't remember much about the next scenes:

the girl from the chambre séparée visits a young playwright in his apartment;

the playwright spends the night with a famous actress;

the actress receives the Count, an elegant, graying captain of dragoons, in her flower-filled bedroom. . . . She teases him about another woman. . . . He wants to make an appointment, dinner after tonight's performance, but the actress doesn't want to wait that long. Just like the girl in the chambre séparée, the Count is afraid that somebody might come in.

"That door won't open from the outside," she assures him.

He still holds back: Love by daylight?

Just close your eyes, she suggests; pretend it's night. . . . These two casually fencing debauchees delighted Helena and Christoph, who chuckled at every line. Sigrid and Alfred looked amused. Lili glanced across me at Helena, just for an instant, and then she looked back at the stage without changing her expression.

The lights go on again, the Count, buttoning up his uniform and buckling on his sword, still wants his dinner date — day after tomorrow!

Christoph and Helena roared.

"Did you really think you could play all these women?" asked Christoph.

"Why not?" replied Helena.

"You're conceited," murmured Christoph. "But I love you."

"Shut up, Herr Oberleutnant!"

That was the first time either of them expressed affection in front of me.

In the last scene the circle is closed. It is six o'clock in the morning in the small shabby bedroom of Leocadia, the whore from the first scene. Her clothes are strewn all over the floor and she is sound asleep in bed with only her head and naked arms exposed.

On the sofa is the Count, fully dressed in his greatcoat, boots crossed, also asleep. Half-empty glasses. A pitcher of stale beer.

The Count sits up, stretches and groans, tries to understand where he is and what happened. Hangover. He talks to himself, admires the sleeping girl: "It seems to me that sleep makes all of us equal, just like sleep's brother, death . . ." but he can't remember whether he *did* anything. First it bothers him, but then he rather likes the idea that he didn't. He puts some coins on the nightstand and begins to leave. The girl moves. Who does that remind me of? A girl moving in her sleep, easily moving her arms, stretching her naked arms, her eyes still shut. Who? The girl is awake. They chat casually, he asks the usual how-did-a-nice-girl-like-you? questions, he thinks she reminds him of someone.

Who? She reminds me, too!

He kisses her eyes, he wonders if anybody else has left her without . . . No, she says proudly, that's never happened to her.

"Well, did you think I didn't like you?" asks the Count.

"You liked me fine last night" — and now he seems a little disappointed to learn that, drunk as he was, he performed on the sofa. He gets up to go, a chambermaid opens the door for him, he gives her a tip and says, "Good evening."

"Good *morning*, sir!"

"Oh yes, of course, good morning. *Good morning!*"

Curtain.

Loud, strong applause.

The play is over, and I know who.

It was still pouring rain, and we were lucky to get one of the taxis in front of the theatre. Christoph sat up with the driver, Alfred between Helena and Sigrid in back, Lili and I sat on the jump seats.

"Peter, what did you think?" asked Alfred.

What did I think? "Well —" I began, but Helena interrupted.

"You can't really understand the best part, because the best part is the *patois,* the expressions they all use, it's pure Vienna. All the different levels of society, from the little prostitute all the way up to the Count, they are all exactly *right,* each person speaks differently but they all are Vienna. My idea was to rewrite it all for Berlin accents, but then of course it wouldn't have been Schnitzler."

"I had some trouble with the dialect," I admitted, "but I think I understood the general idea."

"But did you like the play?" asked Alfred. I sensed that they were all watching me. Should I be polite or honest?

"Well . . . I guess not so much." Lili's cold little hand clasped mine in the darkness.

"I hated it!" she said. "They all use each other, like *animals!* Every single person lies to the other person, every single person cheats, the men say anything at all to make the women do it, and when they're finished they don't care anymore —"

"But sometimes it's the women," Alfred reminded her. "The actress, the streetwalker —"

"I thought they were horrible," said Sigrid. "I agree with Lili. Why write a play about such awful people?"

"Because that's how people are," said Helena.

"Is that how people are?" asked Lili. "Really?" but before anyone could answer we were distracted.

The taxi was stopped in the heavy traffic around the Kaiser Wilhelm Memorial Church — cars, crowds of people with umbrellas, the blazing lights of the Kurfürstendamm.

"What are we doing over here?" demanded Helena. "Why. didn't he go straight through the Tiergarten?" and we heard voices singing, a sizable group of young men just emerging from a beer hall, sort of marching in step or trying to, marching bareheaded through the crowded sidewalks, brushing past the people with umbrellas, pouring across the street directly in front of our taxi, all singing — bellowing — some song. I could not understand the words except something about "Walther Rathenau" . . . Lili dropped my hand . . . and then they were gone, their voices gone too, the traffic began to move, and nobody in the taxi said a word for what seemed like several minutes.

I guess it was only a few seconds. Lili had covered her face with her hands and Sigrid leaned forward to put her arms around Lili. "It's just nonsense, dear. Just politics."

"They are swine!" said Christoph from the front seat. "Exactly the same as the ones in the theatre."

"You didn't understand, did you?" asked Helena.

I shook my head.

"A nice new marching song, invented by the Freikorps people. All the things that should be done to Chancellor Wirth and his cabinet. And the last lines are:

> *Knalt ab den Walther Rathenau*
> *Die gottverdammte Judensau!* which means
> *Knock off Walther Rathenau*
> *The god-damned Jewish sow!*"

"Is that really necessary, Helena?" Sigrid still had her arms around Lili.

The taxi driver and Christoph and Alfred were all staring straight ahead.

"Yes," said Helena. "I think he should understand."

Nobody said anything until the doorman of the Hotel Adlon came running out from under the big canopy with his umbrella.

My dinner party was a disaster.

We were kept waiting for a moment because the head-waiter seemed confused when he saw that Alfred and Helena were in my party and then I noticed them all looking into the huge glittering room, white tablecloths and chandeliers and the tailcoated orchestra softly playing dance music and then Helena turned to me, said, "The ladies will retire for a few minutes," and all three of them swept away. Couldn't they wait until we ordered? But then, as we followed the headwaiter into the room, I saw that Bobby von Waldstein, in white tie and tails, was sitting in a distant corner table with a perfectly beautiful young woman.

The headwaiter indicated our table. "If you please, gentlemen?" but I was looking at Christoph, who was looking at Alfred.

"What do we do?"

"We will go over now." Alfred said something to the headwaiter, then grasped my elbow and led me across the room, where Bobby was already standing up.

The girl was very blonde and very young, not much older than Lili. Her pale blue eyes regarded us calmly, perhaps a little suspiciously, but then she smiled as both Alfred and Christoph moved forward to bow over her hand and to introduce me: Countess something Russian, I didn't understand the name. They called her Kyra.

Alfred explained where we had been, that I had kindly invited them to have supper . . . and Bobby smiled his gentle little smile and said what a pity (looking at his watch) they had to leave and could not join us because they were late for another engagement, and Kyra's lovely smile disappeared, she turned red, she bit her lip and looked at the almost-full bottle of champagne in the bucket by the table and rose without another word and made for the door, with Bobby carrying her cape, smiling and nodding goodbye to us and hurrying to catch up.

The band was playing and people were moving past us to the dance floor. We returned to our table in silence. Then I said: "I do apologize, but I didn't know —"

Alfred: "How could you know? Our problems are our problems. You seem to be getting a heavy dose of them tonight!"

Christoph: "All the same, please let Helena make the social arrangements."

I: "May I ask one question? Is that girl really a countess? She's lovely! What's wrong with her?"

A moment of silence.

"You know who the White Russians are?" asked Alfred. "Berlin is full of them, and most of them have lost everything. Kyra's father was a colonel in Denikin's cavalry. He was killed by the Reds, I think in the Ukraine, in 1919. She lives alone with her mother. They haven't got a penny. When Bobby met her she was singing folksongs in a Russian nightclub — but that is not all she was doing. She is completely dependent now on Bobby, and so is her mother."

"But —"

"But in Russia, in the time of the Czars, that young lady and her mother would not *speak* to a Herr Waldstein from a bank. You understand what I mean?"

I nodded.

"So my family . . . we are not exactly enthusiastic about this little Countess although as you say she is beautiful, she is charming . . . but we are not quite ready to embrace her."

And then he looked up and rose. The ladies had returned.

It was a disaster. As host, I should have set the tone, told jokes, told stories, cheered everybody up — but I don't know how to do that.

Christoph and Helena did their best, insisting that everybody start with some champagne, then supervising the orders (everybody ordered something "small" — smoked salmon, or soup, or an omelet) and then I asked Lili to dance.

"You have your answer about Bobby?" asked Lili, moving with her practiced grace to the sound of Marek Weber's foxtrot beat.

"She looks like a beautiful girl," I said.

"Yes. She sleeps with men for money. She could be another scene for *Reigen*."

"I've apologized to Alfred, now I'll apologize to you, but I didn't know —"

"Of course not, how could you know . . . Peter, I think after we eat we'll go right home. You will not mind, will you? It has nothing to do with you, but it has been . . . not a nice evening. Will you understand?"

"Of course. I hope the next one will be better."

She looked up at me with those coal-black eyes, and then she smiled.

"Yes," she said. "The next one will be better. Will you come out early on Saturday?"

We separated in the rain in front of the Adlon with the doorman and two bellboys holding umbrellas as we moved toward the waiting taxis. Alfred was taking Helena home. They made quite a fuss about the fact that I should come with them — "just one more glass" — but I didn't feel like it and I didn't think they really felt like it, so I said goodbye and ran toward the third taxi in the row.

When I let myself into the Villa Keith only the downstairs hall light was on. Kaspar was obviously out and everybody else was asleep. I felt rotten, and tried to figure out exactly why I felt that way. Was it the play? Was it Lili's reaction to the play? Was it the fury of the nationalist students, or the song they were singing about Rathenau, or was it the look on the Russian girl's face when she got up and left the table?

I went to the bathroom, then came back to my room and washed my face, put on my pajamas, got into bed and turned out the light, but I didn't go to sleep. It would have been better if I had.

I lay there in the darkness for twenty minutes or so,

and then I heard the deep purring motor of a powerful car. The car seemed to be moving around the back of the house, right under my window. I had never seen a car down there before. I got out of bed and peered through the curtains.

BOOK TWO

WHAT HAPPENED

Overleaf: Max Pechstein, *Drunken Fisherman* II, woodcut, 1912
Collection, The Museum of Modern Art, New York

17.

THURSDAY, JUNE 15, 1922

I was having breakfast alone when they arrived. I don't know how they got there, but I didn't hear a taxi so presumably they walked from the trolley stop. They didn't come in the front door. They must have gone to the stable first, because I heard them coming in the kitchen door, and then I heard Kaspar shouting at the servants. I couldn't hear exact words, but of course the meaning was clear enough. I held my breath and touched the hard little revolver through the cloth of my jacket, but I needn't have worried: the word of the Herr Oberleutnant was still law at the Villa Keith. The Meiers played dumb, and a moment later Kaspar burst into the dining room, with Tillessen directly behind.

"Good morning," I said.

"Good morning," said Kaspar. "Where is the car?"

"What car?"

"The Austro-Daimler we put into the stable last night! Where is it?"

As I shook my head, wondering if I could bring this off, I noticed the difference in their expressions. Kaspar's pale face was flushed, his eyes distended by surprise and fear. Tillessen, taller, older, still very much the naval officer, regarded me with icy suspicion. Tillessen wasn't going to believe a word I said.

"Kaspar, we were out very late last night, and I don't know anything about a car in the stable. I didn't know you had a car."

"It's not my car —" Kaspar fairly shouted, but Tillessen put a restraining hand on his shoulder and interrupted:

"Excuse me, sir, but may I ask what time you came home?"

"I don't know exactly. . . . We were at the theatre, then we had dinner and went dancing. . . ." This was the bad part, because if they were in the house they might have

155

seen my coat and hat in the hall closet — but I didn't think they had been in the house at all. "I guess it must have been after two o'clock."

"Really? So late? And you came with Oberleutnant Keith?"

"No, he came later."

"Oh, even later? And now the butler tells us he has already gone to his bank?"

"I assume so. They keep bankers' hours, you know."

Apparently bankers' hours don't have the same connotation in Germany. They both just stared at me for a moment, genuinely puzzled. Then a thought struck Tillessen, a thought that probably never left his mind, a thought that may have had some effect on what happened (or didn't happen) later.

"Sir, may I ask, were you in the War?"

"Yes, sir."

"An American officer?"

"No, sir."

"Ambulance driver," said Kaspar, with something of a sneer. Tillessen apparently didn't believe that. "May I ask your rank in the American army?"

"I didn't have any rank in the American army because I wasn't *in* the American army. I was a civilian volunteer, driving for the French. Your colleague here knows all about it. Now it seems to me that if you parked a car in the Keith's stable last night and it isn't there this morning, you might consider calling the police. I mean, that's what we would do at home." By now I had worked myself into a fine state of indignation that made me feel better about telling them a barefaced lie.

"We will of course notify the police at once," said Kaspar, causing Tillessen to look at him without expression.

"Well, I would certainly think so," I said, seeing Christoph had been right, they hadn't told Kaspar any details because Kaspar was too young, too inexperienced, and probably not cool enough for this kind of work. "The telephone is in the pantry."

"You think I don't know where the telephone is in my own house?" Kaspar's face was getting redder, and Tillessen didn't like this conversation at all.

"In Germany it is not customary to send for the police by telephone if there is no emergency," he informed me.

"We will go now and report this situation at the station house."

"Well, Kaspar seems to think there is some emergency, but of course it's entirely up to you." They were not listening. They were already out of the dining room, heading for the front door.

I went up to my room and put the pistol into the drawer of my bedside table. I had gone through the War without a gun — we were not supposed to carry them — but after they let me out of the hospital I bought a snub-nosed .32 Smith & Wesson Hammerless Safety and went out to a friend's farm one Saturday and fired at tin cans until the explosions didn't scare me anymore. I had not used it since, but I kept it, and early this morning I had dug it from the bottom of my Gladstone bag, loaded it, and put it in my pocket. It made me feel a little better, but not much.

What was I doing in the bathtub at nine o'clock in the morning? I was thinking about my conversation with Christoph as we walked out of the Grunewald at dawn. I was too excited to sleep, I didn't want to face Meier, and there wasn't time for the trip to Falke's in Neukölln because I'd promised to have lunch with Christoph downtown. So I took a hot bath.

German forests don't look like American forests. People come and pick up every branch and every pine cone because they need them for fuel. They don't let weeds grow, or underbrush. The Grunewald at the edge of the city and the Tiergarten in the center are manicured, like gardens.

The rain had stopped, and between the tall black tree trunks the sky was getting lighter. Christoph limped along, not following a path but moving straight through the forest, sure of his way. He didn't say a word until we had walked a quarter of a mile or so.

"I want to thank you."

"No need for that —"

"— and to ask for your help again. I will need a lot of help. I would not ask if I did not have to, but I must. I cannot do it without your help, Peter."

"Well. of course I'll do whatever —"

"When I saw that car, I made my decision. I have to

get my brother out of this. Somehow. But I don't know
exactly how."

"Out of what?"

"They are going to kill Rathenau."

"You mean — Tillessen?"

"Maybe not Tillessen himself, but he is part of the
group."

"How do you know?"

"Well, I just know. He's in the O.C."

"You wouldn't tell me —"

"Organization Consul. Don't ask what the name means,
it means nothing. They are extreme Nationalists, former
Freikorps people, mostly Ehrhardt people. Ehrhardt himself is supposed to be the 'Consul.' They are based in
Munich now. The Bavarian government protects them
from the federal government. They collect money from
bankers and industrialists who are frightened of socialism
and communism. And they kill people. You know the
word *Feme?* It's from the Middle Ages. Secret courts of
honor, *Femegerichte.* They held secret trials and con-
demned people to death — people who violated their
code of honor, or just political rivals. That's what the O.C.
is doing to men they think betrayed Germany, men who
made peace with the Allies, men who are running the
Republic. They've killed a lot of people. The most famous was Matthias Erzberger, last summer. I told you
about that — Tillessen's brother?"

"Yes, but how do you know —"

"I *know!* I feel it in my bones. They're going to kill
Rathenau."

"Then we should try to stop them."

"Can't. Can't stop them. Everybody has warned him.
He won't take any precautions, won't allow bodyguards,
rides around in an open car. . . . There is no way to stop
them, but I don't want my brother involved, my *name,*
my father's name —"

He stopped for a moment to catch his breath.

"But if Kaspar's already in with them . . . ?"

Christoph shook his head. "I don't think they've told
him. Wouldn't be safe. He talks too much, he drinks too
much, he's too emotional and too young. They're using
him. They want a quiet place to keep their men, a quiet
place to hide their car. . . . Do you know that Rathenau's
house is only a few blocks from ours? My guess is that

Kaspar's been told they have a secret mission, sealed instructions or something like that. These are navy people and navy people are always giving orders to be opened at sea — you understand what I mean? So I must get him *out*. Before it is too late."

"By force?"

"Yes, certainly. There would be no other way."

"You mean kidnap him or something?"

"Yes, something, but I don't know exactly what. I need your help, you see. Now we have destroyed their car, they will have to find another. It's not so easy to find a big fast car, and very expensive. They will be busy, and it is the last moment to get Kaspar away from them. Will you help? It may be dangerous."

What could I say? The birds were singing as we walked out of the woods, but among the shuttered suburban villas in front of us the street lights were still on.

I had agreed to meet Christoph in a restaurant called Lutter, across the street from the Gendarmenmarkt and just around the corner from his office. The place was very dark and very old and very crowded. It smelled of wine and sauerkraut and sausages. Christoph had already secured a corner table, where he was sitting with a man I didn't immediately recognize.

"You remember Hans Kowalski," said Christoph as they rose to greet me. "Our host that noisy evening in the Nollendorf Platz, my companion behind the wire at La Rochelle."

Kowalski remembered me, remembered our efforts to translate Bertolt Brecht's V.D. song into English.

An ancient waiter came. Black jacket and white apron to his ankles. They told me what I should order here. I watched Christoph as he talked with the waiter. He had worked all day Wednesday, spent the evening at the play and the Adlon, the rest of the night with Helena and in the Grunewald, and now he had worked all morning again. He didn't show it. When the waiter left, he turned to me.

"Peter, I took some funds from your account. I told Hans we need his help and that you will treat us to a good lunch here at Lutter's."

Was he going to discuss this in a restaurant? Why weren't we behind one of those double doors at Waldstein & Co.? He read my mind. "Don't worry, they're all busy shouting about the stock market, and we will talk quietly. You wonder why Hans is here, and Hans wonders the same thing."

The waiter brought rolls and butter and glasses and a bottle of Rhine wine. The cork was drawn, the wine was poured; we sat and watched the ceremony. The waiter left.

"Gentlemen," said Christoph, "I drink to old comrades."

We lifted our glasses. "To old comrades." The wine was too sweet for me.

"Those years at La Rochelle," said Christoph. "We heard a lot about Kowalski's brilliant brother, the research chemist, the fellow who works to develop substitutes for morphine. Is he still doing that?"

Yes, said Kowalski, puzzled as I was. His brother was with Bayer, they were developing barbiturates, not as addictive as morphine. . . .

"Ellis here wanted to give me morphine at Verdun, when the plane came down, you know, but I was so afraid of morphine I rather let the leg hurt . . . and it hurt like hell." He looked down at the white tablecloth and spoke, very quietly. "Hans, we need some of this stuff your brother makes, we need it right away, and don't ask us why we need it." Then he looked up. "All right?"

They stared at each other.

"It's not for Ellis, and it's not to sell to anybody. The less you know the better. We will pay in dollars, and nobody will find out."

The waiter came with plates of Bismarck herring and sliced cucumbers in sour cream. We began to eat in silence.

I decided to ask a question. "Can these synthetic substances be given by injection? You can inject morphine with a hypodermic needle, but —"

"He understands the problem," said Christoph. "We cannot use pills. Does that mean we must use morphine?"

Kowalski's mouth was full. "No idea. I will try to find out but it won't be easy. My brother is in Leverkusen, that's where their laboratories are."

"Leverkusen?" Christoph didn't like that. "Near Cologne, isn't it? Where the British are? Can you get in?"

"I suppose so, but it will take several days to get there and back. If you're in a hurry, there's plenty of morphine right here in Berlin. You know that."

Christoph drank his wine thoughtfully. "I am in a hurry but I hate the thought of morphine. I suppose we can wait a couple of days."

The waiter was back, removing the herring, then serving us from huge platters: steaming veal sausages, sauerkraut, boiled potatoes. The glasses were refilled. The waiter withdrew. We ate.

After a long time Kowalski said: "All right."

"You'll go to Leverkusen?"

"You know I owe you something. If I go, will that make us even?"

"Of course."

"Then I have to go, don't I?" He turned to me. "How much do you need?"

"He doesn't know," said Christoph. "And I don't know either. Your brother will know. Enough to keep a strong young man asleep for — what? Several weeks?"

"*Several weeks?*" Kowalski shook his head.

"Oh, that can be done," I said. "They did it to me."

All eyes on me. Was that necessary? Am I drunk? "Yes, they really did." I gulped what was left in my glass, feeling my face turning red, feeling the wine seeping into my blood.

"Really asleep?" asked Christoph quietly.

"No. Intermittent sleep, general drowsiness, stupor. Most of the time you really don't know if you're asleep or awake."

"Could you eat? Go to the toilet?"

"They fed me somehow. Sometimes they used bedpans, sometimes they helped me to the can. Had to hold me." I shook my head to make the pictures disappear, and tried to peel one of the sausages with my knife and fork, the way they were doing it.

We finished our plates. The waiter offered more wine, which we declined. A cart loaded with desserts was rolled to the table: fresh strawberries, sliced peaches, raspberry tarts, three different kinds of chocolate cake. . . . I couldn't eat any more, but I saw Kowalski's expression as he looked at the cart and I knew that he wouldn't take anything if we didn't so I insisted that everybody have dessert.

After the waiter poured the coffee and we were alone again, Kowalski said: "You mentioned payment in dollars?"

Christoph nodded: "They are in my pocket — and will be in yours after we walk around the Gendarmenmarkt. They come from Ellis, needless to say. One hundred dollars, at this morning's rate, that would be thirty thousand marks — but at that price, Hans, we need something else. We need a small bottle of chloroform."

Kowalski finished his raspberry tart and his coffee. When he put down his cup, he asked: "This is political, isn't it?"

"You know I have no politics," said Christoph.

"Might be better for our country if you did," said Kowalski.

Christoph smiled. *"Your* comrades wouldn't trust me anyway."

And now Kowalski smiled for the first time. "But the Limping Eagle of La Rochelle still trusts in *his* old comrades. All right, gentlemen, I will try to get what you need." He turned to me. "And thank you for the best meal I've had in . . ." He paused to think, then smiled again. "In years."

"Kaspar showed up while I was having breakfast, and Tillessen was with him."

"I know. Meier telephoned. What did they say to you?"

I told him. We were sitting on an iron bench in the Gendarmenmarkt, just outside the French Church. Christoph had taken off his hat and was stretched back, his eyes closed against the afternoon sun.

"Tillessen suspects you of being an American agent? That could be helpful. These fellows want to destroy the Republic, but they have respect for American power. They may want to stay away from you. We'll see."

We sat in the sunshine a few minutes. Then he said: "I must get back to work. I'm falling asleep. Thank you for the lunch."

"Christoph, why did we have to do that in a restaurant? Why didn't we use one of those rooms in your bank?"

He opened one eye. "Guess."

"You don't want the Waldsteins to know about this?"

"I don't want the Waldsteins in any way involved."

The food and the wine and the sunshine had made me drowsy, but now something in my memory floated loose and rose to the surface. "Tell me about Helena's father."

Christoph sat up straight and rubbed his eyes and looked at me. "Where did you see Helena's father?"

"At Havelblick, at lunch."

"Oh yes. Well, what do you want me to tell you?"

"What does he do?"

"What does he do? He expresses opinions." Christoph leaned back again and closed his eyes. He sounded tired now.

"What do you mean by that? What's his job?"

"He has no job, he's a *rentier*. Lives from income on his investments. As a young man he inherited a weekly journal, quite successful, started by *his* father, that's Helena's grandfather. *Waldstein's Woche*. Waldstein's Week. But everybody called it *Waldstein's Stimme*, Waldstein's Voice."

"That was the poet?"

"No, the poet's son. The poet had a literary monthly."

"I'm getting mixed up."

"It doesn't matter, the point is Helena's father owned this excellent highly respected paper, they employed the best writers, they published articles about books and the theatre and politics, it never made a lot of money but it was a *voice*. You understand? A voice of the educated upper-bourgeoisie, and it gave him — and in a way the whole family — a certain position in the town . . . no, in the whole country, really. People read it — I mean they still read it — in Hamburg, in Hanover, in Munich, in the universities —"

"It still exists?"

"Oh certainly, doing better than ever. But it doesn't belong to the Waldsteins, because Helena's father sold it to the Ullstein chain — you know of them? They are also Jews. They own a lot of newspapers and magazines, they publish books — of course they kept the name but everybody calls it Ullstein's Voice now!"

"Why did he sell it?"

"Well, why? Good question. Because he wanted money, I think. His father, his grandfather, they had this name, this famous name; but they never had money like their cousins in the Bank, you see. No Schloss on the Havel, no titles, no places in hussar regiments — and I think as a young man Helena's father didn't like that. The poor relation, the guest at the party. Always invited, of course, but always the guest. So the Ullsteins come along, they want some prestige for their empire, they offer him so much money that he will be rich for the rest of his life . . . but it was probably the wrong thing. Even if he could marry his daughter to a prince. If Helena had a son, he would be the grandfather of a prince. But Helena had no son, her prince is killed in the first weeks of the War, and then the Austrians not only lose the War but abolish their nobility. So Helena's father is just another rich old man. He reads a lot and thinks a lot and talks a lot — but nobody pays any attention to him. No voice. And now the banking cousins produce Alfred: famous writer, Kleist Prize, translations into French and English. . . . Helena's father isn't happy."

"He doesn't like Walther Rathenau," I said.

"No, he doesn't. They are exactly the same age, same schools, very similar backgrounds, both inherited their business from their fathers — but Rathenau is foreign minister while Helena's father gives lectures at family dinners."

"He thinks Rathenau wants to die."

"He said that to you?"

I told him what I had heard.

Christoph nodded thoughtfully. "Yes. He could be right. You see why it is useless . . ." He began again. "You see why the best that I can do is rescue my brother? Or try to."

Above us, church bells began to ring. Christoph stood up, adjusted his jacket and his necktie, cocked his hat at a fairly hussarlike angle and picked up his cane.

"Tell Meier we will have a light supper, just an omelet or something. I think we better sleep tonight." He saluted casually with the cane and went limping across the square.

18.

MONDAY, JUNE 19, 1922

Nine . . . ten . . . eleven . . . twelve? It's Monday and he isn't home yet. Sometimes he doesn't come home at all so why should he tonight? When we're ready for him. If we don't fall asleep. Just like the War: can't sleep when there's time, can't stay awake when you have to. But Christoph won't fall asleep. Sitting fully dressed in his room, waiting. My window is open to the moonlit summer night so that I can hear a car, or footsteps, but my window faces the stable. Unless they bring another car (which they won't), he should be coming in the front door and Christoph will hear him first. Looked funny to rush away like that, before Sunday night tea. Lili thought it was strange. If Helena had been there she would have made a fuss, but Helena was at some fancy reception for Rathenau and Chicherin, Russian foreign minister in town a few days. Lili's parents also invited. Wouldn't go. Bolsheviks. Out in the sloop with Lili, gentle breeze, learning to handle boat by herself. Sitting down in the hull, trying to sketch her. Not much sense to take a sketch pad into a sailboat, bound to get wet and too busy with boat, but I thought I should work every day. Hadn't done anything yet. Big scene with Falke Friday. Not doing any more still lifes, glasses of water and fishbones. Who is student here and who is teacher? Who is paying for the lessons? No more inanimate objects, want to paint people. Funny glint in his eye. New expression. Want to paint people, eh? Shout for Bärbel, asleep in next room. Nothing happened. Falke bounds out of chair into bedroom, sound of hand slapping naked flesh, scream, bare feet hitting floor, Bärbel, dressed only in slip, propelled into studio. Face swollen and red from sleep, contorted in anger. He wants to paint people. Show him what people look like. Take that thing off, and she dodged sideways to avoid the blow, already pulling the

slip over her head. . . . Don't think about it. Think about
Lili, holding the tiller in one hand and the main sheet in
the other, glancing up at the sail as we lost wind coming
into the lee of the island, trying to figure out how to catch
the exact look of puzzled annoyance as the sail began to
flutter, what brought on his rage? Stuck his hands between her thighs and slowly turned her around. You like
that ass? Finest ass in Berlin, definitely not an inanimate
object. Wasn't drunk at all. Middle of the morning, Baby
in school, Mutti Bauer out with the boy standing in some
queue to get groceries, what was the matter with him?
Just don't think about it. Forget about it? Lili turned her
head. There is somebody waving on our dock. Christoph? Yes. No, don't point that close to the wind, we'll
lose our headway, there isn't enough wind here to do
that, point it *down,* that way. I know, but this isn't a
motorboat. Have to go way over there and then come
back on the other tack. No, it's fine, you're doing fine. I
know, I can see him, he'll just have to wait a few minutes. Put your hands against the back of your head, com-
manded Falke. Yes. You like her like that? I want some
coffee, said Bärbel. You know we haven't got any, said
Falke. I'll go get some, said I. No you won't, said Falke.
You're going to begin a pencil sketch in preparation for a
life-size oil figure study. And besides there isn't any coffee in all of Neukölln. Coming back on the opposite tack
we could point almost on the reeds of the beach, that got
us a little closer to the dock and Christoph cups his hands
around his mouth and one word floats across the quiet
water. My hands were shaking, but I tried. You want to
paint her or you want to fuck her? Can't do both at the
same time. Can I take my arms down? asked Bärbel.
Tell him what I'll do to you if you move a muscle while
you're posing. Who is Kowalski? asks Lili as she changes
places with me so that I can bring the boat in. Her sun-
tanned cool hand fastens around my elbow for support.
He's a sculptor, friend of Christoph's. Is he the one who
teaches you to paint? If you don't tell him, said Falke,
I'm going to demonstrate right now. He's a filthy swine,
said Bärbel through her teeth. No, I said, the painter is
Fritz Falke. This one's a sculptor, Christoph has some
business with him. You mean tonight? Christoph has
business on Sunday night? All right, said Falke, heading
for the door. He tries to push a beer bottle . . . into me.

Show him where, said Falke, at the door. You may take
your hands down to show him which hole. She did. Falke
walked out and slammed the door.

One! He isn't coming. Why should he? But he was here
last night, and the night before. Meier told us. And nothing's been seen of Tillessen. Or the third man. Maybe they
smelled something. Me. The American Agent. Unlikely
role, if they only knew. But they don't. What they know is
they obtained a powerful expensive car, hid it in Kaspar
Keith's stable, and it's gone, and they find an American
with no very plausible explanation for his presence in the
household of Generalmajor Keith. If Kaspar isn't already
in on it, the safest thing would be to avoid him, avoid the
Villa Keith. Which may be why he's been home alone so
much lately, while we cursed Kowalski and thought about
the French army in Cologne and worried that I might not
have enough money to buy morphine if Kowalski disappeared because Dr. Strassburger now sent word (through
Christoph) that he felt the mark would drop sharply during the rest of the year. Advised me to put up nearly all
of my dollars in Amsterdam and borrow ten times as
many additional dollars from Waldstein's Amsterdam
bank to buy forward delivery contracts in marks — that
is, contracts to deliver marks in three months and in six
months, on the theory that they will be worth much less
then. But what if the mark stops falling? I asked. What if
Rathenau convinces the Allies to reduce their demands,
or to take raw materials or German products instead of
gold? What happens if I have to cover? I won't even be
able to repay the loan. Christoph said yes, Strassburger is
well aware of that. I'll be absolutely busted and so far
in debt that I'll never get out. I might have to go bankrupt! One of my mother's uncles went bankrupt. He shot
himself in his office in the Land Title Building, corner of
Broad and Chestnut Streets in Philadelphia. Nobody ever
mentions his name, not even his children. Christoph only
smiled, a little sardonically: I don't think anybody expects you to file for bankruptcy, or to shoot yourself. But
you might have to go home. Listen, I said, hearing my
voice shaking, I don't want to paint right now, I just don't
think I can, and she nodded and took my hand and led
me over to the bed. It's all right, she said, already unfas-
tening my buttons. But he's right outside. It's all right,
she said again and pressed herself against me. I feel you

want to, and he wants us to. But why? Lili was upset about the play, what happened at the play. And afterwards. Why do the people hate the Jews so much? Only some of the people. But why? Don't ask me why, he is a swine, a crazy swine. But you let him treat you this way. Yes, don't talk so much, just do that. Yes, like that, oh yes! That's good. Hold me like that. I don't know much about Jews but I know how to sail a boat and when you get too close to the wind the sail will flutter like that. You're pointing too close to the wind. No, the sail is right the way you have it, point the *boat* downwind. Move the tiller. That's right, like that. Do it like that. Harder. But he will hear the springs! Don't think about it. He's gone out anyway. How old are you? Did you know my greatgrandfather was a Jew? He became a Christian. Yes, Christoph told me about your family. His brother hates the Jews. Yes, I know. His brother was to marry Sigrid. Yes, I know. Then we came into the shadow of the island. You liked that? *Did I like it?* I'm a new man, but I can't tell her that. I only smile. You have a cigarette?

One . . . *Two!* Isn't coming. Fell asleep. Sit up and light a cigarette. No, he might smell the smoke in the hall. I'm sorry, Lili, said Christoph as he helped her out of the boat. Peter and I cannot stay to eat, we must go back to town. On Sunday evening? Surely the Bank is closed. No, this is an important client. You are making Peter a banker now? Irritated, didn't believe a word. I busied myself in the boat, taking down the sail, fastening the boom, pulling up the centerboard. Rolled over on her stomach now, propped up on her elbows, smoking the cigarette, blowing smoke at me over her shoulder. You agree it is the finest ass in Berlin? Well, I haven't seen the others. She laughed, breasts swaying between her elbows. Looking at her: Is it true about the beer bottle? Once. Hurt like hell. Why do you stay with him? Didn't answer, put the cigarette in her mouth, got off the bed and stooped to pick up her slip. Now I've got to have some breakfast. With the money I give him and the money you give him, at least that Schweinehund could have some coffee in the kitchen. Peter has to change his clothes and you can have a cup of tea, said Lili. They are just bringing it down now. On the other side, the shadow of the island had reached the public beaches. People take down their parasols. Women wrap towels around themselves and manage to get their bathing suits off and their clothes on while wrapped in damp sandy towels. Then they hold up the towels so that the men can change in more dignified privacy. On the other side of the Tea House, the Waldsteins have comfortable dressing rooms for the guests. I step out of the shower and find Christoph looking at his wristwatch. I don't want to go out there, I said, I can't look him in the face. He won't be there, he's gone out to find a drink, he'll drink all day now, we won't see him until tomorrow. Why tonight? Because Kowalski has the stuff, we've delayed too long already, I just can't stand to wait another night! Did he call here? No, he called the house and told Meier he had to reach me, so Meier called out here. Just now. How are we going to get in there? Bobby's up at the Schloss, he says he'll run us over the Nikolassee in the Horch. They all think it's a little strange, Sunday night, such beautiful weather, I already told her Kowalski is a sculptor, so now you've got to explain why a sculptor is such an important client that we've got to rush into town on Sunday evening without staying for dinner. On the contrary: the best advice is never apologize, never explain. On Saturday I had rigged up a pulley to connect the buoy with the floating dock, and Lili was using it as we said goodbye, hauling the sloop out to the buoy, and a big motor launch was passing, moving slowly but drawing a lot of water, making a deep wake, and the sloop rose and fell in the wake, and as we climbed the gravel path I heard the boom clanking in its socket, realizing I hadn't strapped it down tight enough and it will go on clanking like that every time some waves come in and maybe she will think of me when she hears the boom clanking like that. Bärbel eating a slice of black bread with lard on it, drinking tea made out of herbs. Will you let me take you out for breakfast? No, too lazy to get dressed and then undressed. You draw my picture now and then you take me out to lunch. What will Fritz say? You don't worry about Fritz. What will Bobby say, driving us in the huge old Horch, driving us across the clunking wooden bridge and up into the Scotch pines toward Nikolassee?

Jesus, is that the door? Screaming silence. On the other side of the house a car drives by, but it didn't stop, did it? Was that the door? Is Christoph moving? I can't hear anything now, but it sounded like a door. Where is the stuff? For Christ's sake don't knock over anything in the dark, it's all right here, it doesn't help to use the Redeemer's name in vain my old man says exasperated, it's just the sign of a limited vocabulary. Silence. False alarm. He's not coming anyway, we could have stayed, I could have spent the evening with Lili. What do you think about Jews? I don't know. I don't think I think anything about them. How can you not think anything about them? Well, what do you want me to think about them? Well, do you like them, or don't you like them? Want to hear a story? Yes. My parents have a friend, Miss Boatwright, well you know her, she was just here the other day. Yes, I know Miss Boatwright. All right, well, Miss Boatwright, she's a wonderful person, always trying to help good causes, raising money for all sorts of things, and one time she was raising money for a Conference of Christians and Jews, you see, to promote understanding between the Christians and the Jews. And she came to see my father, although she has much, much more money than my father, her family owns the Locomotive Works, but anyway she asked my father to contribute money to this conference and he wouldn't because, he said, he didn't like Christians *or* Jews! Is that supposed to be funny? I thought it was sort of funny, yes. But your father is a Christian, isn't he? Yes, of course. Then why is it funny if he says . . . Oh never mind, I didn't tell it right. There is an American lady here, said Mutti Bauer, putting her head in the door. Bärbel has one stocking on and nothing else. She asks for Peter Ellis. An American lady? Get dressed, said Mutti Bauer to Bärbel. She said it angrily. He's painting me, Mutti, I'm his model, but she slipped past her mother into the darkness of the bedroom and as I follow I hear and feel and smell her putting on the kimono and in the kitchen Miss Boatwright is still panting from the climb, trying out her German on the boy. Wie alt bist du, kleiner Junge? Good morning Peter, I hope this visit is not inconvenient. Bobby didn't ask any questions. Drove the Horch. I had not been alone with him since we met his Russian countess at the Adlon, and they'd had to leave because of us. I wanted to say something to him, but I just didn't know what to say. He and Christoph talked politics. Silesia. The people in Silesia voted to stay with Germany, but the Allies were going to give half of it to Poland anyhow. Uproar in the Reichstag tomorrow.

What will Halfferich say? Leader of the Nationalists, been making personal attacks on Rathenau. Not a bad man, actually, says Bobby. Used to be in the Deutsche Bank, friend of Father's. Often been to the house. But these attacks, always picking on Rathenau . . . Bobby shakes his head. I think of Lili, pulling on the boat rope. Goodbye I said. Goodbye she said, not turning around. Thank you for a lovely weekend. You're welcome. Are you angry with me? Why should I be angry? You teach me how to sail, now you have Bank business in town on Sunday night. Men do the things they want to do. I didn't say it was Bank business. Peter, we're going to miss the train. Bobby's eyes look sad. Mutti Bauer's eyes look puzzled, what is this lady doing here? This is Frau Falke, the wife of my teacher who is out on an errand, Miss Boatwright. And this is her mother, Frau Bauer, Miss Boatwright of the American Friends Service Committee . . . *Die Kwäker?* Both women say it in unison, almost a gasp. Atmosphere changed. Cupboards are flipped open, plates and cups appear, apparently some sort of meal must be served although Miss Boatwright keeps protesting that she just ate, she wants to see my pictures, Herr Falke's pictures. They serve the herb tea, and the bread with lard, and potato soup with a sausage cut up in it, and Mutti Bauer explains that but for the Quakers this grandson and her younger daughter would have starved in 1919. Not this one, this one was older, we got enough meat on her before the times became so hard, she even nursed her baby but the younger one was only eleven when the hunger began, she didn't gain one kilo in two years, she's still as thin as a boy, but when your people served milk and pudding in the schools she began to grow. . . . As we got out of the Horch at Nikolassee, Bobby looked at us and smiled a sad smile and said Hals-und-Beinbruch and roared off. Does he know something? I think he knows we are not going on a picnic, said Christoph. And for the first time I wondered how many people Kaspar Keith has killed. His photograph albums. We got off the train at Bahnhof Zoo and took a taxi down to the Nollendorf Platz but the minute we got into the taxi and had to give the driver the address of Kowalski's apartment, we knew we were in trouble. We had both forgotten it. A lovely summer evening, crowded streets. Would Kowalski have a telephone? Frau Bauer proudly

told Miss Boatwright that I was painting her daughter. Oh
good, may I watch you doing that? What does she want,
the American lady? Oh no. Retreated to the bedroom.
Stand naked in front of that lady? So siehst Du aus!
You're just proving you're not really a model. A professional model wouldn't give it a thought, her body's just an
object for the artist to paint. Kowalski had no telephone.
Maybe he left his address with Meier when he called.
Christoph came out of the telephone kiosk of the café and
shook his head. You invited him for lunch at Lutter's. How
did you find him? We are sitting in this café on the
Nollendorf Platz and Christoph is leafing wildly through
his address book. How did you get him down for lunch so
fast if he doesn't have a telephone? Sent a bank messenger. But how did you know where to send the messenger
if you didn't have his address? Drinking coffee. Don't
even have a cup of coffee to offer the American lady.
She doesn't want any coffee, she wants to see my work,
she's already bought one of my pictures, she might buy
one of Fritz's if you will stop acting so . . . I didn't know
the German word for coy. Miss Boatwright, come into the
studio, I'm just working on Frau Falke's face today, this
is eventually going to be a full figure study but as you
know I'm interested in faces so we're working on the face
first. Nobody looks at the tumbled bedsheets until Mutti
Bauer comes in, ostentatiously makes up the bed: Solch
ein Saustall! Pigpen? These are certainly very strong
statements says Miss Boatwright, peering through her
glasses at Falke's phantasmagorias. I have it! shouts Christoph, slamming the marble table.

One . . . two . . . *three!* Well, he's not coming. He's
drunk and asleep in some apartment full of rifles and submachine guns and other sleeping hate-crazed men. But
does this operation really make sense? Trying to cut out
one sick boy instead of trying to stop the whole thing? I
told the messenger to find Kowalski's address at the Pol-
izeirevier Nollendorf Platz! In fact, it was the messenger
who suggested it. The police station? Certainly. The police
have a list of every person in every apartment. And they
let you look at it? If you have a proper reason. You mean
to tell me we're going to the police station now? Why not?
I'm trying to find my old war comrade Kowalski who lives
off the Nollendorf Platz but I can't remember exactly . . .
As I look at Bärbel's face, her modestly downcast eyes, I

feel her legs around me. Frau Falke, please look at me. I
want to see your eyes. You gentlemen took your time,
says Kowlaski as he opens the door. I telephoned the moment my train arrived. . . . He wants to tell his adven-
tures, but we want to leave. Three small parcels wrapped
in newspapers. Had sewn them into the bottom of his
trench coat. Hypodermic syringe. Small bottle of chloroform. A dozen little vials containing clear liquid. Is this
the Amytal? How much do we? One every twelve hours.
But that's only enough for six days! I told you two weeks.
Shakes his head. All he could get his hands on. Not on
sale yet, still strictly controlled in the lab. And he said
better give two ampules the first time. It's the best I could
do, Keith. And it wasn't easy. The British stopped me
twice. If they had searched me I would be in the Fortress
Cologne now. It's good, I understand. And thank you.
Formal handshakes. Hals-und-Beinbruch, says Kowalski,
just like Bobby. Later: Why does Kowalski owe you a favor? Nothing, don't want to talk now. At that party, you
said they are Communists. Was Kowalski . . . Same camp
with you so he must have been an officer. Yes. German
officer who was a Communist? I will tell you the story
some other time. Did the other German officers know this
one was a Communist? Long story, Peter. Tell you another time. We have a hard job tonight. Did you save
Kowalski's life at La Rochelle? Maybe he thinks that.
Well, tell me about it. Not tonight. Tonight we make our
plan. And he didn't bring us enough Amytal. I have
watched Mr. Ellis paint before, so I don't believe it dis-
turbs him. Miss Boatwright's German is not as good as
mine. Bärbel's eyes move back and forth, the green eyes
of a cat. A cat who smells money. American money. What
if Falke comes back? How can she love a guy who treats
her like that? Somebody told me the worse you treat them
— But is that true? Animals? Pigpen? Beginning to look a
little like her? Putting on her stockings. Long way from
the azalea gardens at Friends Hospital, hot summer afternoons, long hot summer afternoons, trying to capture
the real face behind the mask of tissue and bone, concentrating so hard on trying, concentrating so hard that the
other things recede, little by little the other things recede
so I can sleep at night, even when the nights are very
hot. . . .
     "WANT . . . HIM . . . OUT . . . OF . . . THIS . . .

HOUSE!" Kaspar. Jesus Christ Almighty, fell asleep after all, he's already inside, he's shouting at Christoph! Up and out and — *crash*. Wet. Oh my God that was the chloroform. Don't breathe, *don't breathe!* The sponge, yes, forget the other stuff, just soak the sponge in wetness and don't breathe. Out of the door, hold away from face, take one breath, step silently across the hall — "He cannot stay in this house, it compromises our position, our name!" — burst into the brightly lighted room, Kaspar red-faced, apparently drunk, turns in surprise as I slam the sponge against his face and Christoph comes out of the wicker chair and tackles him below the knees, a neat American tackle, where did he learn that? and Kaspar, crashing sideways, strikes out wildly with both arms, strong arms, catches the side of my head and my ear rings but I've kept the sponge in place, he's taken deep drafts of choloform now and the thrashing stops. All three of us are gasping, lying on the floor, I'm dizzy. . . .

I'm sorry Christoph, fell asleep.

Where's the other stuff? Go get it, quickly! Don't want him to get too much chloroform. Leave the door open. Have the Meiers heard anything? I come back with the filled syringe. The place reeks of chloroform although the window is open. I roll up Kaspar's sleeve.

What are you doing?

Giving him the shot.

In the arm?

Of course. Where else?

We give it here, pointing to chest. Pectoral muscle.

Never heard of that. We give it in the biceps.

Then do it your way, only hurry!

I haven't done this in a long time, my hand is shaking, but somehow I sink the needle under Kaspar's chalky skin and slowly inject the double dose of Amytal. He is breathing heavily, his eyes are closed.

All right, now what?

The night was turning gray and birds were singing.

19.

WEDNESDAY, JUNE 21, 1922

"What the devil is going on here?"

Helena stormed into the dining room as Meier tried to make a formal announcement: "Her Highness *Prinzessin von* —"

I stood up. "Good morning, Helena."

She wore a big straw summer hat and underneath the brim her eyes were blazing. "What is happening in this house?"

"In this house? What do you mean? Will you have some breakfast?"

"At ten o'clock? I've had breakfast! Meier, get out!"

Looking relieved, Meier bowed and left the room.

The Meiers had been our first problem. Although we opened all the windows on the second floor, you could still smell the chloroform, so when we heard them moving about in the kitchen we decided to go right down and get it over with. I stayed behind Christoph and let him do the talking.

Frau Meier looked startled as she saw us coming through the pantry. Her husband was just putting on his gray jacket. "Guten Morgen, die Herren."

"Will you sit down a moment, Frau Meier?"

"Herr Oberleutnant, is something wrong?"

"Yes. My brother is sick. Nervous exhaustion of some kind. Still from the Revolution, of course."

"Um Gottes Willen! He is in the hospital?"

"No, he's upstairs in bed. He's been given sleeping pills. We don't want him in the hospital. You understand? Mr. Ellis was a *Sanitäter* in the War. You remember he saved my life. Mr. Ellis will help me to care for Kaspar until he is better."

Frau Meier twisted a dishcloth in her liver-spotted hands. "But Herr Oberleutnant, we must call Dr. Goldschmidt, we must telephone Frau General —"

"On the contrary, Frau Meier. We are *not* going to call

Dr. Goldschmidt, we are *not* going to worry my mother, we are *not* going to tell the milkman, or the baker's boy, or the servants of the Hansemanns next door. This is a private matter involving the honor of this house, and we are not going to tell *anybody!* Is that clear?"

The old woman began to cry.

"Is that entirely clear, Frau Meier?"

Her husband answered. "We understand, Herr Oberleutnant. We only want to help."

"Meier, how old were you when you came with my father?"

"Fifteen, Herr Oberleutnant. I took care of his horses. The regiment was in the honor guard at Versailles, the winter our old king became the Kaiser. *Anno* '71. We paraded in front of the Palace of Versailles that day. Oh, those were different times, Herr Oberleutnant!"

"Yes," said Christoph. "Very different times. But times always change, Meier. There will be good times again. Right now we obey orders and keep our mouths shut. Understood?"

"Understood, Herr Oberleutnant." Meier could hardly keep from clicking his heels, but his wife was still wiping her eyes. "If the boy is sick his mother must be told, Herr Oberleutnant."

Christoph sighed. "Perhaps you're right, Frau Meier. Perhaps you're right about Mother, but *I* will handle the matter. I will telephone to Kolberg from the Bank. Now you can give us breakfast, please."

The first day wasn't so bad. I had taken my easel, my canvases, and most of my oil paint down to Falke's, but I still had enough equipment for sketching and I had my watercolors, so I made the time pass trying to copy faces from a book of photographs, and every hour or so I went in to check on Kaspar. By the middle of the afternoon he was still dozing and I was getting sleepy and bored. And skeptical about the whole thing. How long are we going to keep him out? How long will I have to sit here like a psychiatric nurse? There must be some better way —

Christoph came home early, and Kaspar began to regain consciousness. "Oh my God," he whispered, "I never had such a hangover in my life. How long have I been asleep?" and then he fell asleep again.

"Let's get him to the toilet before he has an accident," said Christoph, so we did that, and it was awful, just like when it was me (limp as a rag doll, he kept muttering, "I'm so tired, please let me sleep") but we got him emptied out and back into bed. Then Christoph held down the arm while I gave him another injection. He moaned a little as he felt the needle. Christoph sat in the wicker armchair and stared silently at his brother. Christoph's eyes closed. Christoph's head fell to his chest.

What am I doing here?

Some time in the middle of the second afternoon the telephone rang. At the Villa Keith, Meier answers the telephone. He came to my room with raised eyebrows: a Fräulein Bauer wishes to speak with Mister Ellis? He seemed to think I might not want to speak with Fräulein Bauer, but I went down to the pantry.

"Hello?"

"Peter? This is Baby."

"Hello, Baby!"

Meier passed through the pantry into the kitchen, eyes front.

The sound of Baby's almost comic Berlin patois relieved my depression just a little. Bärbel had sent her down to the nearest *Kneipe*, a corner bar in the Kaiser Friedrichstrasse, to call me. Why hadn't I come to paint? Was I sore at them?

I tried to explain: somebody was sick, I had to help, I would be down there in a few days, I certainly wasn't angry at anybody — but how was Fritz?

Pause. I could hear the people in the bar shouting at each other. Fritz was still on a bender. That's why they wished I would come. If he had to give me lessons he might stop drinking. He's given Bärbel such a terrific *Backpfeife* —

What's a *Backpfeife*?

When you slap somebody's cheek with your hand, and Bärbel's face is all swollen and blue and she won't go out —

Where's he getting the money for all this drinking?

Just guess! Oh, and your American lady came back and bought one of his little oils. Paid him twenty dollars, can you believe that? That's six thousand marks. Fritz has plenty of money, but he won't give us enough for food. I have to hang up now. We hope you come back soon, Peter.

I tried to time my sleep with Kaspar's so that I would be awake when the Amytal began to wear off, because then he would be conscious, it was easier to feed him, and sometimes we would talk a little. *Hypnotic state,* Kowalski's brother had advised. He will not sleep all the time, even on 200 miligrams per day. Some of the time he will be in a hypnotic state. I tried to remember what that feels like. 1918? 1919? They did it to me. They did it to find what cracked me up. I remembered a sense of lassitude, an absence of will, but I couldn't remember anything I'd said to them, as if I'd been asleep.

"I've been asleep," said Kaspar.

"Yes. Did you have dreams."

"Oh yes! Am I sick?"

"Yes, you're sick, but you're getting better. What did you dream about?"

He would mumble about his dreams, which didn't make more sense than anybody else's dreams — except the recurring one about the sailors who tore off his epaulets, and the shrieking women.

I sent Meier out for newspapers.

Our shady street was silent and empty, but the country seemed to be in turmoil. The provinces of Upper Silesia had voted to stay with Germany, but the Allies had turned them over to Poland anyway, and thousands of frightened German refugees were pouring across the border. Now the papers were full of speculation that the French were going to expand their occupation of the Rhineland and the Saarland. And whose fault was all of this? It was the fault of Chancellor Wirth's government in general, and of its foreign minister in particular. This is where the policy of "fulfillment" has brought us! It wasn't just the Nationalist papers, it was practically all of them now. The Center Party, Dr. Stresemann, demanded specific answers to specific questions about the government's policies in the Rhineland and the Saar, and Walther Rathenau, his back to the wall, gave a strong and rather nationalistic speech to the effect that Germany would never abandon the people now under French occupation.

"The picture of conditions in the Saar is not a pleasant one," Rathenau told the Reichstag. "But as Germans we can point with pride to the fact that in these difficult years of alien domination the population of the Saar has held together as never before, in order to preserve that which they regard as their most precious possession — their German nationality and culture!"

Christoph Keith called from the Bank to find out if Kaspar was asleep, and to tell me I had purchased contracts to deliver 3,000,000 marks in Amsterdam on September 21, 1922. And I owed the Waldsteins $9,000 I didn't have.

"All right," said Helena when Meier had closed the door. "I want to know what's going on here!" She took off the straw hat and touched her piled-up platinum hair and stared at me.

"What makes you think there's something —"

"Don't trifle with me, Peter, *I will not have it!* I understand that you and Christoph rushed back to town on Sunday evening, supposedly on Bank business that nobody at Havelblick knows anything about. On Monday I hear nothing from Christoph. I am busy, I assume Christoph is busy. On Tuesday I still hear nothing from Christoph, so I telephone the Bank, where I am told that Oberleutnant Keith is in a meeting. I ask that he telephone when the meeting is finished. He does not telephone. I telephone the Villa Keith, where I receive evasive answers from Meier, not only evasive but actually frightened. I am not allowed to speak with Mister Ellis, because Mister Ellis is asleep — at five in the afternoon! And now I find you here alone in the middle of the morning. You *are* alone, are you not?"

"Helena, please —"

"This has something to do with his brother, doesn't it?"

"Helena, you've got to ask Christoph these questions!"

"Why?"

I couldn't look into those eyes anymore.

"Will you not look at me, Peter?"

What could I do? I just shook my head and repeated that she would have to ask Christoph, so she stood up and walked out of the dining room and started up the stairs.

"What is the meaning of this?" shouted Christoph, slamming the living room door.

It didn't take him long to get home. I didn't think it would. When Helena came racing down the stairs she was calling for Meier, and Meier was there before she reached the bottom step.

"I want you to call Herr Oberleutnant at the Bank and I want you to give him this message: the Princess Hohenstein is here with Mister Ellis. The Princess Hohenstein wishes Oberleutnant Keith to come home at once. If Oberleutnant Keith is not home within one hour — *one hour,* Meier! — then the Princess Hohenstein is taking a taxi to Police Headquarters Alexanderplatz. You understand that message, Meier?"

"Oh, Your Highness!" Overwhelmed, almost sagging with relief, Meier waddled toward the pantry as fast as he could get there.

"You have a very loyal friend in Peter," said Helena to Christoph, putting out her fourth cigarette. "He insists that all questions about Kaspar must be directed to you, and as you will not return my calls I had no choice but to send for you. Now I want you to tell me why Kaspar is lying in his bed, asleep with his eyes open, and why there is a hypodermic needle in the bathroom."

Christoph stood there, leaning on his cane and looking at the carpet. He shook his head. "I can't, my dear."

"Why can't you?"

He shook his head again. "Just can't."

They stared at each other. I couldn't look at them. I looked at the walls, at all the grinning death's heads on the caps of all those hussars in their faded photographs, but finally the pressure became too much for me. "Better tell her," I said.

"Peter! You know why she must not be involved."

"She's involved already, and it isn't going to work, your way."

"What isn't going to work?" demanded Helena.

"Peter, I forbid you —"

"You can't forbid him anything!" Helena was shouting now.

My heart was beating in my throat. "Christoph, we can't just sit here and wait for a man to be killed."

"Wait for what man to be killed?" Helena leapt to her feet, stepped across the room and threw her arms around

Christoph. "What man?" she whispered, her face pressed against his chest. She was crying.

I just couldn't stay there anymore. I walked out of the room and closed the door.

We hadn't tried to shave Kaspar, so he had the beginnings of a scruffy blond beard, really just pale stubble fuzzing the bottom half of his narrow face. We hadn't tried to wash him either, and he smelled. It was all we could do to feed him black bread and vegetable soup and mashed potatoes and carefully cut-up sausages. Things like that. And to take him to the toilet twice a day. I didn't see how we could keep this up much longer.

"You hungry, Kaspar?"

Shakes his head. Sighs. "Tired. Always so tired."

Long pause. I am sitting in the wicker armchair.

"From the medicine?" Kaspar points to his arm. We gave him the shot very early this morning. Is it wearing off already? Could he be building up resistance? Does he remember that we chloroformed him?

"Why medicine?" asks Kaspar.

"You were excited," I used the word *aufgeregt*.

Shakes his head: "Nicht aufgeregt. Traurig." Sad.

Why sad?

Closes his eyes and shakes his head.

"Because of the car, Kaspar? The Austro-Daimler?"

Eyes remain closed, but there is a racking sob.

"They are angry at you about the Austro-Daimler, aren't they?"

Silence.

I repeat the question.

Kaspar nods.

"Tillessen is angry."

Kaspar nods again.

"Who else is angry?"

"Kern."

"Who is Kern?"

Kaspar opens his eyes, stares at me. I can see him struggling with the memory, so I try to help him.

"Kern thinks I took the car, doesn't he? Because Tillessen told him I'm an American agent. But *you* know I'm not an American agent, I'm Christoph's friend who pulled Christoph out of the burning airplane."

Kaspar nods again...

"But Tillessen — and Kern — they won't believe you."

"They won't believe me."

"Why would the Americans want that Austro-Daimler?"

Kaspar doesn't know. Neither do I.

"What does . . . Kern? want with the Austro-Daimler?"

"Have to get another car now!" Kaspar's eyes widen.

"Why? Why do they have to get another car now?"

"Geheimsache," says Kaspar. Secret matter.

"But *you* know, don't you?"

Kaspar shakes his head.

"But Kern knows."

"Kern knows."

"Because Kern is the leader."

Am I learning something or am I just putting words into his mouth? I try a long leap: "I thought Captain Ehrhardt was the leader."

Kaspar looks puzzled. "Of course. Captain Ehrhardt."

"But he's down in Munich and Kern's up here?"

"Kern's up here."

"Who else is up here?"

"Fischer is up here."

"Which Fischer is that?"

"Hermann Fischer, of course!"

"The one who was in the Brigade?"

"Of course!"

Something clicked. "Are Kern and Fischer the men Tillessen wanted to put up in this house?"

"Old comrades."

"Old comrades on a secret mission."

"Old comrades on a secret mission."

Hypnotic state.

"But Christoph would not let them come here."

Kaspar sighs.

"And then their Austro-Daimler disappears."

Kaspar sobs.

"And they are angry, and won't tell you what the mission is."

Kaspar turns his head away and puts his hands over his ears.

"Your brother works for the Jews and his friend is an American agent so they don't trust you anymore, your old comrades!"

Kaspar's head is pressed between his hands, his face is buried in the pillow, his shoulders are shaking. I decided to give him another 25 milligrams, to put him back to sleep.

If he really doesn't know, then he's out of it, isn't he? He knows Tillessen's brother killed Matthias Erzberger. He knows that the O.C. kills people. He must know they're going to kill *somebody*.

Suppose Christoph is wrong, and they're really after somebody else? The leader of this government is Chancellor Wirth.

"What man?" Helena had asked, but it wasn't a question. If Helena knows and Christoph knows, how can Kaspar — after all those nights of drinking and talking and planning — how can Kaspar *not* know?

When I returned to the living room, I found Helena alone. She was smoking another cigarette and staring out into the garden. When she turned, I saw that her eyes were red and swollen. This was a new and different Helena.

"Christoph's gone back to the Bank, but he made me promise I would not go to the police. Oh, Peter, I just don't know what to do!"

I sat down and told her what I had extracted from Kaspar.

"Helena, I think that Christoph is all wrong about this. If these people kill somebody important — whether it's Rathenau or Wirth or whoever — and there is a serious investigation, we're never going to keep Kaspar out of it this way. If they catch any of the others, they'll implicate him. Even if he doesn't know exactly who the target is, will that be a good defense?"

Helena looked out of the window and shook her head.

"And even if that is a defense, how would he establish it? How do you prove you didn't know something? And what about the rest of us? We go out and smash a car because we think it's going to be used in a murder. Doesn't that implicate *us* in some way, if they find themselves another car and actually commit the murder? I'm not a lawyer, but these are legal questions. You know what we would do at home, if we got into a mess like this? We'd go and see a lawyer."

20.

FRIDAY, JUNE 23, 1922

Although he was doing his best not to show it, Herr Ober-verwaltungsgerichtsrat Dr. Friedrich-Karl von Winterfeldt was disturbed by the story he had just heard. It didn't show in his face, the kind of face Americans think all German bureaucrats have, right down to the monocle and the little white dueling scar on his left cheek. It showed first in the way he began to tap his fingertips together, then in the way he rose abruptly from behind his enormous oak desk to pace around his book-lined study.

"This is a serious matter, Helena! Very serious. This could bring unfavorable attention, public criticism — who knows what else? upon the *entire family!*" He meant his own family.

"That is why we came to see you, Dr. Von Winterfeldt."

(I was beginning to understand all these little nuances: he calls her "Helena" because he has known her from childhood; she calls him "Dr. von Winterfeldt" instead of "Herr Oberverwaltungsgerichtsrat" for the same reason.)

When I said that we should consult a lawyer, Helena had turned quickly to look at me, had opened her purse, blown her nose into a lace handkerchief, opened a silver compact, studied herself critically in the mirror, powdered her face carefully, produced a tiny comb with which she subdued the few strands of loose hair — and turned to look at me again.

"I think you have the answer, Peter. We need a lawyer. And not just a lawyer — a judge. Gerichtsrat Dr. Winterfeldt, of the Oberverwaltungsgericht — Oh, I can explain it exactly, the supreme court for government matters, the highest court for the government ministries? It doesn't matter, they are very important, and Dr. von Winterfeldt is a famous jurist, a classmate of my father, a man who

knows everybody at the Ministry of Justice, everybody in
the Prussian state administration —"

"Now wait a minute, Helena. You're going to see a
judge about this thing? Isn't that the same as going to the
police?"

"Not quite the same," said Helena, in full control
again, biting her lips to make them red, putting the handkerchief and the compact and the comb and the cigarette
case back into her purse. "This particular judge is the
brother of Frau Keith — and therefore the uncle of
Christoph and of Kaspar!"

But you don't just run across town and drop in on a
judge of the Oberverwaltungsgericht, we discovered. Helena decided to telephone for an appointment but we
agreed that she had better not call from the Villa Keith,
because the Meiers would tell Christoph, so she left and
went back to her apartment. I didn't hear from her until
the middle of the afternoon. The court was adjourned for
the summer. Gerichtsrat von Winterfeldt was at his summer house in Wannsee.

— Well, let's go out there and see him.

— No, we can't, because his wife will find out. She's a
frightful Nationalist, a cousin of General Ludendorff,
she'd happily shoot the whole cabinet herself.

— But her husband is all right?

— Yes. He's stuffy but he's all right. People don't
marry women because of their political opinions, you will
discover.

— Well then, what are we going to do?

— It so happens that he's coming into town for lunch
on Friday, he plans to work with his law secretary in the
office on Friday afternoon, and he has agreed to see us at
four o'clock. Will you be able to leave the house? Can we
meet at my apartment?

— Now wait a minute, Helena, you really want me
along on this? A stranger, and a foreigner? What's he going —

— Oh yes, yes, Peter, *please!* I cannot do this behind
Christoph's back all alone, and you know the whole story,
and the names that Kaspar has told you, and where the
Austro-Daimler is, and everything, and also you are
American, you have no personal involvement, you did it
only as a friend, it makes a completely different impres-

sion than if I come alone, he *is* an old friend of my father but he thinks of me . . . Oh, I can't explain it, Peter,
I am an actress, and I have been the friend of his nephew
for many years — but not the wife — and during the
War I did go out with other men —

— It's all right, Helena, I understand. What time shall
I be at your apartment on Friday?

"One thing is certain," announced Dr. von Winterfeldt.
He had finally stopped pacing and was staring out of the
window. "If a crime is actually committed, persons who
had advance information about such a crime, and with-
held such information from the authorities, have committed a crime themselves. That is the law. It has always
been the law. And it is my sworn duty to uphold the law,
and I cannot permit any member of my family to involve
himself in a criminal offense."

Pause. Dr. von Winterfeldt neatly dropped his monocle
into the palm of his hand and began to polish it with his
handkerchief, still staring out of the window. "However!
Do we *have* advance information about a crime? What
information? What crime? A brother of the man who
killed Erzberger appears in Berlin. He obtains an automobile. He seeks living quarters for two friends. All three
of them belonged to Ehrhardt's Marine Brigade, which
was dissolved two years ago. Kaspar Keith is told about a
secret mission." He turned to face us, neatly replacing the
monocle. "Are those the hard facts we know?"

"Yes, sir," I replied.

"And what's the rest of it?" asked Dr. von Winterfeldt.
"The rest of it is Christoph's conjecture, is it not? Organization Consul? In well-informed circles we hear a lot of
talk about the O.C. But is there anything more than talk?
Any arrests? Any documents? Any court determinations?"

"Just a lot of corpses," said Helena.

"But that is not enough, my dear girl. The question really is: Can the police arrest this Lieutenant Tillessen and
his friends on the basis of the information you have given
me? And the answer is No."

He began to pace again, hands folded behind his back.
When Helena introduced me he had been polite but very
chilly, what the Germans call "correct." *Another one of
her men* was the first reaction I read in his expression.
Why else would an American involve himself in this sit-

uation? After that, for a moment, he may have shared
the suspicion of Lieutenant Tillessen, but by the time we
finished our story he had reached a different, right, con-
clusion: an innocent abroad, a stranger in a strange land,
getting in over his head.

"Despite the fact that there are no grounds for arrest
— at least we are not aware of grounds sufficient for arrest — it would seem the better part of wisdom to notify
someone. Yes, we must notify someone," said Dr. von
Winterfeldt.

"You don't need to notify the victim," said Helena.
"That's been done."

Both of us turned. *"What did you say?"* whispered Dr.
von Winterfeldt.

"I have told Walther Rathenau everything we just told
you. I went to his house in Grunewald last night. You
cannot guess whom he was entertaining for dinner: Dr.
Helfferich, and another man from the Nationalist party.
I think my appearance rather surprised them."

Dr. von Winterfeldt was incredulous. "Rathenau was
having dinner with Helfferich? Helena, I find that a little
hard —"

"I saw it with my own eyes. It seems they have known
each other for years, the Rathenau parents befriended
Helfferich when he was an apprentice at the Deutsche
Bank. They are political enemies, the bitterest enemies,
but they've maintained contact, and when Walther Rathenau asked Helfferich for dinner, he came. With an aide."

"But why —"

"Because Walther Rathenau has so much faith in the
logic of his ideas, he thinks he can persuade the devil
himself. He just tried to reason with Helfferich, to explain
that these endless attacks from the Right are making it
impossible to conduct Germany's foreign policy, that
Helfferich is actually hurting the nation by his tactics —"

"And he expects Helfferich to listen?"

"Yes, he says Helfferich did listen, did agree to stop
these personal attacks —"

I interrupted her: "But what about these O.C. people?
Did you tell him all that? In front of this . . . Helfferich?"

"Of course not. I apologized for bursting in on them, I
asked to see Dr. Rathenau alone for just a minute, and of
course he had to get up from the table and take me into
his library. And I just told him."

"And what did he do?" asked Dr. von Winterfeldt.

"He shrugged his shoulders," said Helena.

We stared at her.

"That's right. Shrugged his shoulders. 'My dear,' he said, 'I'm told these stories every day now. What should I do? Go to the Ministry in a steel helmet? Borrow an armored car from the Reichswehr? I love my country more than anything in the world. If I have to give my life in Germany's service — well, I won't be the first, will I?' " Helena choked on the last words and took her handkerchief out of her purse.

"I think that's a little exaggerated," said Dr. von Winterfeldt. "He need not always drive about Berlin in an open car. So he's not going to take any precautions?"

Helena shook her head. "He only asked if I could go to dinner with him tomorrow — that is tonight — at the American Embassy."

"Very gallant," said Dr. von Winterfeldt dryly. "You warn him that he is to be shot and he invites you to join him for dinner!"

"Dr. von Winterfeldt! That never entered his mind —"

"I'm sure it will enter Christoph's mind," I said.

"We are not going to tell him," she said.

"Maybe *we* aren't, but I'm certainly going to tell him."

"Peter, I *forbid* you —"

Dr. von Winterfeldt silenced us by clearing his throat. "I believe you came here to seek my advice, Helena."

"Yes, of course, I'm terribly sorry —"

"I think we had better take some action in this situation. For the sake of record, just in case — ah . . . something happens, we will make a report of these admittedly meager facts, but make this report at the highest level. At the same time we will see if the Prussian State Police can locate these gentlemen and keep them under observation." He turned to me: "May I have those names again?"

I gave him the only names I knew: Karl Tillessen, Hermann Fischer, and Kern.

Back behind his desk, Dr. von Winterfeldt wrote down the names and picked up the telephone. "Schulenburg? Please connect me with the Minister of the Interior."

Long ago and far away the doctors always told me, "Don't *ever* take a drink if you feel you've got to have

one," but when Helena offered tea I diffidently asked if
she had any gin.

"Of course I have gin! What an excellent idea. . . .
Clara, the English bottle at the very back, please, and the
green bottle of Martini & Rossi, and a glass pitcher with
only pieces of ice. You understand? No water in the
pitcher, only ice. And a long spoon, please. And you can
use the sherry glasses, I think."

The maid went out and left us alone in the big sunny
living room of Helena's apartment: yellow wallpaper,
fresh flowers on every table, tall french windows leading
to a little balcony, a view of treetops along the Lützowufer, the Landwehr Canal, and the old townhouses on
the other side. The french windows were open, and we
could hear the traffic in the street below.

It was a beautiful room, filled with elegant and expensive things from different periods: Biedermeier furniture
and Oriental carpets she must have inherited, a few small
paintings — a Degas figure study, a brown girl by Gau-
guin, a Pascin watercolor of two women on a bed, a large
formal portrait of a statuesque blonde woman in the black
robes of Mozart's Queen of the Night — presumably Helena's mother — and a great many photographs of Helena
in stage costumes, Helena with other actors, with theatre
directors, with bemedaled officers. There was a grand piano, and more silver-framed photographs on top of the
piano: Helena's father, much younger, sitting on a beautiful horse with a blonde little girl up front: Helena in her
wedding veil beside a boy in a splendid white uniform;
Walther Rathenau, black eyes, black goatee, white tie and
tails, scowling above the bold inscription to "Die *Schönste*
Helena!" and Christoph Keith, bareheaded, grinning, his
fur-lined flight jacket unbuttoned to reveal the new Iron
Cross dangling just below his collar button. . . . I turned
around. Helena was looking out over the canal.

"I just don't know what to tell him," I said.

"Tell him the truth."

"But he'll be furious! He'll say we've betrayed him."

"Just blame it on me."

"Are you really going to dinner with Rathenau tonight?"

"Yes, why not?"

"But what will Christoph say?"

"He's busy guarding Kaspar. Why shouldn't I do something else?"

"Does he like you going out with other men?"

"With other men?"

"Well, Dr. Rathenau is certainly another man —"

"Oh, I understand your question." She smiled. The maid came in with a tray. "Just put it on the coffee table, please. Mister Ellis will mix the cocktails."

I poured the gin and a little vermouth over the few pieces of ice in the pitcher, stirred gently, filled the two little sherry glasses, and handed her one of them.

She raised it and looked at me. "Thank you for coming with me. And thank you for being such a good friend."

The first martini in a long time. Although it wasn't cold enough, it warmed my heart a little.

"Christoph is not jealous of Dr. Rathenau," said Helena. She sipped her drink, then looked into the glass. "A little hard to tell you . . . Dr. Rathenau has many close friendships with women. Women like him, they admire him for his imagination, for his brilliant intellect, perhaps even for his fortune and his position, but these relationships are not —" Helena suddenly swallowed all of her drink, put her glass back on the tray, folded her hands and looked into my eyes. "His relationships with women are not . . . physical relationships." Her cheeks were turning red.

"Are you sure?"

"*Quite* sure. People in our circles know about it, it's not such a terrible thing, though sad for him, and lonely."

Silence, broken by the ringing of the telephone in the hall.

The maid appeared: "Herr Oberleutnant, Your Highness."

Helena stood up and walked out into the hall, leaving the door open.

— He's right here with me. . . . Because we have just made a visit — to your uncle. . . . Which one do you think? Dr. von Winterfeldt. . . . Yes. . . . Yes. . . . More or less the whole story . . . Yes. *I said Yes!* . . . Tillessen, and I think two other names that Kaspar has told to Peter . . . .

— Are you finished now?

... ...

— I know. . . . I know, yes.

... ...

— May I say something now?

... ...

— Oh my dear, how can you talk that way? I *do* understand, I understand only too well!

— Christoph, I'm sorry, I don't agree with you. And Peter does not agree with you. . . . Your uncle telephoned the Minister of the Interior. . . . Yes, the Minister himself . . . Yes. . . . Yes. . . . Apparently the state police are going to look for Tillessen and the other. . . . I did not call them, *your uncle* called them. That's *his* opinion about how to protect your precious name. And he is a judge! So will you please stop shouting at me? . . .

— How is Kaspar? . . . All right, yes, I will send Peter home now. . . . No, you will not! I will not be here, I'm going out to dinner. . . . Mr. Houghton, the American Ambassador . . . No, with Walther Rathenau . . . Because he invited me. You are busy on your watch duty, aren't you? . . . last night . . . At his house . . . Rathenau's, of course . . . Because I went over there to warn him again, and you know what? You know who was there for dinner? Dr. Helfferich. *I swear it!* I was in the same room. . . . To ask Helfferich to stop these endless attacks, to persuade him that they cannot conduct our foreign policy under this pressure from the Right, and Helfferich agreed, although he is sure that Rathenau is wrong he promised to stop these attacks —

. . . .

— What?

. . . .

. . . .

— Oh my God, Christoph! It's in the paper? Oh that *swine!* The very next day?

I ran down to the corner, bought the night edition of the *Berliner Tageblatt* and carried it back to Helena's apartment. She read the story to me while I drank another martini.

Just after lunch Dr. Karl Helfferich, leader of the Nationalist party, had addressed a crowded session of the Reichstag and delivered what was so far the most savage attack against the Wirth cabinet, its foreign policy, and the architect of that policy:

The people of the occupied Saarland are supposed to depend upon their German culture? What a helpful suggestion! What about their German government? After what *this* German government has done (or *not* done) for the Germans of Silesia, there's nothing left for the Germans of the Rhineland and the Saar except *absolute despair!*

The whole world — not just the people of our occupied provinces — must have the feeling that this government has abjectly surrendered to the League of Nations — that is, to the Allies. Herr Dr. Rathenau's policy of fulfillment has caused the appalling depreciation of our German currency;

it has utterly crushed the German middle class;

it has brought poverty and misery upon countless families;

it has driven countless men and women to despair, to suicide;

it has sent abroad enormous portions of our nation's capital;

and it has shaken our industrial and social order to its very foundations!

Roars of applause in the Reichstag.

Helena dropped the newspaper to the carpet. "Oh, the swine! Hypocritical swine! Everything that's been done to Germany is the fault of Walther Rathenau. Isn't it convenient for them!" She rubbed her eyes and slumped back in the sofa. "You'd better go now, Peter. I must dress for dinner, and I don't want you here when he arrives. He will be in a terrible mood."

"I really don't think you ought to be with him tonight, Helena."

"On the contrary, I *must* be with him! You understand that, don't you, Peter? Do what you can to quiet my angry friend, will you please? He's going to the Bank in the morning, isn't he? Tell him I expect him here for lunch. Good night, Peter — and thank you."

21.

SATURDAY, JUNE 24, 1922

— Hello?

— Hallo?

— Yes?

— Villa Keith?

— Yes, Villa Keith.

— Peter, is that you?

— Helena? Where are you? What time is it?

— I'm back in my apartment, it is . . . let me see . . . twenty minutes after twelve, and I want to know what is happening over there.

— Over here everybody's asleep. Had a bad evening. I made some Kraut martinis.

— You made *what?*

— Invented a new drink. They had no gin, we sent Meier down to the bar in Roseneck, only thing he could get there was potato schnapps, so we made a pitcher of martinis with vermouth and schnapps, you see, a Kraut martini — I don't think it will become very popular. . . .

— And you got drunk!

— Helena . . . What else was there to do? Christoph was . . . he was just beside himself when I got here —

— About our visit to his uncle?

— About *everything!* About his uncle, about Kaspar, about Helfferich's speech in the Reichstag, about your driving around in Rathenau's car. . . . He was going over to the American embassy to fetch you out.

— Peter, he wasn't!

— Yes he was! I told him you wouldn't come, he'd just make an ass of himself. Then he was going over there to stand in front of the embassy gate to guard you when you came out, but by that time he couldn't stand up himself. . . . I've never seen him like this, Helena.

— Poor Christoph. I think he loves me.

— Of course he loves you. How was dinner?

— Oh it was a mistake for me to go. They didn't want ladies, they wanted to talk politics. Economics. I spent the whole evening in a corner with Mrs. Houghton and two other women. . . . Walther Rathenau had Mr. Houghton send for Hugo Stinnes.

— Hugo who?

— You don't know Hugo Stinnes? He is the richest man in Germany now, coal mines and steel mills and factories, and he's made it all out of the inflation. He borrows millions and millions of marks from the banks, he buys these coal mines and factories, then he pays back his debts with money that's worth only a fraction of what it was worth when he borrowed it — or better still he simply borrows *more* money to repay the debts, and those idiots, they go right on lending to him, supposedly because he employs thousands of workers, he provides work. . . . I think they have all become a little crazy. . . .

— And Rathenau wanted him at this party?

— Yes, because Stinnes is like Helfferich, a violent opponent of Rathenau's policies, and they were talking about how to pay our reparations to the French with coal, and Rathenau said "Let us see how Stinnes would do this" and the ambassador called him, he was at the Hotel Esplanade, he came over and they talked and talked and it got so late I said we cannot keep the Houghtons up all night, so we left.

— Who left?

— Well, everybody, the party was over, we took Stinnes in Walther Rathenau's automobile, they dropped me here at my place, and then they went on to the Esplanade to continue talking.

— You think they're still there?

— I don't know, I suppose so. Walter Rathenau keeps trying to convince these people, he was terribly depressed about Helfferich's speech but he felt he was making progress with Stinnes, I think. . . . Peter, I'm so grateful to you for distracting Christoph, he should not worry so much about me.

— Well, but what about Kaspar? What are we going to do about Kaspar? We've only got two hundred milligrams left, that's about one more day, maybe. Are we going out in the street to hunt for morphine after all?

How long can we keep this up?

— I would stop right now, Peter.

— Stop giving him Amytal?

— Yes.

— What happens when he wakes up?

— Who knows? But he must wake up eventually. What is the use of postponing it — and maybe causing an addiction?

— It's not up to me.

— Peter, you are giving the injections!

— Not my brother.

— Oh I *know* it's not your brother — and it's not your country, it's not your trouble, I just *wish* we had not dragged you into this!

— Helena . . . I can't say this clearly but I want you to know . . . I want you to know I'm not sorry that you trust me, that Christoph trusts me . . . and I feel sort of . . . like I'm part of your life. In Paris I was nothing, a tourist, I didn't know anybody except some Americans who were tourists too, but here . . . I don't know how to say it —

— You say it very well, my dear. Now go to sleep, please. It is already tomorrow.

Christoph was sound asleep on the living room sofa, mouth open, snoring. Kaspar was sound asleep in his bed. My head ached and my mouth was parched. In the bathroom I drank a glass of water. Then I took the box with the remaining Amytal and the hypodermic syringe out of the medicine chest. I went downstairs and turned off all the lights and then I went out into the silent street and walked along the sidewalk under the big old horse chestnuts until I came to a rainwater culvert. I leaned over, carefully dropped the box behind the grating, heard the splash. Then I returned to the Villa Keith and went to bed.

Knock at the door.

Headache.

Another knock. "Mister Ellis!"

Headache. Dry mouth. Faint nausea.

"What do you want, Meier?"

"Telephone, Mister Ellis. Herr Oberleutnant. Very urgent, sir. He told me to wake you, please. He is waiting on the telephone."

"Well, where is he? What time is it?"

"He is at the Bank, sir. It is after eleven o'clock. He says it is very urgent."

"All right, all right, tell him I'm coming."

22.

WHAT HAPPENED?

I didn't know what happened. Sometimes in my dreams I dream that I heard the shots, but I couldn't have heard them. I was sound asleep, half a mile away. I do remember — I *think* I do remember — that as I went downstairs to take the telephone call I heard the loud distinctive klaxons of the Berlin police cars.

I didn't know what happened, and neither did most of the people who wrote the hundreds of thousands or millions of words that were published during the uproar of the next weeks, so I think the best way to tell this part is to quote three very different witnesses.

Ernst von Salomon was sentenced to five years in prison for his part in what happened that morning. A veteran of the Freikorps, same age as Kaspar Keith, he eventually became a writer, and in 1930 he published *Die Geächteten,* which means "The Outlaws." He called it a novel.

On Saturday the 24th of June, 1922, about half-past ten in the morning, the car was parked in a side street off the Königsallee in the suburb Grunewald, not far from Rathenau's home. Fischer stood on watch at the corner where the street joined the Königsallee. Kern took his old rubber coat out of the car. Techow was fastening the hood. He reported to Kern that the oil pump was busted, but it would do for a short, fast ride.

Kern remained cool and unconcerned. I stood in front of him and looked at him. I was leaning against the car, trembling so hard that I thought they had

started the motor. Kern put on the overcoat. I wanted
to say something to him, anything warm, reassuring.
Finally I asked: "If we're caught, what shall we say
the motive was?" . . .

"If you're caught, just blame it all on me," said Kern
cheerfully. "That goes without saying. Under no circumstances tell them the truth. Say anything at all.
God, it makes so little difference what you say. Say
what the people will understand, the people who believe what they read in the papers. As far as I'm concerned, you can tell them he was one of the Elders of
Zion, or that he married his sister to Radek, or any
other nonsense you can think of. . . . They're never going to understand what motivated us anyway. But don't
let them catch you. Soon, every man will be needed."
He pulled the leather flying cap over his head. Encir-
cled by the tight brown frame, his face looked bold and
open. . . . He lifted the submachine gun out of the
trunk and slid it carefully between the front seats. Then
he turned and looked directly into my face: "Take it
easy, kid. You're a sharp one, don't let them grind you
down. And I've got one request: let Wirth stay alive;
he's a brave man, and quite harmless." He leaned
closer, grabbed my jacket, and said quietly: "You can't
imagine how glad I am that it's all behind me."

At this moment a small maroon automobile drove
slowly up the Königsallee. Fischer raced back from the
corner and silently climbed into the back of the car.
Techow got behind the wheel; his face was suddenly
gray, looking as if it were carved from wood. Kern
shook my hand, then stood up in the car, tall, his overcoat flapping. The car began to tremble. I jumped to
the door and put my hand in, but nobody took it. Kern
sat down. The car began to move.

The car began to move; I wanted to stop it. It moved
with a humming tone. I wanted to scream, I wanted to
run, I stood there paralyzed, empty, numb, completely
alone on the gray street. Kern looked back once more.
I saw his face once more. Then the car roared around
the corner.

A new house was being built on the Königsallee. One
of the bricklayers gave this account to reporters from the
Vossische Zeitung:

About 10:45 two cars came up the Königsallee from the Hundekehle. The first carried a single, older gentleman in the back seat. We could see him clearly because the top was down. The second car was bigger, a high-powered six-seater open convertible. There are always lots of cars in the Königsallee, but we all noticed this one because of the fancy leather outfits these men were wearing — the driver in front, two others in the back. They wore long leather driving coats and leather caps that covered everything but their faces. . . .

When the smaller car slowed down for the S-curve, the larger car began to pass, forcing the smaller one all the way over to our side of the street. The gentleman in the back seat turned to see if there would be a crash. At that moment, one of the men in the leather coats put a machine pistol to his shoulder, leaned forward, and fired a burst directly at the gentleman in the smaller car. He was so close that he really didn't need to aim. I could see his face as he was shooting. It was a healthy open face — the sort of face we call an officer's face. . . . Then the other man in leather stood up and threw a hand grenade into the smaller car, the big car pulled away, turned the corner, and disappeared down the Wallotstrasse.

In the meantime, the chauffeur of the little car had brought it to a stop, shouting "Help! Help!" The gentleman in the back was slumped down, covered with blood — and then the grenade exploded, throwing him into the air. . . . I don't know why the whole car was not destroyed. . . . A young girl ran over from the trolley stop, climbed into the back of the car and tried to help, but the gentleman was unconscious — if he wasn't dead already. The chauffeur turned the car around and drove to the police station, which is only thirty yards back down the Königsallee. . . .

When Christoph telephoned, he had just heard the news from Helena. Rathenau's butler had called; he wanted her to tell Rathenau's mother before somebody else did, and Helena had rushed off to do this in person. Christoph asked me to meet him at Helena's apartment as soon as I could get there. Then he hung up.

What about Kaspar? No Amytal in over twenty-four hours. Might he just get up and disappear?

I looked in. Meier had brought a glass of milk and a roll.

"You awake, Kaspar?"

His eyes were open and he nodded, but he didn't focus on me.

Should I tell him? Yes, I should tell him, but I was afraid to, so I didn't. He still seemed to be thoroughly under the influence of the drug, and after a week in bed his muscles would not get him very far. I told the Meiers where I was going, and walked down to Roseneck to catch the trolley into town.

People were pouring into the streets. The traffic clogged. Nobody knew exactly what had happened, or where, and people shouted every sort of rumor at each other: a bomb had gone off in Rathenau's car; a bomb had gone off in the Reichstag; Wirth and Rathenau were both dead; the Reichswehr had declared martial law . . . men were climbing up on tables of the sidewalk cafés, making speeches to the crowds that formed around them. The Republic is in mortal danger. This is another Putsch from the Right. The workers must stand together again. Flags in the streets and flags in the windows.

Somewhere along the Kurfürstendamm I got out of the trolley and walked the rest of the way, through streets that became hot and increasingly crowded with worried, confused-looking people who didn't seem to know what to do but wanted to do *something*.

That is what I saw. Here is what Ernst von Salomon saw:

Mobs swirling around in the squares of the city, marching, driven by the sudden collapse of their orderly world . . . I felt within me a glow of unbearable pain, the insane desire to shoot right into the mob, to throw myself in as a blazing wedge that would split open the impacted core of this madness. Trembling, I reached for my weapon, but no worthwhile target appeared in the mass of empty faces; I tried to telephone others of our group, but the secret power had swallowed them too; filled with seething hatred, I ran through the streets, ready to murder the first person I met . . . but the racing seconds cheated me of that last compulsion. I wanted to pick off my sacrifice from a level above the nameless masses, President Ebert or

Chancellor Wirth, but then one single thought singed my blood; bathed in cold sweat, I stood crowded up against a wall, and I thought "Kern," I could only think of "Kern." But Kern was lost.

Years later, as I read those words, I could only think of Kaspar Keith, just waking from his amobarbital dreams while von Salomon and maybe Tillessen and who knows how many others were skulking through the crowded streets, grinding their teeth, looking for other worthy targets. . . .

Helena's maid told me that she had not returned, but Christoph was out on the balcony, hands in his pockets, staring down at the marching columns now forming on both sides of the canal.

"We can get rid of the Amytal," he said, without turning around. "We had enough after all."

I told him I had already done that. I didn't tell him when.

"What did Helena say when she called you?" I asked.

"She said: 'You can let your brother out now. The deed is done.' "

"Christoph . . . this business with Kaspar —"

He turned. "Peter, I want to express my deepest gratitude for what you have done —"

"Thank you, but I want to make my point: They got Rathenau. Who's next? Wirth? Ebert? You can't keep Kaspar under supervision forever. We kept him out of this one — maybe — but we can't do it again. He's a grown man. There's no way you can control his life."

Christoph nodded. We remained on the balcony silently watching the turmoil until a taxi nudged its way through the crowds and stopped directly below. Bobby von Waldstein climbed out and held the door for Helena, who was dressed entirely in black; even as she glanced up at us we could not see her face, because she was wearing a veil.

We were at the door of the apartment as they came up the stairs. Helena walked into Christoph's arms without a word, and through the veil I could see that her eyes were closed as she leaned against him. Bobby walked past me into the apartment, also without a word, and without looking at me. The maid and I stood there, not knowing what else to do.

After a moment Helena stepped back, removed her hat and her veil, handed them to the maid, and walked into the living room touching her hair. "I have to wash my face. Peter, will you make me one of your martinis, please."

"How was Frau Rathenau?" asked Christoph.

"A pillar of ice. 'My son gave his life for his Fatherland,' was all that she would say."

"Did you have to tell her?"

"No, two police commanders were already there, then the police president, then Chancellor Wirth came with police on motorcycles — the house was full of people, his sister came, there was no use my staying so I left, and as my taxi passed the spot in the Königsallee where it happened, there was Bobby in the crowd."

"What was Bobby doing there?" asked Christoph as he followed her out of the room.

The maid brought the gin and the vermouth and a pitcher of ice, and I walked over to the balcony, where Bobby was looking down at the marching people.

"Bobby, may I fix you a drink too?"

He turned and glared at me. I hardly recognized him. "Am I to understand that you knew this was going to happen?"

"Bobby, everybody in Germany knew it was going to happen."

"But you had specific information? Names?"

"We reported them, Bobby. Didn't Helena tell you? We went to see Dr. von Winterfeldt, and he called the Minister —"

"When was this?"

"Yesterday."

"*Yesterday?*"

"That was the first time we had names. . . . I mean that was the first time we could see Winterfeldt, but even *he* said there wasn't enough to arrest anybody —"

"You knew something Sunday night, a week ago, when I drove you to Nikolassee!"

Jesus Christ, I thought, feeling a cramp around my heart. If *he* doesn't believe us, who will?

The telephone rang and the maid went to answer it. We heard her knocking.

"Herr Oberleutnant? Herr Meier, bitte?"

Christoph took the call in Helena's dressing room. I

couldn't hear what he was saying, but a moment later he
appeared.

"That was Meier. The police were just at our house.
They took Kaspar to the Alexanderplatz."

I spent the next few days in and out of central police
headquarters, so Count Kessler must complete this part of
the story.

Count Harry Kessler was a rich, cosmopolitan patron
of the arts, diplomat, diarist, possibly the illegitimate son
of Kaiser Wilhelm I . . . an aristocrat with liberal political
leanings, a sensitive observer who went everywhere and
knew everyone of importance. He was a close friend of
Walter Rathenau, whose biography he published in
1928.

The Reichstag met at three o'clock. Helfferich's appearance was greeted with shouts of "Murderer! Murderer! Out with the murderers!" The tumult subsided
only when Helfferich had disappeared. Later in the day
Wirth spoke. "Ever since we first began to serve this
new state under the flag of the Republic, millions have
been spent in pouring a deadly poison into the body of
our people. From Königsberg to Constance the campaign of murder has menaced this country of ours, to
whose service we have devoted all our powers of body
and mind. In return we are told that what we are doing
is a crime against the German people, and that we de-
serve to be brought to justice [cries of "No, Helfferich!
Helfferich!" from the Left]; and then people are surprised when mere deluded boys resort to murder."

Next day, which was Sunday, there was a special session of the Reichstag. Wirth did not intend to speak.
But when he entered the House it was almost empty,
most of the members being in the lobbies discussing the
situation. He turned to me and whispered that as there
seemed to be nothing in particular going on he would
seize the opportunity of saying a few words in memory
of our poor friend Walther Rathenau. As soon as he
began speaking members flocked in, and then he
launched his indictment against the Nationalists. "When
a statesman of the rank of Dr. Helfferich speaks here as
he did, what must be the effect on the brains of youth
who have combined in secret or semi-secret Chauvinist,

Nationalist, Antisemitic and Monarchist organizations? It is evident that the result is a sort of *'Feme'* . . . The real enemies of our country are those who instill this poison into our people. We know where we have to seek them. *The Enemy stands on the Right!"* he exclaimed, pointing at the empty benches of the Nationalists, only a few of whom had dared retain their seats, sitting there ill at ease and pale as death, while three-quarters of the House rose and faced them. The effect was tremendous. . . .

Not since the assassination of Abraham Lincoln has the death of a statesman so shaken a whole nation. The trades unions had decreed a general holiday throughout the Reich from midday Tuesday to early Wednesday morning. Stupendous processions, such as Germany had never witnessed, marched in order under the Republican flag through all the cities of the land. Over a million took part in Berlin, a hundred and fifty thousand in Munich and Chemnitz, a hundred thousand in Hamburg, Breslau, Elberfeld, Essen. Never before had a German citizen been so honoured. The response which had been denied to Rathenau's life and thought was now accorded to his death.

Count Kessler died in 1937, an exile in France. His diaries were published in 1971. This is the entry for Tuesday, 27 June 1922:

Rathenau's funeral. From noon on all work stopped as a token of mourning and protest against political murder.

The funeral ceremony was held in the Chamber of the Reichstag. The coffin lay in state, mounted behind the speaker's rostrum and under a large black canopy suspended from the ceiling. The Chamber was hung with black and transformed into a sea of flowers and plants. Enormous palms flanked the coffin at its four corners. The speaker's rostrum was shrouded in black and buried, as was the Government Bench, beneath magnificent wreaths with ribbons in the Republican colours, black-red-gold. The galleries, draped with crepe, were decorated with banks of blue and pink hydrangeas. Long crepe veils hung from the ceiling arc-lights. . . . The galleries, like the Chamber itself, were packed. There was not one empty seat, not even among Nationalists. The focal point was the coffin, draped with a huge flag in the national colours. At its foot there lay two immense wreaths of red and white flowers, to right and left of the colours.

At noon the Chancellor led Rathenau's mother into the Imperial box. She sat down in the seat whose back was still embellished with a crowned W. The old lady was evidently in full control of herself, but her complexion as pale as wax and the face behind the veil might have been carved from stone. These features, all colour drained from them through grief, touched me most. She stared motionlessly at the coffin. Kreuter, who visited her yesterday, says that she is the embodiment of retribution. Her sole desire is to take time to write to Helfferich, condemning him as the murderer of her son, and then die.

Wirth, having escorted her to her place, left the box. A moment later he was to be seen below in the procession led by Ebert. The orchestra, out of sight in the vestibule behind the coffin, played the Egmont overture. Ebert stepped in front of the coffin and spoke, very softly, almost inaudible from emotion, but well. After him came Bell, representing the Reichstag, his tone clearly articulated, his words moving. Lastly, and mediocre, a Pastor Korell on behalf of the Democrats. Then the musicians played the Siegfried Funeral March from Götterdämmerung. This undoubtedly brought the ceremony inside the Chamber to its highest pitch of emotion. In the circumstances the effect was overwhelming. Many of those around me wept. The historic significance of his death echoed from the music in the hearts of those present.

The coffin was carried through the lobby to the entrance stairway. At the foot of the steps stood a Reichswehr company, in field-grey uniform, steel-helmeted. The drums rolled and the resonant tones of a funeral march rose muffled into the air, strangely like a distant thunder. The coffin, wrapped in the national colours, was laid on the hearse which was swathed in red roses. Slowly, to the accompaniment of drum-beats, the cortège set off. In spite of the rain, or perhaps because of this grey gossamer appropriate to the muffled roll of the drums, the impression made upon the spectators was almost even more intense than it had been in the Chamber. Lassalle's dream of passing through the Brandenburger Tor as President of a Republic of Germany was today fulfilled by the Jew Rathenau because of his martyrdom in the service of the German people.

BOOK THREE

FASTNACHT

THE WITCHES'
SABBATH

I was already on vacation in Westerland. Hundreds of bathers were splashing in the surf. It was exactly like the day the murder of Franz Ferdinand was announced. A band was playing for the holiday crowds when suddenly, like white petrels, a flock of newsboys stormed across the boardwalk: "Walther Rathenau assassinated!"

Panic broke out and shattered through the whole Reich. Instantly the mark plunged — and continued straight down until it reached the millions and billions and trillions of fantasy, of madness. Only now did the real witches' sabbath begin; by contrast, our Austrian inflation — 15,000 to 1 — was child's play. It would take a book to describe what happened — and today such a book would sound like a fairy tale. . . .

—Stefan Zweig, *The World of Yesterday*

23.

SILENCE—WITH VOICES

If you are raised in the Friendly Persuasion you learn to sit in silence. The silence can continue for a long time if nobody is moved to speak, but even as a little kid I was not restless or fidgety because I enjoyed the silence. They tell you to "Heed the intimations within."

What was I doing at First Day Meeting after all these years? And what a very strange one: the spartan living room of a third-floor apartment in the Dorotheenstrasse, a dozen miscellaneous benches and chairs arranged to form a hollow square around the iron stove, from which a handful of glowing coals gave forth a little warmth and a little light, the cold November rain streaming against the windowpanes — and the faces. A few were sedate, serious, well-fed Philadelphia faces, appropriately composed; the rest were mostly gaunt, politely puzzled, the faces of the German guests.

I had fought it as hard as I could.

"Miss Boatwright, there must be a thousand people in Berlin who could interpret what is said at a Meeting."

"Not a thousand, I think, who were born into the Society of Friends, who have attended Meeting all their lives —"

"Does that really make such a difference?"

"I think so."

"Miss Boatwright, I haven't been to Meeting in . . . years."

"I know that." A long look. I understood what it meant. I dropped my eyes.

"Miss Boatwright, my German's not that good —"

"The people here assure me that thy German is the best they've ever heard from an American. That handsome Fräulein did her job. What was her name?"

It was only an experiment, Miss Boatwright told me. In
addition to providing food, the American Friends Service
Committee wanted to spread the Quaker Message to the
Germans. "Our task is to interpret a friendly Germany to
the rest of the world, and a friendly rest of the world to
Germany. The Germans feel terribly isolated. We want
to change that, by bringing all kinds of people into normal
personal contact." A few Americans directing the food
distribution had started gathering for Weekly Meetings,
and now they wanted to include some German "friends
of Friends." Miss Boatwright therefore composed a polite
letter of invitation, explaining the simple procedure of a
Meeting for Worship — and here we were, a room full of
silent faces including, to my surprise, the faces of Alfred
and Sigrid von Waldstein.

Heed the intimations within?

In retrospect, the death of Walther Rathenau was a
watershed not only for the Germans but also for me.
Whether I had done right or wrong, I had thrown myself
into their lives and into their history.

We only accomplished part of Christoph's mission.
Kaspar was arrested, all three of us were grilled for hours,
first by detectives, then by an icy middle-aged *Unter-
suchungsrichter,* the investigating judge who was prepar-
ing the case against the murderers, but the call on Dr.
von Winterfeldt made the difference for us.

Within a few hours the police had caught all the partic-
ipants except the actual killers. It was not the names I
had obtained from Kaspar; it was their car again. They
had rented the second car. Techow, the driver, returned it
to the garage and carried off a duffel bag containing the
long overcoats and the flying caps which had disguised
them, but before he dumped the bag into the Landwehr
Canal he checked the contents. One of the flying caps was
missing. Techow sent his sixteen-year-old brother, a high-
school student, back to the garage to look for the cap. By
that time news of the murder was all over Berlin, the
garage owner became suspicious, the boy became pan-
icky, the police were called. . . .

Each arrest led to others. Over eighty people were
pulled in. Two weeks later the investigating judge released everybody except the inner circle: Tillessen, von
Salomon, the Techow brothers and a few more. They

were held for trial by the Constitutional Court in Leipzig.

Kern and Fischer disappeared. We heard later that they sailed far out into the Wannsee and spent hours sleeping in the sunshine. They left Berlin, made their way to the Baltic, missed their connection with a boat that was to take them to Sweden, then switched back toward central Germany, hiding in the daytime and walking through the forests at night, the objects of an enormous manhunt. One night in July people noticed a light in what was supposed to be an empty castle on the river Saale, in the province of Thüringen. The police were called, the castle was surrounded, Kern appeared at a tower window, the police opened fire, and Kern was killed. Fischer put Kern's body on a bed, sat down on the other bed, and blew his brains out.

When Kaspar Keith was released from the Alexanderplatz he didn't come home.

The rain beat against the windows and nobody seemed moved to speak. The Germans were certainly not going to say anything before the Americans, and the Americans — I was pretty sure — would wait for Miss Boatwright, so the question was: how long would *she* wait?

One obstacle to the self-awareness that is supposed to develop inside you during silent worship is "selfish or degrading desire." That's what we were taught.

Here I am waiting for God to speak within me, but the emotions I feel are insatiable appetite — and shame. The thing with Bärbel and with Baby is completely out of control. Does Miss Boatwright know? If not, it won't be long. But the worst is that Falke knows and Mutti Bauer knows, and they seem to be all for it! Baby goes to school now, Bärbel poses, Mutti cooks, Falke runs around to the galleries trying to sell the pictures we produce — and I pay for everything, because I've never had so much money in my life.

The money doesn't come from painting.

When my forward delivery contracts came due in September the mark had fallen so far that one dollar bought 1,200 marks on the Amsterdam Exchange. After I settled my contracts and paid Waldstein & Co. what I owed them I still had a profit of $2,000.

"No more forward contracts," said Dr. Strassburger. "Nobody wants to take the other side. I would advise you

to leave five hundred dollars in Amsterdam and use the
rest to purchase stocks on the Berlin Exchange. That only
requires twenty-five percent margin. You can give us a
note for the balance. If the stocks go up in price, you sell
enough to pay your note."

"And what if they go down?"

He shrugged. "You still have five hundred dollars in
Amsterdam."

"But I'll owe you more than that."

"Correct," said Dr. Strassburger, looking at me calmly
across his folded hands.

I did what he suggested. By the middle of November
my shares had gone up but I didn't reduce my note. I
bought more stocks.

It is hard to explain how it was. I didn't even have to
go to a bank like the other speculators. I would get up
quite late and Meier would serve my breakfast and then
I would telephone Christoph, who would tell me how my
stocks were doing, I should sell this and buy that, pay off
one note and renew another. . . . I tried to enter each
transaction into a little cash ledger I carried around with
me.

Each time a note came due the marks in which it was
payable had depreciated to a fraction of the original principal amount. I didn't understand how the banks could
operate this way until it was explained that they were allowed to discount — that is, *sell* — their customers' notes
to the Reichsbank, so in effect the government was financ-
ing the whole crazy system. In any event, I kept accumulating more stocks in steel companies and coal mines
and chemical plants — and more debts to Waldstein &
Co. Once in a while I sold some stocks to pay my expenses, which amounted to very little in terms of dollars
but which had become the principal support of the Keith
and Falke households.

Heed the intimations within.

Sigrid von Waldstein had smiled when she saw me, and
I was glad. Bobby's reaction on the day of the murder
had reflected the reaction of his family: an instinctive
drawing back, sort of looking at us with different eyes.
Despite Dr. von Winterfeldt, Kaspar's name appeared in
the newspapers. Only once, when he was released, but
that was enough. The Waldsteins didn't like this connec-

tion. Christoph felt it at the Bank. I felt it when I telephoned Lili to ask if she wanted to go sailing on Sunday. She would like to go sailing but she had to visit a cousin in Potsdam. . . .

Helena and Sigrid intervened. Of course I wasn't there, but I could imagine Helena shouting at Baron Eduard: Christoph was trying to keep his crazy brother *out of it!* And he did keep him out of it, the judge let Kaspar go, and Peter Ellis wanted to help the family —

— and Walther Rathenau is dead! They should have called the police.

The police would not have done anything! I told you what Gerichtsrat Winterfeldt said —

That's his uncle. The wife's a Ludendorff. . . .

In the end they let Alfred make the decision.

Miss Boatwright stood up.

As she had suggested, I stood up too. She spoke very slowly and paused after every phrase, and I tried to translate.

They told me that I did all right, but of course I can't remember any of it. She didn't offer any words of welcome or explanation — nothing of that sort. She must have plunged right into her thoughts; they might have been about anything at all, just a few simple sentences, perhaps about the need for individuals in different countries to speak to each other as *people,* instead of nations speaking to each other through emissaries. Then she sat down, I sat down, the room was silent again.

"Do you think I should resign from the Bank?" Christoph had asked one evening in July. His parents had returned from Pomerania, and his mother was eating dinner with us.

"Why should you do that?" I answered.

"In view of the circumstances, perhaps it would be the honorable thing."

"What circumstances? You haven't done anything wrong, you haven't done anything dishonorable —"

His mother suddenly spoke up: "Of course this would never have happened under the Kaiser."

"What wouldn't, Mother?"

"This whole . . . scandal. They would not have made a Jew the Foreign Minister."

"*Mother!* You think it was Rathenau's fault that they shot him?"

"These people are powerful enough already. The banks, the law courts, the newspapers, the department stores . . . now they are going to be cabinet ministers, they are going to govern Germany?"

"The Kaiser had no more faithful servants, Mother. You know that."

"Perhaps. That doesn't mean we want them to *rule* us, does it?" Frau Keith wiped her mouth with her napkin, rolled it into the silver ring and left the table. She was crying.

We had not heard a word from Kaspar.

One of the Americans stood up, a reedy pale young man with heavy spectacles. The past months in Berlin reminded him of a poem by Rainer Maria Rilke. He had translated it into English. He then began to read his English version without pausing for me to translate, but of course I could not have translated back into Rilke's words anyway. I didn't know what to do.

Alfred von Waldstein stood up. "If I may do so, I would like to repeat that poem in German, as Rilke wrote it."

> *Herr: es ist Zeit. Der Sommer war sehr gross.*
> *Leg deinen Schatten auf die Sonnenuhren,*
> *und auf den Fluren lass die Winde los. . . .*

Alfred recited all three verses from memory. Then he sat down. And he looked at me.

On the eighteenth of July all the newspapers reported the deaths of Kern and Fisher at Castle Saaleck. I was with Bärbel that evening and didn't get back to the Villa Keith until after midnight. On my bedside table was a piece of crested notepaper.

Dear Christoph,

My father has asked me to discuss the Rathenau matter with you and Peter Ellis. I would be glad to see you both at No. 4, Pariser Platz on the 20th at six o'clock.

Alfred

Their townhouse, in the shadow of the Brandenburg Gate, was supposed to be closed for the summer, but the moment we rang, a young underbutler opened the door, led us through huge echoing hallways, through a living room filled with ghostly lumps of white-draped furniture, into a cool dark library. The curtains had been parted just enough to let in some evening sunshine and to reveal a glimpse of city garden — grass and shrubbery and a fountain in front of a high brick wall.

Alfred turned away from the window, shook hands politely, and motioned us into the leather armchairs by the empty fireplace.

"I'm drinking some sherry. Will you join me?"

"No, thank you," said Christoph.

"No, thank you," said I.

Alfred nodded to the butler, who backed out and closed the door.

A woman stood up, a small thin woman of middle years, with transparent skin and mouse-colored hair tied back into a bun. She spoke in German, very slowly, so I stood up and tried to translate.

"I feel that the people of other nations hate the German people and I wonder why this is, because we do not hate the people of other nations. My son was killed in France, but he did not hate the French soldiers, and I do not hate the French soldiers. The War was not started by the people; the War was started by the kaisers and the ministers and the generals. Germany fought alone against the world, fought alone four years, and of course we were beaten, and now the people who beat us want us to pay enormous unbelievable sums in gold and coal and iron and steel, sums so high we cannot possibly pay them. Why is this? I do not understand it. I want to say that the Quakers are the only people from the other side — the only people I have met — who brought not only food for our starving children but also offered us a hand in friendship. And we will never forget it."

She sat down. I sat down.

The day after our interrogation at the Pariser Platz I got up later than usual, ate breakfast alone, and telephoned Christoph at the Bank. There was not much to report: the mark was falling steadily, my German stocks were becoming more valuable every day, I was to sit tight. Neither of us mentioned the Waldsteins.

"Are you going to Neukölln this afternoon?"

"Yes, of course, my lessons . . ."

"My friend, you are not getting in trouble, are you?"

"What do you mean?" Of course I knew what he meant, but why bring it up now, in the middle of a business call?

"Helena has heard stories about you. The artists are beginning to talk."

"About my pictures?"

"Not so much about your pictures as your models."

"Have you heard from Helena today?"

"No . . . I'm sorry, Peter, there is another call for me —"

I finished my coffee and went upstairs for a moment. The telephone rang. Meier appeared in the hall below. "Fräulein Elizabeth von Waldstein, Mister Ellis."

Oh look how *brown* you are! she said. And look how white I am, like chalk. Sailing on the Havel again? Oh I would like that so much. Will you ever take me sailing? You'd take Bärbel if she asked. You don't really like her better, you like her boobs and her ass. In that last picture, the two of us on the bed, you made me look like a boy. It's because we didn't have food, you know, when I was growing. I was hungry all the time, so hungry I couldn't go to sleep at night, and when I did sleep I had dreams about chocolate cake . . . one time, I was very little, some fellow brought Mutti a chocolate cake and it was so good but it made me sick to my stomach, I had to puke. . . .

Don't worry, they won't be home for an hour at least. You like me to do that? Mmmm . . . You like that? That's better than Bärbel does it? Mmmm?

Now that you're giving us the money for butter and eggs, I'm going to look like Bärbel, you wait. It won't be long. Yesterday Mutti beat an egg into a glass of milk and I drank the whole thing and I wasn't sick. And she wouldn't let Bärbel have any. It was all for me.

Or would you *rather* have me looking like a boy? Is that why you painted me that way, lying on my stomach like that? Bärbel on her back and me with my popo in the air . . . You want to do it to me like I was a boy? Hm? You *sure?* Some men just love that — pretend I'm a boy

when I'm really not a boy, so it's all right to do it that
way. It hurts a little but I'll do it with you. . . . No?
You sure? Why did you pose me with my ass like that,
looking like a boy? Oh don't be mad. I know you're not
a homo, I'm teasing you. . . . But you like *this,* don't
you? . . . Mmmm? . . . Just tell me I do it better than
Bärbel. . . . Tell me you love me better than Bärbel —
or I'll stop!

One of the older Americans stood up, so I stood up too.
Again I don't remember exactly what he said, but it was
something appropriate to the occasion and he said it
slowly, waiting for me to translate. I think he spoke about
the history of the Society of Friends, how it originally
developed under extreme oppression in England, how it
prospered in the United States, how it has changed, how
it is organized today, that it was the intention of certain
Friends here today to continue Weekly Meetings at this
location and that *all* persons interested in participating
were sincerely welcome. For those who would care to stay
for a short visit, coffee will be served in the room next
door.

He sat down and shook hands with Miss Boatwright.
Miss Boatwright turned and shook hands with me. The
Meeting was over.

24.

THE JUDGMENT OF PARIS

Germans take Christmas seriously, and they celebrate on
Christmas Eve, which created a problem for me: I
couldn't be in three places at the same time. I worried
about that for several weeks, which demonstrates how in-
sulated I was.

For most Germans, the Christmas of 1922 was turning
into a nightmare. By the middle of December one dollar
was worth more than 7,000 marks — and a pound of

butter that had cost 800 marks in November now cost
2,000 marks.

When I went shopping I had to pick up money at
Waldstein & Co. The cashier's messenger came into the
little consultation room carrying a maroon tin box, and
the wad of bills he put on the table had to be divided into
separate bundles, which I then distributed among the
pockets of my suit and my new double-breasted overcoat.

It was snowing. The faces in the streets looked cold
and gray and worried. The word *Ruhr!* was a scream in
the headlines of every newspaper, every day. The French
announced that if the Germans did not catch up in their
deliveries of coal and steel and telephone poles, the
French army would move into the region of Essen, Duis-
burg, Gelsenkirchen, Mülheim, Bochum, Dortmund —
the smoke-blackened cities, the valleys of factories and
coal mines and steel mills: *Ruhrgebiet*, industrial heart of
Germany.

Those were the headlines. Inside, the newspapers were
filled with offers to purchase gold and jewelry, wedding
rings, engagement rings. . . . "Unbelievable Prices!"

And yet the stores were filled with people buying
things. At the Kaufhaus des Westens, the huge department store, business was frantic; people streamed through
the revolving doors from the Wittenbergplatz, jammed
the aisles, packed into the elevators, pushed and shoved
each other to admire the displays: jewelry and evening
gowns and linen, glass from Bohemia and porcelain from
Saxony, beautiful books, toy trains pulled by real steam
locomotives, armies of lead soldiers arranged in battle
scenes from more successful wars. . . . While some people
had to sell their wedding rings to eat, other people —
people like me, people with the resources to speculate,
Americans, Englishmen, Frenchmen, Dutchmen, Bel-
gians, people from eastern Europe whose nationalities I
could not distinguish — all of these and many Germans
seemed to be loaded with paper marks, spending them as
fast as possible, converting them into Christmas presents
that would cost much more tomorrow than they cost today.

I bought: a brown cashmere cardigan for Frau Keith;
a leather handbag for Frau Meier; an identical handbag
for Mutti Bauer; and a tiny gold wristwatch for Lili. The

only problem was Bärbel versus Baby. Should I give both of them the same present? If I didn't, then whatever I gave one would seem better to the other.

Clutching my packages I allowed myself to be swept along in the crowds as I pondered my special puzzles. There was a giant Christmas tree in the central hall of the Kaufhaus des Westens. In front of the tree a chorus of children sang carols.

It was harder to see Lili in the winter. She lived with her parents in the mansion at No. 4, Pariser Platz. On weekdays she was driven to school in the Horch. After school she was either picked up in the Horch or she went to visit one of her classmates. On Saturdays she went riding in the Tiergarten — always with a group of girls under the supervision of a bony, sullen young woman from the Baltic, a war widow who supported herself by giving riding lessons. In the evenings Lili went to dancing classes — or to parties.

"Couldn't I rent a horse and ride along with them?" I asked Helena.

"*Rent* a horse?" Helena wrinkled her beautiful nose. "I've never heard of anyone renting a horse. Sounds unsafe. But in any event they wouldn't allow it. What if every young man wanted to ride along? Where would it end?" Helena giggled. We were drinking martinis in her apartment, waiting for Christoph to come over from the Bank.

"Helena, you've got to help me see her. I mean, be alone with her. I can't stand this. The only time I can see her is Sundays at tea, with everybody sitting around that huge salon talking about whether the French will really move into the Ruhr —"

Helena produced a cigarette. I lighted it for her. She glanced at me through the smoke. "Why, if I may ask, *should* I encourage you to see my cousin alone, Mr. Ellis?"

"What?"

"I think you heard my question."

"But I don't understand it!"

Her eyebrows went up. "Really not?"

"No, I really don't. You know I'm crazy about Lili."

"And what does that mean?"

"What does it mean?"

"Mmmm." She blew out another cloud of smoke and gazed at some spot above my right shoulder. "What are your intentions for Lili, Peter?"

"Well! My intentions? . . ." I guess the only word is "spluttered." I spluttered, reached for my glass, finished the martini and announced: "My intentions toward Lili are honorable!"

"Honorable . . . How nice. In English, in American, that means you wish to marry her?"

Up to now I had avoided it. I considered squirming sideways: was this really Helena's business? But I couldn't squirm in front of Helena.

"Yes," I said.

"Are you quite sure?"

"Yes, I'm sure." And then, suddenly, I was.

Helena nodded. "Will you pour me another drink? . . . Thank you. I met Professor Liebermann at a tea the other day. He lives in the Pariser Platz also, you know. And he is a charming old man, very much still interested in the ladies. And he took me aside. 'What is the name of Leutnant Keith's American friend?' and I told him. And he nodded, very amused. And he told me that he sent a student, former student of his, very modern artist, very political, he said he sent this student to give this American lessons because he knew the artist needed money badly, but now this American — meaning you, of course — is producing pictures quite the opposite extreme of his teacher — and Professor Liebermann looked so *amused*. And he gave me the name of a gallery — Joseph Ansbach in the Potsdamerstrasse?"

Helena's eyes twinkled over the edge of her glass. I knew what was coming so I said, "Did you like them?" and I heard that my voice sounded defensive.

"The pictures . . . or the girls? The pictures are — well, not exactly modern, are they? Almost photographically accurate, one can almost smell the perfume, and they show tremendous skill, Peter. Tremendous skill! But they are so realistic that I don't think . . . I don't think I would want them in *my* living room, not those two girls, I think. Though many other people apparently do want them, according to Herr Ansbach."

"You don't like my pictures?"

"Oh Peter, it's not a question of liking your pictures.

You are obviously going to be a successful painter, you paint a woman's face, a woman's body exactly as she would like it to look — but we are talking of your life. And your interest in Lili."

"What have my pictures got to do with Lili?"

"Peter!" Helena slapped her hands, exasperated, and leaned toward me. "Look, dear boy, everybody knows that painters sometimes sleep with their models, but must you make it so obvious? This study of the two girls on the bed, the hazy feeling, the sleepiness, the softness . . . *everybody,* Professor Liebermann, me, everybody who sees that picture knows you have just made love to them, both of them, it positively screams it! And what do you think Lili's mother will say, or her father?"

That had not occurred to me. "You think I should paint some different way?"

"No, my dear, of course not. A painter paints what he feels, your paintings show what you feel. But where does that leave my little cousin Lili?"

I thought about that. "Maybe I should paint Lili," I said, and then the doorbell rang.

One third of my Christmas Eve problem resolved itself, rather sadly, just before dawn on December 24. I woke up hearing shouts, hearing the doorbell ring several times, hearing doors slam, hearing people in heavy boots running around the house. My first thought was that Kaspar and his friends had returned. I put on my bathrobe, transferred my little Smith & Wesson revolver from the bedside table into my bathrobe pocket, and peeked into the hall. I felt a cold draft. The front door was open. I walked to the top of the stairs, just in time to see two soldiers wearing Red Cross armbands and forage caps carrying a stretcher out the door, followed by Christoph and his mother and Dr. Goldschmidt.

Meier closed the door as I came down the stairs. "Herr General collapsed in his bathroom this morning. Dr. Goldschmidt came immediately and diagnosed a heart attack. He is being taken to the military hospital in Potsdam." Meier looked pretty sick himself, but he served my coffee, and about an hour later Christoph telephoned: His father's condition was stable, his mother insisted on spending Christmas Eve at his side, Helena had now arranged for Christoph to be at the Waldstein's big family celebration — to which I had already been asked by Lili. We were to present ourselves at six, in evening dress.

At four I was still down in Neukölln, not in evening dress and not quite sober.

Falke and I had picked up a little Christmas tree at an outdoor stand in the frozen slush of the Hermann Platz. I paid 1,500 marks for the tree and bought six candles for 100 marks each.

The square was cold, the square was dark, the square became crowded as tired men and women stepped off the trolley cars. Sullen anger, threadbare clothes, the smell of hunger, of unwashed bodies, of cheap alcohol . . . Falke was drunk. He tried to help me carry the tree, but he kept stumbling and bumping into people who turned and cursed at us, so finally I just slung the tree over my shoulder and tried to keep out of his way.

As we started up the endless flights of cement stairs, Falke tried to help me again. At each landing, children came out of the doors and looked silenly at our tree. Falke began to sing, his voice echoing up the icy stairwell:

> *O du fröhliche*
> *O du seelige,*
> *Gnadenbringende*
> *Weihnachtszeit!*

Baby yelled, "Hurrah, ein Weihnachtsbaum!" and kissed me on the mouth. Behind her was little Ferdi in his shorts and his ragged sweater. My God, I had forgotten to get a present for Ferdi! What should I do? There wasn't time to go out again.

The kitchen was full and warm and smelled wonderful: I had given the girls enough money to procure a goose — I didn't ask how or where — and Mutti Bauer was cooking and there was a lot of noise as the girls shouted and Falke continued to sing. Mutti Bauer's face was beet red but I couldn't tell if it was from the heat of the stove, because her eyes were red too.

Bärbel kissed my ear. "The neighbors smell the goose, you see, and they have been making remarks all morning. Mutti's running a *Puff*, they're going to call the po-

lice! Can't we move out of this stinking monkey house?
Why don't you buy us a cottage, in Schöneberg or
Wilmersdorf? You wouldn't have to climb those god-
damned stairs, and we wouldn't have this jealous bitch-
ing all the time. . . ." She leaned against my back and put
her arms around me.

Falke took a bottle of schnapps from the closet. His
hands shook as he filled the little glasses on the table.
Over my shoulder Bärbel watched, her hair brushing
my cheek, and he knew she was watching. I moved away
and helped the boy, who had filled a bucket of water.
We put the tree into the bucket, and Baby attached the
candles with long hatpins.

"Do you want the tree in the studio?" I asked.

"No!" they all shouted. "It's freezing in there. Christmas in the kitchen," said Falke, handing around the
glasses.

Mutti Bauer lifted the lid of the heavy roaster and
poked the goose. "Another hour," she said, turning her
glistening face to me. "You will stay to eat some of your
goose?"

"What do you mean?" asked Baby, who was lighting
the candles on the tree. "Of course he'll stay."

Falke raised his glass. "Meine Damen und Herren, a
toast!" He was swaying slightly. "I suspect that my hardworking pupil is awaited at another feast — a Christmas
carp on the Pariser Platz? and so I ask that we lift our
glasses to thank him for what he has done here and wish
Fröhliche Weihnachten!"

They raised their glasses, even the boy.

Was I supposed to drink to that? And how exactly did
he mean it? I wondered, picking up the little glass of
clear liquid after all, looking around into their eyes, looking particularly at Falke's ironic expression, trying to
fathom his feelings. . . . They drank, I drank, the
schnapps burned, we put our glasses down — and Falke
immediately refilled them — all but the boy's.

"Well, thank you very much," I began. "I want to
thank you for all you've done for me —" We stood so
close together in the tiny kitchen, it was warm, the candles were reflected in Bärbel's eyes but it was Baby's
hand that crept into mine. . . . "I want to wish you a
Merry Christmas, and I've brought a few things. . . ."

I was so late that I had to take a taxi back to the Villa Keith. My head was full of schnapps, and my conscience hurt. Why couldn't I have stayed with them? They needed me, and the Waldsteins didn't.

They liked my presents. At the last second I remembered the fat black Mont Blanc fountain pen I'd just bought myself, so I pulled that out and presented it to the boy, who gasped, held it reverently in both hands, and sat right down in the corner to try it out.

Mutti Bauer seemed overwhelmed by the handbag, she burst into tears again, while Bärbel and Baby tore away at the elaborate wrappings the people at Waldstein & Co. had contrived for me. At my wit's end, I had finally decided to give them money so that they could buy whatever they wanted — but money in slightly romantic form, so I persuaded Waldstein's cashier to find me some rare items — a couple of five-dollar gold pieces.

Now each girl stared at the coin in her palm while I made my little speech: just couldn't think what you might like . . . pick out whatever you want . . . might be a good idea to hang on to these for a little while. . . .

They both kissed me and thanked me profusely, but there was something odd in the way they reacted. Both of them. Was it the fact that I gave them money — as of that morning each coin was worth about 40,000 marks — or was it something else?

Falke had poured the third round. Now he said: "We have something for you, too," and disappeared into the bedroom. Instantly both girls pressed against me and slipped their coins into the pockets of my jacket. Mutti Bauer watched, then turned away to busy herself at the stove.

"Please keep them for us," whispered Bärbel. "Otherwise he'll take them the minute you're gone."

"Do you really have to go?" Baby looked frightened. "He's acting nice while you're here but underneath he's in a rotten mood, he'll kick the shit out of us —"

"Not out of me, he won't," said Bärbel. "I'm going to eat some of that goose, but after that I'll do my celebrating on the Friedrichstrasse!"

"You're going to leave me and Mutti up here to get our asses whipped all evening?" asked Baby, but then Falke returned to the kitchen, and with a bow he handed me a parcel.

I removed the paper and looked into my own eyes: a framed charcoal sketch, done in Falke's inimitable cartoon style, very carefully done with much attention to detail, certainly not flattering but also not as bitter as it might have been (should have been?), the picture of a rather conventional-looking young man in a striped suit, white shirt, dark necktie, neatly combed hair, suggestions of money in the clothes and lechery around the eyes . . . but the inscription said it all: *The American as Paris in Berlin. Falke. Christmas '22.* It was a damned good picture. (I still have it. It is not over my mantelpiece, but I have it.)

The women didn't understand the reference to Paris. I understood it. "You should have drawn in Venus and the other two," I said as I thanked him. "Who were the other two anyway?"

"Well, you have already drawn the other two, I think."

We laughed. The girls looked at us, puzzled. Mutti Bauer poked the goose. I consulted my watch.

"Listen, Fritz, it was stupid of me to think the girls could carry those coins around, down here. Somebody will knock them over the head, or break in. . . . I'm going to lock them up in my vault, they can get them whenever they want them, of course, or we can have the Bank change them into single dollars, but I don't think they should carry them around —"

Falke said nothing as I babbled. He looked into his glass, poured the contents into his mouth, swallowed, grimaced — and then turned his face toward the ceiling, bellowing:

> *Stille Nacht,*
> *Heilige Nacht,*
> *Alles schläft,*
> *Einsam wacht . . .*

I had to go. I kissed all three women, shook hands with the boy, and asked Falke to step into the hall for just a moment. He followed me out and leaned against the dirty plaster wall. He looked at me, waiting. I could hardly see him in the gloom. I didn't know what to say before I said it.

"I really do appreciate this picture, and I thank you very much."

"Bitte, bitte," mumbled Falke.

"You've been a wonderful teacher."

He shook his head. "You don't need a teacher. But I need the money."

"No, I do need a teacher, Fritz, and I want to go on with you. But if there's any trouble here tonight, I'm not coming back. Is that clear?"

"What do you mean?" Were his eyes turning yellow? It was too dark to be sure.

"You know what I mean. I don't want to go, I want to stay here, it's just that I've *got* to go. But if there's any trouble — and you know I'll hear about it — then I'll rent my own studio, you won't see me again!"

Falke bit his lip and looked down at the cement floor. He should have thrown me down the stairs, but all he did was shrug and turn around and walk back into the apartment.

I paid the driver with a handful of 100-mark bills, ran up the walkway, slipped on the ice, and fell flat on my face. As I struggled to my feet, the door opened and in the bright light stood Christoph Keith and Meier. For a second they just stared at me, then they both came forward.

"My God, man, what's happened to you?" asked Christoph.

"Nothing happened, I slipped on the ice, I'm perfectly all right —"

"You've got blood all over your face."

"Herr Oberleutnant, please!" Christoph was immaculately dressed: white tie and tails and medals. Meier, who didn't want my blood to spoil the effect, pushed himself between us and tried to help me into the house, but somehow his feet got in front of mine, and I fell down again.

"Draw a bath for Mr. Ellis," said Christoph. "A cold bath."

25.

SAME SONGS, DIFFERENT SINGERS

Falke was right about the carp. They were rolled into the dining room on special serving tables. Silver lids were lifted to reveal enormous steaming fish that had been poached, I was assured, in beer. The tables were moved around the room, the butler dissected with the precision of a surgeon, an underbutler served hot Meissen plates with slices of carp, waitresses passed vegetables — but all that was later. First, the *Bescherung*.

A Christmas tree stood in the central hall. Marble stairs curved up behind it. The tree was lighted with a hundred candles, and their light shimmered on the silver tinsel, on the colored glass balls and on an infinite variety of carved moons and stars and flying cherubim. The big gold angel at the top of the tree spread its arms only a few feet below the skylight. All around the bottom of the tree were piles of presents, beautifully wrapped and carefully labeled.

The hallway and the curving stairs were packed: Waldstein aunts and uncles and in-laws, children and grandchildren, friends and friends-of-friends, servants. As the heads of the house, Lili's father and her Uncle Fritz had moved to their places on the bottom step, near the entrance to the big salon, where a small ensemble had been placed around the grand piano. From our places in the middle of the hall we couldn't see the musicians, but it didn't matter, because we could see Baron Eduard turn to give them the signal. They began to play, and a hundred voices joined in:

> *O Tannenbaum, O Tannenbaum,*
> *Wie grün sind Deine Blätter. . . .*

"What happened to your nose?" was the first thing she said when we arrived. The hall was filling with people, and as our coats were taken I was separated from Christoph and pressed toward a corner with Lili.

"I slipped on the ice. Are we very late?"

"No, we just got back from church."

"From *church?*"

The black eyes flashed. "You think we should celebrate Christmas in a synagogue?"

"No, I mean —"

"It was my great-grandfather who was Jewish. Remember?"

"Yes, of course —"

"All the same to you, though, isn't it?"

"Lili, it doesn't *matter* —"

"Are you sure? Or do you think this much Christmas display is in questionable taste?"

"Are you mad at me?"

She shook her head. "I just wonder what you think, sometimes."

"I think all this is . . . splendid. My family makes very little out of Christmas —"

Lili interrupted, still compelled to explain. "My mother's family were Huguenots. From France. You have heard of the Huguenots?"

"Well, I guess I've heard something —"

"But not very much. They were French Protestants. They were persecuted there, by the Catholics, they were driven out of France by Louis XIV. A lot of them came here, the Electors of Brandenburg welcomed them. They did well for themselves, as artisans, in the civil service, in the law, in the army. My mother's father was a professor of law. . . . Well, in any event my mother and I attend the French Church you have seen in the Gendarmenmarkt, and my father — who frankly doesn't care what church he goes to — my father goes with us on Christmas and Easter." Lili looked down. "And on the anniversary of Max's death. He goes then too. Which is a little strange since Max and Alfred's mother came from a Jewish family. Are you sufficiently confused now?" She suddenly smiled.

"Alfred and Sigrid have been to Friends Meeting," I said, just to say something after all that.

"Alfred is always interested in new things, and Sigrid goes where Alfred goes. The good German wife. *Her* family have their own church, right in their castle."

The fall on the ice and the cold bath had neutralized
the afternoon: the schnapps was gone, the smell of the
goose was gone, the feeling that I should be down there
instead of up here was gone. I looked at Lili. In Friends
Meeting the bride and groom stand up and marry each
other. They stand up and say something: "I take thee
Elizabeth von Waldstein to be my wife before these our
friends promising . . ." What? To be unto thee a loving
and faithful husband until . . . Something like that. Only
of course it wouldn't be in Meeting, it would be here,
presumably the French Church in the Gendarmenmarkt. . . . Until death shall separate us, that's what you
have to say. Am I prepared to say that?

"Isn't that Miss Boatwright up there?"

"Yes, and she's brought a gentleman with her. An
American banker" — The music began again, the voices
rose:

> O du fröhliche
> O du seelige,
> Gnadenbringende
> Weihnachtszeit!

Four verses. Then Baron Eduard spoke: "This year I
have asked Alfred to read the Christmas story."

Alfred stepped out of the crowd, turned to stand beside
one of the candles of the tree, and began to read the
chapter from St. Luke about how it came to pass that
there went out a decree from Caesar Augustus that all
the world should be taxed and how Jesus was born in
Bethlehem, what the angels said to the shepherds, what
the shepherds told the people, and how Mary kept all
these things and pondered them in her heart.

Alfred stopped there and closed the Bible. For a moment there was silence in the darkness, but you could see
all the faces up the stairs reflected in the candlelight, and
I was surprised how many of the faces I recognized now.
Then the music began again, and everybody sang.

> Stille Nacht,
> Heilige Nacht,
> Alles schläft
> Einsam wacht . . .

They sang all of the verses. When the last note sounded, the electric lights were turned on and Baron Eduard began to reach for the presents, reading the labels through his pince-nez, calling out the names: the youngest servant girls first, the older servants, the children, the guests. . . .

"Mr. Peter Ellis!"

Lili pushed me forward. Her father gave me a look over the top of his glasses, and handed me a box. By its shape, I judged it to contain a bottle. I put it on a table.

Everybody came down the stairs and milled through the hall into the big salon.

Sigrid said: "Bobby and Alfred are having a small martini in the library. I have been sent to invite you and Miss Boatwright's friend to join them."

"Peter's been drinking all afternoon," said Lili. "He fell on his face, just look at him."

"How is General Keith?" asked Sigrid, ignoring Lili.

"They say he's about the same, but I think Christoph is worried. Frau Keith is out there at the hospital —"

"If the General dies, how long must Christoph remain in mourning?"

"Lili!"

"Well, it's a perfectly natural question."

I saw Miss Boatwright looking at me, so I moved in that direction.

Miss Boatwright's escort was called Whitney Wood, a benign portly red-faced gentleman, not much taller than I, with white hair that made him look older than he probably was. The first thing he told me was that my father had taken out his appendix twenty years ago, when Mr. Wood had visited Chestnut Hill to be an usher in a classmate's wedding. They took him straight from the reception to the operating room. My father made such an impression that they remained in touch over the years, and Mr. Wood became a trustee of my father's hospital even before he was made a partner in J. P. Morgan & Co.

It was not the first time I had heard a story like this, but I liked Mr. Wood (can a Morgan partner be benign?) and I liked the way he looked at Miss Boatwright, a radiant, glowing Miss Boatwright who was chattering like a debutante this evening: Whitney, Peter is becoming an absolutely splendid painter, his work is being sold by Berlin galleries, I'll take you to see them. Peter, Whitney has come over to work with a government commission on German reparations, he's already been to lunch at the Gendarmenmarkt, he's extremely concerned about the situation here. . . .

"I had a good talk with the fellow who really runs the place. Dr. . . . What's his name?"

"Dr. Strassburger." I looked around hoping nobody else heard that.

"Strassburger, right. He here? Don't see him here."

"Ah . . . no, sir. I don't see him either, but this is more of a family party, I believe —" and then Helena appeared at my side, was introduced to a dazzled Mr. Wood, and told me that I was taking her in to dinner. Christoph was taking Lili. Miss Boatwright and Mr. Wood had been placed near the head of the table, with Lili's parents.

It isn't easy to study portraits by candlelight, but I tried to find some resemblance between the faces on the walls and the faces around the table. There wasn't much, but there was some: I knew that the gaunt unsmiling man in a black suit and a white stock of the 1790s was David Waldstein, and he had the same slightly skeptical look that Bobby had when Bobby wasn't smiling; I knew that the very young mustachioed hussar of 1813 was Jacob the poet, and something of the sadness in his eyes reminded me of Helena's father, who happened to be sitting directly in front of his ancestor.

Helena seemed unusually quiet.

"I've never eaten carp before," I told her.

"They have been cooked in beer," she told me. "Beer and all sorts of other things. It is a Christmas custom here." Her thoughts were elsewhere.

"Are you worried about the General?"

She sighed. "I am sorry about the General, but life cannot be much fun in that condition. I don't plan to become so old myself."

"Do you think all that about Kaspar —"

"Let us not talk about Kaspar, please! That subject is closed."

"Not for his mother, I think."

"No, you are right. . . . Not for his mother."

"Are you not feeling well, Helena?"

She turned to look at me. "I'm just a little nervous, Peter. Something like stage fright."

"But why?"

She inclined her head toward the top of the table, where the two Barons and their wives were sitting with Helena's father, Miss Boatwright and Whitney Wood. "I think you will find out right now." Baron Eduard was standing up.

"Well, here we are again, another Christmas, another Christmas toast — but this year, I am pleased — No, I am *delighted* to announce that we will first drink another toast, and to propose that toast I ask my cousin Paul to rise —"

Helena's father stood up, a glass in his hand. He stood there for a moment, bit his lips and looked around at the expectant faces. A man who expresses opinions, Christoph had said, and I had never seen this old man at a loss for words, but tonight he seemed to be having some trouble. Under the table, Helena suddenly gripped my hand. Hers was cold.

"My friends," began Paul Waldstein. "My cousins, *our* friends . . . I had prepared some preliminary remarks. Our beloved nation stands in mortal danger. On the inside, our economic and financial system is approaching a state of chaos. On the outside, an enemy army stands poised to seize our most vital industrial territory. These thoughts oppress us, even at this Christmas feast, but life goes on, and for this reason I rise tonight to tell you that I am happy — yes, very happy, very proud and happy to announce to you the engagement of my beloved daughter — my only child —"

"*Hurrah!*" shouted Lili on my other side and leaned across me to kiss Helena, who was still clutching my hand and trembling, and now everybody was standing up, glasses raised, as her father tried, with some difficulty, to finish the formal toast. Christoph and Helena remained in their seats, both trying to smile.

Bobby began the traditional song and the others joined in:

Hoch soll'n Sie leben
Kinder soll'n Sie kriegen
Drei-mal hoch!

We drank, the butlers refilled our glasses, and Christoph rose to make his response. It was short and somber. He did not need to tell this company how long he had loved this lady, but circumstances had been difficult: the War, the Revolution, the present crises — it is not easy to ask a princess to stop being one! And yet, as Herr Waldstein has reminded us, life goes on, and as we see no indications that the circumstances will get better very soon, Helena and I have decided no longer to postpone the inevitable, to share the bad times as well as the good. He raised his glass: to many Christmases, together! We drank.

Sotto voce, Helena said: "Took him eight years to get this far. Will he make it to the altar?" but there were tears in her eyes.

The coffee was served in the salon. Most people clustered around Helena and Christoph, asking about wedding plans, but I sat with Lili, off to one side.

"Have you opened your present?" she asked.

"Oh, my present!" I went out into the hall, came back with my box, and took the other package from my pocket. "This is from me to you. We got into so much religion that I forgot all about it."

We opened our presents. Mine turned out to be a bottle — a bottle containing an exact scale model of the Waldsteins' little racing sloop. I was almost speechless. "Oh, look at that, oh that's terrific. . . ."

"You like it? One of the gardeners made it, it was his idea, they were all *so* happy to see the boat in the water again. . . . Oh my goodness!" She had unwrapped the little wristwatch. "Oh, Peter!" She blew out her breath, slipped the watch over her hand, held it away to admire how it looked, raised her eyebrows and pulled down the corners of her mouth in a very curious expression. Of what? Of doubt?

"Don't you like it?"

"*Like* it? I *love* it! I'm just not sure I'll be allowed to keep it." She glanced across the room.

"Not allowed to keep it? Why not, may I ask?"

"Rather expensive present, Peter."

"Expensive present!" I looked around the salon, the Persian carpets, the inlaid tables, the velvet furniture, the tapestries, the blazing chandeliers, the blazing jewels on the ladies —

Lili reached out and took my hand. "No, you don't understand. Yes, we have nice things, we live in a big house, we are fortunate, but that has nothing to do . . . For a girl to accept such a present —"

"It doesn't commit you to anything!" I was beginning to get angry. "And it wasn't that expensive anyway."

"Not for you, the rich American stock market operator." But she smiled as she said it. "Peter, it's not me, it's my mother. If my mother thinks it does not look correct. But please let us not quarrel over this, I will handle my mother, but she does not need to see it tonight. Will you please stand up?" She was taking the watch off her wrist.

"Stand up?"

"Yes, stand up a moment and stand in front of me, look over there at the others —" and I did stand up but I glanced into the huge gilt mirror over the mantel — to see Lili crouching forward on the sofa behind my back, quickly flip up her dress, spread her legs a little, and tuck the watch into the top of her left stocking, just beneath the inside garter. I couldn't believe my eyes. . . . My heart was pounding. . . . She stood up at my side, asking: "Have you any plans for Sylvesterabend, New Year's Eve?"

26.

THEY'RE ONLY GOING TO HIRE HIS VOICE

At one-thirty in the afternoon of Thursday, January 11, 1923, the German mark was quoted at 10,450 to the dollar on the Berlin Stock Exchange. At three o'clock the rate had reached 11,600 marks to the dollar, but by desperate purchase operations the Reichsbank brought it down to 10,500. Turmoil. News had come by telephone: French troops were moving into Essen. The occupation of the Ruhr had begun. Everybody believed that the mark would continue to fall, so everybody was desperately buying shares, driving their prices up.

I didn't know all that on the afternoon of January 11, because I was standing in the icy bloom of the Potsdam

Garrison Church, watching six Reichswehr troopers in
cavalry boots and spurs carrying General Keith's coffin
away from the candlelit tomb of Frederick the Great, up
the aisle and out the door, as the organ boomed again,
"Ein feste Burg ist unser Gott."

The faded banners of decommissioned Guard regiments moved gently above our heads. Some of the sur-
vivors stood in the pews. Death's heads grinned as the
honorary pallbearers followed the coffin. Spurs and sabers
clicked. Tight-lipped scowling old men, one of them a
field marshal, walking upright, looking straight ahead.
The flag draped over the coffin was the black-white-red of
the Kaiser's Reich, not the black-red-gold of the Republic.

Frau Keith wore a black coat, a black cloche hat, a
black veil. Christoph, whose arm she held, wore a civilian overcoat with a wide black ribbon around his sleeve,
and his medals on his chest. Christoph limped.

Kaspar wasn't there. At least he wasn't in the church,
and mine were not the only eyes carefully sweeping.

Helena, who walked with me, pulled down her veil as
we came out into the blinding glare of the snow-covered
parade, where a mounted military band began to play.

> *Ich hatt' einen Kameraden,*
> *Einen bessern findst du nicht. . . .*

Steel helmets, kettledrums, snaredrums, trumpets and
trombones. A squad of infantry presented arms. The
coffin, still covered by the flag, was carefully strapped
upon a caisson. Horseshoes clattered on the cobblestones;
the band moved off, only the snaredrums beating now,
beating slow march; horses snorted; the caisson began to
roll. The infantry detail did a right-shoulder-arms, right-
face, and stepped off to the beat of the drums.

The old men, putting on their tschakos, their spiked
helmets from 1914, their top hats, began to talk to each
other.

Automobiles drew up. Christoph was helping his
mother into one of them — a car with a military driver
and General Staff pennants — when Helena grabbed my
elbow:

"Quickly, look over there, the big tree where the coffin is passing now!"

I looked. I saw what she saw.

"Don't tell them!" said Helena. "Please don't tell them."

The mood at the Villa Keith was not mourning but partriotic outrage. On the way back from Potsdam, many people had bought newspapers, and Christoph had telephoned the Bank.

"An absolute act of war," said Dr. von Winterfeldt. "We are simply back at war!"

"With an army of a hundred thousand men," said one of the generals.

"This is what comes of it," said another. "Policy of Fulfillment? Spineless appeasement! Socialists! Disbanded the Freikorps!"

"We're going to have to get those fellows back."

"It's being worked on."

"What?"

"Seeckt is working on it. Bringing them back, a few at a time, sending them out for training."

"Out where?"

The speaker moved his head. "Out beyond the sunrise. Far out."

Another voice cut in: "Gentlemen, don't you think Frau Keith serves *exceptionally* good coffee?"

A moment of puzzled silence.

"Do you know what a pound of real coffee costs today, in this glorious Versailles Republic of ours?"

It was interesting to watch their expressions, because they didn't all get the point at the same time. One by one, the faces turned to wood. Monocles glittered. The ancient field marshal glared across the room at me, looking like a furious child.

Frau Keith, without her hat and her veil, looked much younger than the wives for whom she was pouring coffee. Thinking about it for the first time, doing the arithmetic in my head, considering Christoph's age, considering Kaspar's age, considering that the General had served in the War of 1870 . . .

"Christoph, do you mind if I ask? How old is your mother?"

"Interesting, we are thinking the same thing. She suddenly looks her real age today. She is fifty-five."

"That's —"

"That's over fifteen years younger than my father, yes. He was in no rush to get married. Good times as a bachelor."

"Speaking of getting married —"

"Speaking of getting married, I don't know exactly, of course we must wait a few months now, but I would like to ask you, Peter . . . I would have asked before but continued to hope that Kaspar would return, that Kaspar would accept Helena, but since he did not even appear for his father's funeral —"

Why *not* tell him?

"— I would like to ask if you will stand as best man for me?"

"Well of course, I'd be honored, but I'm sure that Kaspar —"

"No. He hates us. He thinks we betrayed Kern and Fischer."

"But we didn't. How can you betray somebody who isn't on your side?"

Christoph shook his head. "It's what he *thinks*. In any case, we compromised his position with the O.C. people, the Ehrhardt people, so he must prove he is really on their side. . . . I don't know, I just don't know, I try to put it out of my mind. At the moment, my biggest problem is not Kaspar but my mother. The *Dollarkurs* went over 11,000 this afternoon. Do you realize what that means?"

"My God, Christoph!"

"Of course it means different things to different people. To you it means you are richer today than you were yesterday. But for widows, for pensioners, for people living on their savings . . . I don't have to explain what it means when a pair of shoes costs thirty thousand marks!"

"But why can't you do for you mother what you've been doing for me?"

"Well, of course to some extent we have been trying to. But she didn't have any dollars to begin with. She has some stocks, they have risen in value, we have put a mortgage on this house and borrowed money to buy Dutch guilders, there is a little gold and a little jewelry we can sell — it is a struggle, I am forced to speculate with her property in a way one should not speculate with the few things a widow has left, but I must or it will simply melt away! And at least I have my salary from Waldsteins', they have been decent about increasing it. But look at the other people in this room. Spent their lives serving their country. Officers, judges, civil servants. Not only served their country, *ran* the country. Everybody honored them, bowed, saluted, received them at Court, gave them titles, gave them medals . . . and they looked down their noses at people in business — not to mention *banking*. Money-lending! Playing the stock market! Not entirely clean. Probably something somebody must do, people from other classes. Like collecting the garbage. Served their country all of their lives on the assumption of a comfortable, honored old age. And now you know what's going to happen to them — unless they suddenly acquire the talents of Erich Strassburger *and* the capital to use those talents?" Christoph looked at the men who had governed an empire. "They will be standing in the soup lines, with the workers from Neukölln and Moabit. Except that some of them will rather starve!"

"It's just like the War," said Miss Boatwright two weeks later. We were having dinner at the Adlon, as Whitney Wood's guests. He had called at the Villa Keith that morning to ask if I would meet her train at Bahnhof Friedrichstrasse because some conference at the Deutsche Bank might not be over in time. I could have his car, which meant his car and his driver, who by now knew where to find me among the tenements of Neukölln.

I'd had dinner with Mr. Wood a couple of times while Miss Boatwright was in the Ruhr, and after cocktails and a bottle of Riesling he told me about his wife, who was hospitalized with incurable schizophrenia somewhere on Long Island.

That's all he said about himself. He wanted to talk about German politics. He told me about his conversations with Hugo Stinnes, with Dr. Havenstein of the Reichsbank, with the Minister of Finance. . . . "The fact of the matter is they don't know what the hell they're doing. They're paying the government's debts by printing money as fast as they can print it. You know what this is? Proudly showed it to me yesterday: this is the first certificate for one hundred thousand marks. You know what it was worth when the market closed this afternoon? A little over five bucks!"

I already knew that, because I checked with Christoph twice a day now. The mark was falling so fast that everybody in Germany was checking the *Dollarkurs* twice a day.

"What they *think* they're doing," said Whitney Wood, "is keeping unemployment down. Keeping people at work, because they're sure that if they have more unemployed workers they'll get communism, and they're more afraid of communism than anything else. But Stinnes is talking out of both sides of his mouth: what he says is that he wants to keep his men at work, he wants to keep German products cheap so they can compete successfully abroad. That's fine. But what he's doing is encouraging the Reichsbank to print more and more money so the money's worth less every day. At the same time he borrows to the hilt, buys up every mine and every steel mill and every factory he can get his hands on — he's been doing that for years now — and then he pays back the loans with marks that are worth a fraction of what they were worth when he borrowed them. He's built an empire out of this inflation."

"But Mr. Wood, why do they lend him the money?"

"Because, they say, he's providing jobs. They don't want the men on the streets. They're afraid of revolution. Stinnes says his men are underpaid, but he claims he could triple their wages if they'd work ten hours a day. And since they won't do that, they've got to be forced, the way they were forced in the War."

"How is he going to force them to work ten hours a day?" I asked.

"Stinnes wants to install a dictator, but not some prince or some king or somebody like von Séeckt. Not somebody with a monocle and medals. He wants a man who speaks the people's language, as he puts it. A man who can rouse the people, set them on fire, persuade them that working sixty hours a week will bring Germany out of this mess."

"And where's he going to find such a man?"

"In Munich," said Whitney Wood. "Already been found."

"In Munich? You don't mean Hitler? Adolf Hitler?"

Whitney Wood nodded.

"Oh no," I said. "He's nuts. He's the one who's screaming about the Jews all the time. Everything that's happened to Germany was plotted by the Jews, he's obsessed —"

"Yeah, that's the part I don't quite understand, because

of course I have to get all this through interpreters. . . .
Why should Stinnes want to back this Hitler against his
own people? I mean, how cynical can you —"

"What own people?"

"Well, Stinnes is a Jew."

"No. He's not a Jew."

"Sure he is. All you have to do is look at him."

"No, sir. He's not. Old family from the Ruhr. Coal
mine operators."

"Who told you that?"

"Baron von Waldstein."

"Well, he ought to know." Whitney Wood looked
thoughtful. "Okay, that makes the puzzle come together.
Stinnes says that Munich is just about ready to blow up.
The Bavarians hate Berlin, they hate the Republic, the
town is swarming with people who want to overthrow the
government, Bavarian monarchists who want their own
king back, a dozen different Right-wing outfits — most of
them armed to the teeth — and Hitler's gang — I can't
remember exactly what they call themselves — they're
disciplined, they carry out orders, they're getting uniforms
and money, but most important of all, Hitler is a *terrific*
speech maker, he draws crowds, he mesmerizes thousands
of people at a time by yelling at them, he's a born orator,
and Stinnes thinks he can get the workers away from
communism, that he'll let the business people run the
economy, get it back into some kind of order, and when
they've done that, they'll be able to raise new capital
abroad. And when he says 'abroad' you know where he
means." Whitney Wood grinned. "I guess that's why Herr
Stinnes is being so nice to me."

I shook my head. "This Hitler . . . You know, he isn't
even a German. He came over from Austria, he was a
house painter or something —"

"So what? The chancellor they've got now, Dr. Cuno,
was the president of the Hamburg-Amerika Line. A
house painter couldn't do much worse, could he? And it
isn't as if they're going to let him run anything. They're
only going to hire his voice, to bring some order. Germans
like order, and what they've got now is chaos, and chaos
could cause revolution." Whitney Wood paused to light a
cigar. "I mean from our point of view, Stinnes's plan is
better than a Bolshevik Germany, isn't it?"

"It's just like the War," said Miss Boatwright when she had finished her hot bouillon. Her cheeks were red again. When she stepped off the train from Essen she looked gray and cold and very glad to see me on the smoky platform. I had persuaded her to come directly to the Adlon and to take a hot bath in Mr. Wood's suite while he and I had drinks downstairs.

"The Germans are trying a kind of passive resistance," said Miss Boatwright. "They just refuse to work for the French. The mayor of Essen is in jail. Directors of the biggest steel companies are in jail. The plants are closed. The workers are wandering around the streets, getting into trouble with French soldiers. There's real hardship, real hunger again, just like 1919." Miss Boatwright looked around the blazing luxury of the Adlon's dining room. "Whitney, I must confess this place makes me uncomfortable. When I think what we could do with what this dinner is costing you . . ."

"Dear girl, you've spent the whole day on a freezing train —"

"Oh, I know, and I do appreciate the way you take care of me, honestly I do, and why, after all, should you — either of you — deprive yourselves when it would just be a drop in the bucket? In any event, I'm glad you've come to know each other while I was away, because I'm very fond of both of you."

"Tell us more about the Ruhr," I said.

"Well, I think it was just *despicable* of the French to do what they did. In the first place, now the Germans simply *can't* pay any more reparations, and in the second place, this invasion drives all the Center Germans to the Right. It's exactly what the Nationalists want. They are streaming into the Ruhr, signing up recruits, blowing up the coal trains going to France, getting financial support from the big industrialists: Thyssen and Kirdorf and Krupp and those people. There are bonfires in the streets, rabble-rousing speeches, great crowds bellowing 'Deutschland, Deutschland über Alles' and 'Die Wacht am Rhein' —"

"That's happening all over Germany," I said. "Right here in Berlin and in Hamburg and in Munich."

"You can hardly blame them," said Whitney Wood. "There's absolutely no excuse for what the French are doing."

"Well, why can't *we* do something?" demanded Miss Boatwright.

"We? You mean Warren G. Harding? The American people are just not interested in all this. We've pulled our troops off the Rhine to show the French we disapprove, but that's as far as we're willing to go. What we *might* do, I think, is push for some changes in this reparations nonsense. The French and the British are never going to pay their war debts to us, and as you say the Germans obviously can't pay these ridiculous sums that have been assessed against them. So we'll have to work something out."

Whitney Wood paused to finish his coffee. Then he wiped his mouth and smiled across the table at us. "What amuses me, I must say, is to discover two Americans — indeed, two Philadelphia Quakers — who rushed to the defense of *La Belle France* even before we got into the War now berating our gallant ally and shedding tears for the bloody Hun! Are you going native?"

27.

INFLATION WORKS IN DIFFERENT WAYS

I may be giving the impression that Dr. Erich Strassburger spent most of his time advising me on my piddling financial transactions. Of course that isn't true. I hardly ever saw him. All the advice came through Christoph, who also carried out the actual orders, so I was surprised, one morning in March or April, when Christoph's telephone report included a request that I call in person at the Bank. Dr. Strassburger had a lunch meeting, but would like to see me at two-thirty.

When I presented myself at No. 4 Gendarmenmarkt the butler was as apologetic as his icy demeanor allowed: Herr Geheimrat's secretary was extremely sorry, the conference was still in progress, would it be inconvenient for Mr. Ellis to wait in one of the conference rooms? Sherry and the newspapers would be brought. . . .

Just then the bell rang and the butler went to open the door. Two men in gray Reichswehr uniforms came in: the first was a tall lieutenant — very young, very blond, with gloves, riding boots, sword handle protruding through a vent in the long greatcoat; the second was a stubby corporal, straining to carry two bulging briefcases, which he put down as both men took off their garrison hats.

"Leutnant Graf Brühl zu Zeydlitz," announced the corporal in a rather loud voice. "Für'n Baron von Waldstein."

"*Which* Baron?" was the butler's obvious question.

"Baron Bobby," said the lieutenant.

The butler was terribly sorry, Excellency, but Herr Baron Robert was not in the house at the moment. Could one of the other —

"Leutnant Keith in the house?"

The butler believed that Herr Oberleutnant was in his office. Would His Excellency care to wait in one of the conference rooms . . . The presence of two different clients in the reception room obviously made the butler uncomfortable. The lieutenant had glanced across at me with no particular interest, but I suddenly realized who this must be — the name, the face, no indentation between the forehead and the bridge of the nose — so I, the innocent abroad, just strolled over and extended my hand.

"Good afternoon, I'm Peter Ellis. You must be Sigrid's brother."

He shook hands firmly, bowed, clicked his heels. "Good afternoon, sir. Brühl." He looked puzzled. The corporal looked shocked. The butler looked horrified, turned on his heels and disappeared.

"I've seen your photograph," I said. "I saw a picture of you shooting a rifle out the window of your cadet school."

A frown, then finally a smile and he looked even more like Sigrid. "Ach yes, you live with the Keiths, you're Christoph's friend, I understand now." Pause. "Well . . . How is it you speak German so well?"

We stood there making conversation while I tried not to look at the bursting black leather briefcases — they were packed so full that they were almost round — and the corporal stared at the carpet and the chandelier and the bust of David Waldstein.

Then the swinging doors swung open and Christoph

appeared, not smiling. He shook hands with both of us, told me that Dr. Strassburger was ready to receive me now, and turned back to Count Brühl, who said: "Old man, I have a little business with Waldstein and Co."

"Yes," said Christoph. "So I see."

I told Count Brühl that I was pleased to meet him, shook hands again, and followed the butler through the swinging doors. Behind me, I heard Christoph say: "Your driver can go back to the car. Our people will take them downstairs."

Dr. Strassburger's office looked the same — the Chinese jade figures, the Böcklin, the view of the French Church in the Gendarmenmarkt — but Dr. Strassburger himself looked different — pale and tired. He had lost weight; the starched wing collar stood away from his neck.

He apologized for keeping me waiting. The banking business today was not exactly easy. Had I heard the *Dollarskurs* this afternoon? Thirty thousand marks to the dollar! The Reichsbank had been stablizing in the neighborhood of 20,000 for the last few weeks and things appeared to be leveling off, but now, *this afternoon,* Stinnes's companies are suddenly in the market, buying huge amounts of dollars, of British pounds, of Swiss francs, of Dutch guilders — in other words pouring out German marks to buy foreign currencies, completely undercutting the stablization purchases of the Reichsbank. . . .

Hugo Stinnes again! I had the feeling that all this was spilling over from the previous meeting. I had the feeling that Dr. Strassburger had somehow lost the magic touch, that Dr. Strassburger was frantic, and I remembered Whitney Wood's remark: They don't know what the hell they're doing.

"Why is he allowed to do this?" I asked.

"Hah! Good question!"

Reichsbank gave him the permits. Said he needed foreign currencies to buy raw materials abroad. Can't operate his factories without chrome and sulfur and rubber and cotton and petroleum and the other things he has to import — but he could have been accumulating foreign currencies slowly and carefully, like everybody else . . . instead, he goes in one afternoon with all his companies and just destroys what little stability the mark had left. Absolutely incredible!

Dr. Strassburger took off his pince-nez, closed his eyes, and rubbed the red marks on the sides of his nose. "I'm sorry, Ellis, I did not ask you to come here for a lecture. I wish to discuss a personal matter. As a matter of fact, I wish to ask your help."

"After all you've done for me, Dr. Strassburger —"

He held up his hand. "Let me tell you a little about my family. My family is not at all like the Waldsteins. For one thing my family is still of the Mosaic religion —"

"Of what religion, sir?"

"Of the Jewish religion, the religion of Moses, that is how we call it here."

"Oh, I see," I said, feeling like a fool.

"Yes, and we are not rich. My father had a little store in Dresden, a good jewelry store, he made enough money so his sons could go to the Gymnasium, the high school. We were not poor but we were not rich. I would say we were exactly in the middle, when I was a boy. Well, things change. My father died when we were quite young, my older brother had to operate the store although he wanted to study medicine, the store produced enough money for me to attend the University, to become a lawyer. I practiced here in Berlin some years, then I was employed by the Waldsteins. The War came. My younger brother volunteered, was killed in Flanders. My older brother had more and more trouble with the store. He was never a good businessman. Revolution, inflation . . . in these times, you can imagine the difficulty in buying silver, buying diamonds, buying watches, then trying to sell them at a profit. In these times. I mean it can be done, people are doing it, but it requires absolutely icy nerves and perfect timing — and my brother — a good man — he was not the least bit gifted in these matters. I tried to help but how can I run a jewelry store in Dresden? So the business failed, last year. And perhaps because the business failed, I don't know, but this January my brother dropped dead. Heart attack."

"I'm sorry, Dr. Strassburger."

"Yes. Thank you. When times were good, before the War, my brother purchased a policy of insurance on his life, quite a large policy for those times, but he wanted his wife to be secure, his children. . . . He married late, young children. . . . He bought a life insurance policy of three hundred thousand marks. Paid the premium every month. When he died, the insurance company paid my sister-in-law three hundred thousand marks — the equivalent of thirty dollars or so!"

Pause. I didn't say anything. What was there to say?

"All right," Dr. Strassburger continued. "Of course I must help them, and I will. I have done well here, I have as yet no family, I will take care of them as best I can —"

The telephone rang. Dr. Strassburger ripped the receiver off the cradle: "I THOUGHT I SAID I WAS NOT — Oh, I beg your pardon, Herr Baron. . . . No. I'm meeting now with Peter Ellis. . . . No, he didn't, Herr Baron, I don't believe he understood. . . ."

Dr. Strassburger had not replaced his pince-nez, and as he listened to what seemed to be an angry long tirade from Baron Eduard I watched his expression very carefully, because he looked quite different without his optical mask, more vulnerable, perhaps more sensitive —and younger.

"Yes, sir. . . . Yes, sir. Of course, of course. . . . Yes, sir, but after all, as a pure business matter he would be foolish not to do it. . . . I know that, Baron, but in that respect *we* were not being quite professional. . . . Oh, I agree with you, sir. The father wouldn't have done it. But this is just a boy, isn't it? The last son? A boy soldier trying to save his House? Perhaps your own sons . . . Yes, of course. Quite different . . . Herr Baron, forgive me, it has been done, it's over, I would not let it upset you so much. We have more serious problems today. Yes. Yes. Of course, Stinnes, yes, a *very* different matter. Of course not. . . . Of course, the times . . . Yes . . . Well, he is sitting right here at my desk, I would think some explanation . . . Yes, of course I will. . . . Yes, of course. . . . Very well, sir. . . . Yes, I will explain. Yes. Yes. Yes, sir. Good afternoon, Herr Baron."

Dr. Strassburger replaced the receiver, slumped back into his chair, and expelled his breath. "I understand you just witnessed an unusual event in German social history."

I must have looked blank.

"You saw a member of our ancient Prussian aristocracy pay off his mortgage in full, and in cash."

"You mean Sigrid's brother?"

Dr. Strassburger raised his eyebrows. *"Sigrid's brother?*

. . . Yes, of course: Sigrid's brother . . . Lieutenant Count von Brühl zu Zeydlitz — as I call him — walked in the door and paid off the entire mortgage on his family's estate out in the Mark Brandenburg: a castle, a couple of farms, a forest, a village for the workers, stables for I don't know how many horses, several thousand acres of not-very-fertile land. . . . We made them a loan of three million marks in 1913, apparently to replace another one they had with Bleichröder. They needed cash because they had to support I think one general — that was the father — plus three sons in the Garde-du-Corps, a regiment in which each officer required at least six horses, a groom, a batman, and possibly a lady friend or two. The principal on the mortgage is not due until 1933, but they paid interest at 4½ percent per annum. That is, they paid interest until the father was killed — an auto accidnt in France — in 1918. The older sons — the cavalry officers — had all been killed already. Just the youngest son left, still in cadet school. What were we supposed to do? Foreclose? Sell the Rittergut Schloss Zeydlitz to some Ukrainian stock market operator? Throw the widowed Countess and her daughter out into the snow? And then, on top of everything, Alfred comes home from the War and marries the daughter! Not an easy situation for Waldstein and Co. You agree?"

I agreed.

"So the Brühls just sit on their estate and the mortgage remains in default." Dr. Strassburger leaned forward, dipped his pen into a silver inkwell, and began to make some calculations on a lined accounting pad. The pince-nez was back on his nose, his brow was furrowed, he almost seemed to be enjoying himself as he did the numbers: "Three million at 4 ½ percent compounded . . . no interest in 1918 . . . 1919 . . . 1920 . . . 1921 . . . 1922 . . . let's say three months of 1923 . . . let's say a 5 percent prepayment penalty . . ." The pen scratched columns of figures onto the paper. He picked up the telephone. "Give me Herr Borgenicht. . . . Borgenicht, have they figured out the Brühl payment? No, I don't mean counted the bills, have they computed the exact amount? Well, what is it? Thank you." He hung up, and actually smiled at me. "I was rather close: 3,930,590 marks. About one hundred and thirty dollars — in any event, the proceeds of Count Brühl's winter potato crop, which he

brought us this afternoon — and freed his estate from debt
for the first time since . . ." Dr. Strassburger stroked his
chin, still smiling a little . . . , "since — I suppose — the
first Herr von Brühl learned how to write his name under
a mortgage! You see, inflation works in different ways."

"Well, I can also see why the Baron is angry."

"Oh, he is just furious. Because you see, it is a family
matter. We are a private bank. The big banks, Deutsche
Bank, Disconto-Gesellschaft, they are responsible to public shareholders, they could not sit there for five years
with no interest being paid on a mortgage of three million
marks. They would have had to do something. But we
just sit there, we do nothing until the brother of Alfred's
beautiful Sigrid, the uncle of the Baron's granddaughter
the little Marie, this gentleman — practically a relative
— this gentleman walks in with two bags full of worthless
money and pays his debt. Apparently the Brühls do not
feel quite so sentimental about a mortgage as the Waldsteins!"

And apparently, for some reason, Dr. Strassburger was
not grief-stricken by this blow to the bank in which he
was a senior partner. In fact, the incident had brought
some color to his cheeks. He looked better.

"You were telling me about your brother's family. . . ."

"Yes, yes, my God, we have become completely distracted —" he glanced at the clock above the mantel. "I
wish to tell you about my nephew, one of my nephews,
who is a bit of a problem. He did not do well in school, he
did not do his *Abitur* so he cannot go to the University, he
is here in Berlin and he wants of all things to become a
film writer!"

"Well, that sounds like fun. They'e making lots of films
here, aren't they?"

"Fun?" asked Dr. Strassburger angrily. "I don't know
if it is fun, I only know here is this boy with very little education and no money and no job, he hangs about out
there at Neu-Babelsberg and tries to sell them his little
scripts for their films, but of course they have not bought
them, and the people in the film business . . . you know,
they are not exactly . . . let us say they are not exactly
the kind of people you will meet at Waldstein's. And I
have the feeling . . ." By now he looked tired again. "I
have the feeling this boy will get into trouble."

"What kind of trouble?"

"I give him money, I give him an adequate allowance, but he seems to have too much money. He has a car, for example. Where does he get money for a car? You know what a car costs in Berlin today? This boy just out of school, he drives around in a car!"

"Maybe he's playing the market, like everybody else."

Dr. Strassburger shook his head. "No, he would talk to me about that. Whatever this is, he won't talk about it. But I think I know." He leaned across the desk and stared at me and formed the word with his lips: "Cocaine."

"There's a lot of it around," I said, remembering Bärbel's nose slowly, lazily descending to just a millimeter above the folded paper, her eyes slightly crossed as she focused on the tiny heap of white powder, her finger holding one nostril shut, the harsh long rasping sniff, and then the eyes coming up uncrossed to smile into mine. "I saved the rest for you," but I had shaken my head, afraid, so she had shrugged her naked shoulders, closed the other nostril, and inhaled what was left of the powder. . . .

"I want him out of Berlin," said Dr. Strassburger. "I want him out of Germany before there is a scandal, but there is only one place where he will go, and that is California."

"Because of the films?"

"Because of the films."

"Does he know English?"

"Yes, his English is quite good, it is the only subject he would study in school because he wanted to read the English plays."

"For a German to go to the United States today . . . I mean the money . . ."

"Of course. It would be quite impossible with German money, but fortunately we have money in Amsterdam, we will use Dutch guilders to buy them tickets from Rotterdam to New York, and from Thomas Cook in Amsterdam we have the railroad tickets, the New York Central, I think —" Dr. Strassburger had taken out his key ring and was unlocking one of the drawers in his desk. "I think it is the New York Central Railroad to Chicago —" He extracted a file folder, opened it, began to leaf through the documents. "Yes, and then the Union Pacific Railroad from Chicago to Los Angeles . . ."

"Did you say *them*, Dr. Strassburger?"

He stopped shuffling the papers and leaned forward. "Now finally I will explain how you can help me. To enter the United States on an immigration visa one must have an American sponsor who will sign a paper saying that the immigrant will not become a public charge. We have such a sponsor for my nephew. It is a distant cousin of his mother's, a dentist in St. Louis who is not at all proud of his German relatives but who has reluctantly agreed to sign the paper, partly because he is assured that my nephew will not stop in St. Louis and partly because he knows that the American authorities have never — we understand never or almost never — enforced these agreements. They are treated as a mere formality. Even so, however, the good dentist in St. Louis will *not* sign such an agreement for a young woman my nephew has persuaded to accompany him, a young woman without whom he will not leave Berlin, a young woman whom he is going to make into a film star in California, a young woman who has been — I am informed — introduced to you!" The open folder came sliding across the desk and Dr. Strassburger leaned back into his chair, out of breath.

A pile of forms.

UNITED STATES OF AMERICA
Immigration and Naturalization Service

The first thing I saw was the photograph, slightly blurred by an official seal. A very young girl, blonde pigtails, the sailor's collar of what I guess we would call a middy blouse. I didn't recognize her immediately and looked at the name. Large letters, blue ink:
KIRSANOFF, *Kyra Aleksandrovna* . . .
"This is Bobby's girl!" I exclaimed. "Isn't this Bobby's Russian countess?"
Sunk far back into his chair, Dr. Strassburger nodded. "Perhaps it would be more accurate to say this is the Russian countess Bobby believes to be his girl. He is certainly supporting her. But when he is not with her . . ." Dr. Strassburger cleared his throat. "I have not met the lady myself, of course, but as you see, she has filled out all the applications, and they are unusually complicated because she is in Berlin on a Nansen passport, her father was in Denikin's Army and the Bolsheviks took away the Russian citizenship from those people —"

I interrupted him. "Are you paying for her too, Dr. Strassburger?"

"Does that matter? I assure you this is a mere formality, she will not in any circumstances become your financial obligation. I think you know us well enough now —"

"That's not my problem, Dr. Strassburger. My problem is that Bobby doesn't know a thing about all this, does he?"

"Of course not."

"And Christoph doesn't either, because Christoph would tell Bobby."

Dr. Strassburger looked at me.

"And Bobby's father is using *his* Dutch guilders to send this girl as far away as he can get her. Is that correct?"

"Correct."

I felt blood flushing into my face. "Well, may I just ask one question, Dr. Strassburger? Why does everybody assume that *I'm* not going to tell Bobby about this? I mean, he's my friend too, you know!"

Dr. Strassburger had touched his fingertips together and now he was holding his hands in front of his mouth in a thoughtful, somewhat prayerful position.

"He is your friend, yes. But how does it help your friend to bring him news that will only hurt him? The feeling seems to be, Ellis, that while Bobby may be your friend, another member of that family is of considerably greater interest to you. The feeling is that in a matter of this delicacy you may welcome an opportunity to assist her father *and* her mother in a project that is, I assure you, very close to their hearts."

"Well then, why don't *they* ask me?"

A long pause while we looked at each other. Outside in the Gendarmenmarkt, church bells began to toll the hour. I stood up and took out my fountain pen. "Where do I sign?"

28.

SMALL CHANGE

It rained so hard the day I left,
The weather it was dry,
The sun so hot I froze to death,
Susannah, don't you cry!

It *was* raining and I *did* feel like crying, but I don't suppose the legless musician knew the words he was playing on his accordion. He was sitting in a doorway, protected from the rain, his leather-covered stumps supporting the accordion, and he was only playing an American song for a passing American. Instead of a tin cup he had an open suitcase, in which a rusty horseshoe was keeping a little mountain of bills from blowing away, and I hardly knew what I should give him.

"Please sir, amerikanische Münzen?" he croaked as he saw me hesitate, and when I found a couple of copper pennies to throw into the suitcase, he dropped the accordion in his haste to fish them out.

I don't remember where this was — somewhere in the financial district, the Jägerstrasse or the Behrenstrasse. I was walking aimlessly through the rain, numb, furious, hating myself, feeling that I had to talk to *somebody*.

I walked for hours. I must have walked all over Berlin. In front of every grocery store, in front of every butcher shop, in front of every bakery, I saw long lines of weary rain-soaked people — mostly women — but at the time I was too absorbed in my own problems to wonder why.

They tell you that you shouldn't drink when you feel depressed. They tell you that, you know they're right, but you do it anyway. The rain was pouring down, I wanted a drink, so eventually I walked down the steps of a Bierkeller.

I wish I hadn't done that.

The place was big and dark and smoky and crowded, a

real cellar with stone walls and a slimy tiled floor. It reeked of beer and wet clothing. I found a place at the bar and ordered "ein Klares" — just a shot of clear, colorless schnapps. I carefully counted out six hundred marks while the burly bartender stared at me in what seemed an unusually hostile manner. I drank the shot, felt the warmth, felt a little better, ordered another — and only then became conscious of some kind of commotion going on at the back of the cellar, shouts and laughter, shrieks, people pushing and shoving to watch something — so I asked the bartender what was going on.

"Some of your countrymen having fun," he said through his teeth. I paid for the second drink, drank it, and pushed my way deeper into the cellar.

This was not a night crowd. These were bank cashiers, secretaries, telephone operators, sales clerks from the big department stores — people going home from work — and they were saying things like "Unverschämt!" and "Schweinerei!" while standing on tiptoe and even climbing on chairs to watch whatever was going on.

Of course I should have walked out, but I was curious and maybe a little relieved to have my thoughts distracted, so I shoved forward and suddenly saw a completely naked woman crawling around on the floor, a heavy middle-aged woman with shaking white buttocks, crawling around on her hands and knees and picking coins off the dirty wet tiles.

Two men were leaning back against the bar, watching the woman on the floor. The others had moved away from them. They wore hats and raincoats, celluloid collars, tiepins, cufflinks, watch chains stretched across their vests . . . a couple of middle-aged traveling salesmen. The one with heavy horn-rimmed glasses was showing a handful of coins — American small change.

The other one was tugging at his sleeve. "Come on, Charlie, that's enough now, let's get the hell outa here!"

"Leave me alone, for Christ's sake," said Charlie, brushing the hand off. "Okay, girls, who's next?"

In the meantime the naked woman was back on her feet, pushing herself into the crowd which surrounded her as she struggled back into her clothes.

"I want to see a bunch of them at once," said Charlie to the fat barmaid who was pouring his drink. "How much you think that'll take?" He was talking English, but

she seemed to understand, because she clapped her hands
and shouted into the crowd: "All right, ladies, this time
there is a chance for everybody. He's going to throw *five
dollars!*" There was a gasp from the crowd. She reached
across the bar and took some coins from Charlie's hand.
"This one is twenty-five cents, one quarter of one dollar,
seven thousand five hundred marks! This little silver one
is ten cents, one tenth of a dollar, three thousand marks!
This one with the Indian on one side and the buffalo on
the other side, five cents, one thousand five hundred
marks! And these copper pennies, they are only three hundred marks, good for one beer. But remember, you are not
allowed to pick them up if you have one stitch of clothes
on!"

The bartender who served me was beside her now.
"Are you completely crazy? That's more money than we
make in a week! You're going to cause a riot with this
Schweinerei, the cops will come —"

"You shut your mouth," the barmaid said, her face glistening with sweat and excitement. "For that much money
I might just strip myself!" and the American reached
across the bar and pressed all of the change into her large
red palm.

"Here you go, sweetheart. You toss 'em for me."

The barmaid grinned and held the fistful of change up
in the air. The armpit of her dress was black with sweat.

"Eins!" she shouted, her huge breasts rising.

"Wait a minute!" I said it in English and the Americans
looked at me, but it was too late, because all through the
crowd secretaries and telephone operators and salesgirls
who worked all week long for the equivalent of one buffalo nickel were pulling their dresses over their heads,
kicking off their shoes, rolling down their stockings . . .

"Zwei!"

What was I supposed to do? What could I do?

"Drei!" A shower of American coins flew across the
room, rattled off the walls, hit the tiles and rolled all over
the cellar, as a dozen naked women — old ones, young
ones, fat ones, thin ones — began to scramble about on
the slippery floor, picking up the coins with their fingernails, shoving each other out of the way, crawling under
the tables, crawling between the legs of the watching
men. . . .

The watching men. I watched the watching men, know-

ing that somebody would pay for this, someday; knowing
that it wouldn't be two salesmen from Chicago — or
wherever they were from. It may sound erotic but it
wasn't erotic at all. It was a nightmare, a painting by
Hieronymus Bosch.

I guess I could have done something, but I didn't.

I didn't do anything at all. I put up my coat collar and
walked up the steps into the rain.

29.

WHY NOT PAINT LILI?

By the time I reached Miss Boatwright's apartment in
the Dorotheenstrasse I was such a mess that her maid
didn't want to let me in. I was forming a puddle in the
dark gloomy hallway when Miss Boatwright appeared,
took one long look into my eyes, grapsed my hand without a single word and dragged me down her corridor into
a large, brightly lighted bathroom. She turned the taps;
steamy water rushed into the iron tub.

"Miss Boatwright —"

"Peter Ellis, I want thee out of those clothes, all of
them! Throw them into the corridor, and get in that tub
and stay in it for fifteen minutes. In the meantime we
will prepare a pot of tea and find something for thee to
wear while Anna dries your things."

"Miss Boatwright, I've got to talk to you."

"I see that, but I won't listen to a word until thee's had
a bath and a cup of tea!"

I didn't say anything about the circus in the beer hall.
Barefoot, wrapped in large Turkish towels and Miss
Boatwright's own mackintosh, I sat on the sofa beside
the iron coal stove in the same plain living room where
the First Day Meetings were held, and I poured out the
story about Bobby and Dr. Strassburger's nephew and
the Countess Kyra Aleksandrovna Kirsanoff.

Miss Boatwright drank her tea and watched me silently until I had talked myself out. Then she said, "Well, they've put thee in a very difficult position, I quite agree, but I'm not sure what else was to be done. *Assuming.*"

"Assuming what, Miss Boatwright?"

"Assuming thee is really that serious about Lili."

"Oh, but I am, Miss Boatwright."

"She's still in school. She's five years younger —"

"I think about her every minute —"

"Every minute? Gracious. Spend much time with her?"

"They won't let me! I'm never allowed to be alone with her —"

"So thee spends considerable time down in Neukölln?"

"Well, that's where I'm painting, Miss Boatwright. That's where I have my lessons."

"And of course that's where the models are."

"Yes, that's right, you've seen them."

"Yes, I've seen them. One very much in the flesh, the others most vividly portrayed in the galleries." A long thoughtful pause. Miss Boatwright drank her tea.

I felt better. She was right. What else could I have done? I owed it to Strassburger. I owed it to the Waldsteins, who were only doing it for Bobby's good. If she's carrying on with Strassburger's nephew while Bobby is supporting her, we're all doing him a favor by sending her to Los Angeles. . . .

Aren't we?

Why didn't Miss Boatwright say something? These were the reassurances I wanted from her. . . .

"Why not paint Lili?" Miss Boatwright put her cup and saucer on the table.

Why not paint Lili?

"Someone might suggest that Peter Ellis would like to attempt a portrait of Lili. . . . He's grateful for the Waldsteins' hospitality. . . . When is the Baron's birthday? One might enlist her mother's support, and if it were to be a surprise then of course the painting couldn't be done at home. . . ."

Helena set it up. Her apartment on the Lützowufer was only a few blocks from Lili's school, and somehow the Baroness was persuaded that Helena or at least her maid would be there all the time, and she liked the idea of a little portrait for the Baron's birthday, which turned out to be in August.

Helena really did stay with us, for the first sitting. It was in her kitchen, where she decided the smell of my paints and turpentine would bother her the least. Of course her maid didn't like it and Lili didn't like it either, but Helena was adamant.

"You're only going to work for a few hours after school, and Clara can do her shopping then. It's a large kitchen, there's a skylight —" so we sat in the kitchen.

"You want me to take my clothes off?"

"Lili!" I had never seen Helena shocked.

"He only paints women with their clothes off!"

"Nonsense. He's going to become our American Magnus, painting only beautiful rich ladies for enormous fees."

"Beautiful rich ladies sitting in their cousins' kitchens?"

I had never heard of Magnus.

"He was the painter of Berlin society," said Helena. "He painted the royal family, he painted Jenny Lind at least three times, he painted the wives of princes and the wives of bankers — and he painted the picture of my mother in the living room."

"All the ladies Magnus painted were beautiful," said Lili. "Apparently there were no ugly princesses in Berlin. No ugly bankers' wives."

"Well, my mother *was* beautiful," said Helena. "You've seen the photogtaphs!"

"Yes, and a *very* successful actress . . ."

While they chattered I began to block out a tentative charcoal sketch of Lili as she sat with her chin propped in her hand, her elbow on the kitchen table, her eyes firmly on me as she bantered with Helena, and after a while I didn't hear them anymore.

I guess I worked up the courage during the third or fourth sitting. I know it was still in Helena's kitchen, so it must have been at the end of April. I had started on the actual painting, and I still had her in the same pose, with her chin in her hand and her elbow on the table and she still didn't like it. Claimed she didn't like it.

"Who ever saw a portrait of a lady with her elbow on the table?"

"Well, that's how you were sitting when we started."

"You're the artist. You're supposed to tell me how to pose."

"I paint people the way they are."

"Yes, I have noticed that."

"Look, are you going to continue on that subject —"

"Not at this moment." She stood up. "I have to go to the bathroom." She walked out of the kitchen and I stood up too and rubbed my hands to loosen up the right one and paced around to stretch my legs and heard the toilet flushing at the other end of the hall, and I walked out to meet her in the half-light out there and took her in my arms and kissed her on the mouth and she put her arms around my neck and kissed me back as if it was the most natural thing in the world and when we stopped she said: "Well, it took you quite some time to get around to that!"

"Lili, I love you, I'm absolutely crazy about you —"

"Ach, you must love me passionately, it has taken you — how long? Almost a year? — to give me a little kiss!"

"Well, where was I supposed to kiss you?"

"Here on my mouth, to begin —"

"No, damn it, you know what I mean, I haven't seen you alone for one minute since last summer —"

"Because you are so occupied with your friends in Neukölln —"

"Oh for God's sake, won't you stop that? I'm really serious about this, I'm in love with you, I want to be with you for the rest of my life, I want you to marry me!"

She moved back a step, out of my arms. "Now really, Mr. Ellis, that is not required, at least not in Germany. You don't have to propose marriage just because you kiss a girl."

The only light was coming through the open kitchen door and I couldn't see her face very well. "Are you taking this as a joke?"

No reply. I reached forward, took her hand and pulled her toward the kitchen under the skylight.

"You find all this funny?" I asked again.

She lowered her eyes and shook her head.

I tipped her chin up and made her look at me. "You want to marry me, Lili?"

She put her hands on my shoulders. "Just look at me.

A schoolgirl, in a stupid uniform. I'm not even allowed to cut my hair. You think I would be allowed to marry?"

"I didn't ask if you would be allowed to. I asked if you *wanted* to."

She swallowed, looked down, looked up again, closed her eyes — and nodded.

"You do! Oh my God, that's *terrific* — but there's one thing I've got to tell you. About myself."

The eyes came up.

"During the War . . . something happened to me . . . I sort of went crazy. They had to put me in the hospital —"

She smiled and shook her head and put her hand over my mouth. "We know all about that, Peter. Christoph told us before he brought you out."

"I think I'm all right now."

"Of course you are all right. Why don't you kiss me some more?"

"May I talk to your father this evening?"

"Talk to my father? Absolutely *not!*"

"But I've got to ask him."

"No-no-no-no-no! You don't ask him *anything!* Not a single word to anyone, or they will just lock me up or send me to school in Switzerland or something and you will not be allowed to come near me! We must be very careful and we must wait."

"Why? Wait for what?"

"First of all, my father is *terribly* upset just now — about the inflation, it is ruining the country, what will happen to the Bank, what will happen to Germany, is there going to be another revolution . . . and he is deeply hurt by Sigrid's family, how they repaid his generosity with worthless money . . . and then there is Bobby, who seems to be almost going crazy because of the Russian tramp. He's had one woman after another — chorus girls and opera singers and ballet dancers — and it's never made much difference to him, but this one leaves him and he just collapses. It's horrible. I don't think a man should hang that much on any woman. He won't even get out of bed in the morning, he hardly appears at the Bank, he stays out all night and gets drunk, and my father just doesn't know what to do about him."

"Well, I understand that your father has problems, but

are we supposed to wait until all of Germany's problems
are solved—"

"Of course not. We have to wait until I am out of
school, until my family is entirely used to you — we have
to wait for exactly the right moment."

"And how will we know when that is?"

"That is my job. When the right moment comes, I will
tell you." She looked at the wristwatch I had given her.
"Now in a few minutes Helena will come home, then a
little later Christoph will appear, perhaps they would like
to be alone together. If you want to take me home, I am
sure my mother will invite you to stay for dinner."

"That sounds very nice."

"But there is time for you to kiss me again."

30.

COLD WIND IN MAY.

It was still cold on the island. The sky was gray and the
water was gray, and the steady wind blowing across the
Havel from the direction of the Kaiser Wilhelm Tower
was strong enough to raise whitecaps. It was Monday afternoon; only a few sails maneuvered briskly along the
empty beaches on the opposite shore.

Sigrid von Waldstein stood with me behind the reeds
and watched a smoke-belching tugboat pulling two barges
of sand toward Kladow.

She still had not come to the point.

She had knocked on my door, apologized for interrupt-
ing me, and asked if I would like to take a walk. Alfred
was working, and the baby was asleep, she would like to
get some air and talk with me. She had never done that
before. In fact, I had never been alone with her before.

Sigrid and Alfred occupied their Little House all winter. On the first of May, Lili and her parents and their
servants had moved back into the Schloss, and that meant
new arrangements for the portrait project. Since she was
still in school, Lili usually rode into town on an early

train from Nikolassee with her father but then was expected to return in the late afternoon, which left no time for the hours at Helena's apartment.

The answer was the Little House. Lili worked it out with Sigrid and since we didn't make any noise, Alfred raised no objections — in fact he asked me to do something about Sigrid's English, to speak English with her at meals, to let her read English plays to me while I worked. . . .

There wasn't much room in the Little House, but they gave me a comfortable garret with a cot and a chair and a desk and a magnificent view across the treetops and the water, toward Potsdam. Of course I couldn't be there every day, but I began with the weekends and they gradually became longer. Lili came up and sat for me whenever she could get away. I made one change in the pose: I still had her sitting at the table with her face in her hand, but now she was contemplating an object on the table — my Christmas present, the wine bottle containing the model of the sailboat.

I bought a Leica and took hundreds of snapshots of Lili's face, and when she could not pose for me I tried to work from the photographs. We went for walks, we talked about putting the boat back into the water, I ate a lot of meals in the Schloss. . . . I don't know what if anything they told her father, but he never seemed surprised to find me at his table, and the portrait was coming along.

"I've been in Berlin over a year," I said to Sigrid, who turned to me as the wind blew golden hair across her face. "The first time Christoph brought me out you were sitting on that bench and Marie was asleep in her carriage."

Sigrid nodded, smiled, brushed the hair out of her eyes. "Was that when he told you about Kaspar? About me and Kaspar?" She stopped smiling and looked at me with steady sky-blue eyes, and I had a feeling she was coming to the point.

"I don't know exactly when . . . I mean, I don't think Christoph —"

"Of course he told you, he must have told you, and Kaspar told you too. I was Kaspar's girl when he was a cadet, then Alfred came home and I fell in love with Alfred and it drove Kaspar crazy. I couldn't help it, Peter! You can't help how you feel about people."

Why all this now?

She took my arm and walked toward the iron bench.

"Peter, I *must* talk to somebody, and there is nobody else. Will you let me talk to you?"

The cold wind blew across the Havel.

"You know I was at home last week — I mean my family's home, Zeydlitz, out in the forests of the Mark, the place where I grew up. I went to see my mother and — well, there was sort of a family celebration, perhaps I shouldn't have gone, perhaps it was disloyal to Alfred and his family, but you can't imagine what it *means* to my mother, to my brother, this mortgage hanging over our heads, year after year with the interest unpaid, the new interest accumulating on the old interest like a stone on your back that gets heavier and heavier, and all the time the feeling that we must be grateful to the Waldsteins, they only don't take our place away because I am married to Alfred, they have the *right* to sell it anytime . . . and now, all of a sudden, with the money from four wagons of potatoes the stone is lifted from our backs!

"Oh, I know that Alfred's father is hurt. He tries not to show it when he is with me, but I feel it and I understand, but in this matter I think my brother was correct. We did not make the inflation, but we would be idiots if we did not pay off this mortgage.

"But Peter, I did not want to talk about the mortgage. Something else. When I was at Zeydlitz, Kaspar was there. With another man from Munich. They were visiting my brother. Kaspar has been in the Ruhr, doing things against the French, blowing up coal trains, I think. He was coming from the Ruhr this time, but mostly he has been in Munich, and he has become a follower of Adolf Hitler. This other man with him, he became the leader of the Richthofen Squadron in the War, he knew one of my older brothers, his name is Hermann Göring, this man has become one of Hitler's top commanders. You know, all these years they have been screaming to each other about the Versailles Treaty and the Communists and the Jews, but they had no leader, no person strong enough to tell them what to do, no person who could make the ordinary worker listen.

"Well, they have found a leader. I listened to Kaspar, I listened to Göring, they talk about this Hitler like the new Messiah! He was nothing but a corporal. A little Aus-

trian with a moustache like Charlie Chaplin. No education. Can't speak German properly. Hermann Göring was
a captain, Richthofen's successor, Kaspar Keith was an
officer cadet, son of a general, and both of them went on
and on about this corporal, how he talks to the people,
how the people listen, how he is going to bring order out
of this chaos, how he is going to unite the Germans, how
he is going to throw out the traitors running the country
— and how he is going to take away the power of the
Jews! First Bavaria, because, they say, the Bavarians are
all behind him; then a march on Berlin. And that was
Göring's mission here, exploring, trying to find out how
the Reichswehr would react, young officers like my
brother, officers commanding troops in the field. Of course
I did not hear the actual discussions, but people like my
brother will always carry out the orders they get, *whatever* orders they get from their generals, so it will all depend on General von Seeckt, what happens."

Sigrid stopped and put her head into her hands. Was
she crying? She sounded excited, disturbed but not tear-
ful. She had not come to the point, so I just waited until
she looked up again, dry-eyed and grim, to continue her
story.

"Why do I tell you all this? Because I am so terribly
worried. About Hitler, yes, all the hatred against the Jews
when my baby is half-Jewish, I just don't know what to
do about all that, I don't even want to *think* about all
that, but there is something more immediate. Have you
heard the word *Feme*? You know what a *Fememord* is?"

"That's what they did to Rathenau."

"And *many* others. They're doing it now in the Ruhr.
Killing people who are cooperating with the French." She
suddenly grasped my wrist. "Kaspar is one of the killers.
He told me. He was drunk one evening, he came into my
room —"

"He came into your room? At night?"

"Yes. He brought a bottle of Cognac and two glasses.
Said he wanted to have a drink with me. What could I do?
Shout and wake the house? And . . . you know —" She
paused and looked down at her shoes, pushing the gravel
around with the heel of her shoe "—you know, I still
have some feeling for Kaspar, I did love him once and I
know I hurt him so badly and I feel so sorry, I feel somehow responsible for what has become of him —" Then

she looked sideways and saw my expression. "No, no, Peter, don't worry, I love Alfred very much. I did not feel *that* sorry for Kaspar, but I did drink with him and let him talk. But perhaps I wish I had not."

"Kaspar mad at us?"

Sigrid nodded.

"Because of the Rathenau thing?"

"Yes. Kaspar is absolutely wild about what you and Christoph did to him. Still! You compromised him with his comrades, you stole their car, you drugged him, you got information from him, you gave Kern's and Fischer's names to the police, you disgraced him, it took him six months of the most dangerous work to prove he's not a traitor too —"

"But why should anybody think he was a traitor when we had to shoot him full of Amytal? It doesn't make sense, Sigrid."

"Of course, but some of these people are quite crazy, you know. It has been suggested that Kaspar wasn't drugged at all, the whole thing was some kind of a trap —"

"A trap? How? For whom?"

"I don't know. I don't think *he* knows, apparently some people think it might have been a trap arranged by Rathenau himself, or perhaps by the Prussian State Police, to make the O.C. expose themselves, to catch them in the act, to catch them just *before* they killed Rathenau —"

"Well, I wish somebody had been that clever!"

"Yes, but Kaspar — he did not tell me this part. This part is what I have had nightmares about —Kaspar hates his brother so much . . . I don't think he hates you, really, you're not a German, you just became involved through friendship . . . but Christoph —"

She stopped and looked at me.

"Sigrid, what are you trying to tell me?"

She shook her head. "Can't say it."

"Well, my God! Why don't you warn him?"

"How can I tell them all I have been with Kaspar?"

"But you haven't *been* with him, have you? You met him visiting your mother."

She shook her head again. "No. They won't like it. They are angry at my family anyway, now here is my brother putting up Hermann Göring at Zeydlitz. And

Kaspar. I thought perhaps to talk with Helena, but she's a Waldstein too." Sigrid kicked the gravel with her foot again. "You are the only one, Peter."

"But what can I do?"

"Get him out of Germany."

"Sigrid, how can I get Christoph out of Germany?"

"I don't know."

"Well . . ." I didn't know either. Where could he go? Why would he go? Would he run away from Kaspar if I told this story?

"What about Miss Boatwright's friend?" asked Sigrid.

"Which friend — Oh, you mean Whitney Wood?"

"Yes. He is a banker in New York?"

"That's right. J. P. Morgan and Company."

"There was some talk of sending Bobby to New York, to learn about American banking methods. They wanted to send Christoph with him. Just for a year or so. But now, with the Russian girl in America, with the dollar so incredibly high . . . there is no more talk about Bobby going to New York."

"Christoph wouldn't do it! Run away from his own brother? He wouldn't think of it!"

"No, you are right. But if he is offered a position in New York, perhaps the opportunity to earn a few dollars for his mother, for his life with Helena —"

I thought about it. Of course I could ask Whitney Wood, but I knew what the answer would be. The people at Morgan (like the people at Drexel) are passionately Anglophile. A lot of their younger men had joined the British or Canadian armies long before we got into the War. They still attended regimental dinners at clubs in London and Toronto. They still detested the Huns. Even now, Herr Oberleutnant Keith, ex–fighter pilot, ex–Death's Head Hussar, would not be welcome at the corner of Broad and Wall streets. And that was only half of it. Although Whitney Wood had been the model of courtesy at the Waldsteins', the people at Morgan's (like the people at Drexel) were anything but fond of Jews — German or any other kind. Would J. P. Morgan's partners hire a man from Waldstein & Co. to learn American banking methods?

"Well, it's an interesting idea, Sigrid. I'll see what I can do, but —"

"But you don't sound optimistic."

"I'm not. I think the best thing would be for you to tell Christoph this story, and let him make his own decision. Why would Christoph care that you've seen Kaspar? Or Göring, for that matter? He knows Göring. He introduced me to Göring, last year. Remember my drawing of 'Hauptmann Ring'?"

"No," said Sigrid firmly. "I don't want to tell Christoph."

"Well then, I'll tell him."

She grabbed my wrist again. "No, Peter, you must not! Promise me you will not! I told you all this in confidence because there is no one else."

"Not even Alfred?"

"Not even Alfred."

31.

ROLLING THUNDER

I spent less time at the Villa Keith now. There always seemed to be a few elderly distinguished-looking gentlemen around, some in uniform, some not. They came for coffee, they came for lunch, they came for dinner. They brought flowers. They were polite to me, but they were not unhappy when I excused myself.

The five dollars I was still slipping Meier every week was worth 1,750,000 marks by now. I knew that it was too much. I knew it was supporting the household and Frau Keith's *salon* and the rest was being salted away, but giving Meier less did not occur to me. Christoph spent almost every evening at Helena's apartment. It was time to find my own place, and yet I couldn't seem to get around to it.

A hot wind blew dust along the streets of Neukölln. Long lines in front of the stores. I knew the reason now: the farmers would not deliver their crops against paper money. Berlin was facing famine.

"It's just like 1919," said Miss Boatwright. I wanted to

talk to her about Kaspar Keith, but she was too busy to listen, or maybe she was tired of being my sounding board. She insisted that I take her to the municipal soup kitchen in the Warschauerstrasse, which she had helped to organize.

An enormous hall, big as an airplane hangar and echoing with noise. Three endless queues waiting to get in, men and women and children carrying containers of every kind: water pitchers, buckets, washbasins, cooking pots, anything that would hold the quart of boiled rice they were allowed to buy when they finally reached the head of the line. Some of these people sat right down at the long tables in the center of the hall and ate the only meal they would get that day, but most of them rushed home to bring the rice, still steaming, to their families. At the other end of the hall about thirty women were peeling potatoes and chopping carrots for tomorrow's soup.

"We have to charge them something," said Miss Boatwright. "Otherwise the place would be simply overrun. Last week the vegetables did not arrive in time and the people went mad. They turned into a mob, they smashed the tables and one of the cooking vats. . . . The only way we can keep some control is to adjust the price every day, so we just charge the same as the trolley fare; that is announced in the newspapers. They've become accustomed to it; they know when they get here the soup will cost the same as a trolley ticket."

I left Miss Boatwright in a deep discussion with a lady from the Berlin Ernährungsamt: What could be done about families that sent each child to stand in line for a quart? Should they require resident passes? It would take forever to check all the addresses. . . .

I saved the trolley fare and walked from the Warschauerstrasse across the bridges over the Spree and the Landwehr Canal into the tenement canyons of Neukölln.

The wind blew dust along the streets, the air was moist, the sky was turning black, and rolling thunder promised the kind of storm we have on summer evenings at home. Fat raindrops were beginning to hit as I swung into the first gloomy courtyard of Kaiser Friedrichstrasse 101 and started the long climb.

I had a key but I always knocked first because you never knew what might be going on in there.

The door opened. *"Mensch!"* Baby threw her arms around my neck and wrapped her legs around my legs so that I almost fell over while she was kissing me. "Where the hell have you been?"

"Oh, I've been working on a special commission. . . . What are you doing? Where is everybody?"

"What am I doing? I'm washing the god-damned dishes! Mutti's out standing in a food line and the kid is with her. . . ."

She followed me through the body-smelling little room full of unmade beds into the studio. Rain was pelting the windows now. Water dripped into the bucket.

"Where's the picture?"

"Fritz took it. He took it to sell."

"But it wasn't finished! He took *my* picture to sell before I finished it?"

"He said it was done enough to sell. He said he wasn't sure you were coming back, and we need money."

"Bärbel putting on her stocking, my best full-length of Bärbel . . . where did he take it? I'm going right out and get it back —"

"Come on now, you haven't been here for weeks, you don't even know what's going on here," said Baby angrily.

"What do you mean? What is going on here?"

"In the first place, Fritz beat the shit out of Bärbel. He made her strip and he tied her wrists to the bedstead and he beat her ass with the steel ruler until it was all red and purple. And her legs too. Boy, you should have heard her!" Baby seemed to relish the memory.

"But why?"

"Because of you."

"Of me?"

"Partly you. You paid her to stay home. She couldn't do it. Bored her. Began working the Adam und Eva again, and then Fritz got the idea she'd given you the clap and that's why you weren't coming around."

"Why would he think she'd given me the clap?"

"Because she gave it to him! And now they *both* have to go to the Charity and get shot with some arsenic drug that makes them puke." Baby put her arms around me. "Bärbel's got the clap, the clap, the clap," she chanted softly in my ear. "So sorry, but she's finally got it, you're lucky, Peter, because I've been a very good girl, and you haven't got the clap, have you? You couldn't have it!"

"You knew I couldn't have it!"

Baby nodded solemnly. "Oh Christ, Peter, you're not really going to leave us, are you? I couldn't stand that!"

"I came to finish the picture," I said, but the picture was gone and Baby was pulling her dress over her head.

"Is this what you call 'necking'?"

"Mmm . . . Like it?"

"Oh yes . . . but why 'necking'? You are not even touching my neck."

"I don't know. . . . Where did you hear that word?"

"I read it in a story Alfred gave me. A new story by a young American."

"What was it called?"

"I don't know. . . . Do that again, I like it when you do that. . . . His name was Fritz something."

"An American called Fritz?"

"No, it was his last name. Fritz with something behind it."

"You don't mean Fitzgerald? Scott Fitzgerald?"

"Yes, I think so."

"Have they translated him into German?"

"No, what do you think? I read it in English. What does 'Fitz' mean?"

"That's Irish, means 'son of.' "

"Like Mendelssohn means 'son of Mendel'?"

"Yes. Just like that."

"Is this all they do, in America?"

"Is what all they do?"

"This necking. What you are doing to me. Don't they take their clothes off?"

"Lili!"

"How can they do anything with all their clothes on? I mean, doesn't it make them nervous?"

"What makes me nervous is that somebody might walk in here, and then what would happen?"

"You are afraid? We can hear anybody moving in this tiny house."

"Lili, I don't want to get thrown out of here."

"Such a passionate cavalier! All right, you want to paint me some more? I don't think this necking is healthy sport."

She suddenly stopped kissing me, moved her head and bit me just as hard as she could bite, at the place above the collarbone where the neck and shoulder come together.

"Think of *me!*" A flash of lightning illuminated the room, and I saw my blood smeared across her mouth. "Open your eyes and see it's *me*, not Bärbel!"

"I wasn't thinking of Bärbel," I said.

"Don't stop," she said.

I didn't.

Later she boiled some water and cleaned the throbbing wound.

"How am I supposed to explain that?" I asked.

"Just keep your shirt on," said Baby placidly.

As usual, her timing was perfect. We had finished dressing and were in the kitchen, looking in vain for something to eat. A key turned in the lock and Mutti Bauer came in, followed by the boy. She was soaking wet and panting from the climb. Her face was scarlet — and streaked with tears. "The Schweinehund!" she gasped. "The filthy, dirty, stinking Schweinehund!"

The boy was pale and silent. They both saw me, but they didn't really see me.

"Who, Mutti?" asked Baby. "What's the matter? Who's a Schweinehund?"

"Schultz the butcher. You know how long I stood in his line? *Four hours!* In the lightning, in the rain, I have water running down inside my legs. And when I got to the front he still had a few sausages behind the glass and you know what he said to me?" She began to cry again, holding out the shopping net packed full of sodden bundled banknotes.

"He said to me, 'Oh no, Frau Bauer. We don't take marks from *you*, Frau Bauer. You've got dollars up there. Those girls of yours, they bring you dollars, and you could buy everything I have left today with a few American coins, so don't bring me a bag full of German marks, Frau Bauer,' and I said, 'This is all I *have*, Herr Schultz, I haven't got any American money,' and he said, 'Na ja, Frau Bauer, you'll just have to send out those sluts of yours to get you some,' and I said, 'I'll call the police on you, you profiteer, you *gangster!*' and then he told me to get out of his store, he did, in front of all the other ladies. . . ." and with that she sank into a kitchen chair and began to sob into her hands.

"Mutti broke the glass," said the boy in a quiet voice.

"Oh God, oh God, I was so ashamed, so ashamed in front of the people, and so angry that I just couldn't stand it and I took my umbrella and I swung it over my head and I smashed the glass case where he had the sausages and then we ran out of the store and Schultz was yelling, 'Police! Somebody call the police!' and now they're going to come up here and drag me to the Alexanderplatz. . . ."

It took us quite a while to calm her down.

My first instinct was to send the boy back with some American change, to placate the butcher and get something for them to eat. But if I did that, I would just be proving the butcher's point, wouldn't I?

"It's all because of the Jews," said the boy suddenly.

"What?" I turned to him. "What about the Jews?"

"That's what the man in the line was saying. The Jewish middlemen have bought all the meat and they're holding it for higher prices, they borrow the money from their Jewish banks and they're making all this profit —"

I thought of all the people standing in lines all over Germany, and I felt a chill. "Why don't we all go out and get something to eat?" I suggested. "Look, the rain has stopped and the sun is coming out. Isn't there a nice Gasthaus around here somewhere?"

"Treptow Park!" Baby shouted.

"But the police . . ." Mutti Bauer was still sobbing and wiping her eyes.

"Well, they can't arrest you if you're not here," I said. I also had a feeling that butchers were not permitted to demand payment in American money. Maybe the police were not coming.

"Hurry up and put on your other dress," said Baby. "And your good hat. Peter's going to take us over to Treptow. We'll sit along the river and have supper and listen to the band, and maybe he'll dance with us." Her eyes were shining.

My shoulder ached. So did my heart.

32.

WALDSTEIN'S VOICE

"Herr Reichskanzler, Herr Generaloberst, Your Excellencies. . . . my dear cousin Eduard, to whom we lift our glasses . . ."

Helena's father was making a speech. He was not supposed to be making a speech. He was supposed to be proposing the last of many birthday toasts to Lili's father, the toast on behalf of the family, but as I looked at the family faces — especially the face of Lili's mother — I saw them realize they had made a mistake. The audience had gone to his head: not only all the Waldsteins and all the people they had married; not only the other landowners on the island; not only all the partners of Waldstein & Co, and their biggest clients; not only the heads of the Deutsche Bank and the Disconto-Gesellschaft and the Dresdner Bank and the Darmstädter Bank and Mendelssohn & Co. and Hardy & Co. and Delbrück Schickler & Co. and S. Bleichröder & Co.; not only incidental guests like Miss Boatwright and Whitney Wood and Christoph Keith and his mother and me; but also the new Chancellor, Dr. Gustav Stresemann, who had just formed a coalition when Dr. Cuno's government fell, a few days ago; several of Stresemann's cabinet ministers — and Colonel-General Hans von Seeckt, head of the General Staff, commander-in-chief of the Reichswehr.

If I had guessed what kind of party this was going to be, I would never have agreed to Lili's plan and now I didn't want to go through with it. Watching me, she knew it.

Helena's father faced the guests from the edge of the terrace, his back to the glorious August evening, horse chestnuts and weeping willows, cloudless sky and miles of water still speckled with white sails; on the opposite beaches the sun was still warming the picnickers. . . .

"Peter, he's going too fast for me," said Miss Boatwright into my ear. "What's he saying?"

What was he saying? Trying to interpret while somebody is talking is one of the hardest things in the world and of course I couldn't do it, but I tried.

At noon I had beached the boat in a sandy, shady cove on the west bank of the Havel, a few miles above the island. The girls wanted to swim before lunch.

"You didn't get much tan yet," said Helena as I took off my shirt.

"He read somewhere that sunlight hurts your skin," said Lili. "Isn't that nonsense?"

The tooth marks were practically invisible by now, but Helena spotted them instantly. "Sunlight? I can imagine things that hurt more." She gave me a mocking glance as she fastened her black cap, and then she stepped out of the boat with Lili. They sloshed into the sunlit water.

Christoph stood up to drop the slacks he was wearing over his two-piece bathing suit, and with a shock I realized that I had not seen his bare legs since that morning at Verdun.

His eyes followed mine. "Healed pretty well, don't you think?"

White scar tissue where the bullet had gone in and where the shinbone had come out. The wounded leg was thinner and shorter than the other one.

"Yes, it looks very good," I lied. "Can you swim all right?"

"You'll see. I paddle around a little."

The girls had walked in to their hips, launched themselves, and were now swiming breaststroke and shouting to each other. White arms and a black cap, brown arms and a white one.

I realized that Christoph was hesitating. His feet already in the dark wet sand, he sat down on the gunwale and turned to look at me.

"Peter . . . I think perhaps it is time for you to go home."

"Go home? Where?"

"Home to America. I think it is time." He looked straight into my eyes.

"Why, Christoph?"

"I feel, perhaps, your life may be in danger."

"*My* life? Christoph, has this got something to do with Kaspar?"

He pursed his lips and nodded, looking down into the sand. "Remember the heavy blond man to whom I introduced you in the Romanisches Café last year? The aviator? You drew his picture, called him Hauptmann Ring —"

"Of course I remember him. Hermann Göring, he's become one of Hitler's boys—"

"Not just one of his boys. He's one of the inner circle, he's become the chief of Hitler's Sturmabteilung, the S. A. He's got thousands of men in brown uniforms —"

"Well, what about him?"

"I had a drink with him the other evening."

"You had a drink with Hermann Göring?"

Christoph nodded. "Called me at the Bank, if you please. Asked if we could meet someplace where neither of us would be known, he had something to tell me. So we remembered a little bar near the station down in Steglitz where cadets used to meet girls, and I took the Stadtbahn after work and there he was, in civilian clothes, and we sat in a dark corner and had some drinks and talked. He talked; I mostly listened."

Lili and Helena were swimming out into the stream. We could hear their voices but not what they were saying.

"Göring really had two messages. One was an invitation. The other was a warning. The invitation was to change sides. He says they're really going to make a Putsch in Bavaria this year. The Bavarians hate Berlin. They hate the Republic, and so far as they're concerned, Berlin is the Republic, the Republic is Berlin. The Reichswehr commander in Munich is General von Lossow, and he's a Bavarian. Of course he is supposed to be under von Seeckt, but Göring's not so sure that Lossow is going to obey Seeckt when the shooting starts. So Göring thinks there is a good chance that Bavaria will go for Hitler this year, and then it's the March on Berlin, and then — who knows? Things can't go on this way, we all agree on that. Is Seeckt going to back up Stresemann if the whole country rises? Who knows? But in any event, Göring says they need somebody with my training, in other words they need somebody to manage the money that's coming in now, and he says that Hitler is absolutely fanatic in his anti-Semitism, there's just no reasoning with him about it, and if he gets into the saddle he's going to take serious action against the Jews."

"What does that mean?" I asked.

"He didn't say. I don't think he knows. Maybe Hitler doesn't know himself. He's already blaming the inflation on the Jews, and the people *need* somebody to blame. But Göring's point is I'm on the wrong side, and I'd better switch while there's time."

"And what did you say?"

"I thanked him for his advice."

We were watching the girls. Their faces were turned toward us. "WHAT ARE YOU TWO TALKING ABOUT?" shouted Helena.

"I thanked him, but I said it was a little late for me to change sides. He meant it well. He's convinced they're going to win, that Hitler has the answer because Hitler can bring the people together again. Maybe he's right. But he also came to talk about Kaspar and that is really what I want to tell you. Kaspar has been making threats."

"Is Kaspar in the S.A.?"

"Well, the answer is yes and no, apparently. They're having trouble with Kaspar and his friends. They've joined the S.A., but now the S.A.'s not good enough for them. Too many unemployed mail carriers, bus drivers, factory workers — ordinary fellows who just want jobs. Kaspars' friends don't want jobs, they want to be soldiers. Some sort of elite corps."

"Only for killers."

"That's right. They are trying to transfer into something the Reichswehr has set up, a secret command where they train troops that the Allied Control Commission doesn't know about, nobody knows quite where they're training — but it's run from the Bendlerstrasse, it's called the 'Black' Reichswehr, it's run by Seeckt's officers — but it seems they won't take Freikorps people. They never have wanted Freikorps people in the Reichswehr and they don't want them now, so Kaspar is frustrated again."

"Is Sigrid's brother in this Black Reichswehr?"

Christoph rubbed his hand across his mouth, thinking. "Brühl . . . No . . . No, he's regular Reichswehr, they took him straight from cadet school, same time poor Kaspar ran off with Ehrhardt's Brigade . . . but he could be mixed up in the project, it's definitely being run by regular officers —"

Maybe I wouldn't have to tell him about Sigrid's meeting with Kaspar. Had I promised her I wouldn't? "What did Göring say about Kaspar? He's made threats against me?"

"Well, both of us, apparently, but of course he wouldn't do anything to me. Göring says that Kaspar is still berserk about the Rathenau thing, the idea that you and I betrayed Kern and Fischer, gave information to the police, betrayed our name, if you please, my name, I betrayed my own name! . . . and that he's not controllable, I mean even though he is enlisted in the S.A. they can't control him, he's done things in the Ruhr — as a matter of fact, Hitler blows hot and cold on the Ruhr, sometimes he is more interested in bringing down our government than in getting the French out of there, and all this dynamiting coal trains and shooting collaborationists is not necessarily what Hitler wants done —"

"But Kaspar does it anyway."

"Kaspar and the other Freikorps people, especially the Ehrhardt O.C. people — they do what they want."

"Let's get back to the point, Christoph. Göring warned you, didn't he? He thought it was serious enough to warn you. And you can't tell me that Hermann Göring gives a damn what happens to *me*. Göring told you that Kaspar's made specific threats against *you!* Didn't he?"

Christoph shook his head. "It's complete nonsense, it's only little-boy talk, he's a boy who has been through a great deal, but nobody is going to tell me that my little brother —"

"It is not nonsense, it's true," and then I had to tell him Sigrid's story and I had to tell it very fast because the black bathing cap and the white bathing cap were moving toward us.

"WHAT'S WRONG WITH YOU TWO? THE WATER'S NOT COLD! CAN'T YOU AT LEAST OPEN THE WINE?"

Trying to translate for Miss Boatwright:
". . . ladies and gentlemen: with the possible exception of my cousin Fritz, who was a baby, I must be the only person here today who remembers Eduard's *eleventh* birthday, on this very terrace, anno 'seventy-one. And what a summer that was! Our victorious army back from France, some of our fathers still in their uniforms . . . I remember an excursion steamer out there on the water,

band playing 'Die Wacht am Rhein' . . . a new nation,
ladies and gentlemen —"

Dr. Stresemann and General von Seeckt look like caricatures of what they are: the balding shiny-pated German
Bürger, small moustache, small saber scar, creased neck,
wing collar; the slim Prussian Junker, thick short white
hair, clipped white moustache, icy blue eyes, monocle,
Pour le mérite dangling at his throat . . .

"What have we today, ladies and gentlemen, on
Eduard's sixty-fifth birthday? Our nation, united in eighteen seventy-one, is about to break apart, our nation is
about to explode! The French are in the Ruhr, trying to
organize a separate state. The Poles are in Silesia. And
in Munich? In Munich the fanatics of the Right and the
Bavarian royalists are getting ready to cut Bavaria out of
the Reich, getting ready — we are told — for a march on
Berlin. This evening we look out on a peaceful scene
which has not changed in my memory — the sailboats
and the water and the sky — but all of us know what is
going on behind that scenery. And what is really worst,
no longer the result but now the *cause itself!* This nightmare! *This disaster!* The death of our money! Every person on this terrace knows what the *Dollarkurs* was on
Friday afternoon: Five million marks to the dollar!
What will it be on Monday morning? Every printing press
in Germany is printing banknotes for the Reichsbank,
printing money twenty-four hours a day. All of you are
paying your employees twice a day so they can rush out
to the stores and buy something before that money becomes worthless a few hours later. And now we reach the
point where people simply won't *take* these paper marks.
First it was the farmers, now even the stores don't want
them. In the meantime, every town and city is issuing its
own money, many business firms are issuing their own
money. I understand that Waldstein & Co. pays its employees with Waldstein's own notes. The name of some
village in the Black Forest is worth more than the name
of the German Reich! The name of Waldstein and Co. is
worth more than the name of the German Reich!

"Your Excellencies, ladies and gentlemen, I am not
telling you anything you don't know, but I am begging
you — on this quite inappropriate occasion — to *do
something about it!* We are watching the destruction of
the entire middle class. Their savings have disappeared.

Their pensions have melted away. Hardworking honest
people who saved their money according to rules we all
grew up on — these people are today wiped out. Without a penny! On the other hand, people who threw their
money away to buy things — houses, paintings, diamonds, automobiles — they at least have the things they
bought. And the people who *borrowed* to buy things!
Well, ladies and gentlemen, the more they went into debt,
the more they borrowed, the more they bought, the richer
they are today! All the rules we learned in school were
nonsense. Thrift is nonsense. Debt is virtue! And those
people who followed the rules have been cheated and betrayed; the people who violated the rules are rich! The
world's turned upside down and I wonder if you really see
what it means? It means we are in a revolution that is
worse than anything we saw in 1918. We saw mobs then,
we saw red flags, we thought that Liebknecht and Rosa
Luxemburg and the Spartacus Bund were going to take
our property away — but now it's the Reichsbank that's
done it! Oh, I know all the reasons: Versailles and the
Reparations and the French in the Ruhr — but knowing
the reasons will not help us! The French are not printing
all this money. We are doing it ourselves. We are destroying our money ourselves, we are destroying our country
outselves!

"Your Excellencies, I am not a minister and I am not
a banker, *you are the ministers, you are the bankers,*
you gentlemen on this terrace this evening can do more
than anyone else in Germany to stop this madness, and I
seize this opportunity to implore you: STOP IT!"

Silence. Helena's father was out of breath. The glass
was trembling in his hand. "Well, Eduard . . . my dear
cousin . . . I really did not plan this outburst. I drink to
your good health and wish you a happy birthday. *Prosit!*"

Gustav Stresemann rose to his feet and held his glass
toward Lili's father.

At the same moment General von Seeckt, sitting between Helena and Frau Keith, rose too. Everbody else
rose. It was so quiet that we could hear a motorboat buzz-
ing out across the water. We drank the last toast.

Baron Eduard spoke very quietly: "My dear friends
. . . I think we have just heard an echo of Waldstein's
Voice. . . ."

A roar of laughter cut the tension.

"I wish to express my gratitude for the honor you have done me by coming here today. I am deeply moved by it. I do not speak as fluently as my cousin, who carries the blood of a poet in his veins."

More laughter, but quiet laughter.

"However, I wish to say that I share the sentiments which my cousin so eloquently expressed. He is not, as he told us, a banker. I am one. Herr Reichskanzler, Herr Generaloberst, Your Excellencies — and my dear cousins: I think I speak for every banker on this terrace when I tell you that we lie awake night after night this summer. Night after night. In the daytime we meet, we talk, we rack our brains, we study plans that have been submitted, some of these plans have possibilities. . . . This is not the place to discuss the various ideas, but I can only tell you that we know that things cannot go on this way, we know there *must* be a solution, but we also know that any solution will require drastic measures. *Drastic measures,* ladies and gentlemen! And a strong government to adopt such measures, and a strong army to enforce them!"

Dr. Strassburger, standing by a distant table, put down his glass and began to applaud, and then everybody was applauding — even the new Chancellor, his ministers, and General von Seeckt.

"And now," said Baron Eduard, "after so much seriousness, I think we will have some dance music —" The Baroness said something into his ear and Lili shouted:

"Oh no, Papa!" rushing through the crowd, and I knew it was too late. There was nothing I could do to stop her, but I prayed that she would have the sense to do it quickly.

She did. She took her father's arm and turned to the crowd and said "Ladies and gentlemen, we have one more birthday present, and our friend Peter Ellis will bring it now," and the butler was beside me with the package and feeling like a perfect fool I walked up to the Baron and unwrapped the little portrait I had done of Lili — of Lili looking at the sailboat in the bottle — and handed it to him. I guess I must have said something too, something about wishing him a happy birthday and thanking him for his hospitality and then I fled back to my place and as I passed Helena she grabbed my arm and whispered: "If your shoulders are as red as your face now, the marks wouldn't show!" and then she turned and introduced me to General von Seeckt.

Firm handshake. Monocle. *Pour le mérite.*

I gulped. ". . . great honor, sir."

He took the monocle out and glanced over my shoulder. "So. He *is* an artist, after all!" He said it in English.

I turned. The Baron was holding up the portrait, beaming. It did look pretty good. I had worked hard. Of course you never get anything exactly the way you see it in your head, but this was as close as I had managed so far.

"Yes sir, I'm trying to become a painter."

"Yes. Glad to see it." He replaced the monocle and stared right into my eyes. I managed not to drop mine . . . two of the ministers were at his elbow. "Herr Generaloberst —" and the commander-in-chief of the Reichswehr said, "Please excuse me, sir."

They were dancing in the big tiled foyer. The music came from the living room, where Bobby was grimly playing the piano, pounding out American foxtrots with a cigarette in his mouth while the professionals — two violins, a bass fiddle, a saxophone and a set of drums — tried their best to follow.

I felt too many conflicting emotions tearing at me. I'd drunk too much champagne. Helena was dancing with General von Seeckt. Miss Boatwright was dancing with Whitney Wood. I had never seen Miss Boatwright dancing before. I walked through the people, looking for Lili.

Dr. Strassburger obviously wanted to speak with Dr. Stresemann, but the crowd around the Chancellor was too tight.

"Dr. Strassburger, what did you think of Waldstein's Voice?"

He looked over his shoulder before replying to my question. "It is easier to give advice from outside the arena, do you not agree? I heard no specific suggestions."

"But surely something's got to be done."

"Agree. But whatever's done must be done by the government. We are not the government. We are not printing the money. Those gentlemen over there, as of this week they are the government. All we can do is give advice."

"And what advice are you going to give them?"

Dr. Strassburger permitted himself a little smile. "If they ask for it?"

"You're being awfully modest tonight, Dr. Strassburger."

"No. Perhaps a little sad." He looked down into his glass.

"I'm sorry. May I ask why?"

"I don't know exactly. Perhaps I have drunk too much champagne, which usually depresses me. Or perhaps I have heard an undertone in Waldstein's Voice that the others did not hear."

"An undertone?"

"Yes. Something that he did not say, but he thought it, and I heard it."

"What did you hear?"

"A warning. A warning that this disaster, this chaos, this death of money, this destruction of the middle class — one day it will be discovered to have been caused by the Jews. Deliberately brought about by the Jews. Never mind that the Jewish middle class is wiped out too. Never mind that the capital of Waldstein and Co. is less than twenty-five percent of what it was in 1914. At Schloss Havelblick, champagne still flows, the general staff still foxtrots with the granddaughter of the original Voice!" Dr. Strassburger peered at me over the tops of his glasses.

I had to blurt out the first thing that came to mind. "Have you heard anything from your nephew? How does he like Los Angeles?"

"One postcard, reporting that your protégée the Countess Kyra has obtained a role in a film, as a dancer, apparently. If my nephew has found employment, he said nothing about it."

Just then a waiter carrying a tray with clinking glasses approached the group around Dr. Stresemann. As they stepped back to let the waiter in, the Chancellor's shiny face turned toward us. "Strassburger!" he called. "Will you come over here a moment? We need your advice."

"Where's the can?" asked Whitney Wood.

"It's down in the basement. You have to go through those swinging doors and there's a little staircase. . . . I better show you, Mr. Wood. This way."

"Want a cigar?"

"Thank you, sir."

"I liked that portrait you did of your girl. Want to do one of mine?"

"Sir?"

"Want to paint a little portrait of Susan Boatwright? I'm not sure where I can hang it, is the only thing. . . . I keep a bedroom at the Union Club — what's the matter?"

I had stopped in my tracks. "You're teasing me, aren't you?"

"Teasing you?"

"You're serious?"

"What the hell do you mean? Why wouldn't I be —"

"Miss Boatwright just asked me to paint *your* portrait."

Whitney Wood's face crinkled into laughter. "Two commissions in one night! Both payable in dollars. You're a pro, son. You can forget about the stock market."

The Schloss and the gardens teemed with Waldsteins. One was an ancient lady with an ear trumpet.

"Is that Lili's American spy?" I heard her shouting to a younger woman.

"Sssh, Aunt Etta! He'll hear you! He's not a spy, he's a painter."

"He's what?"

"A PAINTER! He painted that portrait of Lili."

"The picture of Lili? I thought Max Liebermann did that."

"No, dear, the professor was only looking at it. The young American painted it."

"He's not a spy?" Aunt Etta was clearly disappointed.

"No, dear. He's a painter."

"Can't he be both?"

Christoph was alone on the floating dock, smoking a cigarette. The stars were out now. Christoph turned when he heard my steps on the gangplank, but he didn't say anything. We stood there looking at the night, listening to the music.

Finally I asked: "What did you think of Waldstein's Voice?"

"He has the best of intentions, but he is naïve. He thinks what everybody else thinks: the bankers make money from the inflation. Not true, unfortunately. The big industrialists have made money from the inflation:

Stinnes, Krupp, Thyssen, Kirdorf, Stumm, those fellows, but on the whole the bankers have lost money."

"Dr. Strassburger just told me that Waldstein's capital is down to twenty-five percent of what it was in 1914. Are they in trouble?"

"They have done pretty well with foreign currencies, and in the stock market; but in straight commercial banking they're losing money. I'll tell you something in confidence: Strassburger wants to merge with one of the giants — Disconto-Gesellschaft — but the Barons won't do it."

"Selling the Bank would be like selling the Voice."

"Exactly. But it will be harder and harder to compete with the Disconto and the Deutsche Bank and the others. We just don't have the capital."

"I still agree with Helena's father. What are they going to do about the inflation?"

"And you heard the answer. If these gentlemen knew how to get the genie back into the bottle they would gladly do it. *They don't know how to do it!* The government is trying to pay its debts by printing more and more money, the more money is printed the less it is worth, the situation is out of control, and whatever is done will require . . . what did he say? Drastic measures."

"Does that mean destroying the Republic?"

"The people on the terrace are not so crazy about the Republic, you know."

"Do they want the Kaiser back?"

"Some of them wouldn't mind, but they know it's not a possibility."

"Well then, what —"

"You heard what the Baron said: drastic measures, strong government, strong army."

"What's that mean? A military dictatorship? These people want a military dictatorship?"

"Depends on the military dictator," said Christoph. "Adolf Hitler? No. Hans von Seeckt? Why not?"

"General von Seeckt is up there dancing with Helena right now."

"Yes, they're old friends. From the War."

"Christoph, may I ask a personal question? This business about Kaspar, Kaspar's threats . . . is that the reason you haven't married Helena yet?"

He turned, but it was too dark to see his expression.

"I am in mourning for my father."

"Your father died in January. This is August."

"We've waited many years —"

"Christoph, suppose I could arrange a job for you in New York."

"In New York? When each dollar costs us five million marks?"

"Well, they'd pay you in dollars."

"Who would pay me in dollars?"

"Well, some bank, say. Suppose I could arrange that. Would you go?"

He reached out and put his hand on my shoulder. "Look, my friend. Each person belongs in his country. It's nice to visit other countries, but an American belongs in America, and a German belongs in Germany. And nothing that my little brother tells his friends when he is drinking is going to make *me* run away from my country. You understand?"

"What about Helena?"

"Same applies to Helena."

"But you told me I ought to go home."

"Yes, because that's your country. That's where you belong."

"Right now I feel I belong right here," I said. "I've never felt as close to any place in my life!"

We heard a deep throbbing diesel engine, saw red and green running lights. A huge cruiser approached the dock.

"Boat for Dr. Wassermann," a voice called.

"The Deutsche Bank is going home," said Christoph.

The last door had been slammed by the last chauffeur. The last limousine had crunched over the gravel driveway into the darkness. The last bank president was gone. The last cabinet minister was gone. General von Seeckt was gone, having taken Frau Keith and Christoph and Helena along in his staff car. Bobby von Waldstein had driven off in his Bugatti, silent and alone. The musicians were loading their instruments into the landau for the drive to Nikolassee station. On the terrace and in the big dining room and out in the maze of pantries and kitchens the bustle of cleaning up had not ended, but the brightly lighted front of the house seemed empty and quiet.

When Alred and Sigrid said goodbye I assumed that I was to walk up the hill with them, but as we stood in the hall Lili announced: "Papa, I think that Peter would like to have a talk with you in the library."

"You mean tonight?" asked the Baron, looking startled.

Lili's eyes were on me. "Yes, Papa, I think he would like to talk to you tonight."

Significant looks were exchanged, Alfred and Sigrid said goodnight again, and the Baroness fled upstairs.

"Papa, should some Cognac be brought into the library?"

"Yes, yes, by all means. Some Cognac!" The Baron, who had been glowing, seemed nervous now as he led me into the dim silent library. He was no more nervous than I.

My portrait of Lili was on the table, leaning against the wall of books.

"I like your picture very, very much, Mr. Ellis. Professor Liebermann also liked it. He said you looked beneath her skin. He finds that important."

"Yes, sir. I'm honored that he liked it."

The Cognac was brought. The doors were closed. The only sound was a slow tick-tock from the clock in the corner.

"Will you pour some Cognac for us?" The Baron looked increasingly uncomfortable.

I watched my hand tremble as I poured, as I handed him his glass.

"*Prosit*, Herr Baron. A very happy birthday, and again, my thanks for everything."

He inclined his head. A forced smile. Tick-tock. There was no way to stall any longer.

"Baron von Waldstein, I'm in love with Lili, I've asked her to marry me, she has accepted. . . . I mean . . . I would like to have your permission to marry Lili, I'm very much in love with her, I'll take good care of her, of course I cannot support her in the style . . . I mean in this style of your house . . ."

He let me prattle on because, I felt, he couldn't think of how to stop me. He did not look surprised, he looked embarrassed. He sipped his Cognac, put down his glass, and began to tap the fingers of his right hand on the inlaid wood of the table top, producing a nervous tattoo.

Nobody ever tells you how to make a speech like this. What are you supposed to say? If I'd had some warning I might have made a list, or something. . . . When I started to tell him about my family, the Baron stopped tapping and raised his hand.

"That's quite all right, Mr. Ellis, Miss Boatwright has given us considerable information about you."

"Oh?"

"Yes. My wife and I have every reason to believe from your behavior and what we have heard, that your background will present no problem. . . . I mean we understand you belong to a distinguished family —" Now he began to fidget with his pince-nez, removing it from his nose, pulling a folded white handkerchief from his breast pocket, unfolding the handkerchief, polishing the lenses of the pince-nez. . . .

"Mr. Ellis, my wife and I are not blind, we have observed you and Lili, we are not — as you see — entirely overwhelmed with surprise by your announcement — and, to be honest, we have discussed what our position should be if this — ah, if this subject should arise."

Pause. The Baron cleared his throat. "We have decided — my wife and I have decided — that *in principle* we have no objection —"

"Oh, that's wonderful —"

He raised his hand. *"In principle,* I said. In practice is another matter. The girl is barely eighteen, she has one more year of school, she can under *no circumstances* become engaged — that is publicly, officially engaged — to *anybody* before she has completed school!"

"But Baron, that won't be for a year from now!"

"Less than a year. Next June. Not a lifetime, I think. And during that year, assuming of course that Lili attends to her schoolwork so she does in fact complete her examinations in June — during that year my wife and I will continue to receive you in our house . . . what shall I say? On a regular basis?"

"And may I take her out?"

"Take her out? Where?"

"Well . . . May I take her to the theatre?"

"I think that would depend upon the play," he said. "But there is another matter. More serious matter." He paused. "You're a stranger in our country, Mr. Ellis. A visitor. You speak the language well, and through your personal friendships you have become involved in the . . . let us say the *situation* here. . . . You have become involved more than the ordinary visitor. Of course I refer

to the incident with the Keith brother and the murder of
Walther Rathenau."

"Baron von Waldstein —"

The hand came up again. "A moment please! The incident is closed. We made a decision, about Christoph Keith
and about you. I do not suggest we made the wrong decision, or that we are having second thoughts. *However,*
Mr. Ellis, under no circumstances, none whatever, can my
daughter — or indeed any member of this house — become involved in scandal or political action of any sort!
Do I make myself clear?"

"Not exactly, sir. I'm not involved in anything like that,
I haven't got any political connections at all —"

"There seems to be some question of your association
with what might be termed shadowy elements on the
Left —"

"Shadowy elements on the Left?"

"Possibly criminal elements —"

"*No sir!* Absolutely not!"

"— and there seems to be a suspicion in some official
circles that you may be . . ." He paused a moment to
choose his words. "That you may be in the service of your
own government."

"Sir, that's absolutely untrue! My word of honor."

He had finally finished polishing his pince-nez, replaced
it, and regarded me sternly.

"Yes. I believe you, and our own sources confirm what
you say. But I bring the matter up . . . I wish to call
your attention to the special position —"

A knock at the door: *"Herr Baron?"*

Frowning, he turned. "What is it?"

The butler glanced at me. "Herr Baron?"

"Well, what's the matter?" demanded the Baron angrily, but he stood up and walked out of the room to hear
what the butler wanted. Inside, the grandfather clock's
machinery began to grind, and then the chimes struck:
One . . . Two . . .

33.

THE MATTER OF A DOWRY

I waited in the library because I thought the Baron was
coming back. When I realized he wasn't, I stepped out into the living room. The first thing I noticed was the smell
of coal smoke. The second thing I noticed was that the
Schloss was completely empty. All the lights were on, all
the french doors stood open, all of the people seemed to
be gone. A cool night wind blew through the house and
carried the curious smell of coal smoke.

When I reached the edge of the terrace, I saw that
everybody was crowded along the waterfront, which was
illuminated by the blinding searchlights of a small steamboat belching smoke and chugging slowly in a circle, just
a few yards off the floating dock. The searchlight beams
swept the misty water, the weeping willows, the people on
the dock, the people on the Tea House terrace, the sailboat bobbing on its buoy, and other boats milling around
out there — the Waldsteins' motorboat, several rowboats,
another motor boat with what looked like policemen. . . .
I was walking down the steep grass hillside now, and I
saw that the steamboat was official too, a limp flag, white
naval uniforms. . . . A violent memory came bursting forward from my childhood but it hadn't been night, it had
been high noon right in the basin of Northeast Harbor,
and nobody had to tell me what it means when police
boats and Coast Guard boats move in wider and wider
circles, dragging lines through the water.

The people in the boats were calling to each other; the
people on the shore watched in silence. I looked for Lili,
then in the sweep of a searchlight saw that she was at the
wheel of her motorboat, still wearing her party dress. One
of the gardeners was lying on the forward transom, prod-
ding a boathook into the water.

I heard somebody sobbing and then I saw that it was
a short dark woman in a black dress who was leaning

against Alfred's chest, and Alfred had his arms around her, and in the darkness it took me a moment to recognize Ma, the old nurse from the Spreewald, because I had never seen Ma without her huge lace bonnet. These two stood on the terrace of the Tea House, and the others were obviously keeping back a little.

"We were just going to bed when Alfred saw the lights," said Sigrid. She had put on an English trench coat and black riding boots.

"Do they know who it is?"

"One of the kitchen maids. Emma something. Been here several years. She's a relative of Ma's, from the same village. I think Ma got her the position."

"Does anybody know —"

"We just came down, all I've heard is they missed her when the dishes were being washed, *now* they tell us she's been crying for a week, threatening to drown herself."

"Do they know why?"

"I think that's what Ma is telling Alfred."

The dragging went on and on. We watched. The other servant girls were whispering among themselves. Lili's mother said: "Eduard, she can't stay in that motorboat all night in her evening dress!"

No reply. The Baron scowled.

The whole operation didn't make sense to me. If Emma was really drowned here, wouldn't the current have moved her toward the bridge by now, or even under the bridge into the Wannsee? I wanted to ask somebody.

"I don't know why this has to be done at night," the Baron suddenly exclaimed. "It is *inconceivable* that the police were called before I was notified!"

"They thought to save her, Eduard. They thought she might be swimming, trying to swim out there. . . . My dear, there's nothing we can do to help, why don't we go back to the house —"

"Inconceivable!"

There were too many people on the floating dock already, but I pushed my way to the end and shouted to Lili. The searchlights were pointed somewhere else, so I didn't get a good look at her until she brought her boat alongside. I asked the gardener to get out, replaced him, and pushed off again. Then I touched her arm; she was shivering. I took off my jacket and wrapped it around her.

"Why don't I put you ashore? You're freezing, you don't need to do this —"

"Don't tell me what to do!" she said, and I realized she was crying.

"Did you know this maid?"

"Of course I knew her. I know them all."

"Did you know what . . . what her problem was?"

"Yes. The same problem as every woman. A man. Men are beasts, you know that?"

"Well, that's a very romantic thing to tell me tonight, when you just sent me in to talk your father —"

"I don't feel romantic now, I feel furious, I feel *sad,* I feel furious *and* sad, can't you see how I feel?"

"Not exactly. I can't see why you have to find her. I mean why not let the police —"

"SUPPOSE THEY DON'T FIND HER?" Lili screamed, so I gave up and pulled alongside the little steamer, conferred with the tired middle-aged officer in command, then steered our boat south toward the bridge, barely moving, going just as close as I could get to the various seawalls and landing stages that belonged to the medieval castles and the Spanish haciendas and the Florentine villas of bank presidents and steel barons and stock market speculators. The steamer had to stay farther out, but his searchlights illuminated the black water in front of us, the green slime on the pilings, the moored sailboats, the weeping willows. . . .

"I'm sorry," said Lili. "It was the contrast between her fortune and mine. Perhaps I feel ashamed, or somehow guilty, although how can I help it? You know, in the War the servants put all their savings into German war bonds, and when we lost the War, those bonds were worthless, and you know what my father did? He paid them himself, with his own money, so they would not lose their savings. Now is he supposed to do that all over again? I don't think he has that much money!"

I waited to hear what all this had to do with Emma.

"I don't know how it is in America," said Lili. "In Germany, if a girl wants to get married, she must bring something. A dowry. Of course it depends on her position, but she must bring something. And since the War it is worse, not better, because so many men were killed that the men available have a wider choice. Too many women, not enough men. You understand?"

"Of course."

"All right, Emma found a man, she was lucky, she was not very pretty but she worked hard and this man — he is the second son of a farmer, also in the Spreewald somewhere — he will get a piece of the farm because the older brother was killed, and they were to be married next year, and Emma has worked here since she was sixteen, her family has no money at all, there are six children and the father is the mail carrier in the village. . . . Well, Emma has saved every penny of her wages, I mean every penny, for her dowry —"

"Oh no!" Steering the boat, peering through the increasing mist, I understood.

"Oh yes! Last week Emma got a letter from the Sparkasse, the savings bank branch in Nikolassee, they were sorry but they had to close her account because it was too small for them to carry on their books, and they enclosed a money order, and Peter, *the stamps on the letter were worth more than the money order!* All her wages since she was sixteen!"

"And then what happened?"

"Yes. You can guess, can't you? Her young farmer is terribly sorry, but he cannot get married unless he can buy some animals, and it seems there is another girl, the daughter of another farmer. . . . Can you imagine how Emma feels, in our house, the way we live, and you are there all the time now. . . . Oh yes, they all know that. . . . What's the matter?"

We were coming up on the bridge now, and as the searchlight beam touched the pile of driftwood caught against the right abutment I saw just what I expected to see, and from the commotion behind me I knew that the men on the steamer had seen it too, so I turned the boat around, pushed the throttle all the way down and roared away from the lights, away from the other boats, away from the island, planing bow-up toward open water and the first hint of sunrise.

34.

A RUSSIAN WORD AND
A GERMAN WORD

"Nothing could be finer than to be in Carolina in the morning . . ." Marek Weber's musicians apparently knew the song by heart, because they didn't miss a beat when the lights went out. At the tables, nobody even stopped talking as the Adlon's waiters quickly lighted candles, transforming the crowded glittering room.

It was the middle of October and the lights were going out all the time. Everybody was accustomed to it. Sometimes the water pressure was turned off. Sometimes the streetcars or the Stadtbahn stopped running. Sometimes the mail was not delivered. All it meant was that a group of public employees had not been granted a raise that week, so they had gone out on strike.

At our table — I guess technically it was my table — Christoph Keith was telling a story he had just heard. He wore a white carnation in his lapel and Helena had put a flower from her bouquet into her hair. Those were the only signs that they had been married that afternoon, a civil service at the Standesamt Berlin. Lili and I and Alfred and Sigrid had been the only witnesses and now, at my invitation, the wedding party was conducting the only celebration of the event.

I had assumed a big wedding and a big reception out at Havelblick, or at the Pariser Platz after the family moved back to town, but neither of them wanted that. "For the second one you don't make such a production," Helena had said. "And certainly not in a situation where everybody says, 'It's about time!'"

As a matter of fact, Christoph had been more or less living at Helena's apartment on the Lützowufer for months, leaving me awkwardly with his mother in Grunewald. The number of Frau Keith's constant visitors had been reduced to one: a well-preserved, tight-lipped colonel with red General Staff stripes on his breeches, a widower, perhaps a little younger, who now kept two riding horses in the stable and his orderly in the kitchen. Although he was meticulously polite to me, he obviously did not share his chief's opinion that I was really a painter. Doors were kept shut; nothing more controversial than the weather was discussed; and even when Herr Oberst was not on the premises, Meier and his wife seemed more reserved now. My five dollars were still accepted, but with just a trace of condescension.

It was time to get my own place. I knew it, both Helena and Miss Boatwright were looking, I suppose I could have been looking myself . . . but I wasn't. In the mornings I was supposed to be painting Miss Boatwright. I had set up my stuff in her apartment for that purpose, but it was impossible to keep her still for more than twenty minutes at a time. Visitors came, usually visitors who wanted something, or she would rush off to help somebody, somewhere. . . .

Christoph was telling his story: "When Stresemann announced that the government was calling off passive resistance in the Ruhr, they expected an uproar from the Nationalists, all shades of the Right, so President Ebert called an emergency meeting of the cabinet at five o'clock in the morning. Half of the ministers showed up unshaved or without their neckties — except Seeckt, who appeared in immaculate uniform, all his medals, polished boots with spurs. . . . There was a lot of talk about a Putsch from the Right, Ebert turned to Seeckt and asked: 'General von Seeckt, will the Reichswehr stick with us?' and Seeckt replied: 'Mr. President, the Reichswehr will stick with *me*.' He let that sink in for a moment. Then he said: 'I'm the only man in Germany who can make a Putsch, Mr. President, and I'm not going to make one.' "

We looked into the candlelight.

"What kind of person is General von Seeckt?" I asked.

"Ask Helena," said Lili, laughing, and Alfred's hand crashed down on the table so hard that the cutlery clanged. People turned to look at us.

"If you cannot behave yourself like a grownup you don't belong in grownup company!" Alfred said to Lili, very quietly, his eyes blazing. "If Peter were not our host I would suggest that he take you home now."

"It's all right, don't make such a fuss," said Helena, but she had paled, compressing her lips.

A terrible moment. Nobody knew where to look or what to do.

"I'm sorry, Helena," whispered Lili. "I didn't mean anything."

"Yes, you did, dear, but I have a reasonably clear conscience, in this case." She smiled. "Will somebody give me a cigarette?"

Christoph supplied the cigarette and lighted it for her.

"All right," she said, blowing smoke toward the candles. "Hans von Seeckt destroyed the Russian army as a factor in the east. Battle of Gorlice. Hindenburg got the credit, but in our staff everybody knows who planned Gorlice and who carried it out. After we lost the War, he was put in charge of the Republic's Reichswehr, our hundred thousand men. He's built an elite corps, only the best officers. No political people. No Freikorps people. No socialists or Communists either, of course. The sons of peasants, not the sons of factory workers. A small, efficient, completely nonpolitical fighting machine —"

"That obeys only its officers," interrupted Alfred.

"Who *else* should it obey?" asked Sigrid.

"Peter asked what kind of a person he is," said Helena, putting out her cigarette. "As you have seen, he looks like a film version of a Prussian general, and he is, as I've said, the most efficient Prussian general we have. But he's other things too. He loves to read books. He loves to play the piano. He loves beauty in all forms — pictures, horses, music —"

"— and women," said Sigrid.

"— and women," said Helena.

"In any event," said Alfred, "this lover of beauty is today, for practical purposes, in command of Germany. These emergency decrees the Reichstag adopted give the Minister of Defense unlimited power, supreme power, they abolish all constitutional rights — but of course the Minister of Defense *has* no power without the Reichswehr —"

"— and Seeckt is the Reichswehr," said Christoph.

"And what does he want?" I asked.

"*Peredyshka,*" said Helena.

"What does that mean?"

"That's Russian," said Alfred. "A chance to catch your breath?"

"A breathing space," said Helena. "What he is most

afraid of is civil war between the Left and the Right, between the Nationalists and the Reds, another Thirty Years' War to destroy Germany again, or bring an Allied occupation. That's his nightmare. He wants peace and quiet, to rebuild."

"Rebuild what?" I asked.

"His army of course."

"What for?"

They all looked at me.

"What is the army for?" Sigrid replied. "To protect us from our enemies. We are surrounded by enemies."

Who was I to dispute her? Nobody else did.

"Hans von Seeckt says the Reichswehr stands in the service of the government," said Helena.

"That's what he says," said Alfred. "But he can't do anything about the inflation, and if *somebody* doesn't do something about the inflation, there's going to be no government to serve."

I ordered more champagne. We drank more toasts. Christoph danced with Helena. Of course he couldn't really dance — they held each other, swaying to the music.

"It's a shame they're not going on a wedding trip," said Sigrid. "They could at least go to the mountains —"

"In October?" asked Lili. "I'd rather go to Nice."

"No money for Nice," said Alfred. "And no time. They're terribly busy at the Bank. This thing has become a nightmare."

"No longer a princess," said Sigrid. "Just plain Frau Keith."

"She looks happy," said Alfred. "So does he. As she says, 'It's about time.' "

"I liked your toast," I said. "A long life, and a happy one."

"Unberufen," said Alfred, expressionless, staring at the dancers.

Unberufen? Else Westerich would say it "Unberufen *toy-toy-toy*" as she knocked on wood.

"Everybody is angry with me," said Lili into my ear as we began to dance.

"Wasn't very tactful."

"I didn't mean she went to bed with him."

"Her wedding day, after all."

"Poor me. They won't say such things on *my* wedding day, will they?"

"Shall we go someplace else?"

"You all can go," said Helena. "The bride and groom are going home. In a taxi."

"I think we should all take the bride and groom home in a taxi," said Lili.

I called for the check. When it came, it was carefully itemized and added to 790,650,000,000 marks. They had helpfully converted it for me: $31.63.

"May I see that bill?" asked Alfred, putting on his reading glasses, and before I could stop him he held it. Christoph stood up, looked over his shoulder, took out his fountain pen —

"Herr Ober!" shouted Alfred.

"Wait a minute," I protested. "This is my party, I know this place is expensive —"

They paid no attention to me. Before they were finished, the maître d', the assistant manager and a night cashier were all grouped around the table.

"Herr Baron, that's the usual procedure here."

"Since when? This is outrageous!"

"It's not our fault, sir!"

"Where'd you get this *Kurs?* You know perfectly well it was twenty-six billion at two o'clock —"

"But it is two o'clock in the *morning,* Herr Baron! We have to cover ourselves —"

"So you invent a new *Kurs?* Adlon's midnight *Kurs?*"

"Works out under twenty-five billion to the dollar," announced Christoph, who had been making calculations on the back of a menu.

"Herr Baron, we have to cover ourselves," said the assistant manager.

"How do we know what the *Kurs* will be when we deposit the money in the morning?" asked the cashier. He was a pale angry young man with bad skin and heavy glasses. He wore a shiny suit. He looked tired.

"You're getting *dollars,* man!" Christoph's parade-ground tone. "They'll be worth *more* tomorrow morning!"

Of course they knew that as well as he did. If I had tried to pay the bill in marks — assuming I could have

carried 790 billion marks into the dining room — they
wouldn't have accepted them. What did people do if they
didn't have dollars — or pounds, or guilders or francs?
One thing they didn't do was dine at the Hotel Adlon.

When the negotiations were over, my bill had been reduced by one dollar and twenty-three cents, which was
hardly worth the little scene that followed.

Christoph and the assistant manager were trying to
smooth things over and Alfred remarked that they were
all in the same boat.

"No, we're not," said the cashier angrily.

"I beg your pardon?"

"Get him out of here!" hissed the assistant manager to
the maître d'.

The cashier, his arms already seized by one of the
waiters and the maître d', shouted: "I don't feel that I'm
in the same boat with an American who has a wallet full
of dollars — or with the Baron von Waldstein!"

Alfred was on his feet, we were all on our feet, the
cashier was hustled away —

"A thousand pardons, Herr Baron, the man will be dis-
charged in the morning —"

Alfred raised his eyebrows. "So he can join the S.A. in
the afternoon? You think that will help the situation? Pay
the bill, Peter. We meant well."

35.

THE MARCH ON BERLIN

A bone-chilling November rain had been falling since
dawn, so I asked Meier to call me a taxi. The financial negotiations began as soon as we turned into the
Königsallee, because the driver noticed that I carried no
bulging briefcase.

"Gendarmenmarkt, mein Herr? The regular fare — I
mean the fare on the old meter — would be about one
mark. . . ." The *Kurs* last night had been 2,000,000,000,-
000 marks to the dollar. As we passed the corner where

Walther Rathenau was killed — sixteen months ago? it seemed a lifetime — we agreed that since I didn't have four of the new 100,000,000,000 mark notes an American quarter would cover the fare and the tip.

I had been summoned to meet with Dr. Strassburger to discuss my investments. I had not bothered much about them. My German stocks were rising. Occasionally I sold some to raise the few dollars I needed to live; occasionally I bought more by increasing my debt to Waldstein & Co. I felt I was in good hands — but suddenly, yesterday, a message came through Christoph to Meier: Herr Geheimrat desired my presence at ten o'clock.

The Kurfürstendamm was jammed with cars, with pedestrians carrying glistening umbrellas. Despite the rain, some workmen with a ladder and long brushes were trying to affix a placard to a Litfasssäule. (I don't know what we call those things because we don't have them. They are fat round pillars, maybe fifteen feet high, erected on the sidewalks and plastered all over with commercial advertising and official announcements.) The sign going up on this one seemed to be a newspaper headline, hugely magnified, black gothic letter on white paper:

HITLER PUTSCH IN MÜNCHEN!

"What's all that about?" I asked the driver, who shrugged his shoulders.

"They don't know nothing. The Nazis cut the telephone lines and the telegraph lines, and all they know is what the people who came up on the night train say, and they don't know nothing except there was a riot in a beer hall. Those damn Bavarians, they do everything in their beer halls."

That was the first time I had heard the word "Nazi."

As we entered the financial district of the inner city, a policeman stopped the cab to let a line of trucks pull out of a courtyard into the Jägerstrasse.

"Look at them," shouted the driver. "Trucks full of money. Trucks full of banknotes with nine zeros behind the number! Last spring they carried the money out of there in baskets, they had hundreds of porters from every bank and every business crowding in there with great big wicker baskets on their backs to lug the money away — but now they send trucks! A truck a day to pay their people, and by the time the people get to the store tonight, all that money won't buy their supper!"

The last truck emerged from the courtyard, the policeman waved us through and a moment later we stopped again, at No. 4, Gendarmenmarkt.

"Ask Baron von Waldstein how this is going to end," said the driver as I gave him his quarter.

"I'll do that," I said.

"Because it's got to end, you know. It's got to end *somehow*." I slammed the door and the taxi drove off in the rain.

The lobby at Waldstein & Co. was full of people. They were well-dressed people. They were important people. They said so. They all had appointments, with one of the Barons or with Dr. Strassburger or with one of the other partners.

The butler had lost some of his glacial aplomb. "Jawohl, Herr Kommerzienrat, Herr Geheimrat knows that you are waiting, he will see you just the moment he is free. . . . Jawohl, Excellency, Herr Baron's secretary has carried your message into the meeting, if you will be kind enough to follow me. . . ." The double-doored consultation rooms were filling up when Christoph appeared.

"I'm sorry, old man, Dr. Strassburger sends his apologies, he just cannot —"

"That's all right, I understand —"

"He asked me to receive you."

Christoph had his own office now, a small white room with a rolltop desk against the wall, a telephone, two chairs, a window looking out onto the back street, and a bare-shouldered actressy professional photograph of Helena gazing soulfully toward the ceiling. We sat down.

"Well," said Christoph, swiveling toward me. "How do the English say it? The balloon has gone up."

I told him about the poster I had seen and asked what was going on.

"That is the problem. Nobody knows what's going on. Most of the lines have been cut. We can't get through to Munich. You know the general picture in Bavaria?"

"Not really. Gustav von Kahr is sort of a dictator, appointed by the Bavarian cabinet?"

Christoph nodded. "Von Kahr calls himself the commissioner-general. He would like best of all to bring

Bavaria out of the Republic, return the crown to the
Wittelsbachs, make Prince Rupprecht King of Bavaria. But
his power depends on the Reichswehr and the Bavarian
Landespolizei. The Reichswehr commander in Bavaria
was General von Lossow, another Bavarian. Von Seeckt
has just replaced him because Lossow refused an order to
close down Hitler's newspaper. So Seeckt sent down General Kress von Kressenstein to take over the Reichswehr
in Bavaria, but Kahr refused to permit that change. Are
you following all this?"

"Not entirely."

"I don't blame you. It's a complete mess. In any event,
Bavaria is — or was as of last night — being ruled by a
triumvirate: Kahr, as commissioner-general; Lossow, as de
facto Reichwehr commandant; and a Colonel von Seisser,
commander of the Landespolizei. All three of those gentlemen unquestionably want to cut loose from Berlin and
establish their Bavarian monarchy.

"On the other hand, the place is loaded with extreme
Nationalists under Ludendorff, Hitler, Göring, Röhm,
Rossbach — all combined now into something they call the
Kampfbund, thousands of armed men: S.A., Freikorps
Oberland, Reichskriegsflagge — different names, same
people. But those fellows are *not* interested in cutting
loose from Berlin. They want to capture Berlin, destroy
the Republic, hang Ebert and Stresemann and even
Seeckt from the lampposts Unter den Linden. Not to mention everybody who signed the Versailles Treaty and
every Socialist deputy in the Reichstag. They've been
pressing and pressing Kahr to lead their march on Berlin, but so far he hasn't marched."

"And what happened last night?"

"All we know is that Kahr held a huge banquet in the
Bürgerbräukeller, one of the biggest beer halls in Munich — it's on the other side of the Isar — they had all
the Right Wing politicians there, all the top police and
army officers in Bavaria, they had Lossow up on the
stage, they had Seisser up on the stage, they had bands
playing patriotic songs. . . . Apparently they were going to
announce *something,* but nobody knows what."

"Was Hitler there?"

"I suppose he must have gotten in because something
happened. There was shooting —"

A knock on the door interrupted him, the door opened

and Bobby von Waldstein appeared. He was frowning. "Heard anything? Oh, good morning, Peter."

"Good morning —"

"No, not a word more, Bobby."

"Well, Father wants to *know*, Christoph! Certainly the Reichswehr wireless must be functioning —"

"Bobby, I can't just call the Bendlerstrasse radio room."

"In the past your connections have always —"

"Tell your father I'll report to him the moment I hear something, Bobby —"

"Herr Baron?" A secretary stood behind Bobby.

"What is it?"

"Dr. Strassburger's office says the Disconto-Gesellschaft has a line open to Munich now. He asks if you will go over to Dr. Salomonsohn's office —"

Bobby withdrew and closed the door.

Christoph sighed, stood up and walked over to the window, his hands in his pockets. "You think they want me for a banker here — or for an intelligence officer?"

"Maybe a little of both," I said. "Bankers have to know what's going on. Don't you remember how the Rothschild carrier pigeons brought the first news about who won the battle of Waterloo?"

Christoph turned and smiled for the first time.

"If I may return a compliment you made me: for an artist, you know a lot of history. At any rate that makes me feel better. Look here, my instructions from Strassburger are to explain about the *Rentenmark*. You've read about the plan in the newspapers?"

"I've read something but I don't understand a word of it."

"Then you have lots of company because nobody really understands it, but I will tell you what we think the *theory* is." He sat down in his swivel chair, leaned back and put his fingertips together. "Everybody agrees the government must do *something* to stabilize the mark, but what? You remember Karl Helfferich from the Deutsche Bank, the man who made those terrible speeches against Rathenau?"

"Yes, of course I do. They hissed at him in the Reichstag —"

"Yes, they hissed at him. But he is quite a brilliant banker, and last summer he came up with an idea of a *Roggenmark*, a rye mark, a new currency tied to the value of a certain amount of rye. Something like that has been done a lot over the last year. The province of Oldenburg did it. Private companies have done it. They have issued bonds that are payable in so many tons of rye, of wheat, of corn, of nitrate fertilizer, so many barrels of wine — at some future date. Of course the price of these bonds will go up and down depending on the price of the rye or the wheat or the corn, but at least you know it's going to be worth *something*. So people have been willing to buy this paper, the farmers have been willing to deliver their crops, factories have been willing to sell their goods, some speculators have even paid foreign currencies — in other words the rye bonds, the wheat bonds, the wine bonds have worked — on a small scale. You understand that?"

I understood vaguely. "Sort of what we call commodity futures?"

"Yes, I suppose so. Now Helfferich wants to issue a whole new currency on this basis, a *Roggenmark*. And to give additional security, he wants to place first mortgages on all the agricultural property and all the industrial property in Germany. These mortgages — they call them *Rentenbriefe* — will form the capital of the new currency bank, separate from the Reichsbank. Well, the government didn't want the rye marks. I'm not sure why, perhaps it's too exotic, perhaps there just isn't that much rye in Germany — frankly, I don't know exactly why they didn't do it, but they modified his idea, they've come up with a very strange animal, the *Rentenmark*. First they have adopted Helfferich's idea and organized a new bank of issue called the Rentenbank, completely independent of the Reichsbank, and this Rentenbank is capitalized with a first mortgage on all the farms and all the factories in Germany."

"That doesn't make any sense," I said. "How can you place a first mortgage on all the property in the whole country? How could you ever enforce —"

"Of course it doesn't make sense! The real question is will it work?"

"So this Rentenbank is going to issue its own Rentenmarks?"

"That's right."

"Convertible into rye?"

"No! Forget about the rye. Convertible — someday — into gold marks."

"At what rate?"

"That's the question. Nobody knows yet. The decision will be made by an independent *Reichswährungscommissar* — I suppose you would say currency commissioner — who hasn't been appointed yet."

"And who is that going to be?"

Christoph looked down at his fingertips. "I only know who it's *not* going to be."

Silence. Our eyes met.

"They asked Strassburger?"

Christoph nodded.

"Who asked him?"

"Dr. Luther, Minister of Finance, former mayor of Essen, an excellent man who is taking a terrible beating because the Reichsbank seems to have gone crazy and he has no power over the Reichsbank —"

The telephone rang and Christoph grabbed the receiver. "Yes, of course, put him through immediately. . . . Keith here! Morning. . . . Yes, of course, we're biting our fingernails, as you can imagine. . . . Well, any news would be gratefully received. . . . Aha. . . . Aha. . . . *What?* . . . . A machine gun? . . . How many men? . . . Aha. . . . Aha. . . " The voice at the other end reported and Christoph listened, looking at me, looking right through me, looking into another country. "Let them *go?* . . . Oh, on parole — well! So we don't know what the situation is this morning? Donnerwetter! . . . Yes, will you be good enough? I don't have to tell you how grateful we are. Many thanks, old boy." He hung up, and instantly the telephone rang again.

"Good morning, Herr Baron. Just this moment, sir. Just hung up. . . . Unclear. . . . I said the situation is *unclear*. Shall I come over and explain? . . . Dining room?" Christoph glanced at his wristwatch. "All right, sir. . . . Herr Baron, I've got Peter Ellis here with me, I was trying to explain the Rentenmark — May I bring him down?"

"So Kahr was making a long speech and all of a sudden Hitler and Göring burst in with a troop of S.A. in steel helmets. With pistols. Pandemonium. Shouting and beer steins overturned and women fainting and Hitler climbed up on a table and fired at the ceiling and the whole place was silent."

The partners' dining room at Waldstein & Co. was silent too. Pale worried faces were fixed on Christoph as he repeated what he had just heard from the Bendlerstrasse.

"The S.A. set up a machine gun in the vestibule. Hitler said the Bürgerbräu was surrounded, he said that Wehrkreiskommando VII had raised the swastika, he said that the Republic was abolished, he said that Ludendorff would head the new government and then he took Kahr and Lossow and Seisser into another room, and Ludendorff appeared and they made some sort of a deal where they apparently would all be ministers in the new government, would ask Prince Rupprecht to become King of Bavaria — and then they would all march on Berlin together."

Pause. Baron Eduard took his heavy gold watch from a vest pocket, then turned to Baron Fritz. "Might as well let them serve lunch. Gentlemen?"

"You want the servants to hear this?" asked Baron Fritz.

"They're going to hear it anyway," said Dr. Strassburger. Somebody opened the door and gave an order, waiters began to carry in trays with steaming soup bowls, and Bobby appeared, still wearing a soaking trench coat.

"The situation is in total confusion down there," he began, as he handed the coat to a waiter and sat down. "Nobody seems to know what's going on."

"Let Christoph finish his report," said Dr. Strassburger.

"So Hitler and Ludendorff brought Kahr and Lossow and Seisser back into the room, and the whole mood was 'On to Berlin,' speeches, oaths of allegiance, military band, everybody singing 'Deutschland über Alles' — and then Hitler was called away. Apparently the Reichswehr garrisons were *not* coming over, nor the Landespolizei. The minute Hitler was gone, Kahr and Lossow and Seisser said they had to leave too. The S.A. commanders didn't want to let them go, but they gave their parole to Ludendorff and Ludendorff overruled the S.A. If you can't trust the word of a German officer, then what can you trust?"

We were eating our soup now and the waiters were pouring the Moselle.

"Is that the end of the report?" asked Dr. Strassburger.

"No, sir," replied Christoph. "Two hours later General von Lossow was at the Headquarters Nineteenth Infantry Regiment, reporting to the Bendlerstrasse by radio, reporting the Reichswehr in Munich is on the streets in combat formation, *against* Hitler. So is the Landespolizei. More troops are being rushed into the city from Augsburg, from Landsberg, from Kempten. Kahr has moved the government of Bavaria to Regensburg. On the other hand, cadets of the Infantry School have mutinied and gone over to Ernst Röhm's Reichskriegsflagge, and they've occupied the old War Ministry on the Odeonsplatz —"

"This is all still General Lossow reporting to Berlin?" asked Dr. Strassburger.

"Yes, sir. The Reichswehr and the Landespolizei have closed the bridges over the Isar, barricaded the entrances to the Odeonsplatz, and surrounded Röhm in the old War Ministry."

"And so far only the ceiling of the Bürgerbräu has been shot?" asked Baron Eduard.

Nervous laughter.

"That's my report," Christoph concluded.

The soup plates were removed and something else was served. I don't remember what it was.

"All right, what's the word from the Disconto?" Baron Fritz asked Bobby.

"We spoke with Dr. Sippell, who is down in Munich working on a dollar loan for the BMW, and for some reason they had an open line. He says the streets are full of soldiers and police, swastika flags are hanging from balconies all over the city. The brokerage firm of Abraham Bleibtreu and Co. in the Kaufingerstrasse had its windows smashed. Julius Streicher is telling crowds in the Marienplatz that Jewish bankers invented the inflation. BMW truck drivers say thousands of Kampfbund people are massing between the Bürgerbräu and the Isar."

Bobby stopped to catch his breath. "Dr. Sippell says the atmosphere is nasty. If the S.A. and Freikorps Oberland try to cross the bridges into the city — will the Reichswehr shoot? Will the Landespolizei shoot? Nobody seems to know."

"What was it von Seeckt said in the Kapp Putsch?"

asked Dr. Strassburger. "German soldiers don't shoot German soldiers?"

"No, sir," said Christoph. "What he said was 'Reichswehr doesn't shoot Reichswehr.' These Hitler people aren't Reichswehr." He paused to drink some wine. I watched the others watching him. "I think the army will hold the town."

Dr. Strassburger nodded thoughtfully. "We'll soon know, won't we? Gentleman, perhaps we should return to work and communicate these comforting thoughts to our clients."

"I don't think I should take up your whole day," I said to Christoph.

"There's not much work being done today. In any event, I was told to advise you on your investments."

"All right, advise me."

Christoph looked at me for a moment. Then he said: "Go home!"

"Go home? What kind of investment advice is that?"

"That is the only honest advice I can give you. What do they say in your country? Cash in your chips and go home."

"Is that Dr. Strassburger's advice?"

"No. It's my advice."

"Why, Christoph?"

"Because nobody knows what's going to happen here. *Nobody!* The French are still in the Ruhr, nobody knows even now what reparations we will have to pay, the German mark is literally not worth the paper it is printed on, and now Hitler has driven the Bavarians to revolt."

"But you just told them the Reichswehr would hold Munich."

"Yes. I told them."

"You don't believe it?"

"I believe they'll carry out their orders. Question is: who's *giving* the orders down there? I don't like this story about the infantry cadets going over to Röhm. And suppose the Reichswehr does put down this Putsch? There are thousands and thousands of people marching for Hitler, thousands more hanging his flags from their windows. Is the Reichswehr going to shoot them all? Is Stresemann's government going to put them all in jail?"

A name and a face hung in the air between us. I avoided his eyes.

"But if *they* win!" Christoph pulled a slim alligator case from an inside pocket and offered me a cigarette, struck a match, lighted mine, lighted his . . . "if *they* win, you're going to see a blood bath."

I didn't know what to say. We smoked in silence for a minute.

"Christoph, I'm not ready to cash in my chips. I like it here. I'm painting. I'm in love with Lili. I feel . . . I don't know, I feel involved somehow."

A grim smile. "Oh, you're involved, my friend. No question about it."

"Well, what should I do about my investments? Should I hold my stocks?"

"The market was off sharply when we went to lunch, because of the Hitler thing, the uncertainty about the Rentenmark —"

"Well, what about this Rentenmark business? Will it work?"

"Who knows? As you saw immediately, it's nothing but a confidence game, a game with mirrors. It will work only if the people *believe* it will work. It might work, it should be attempted, it all depends who runs for it, if he's tough enough."

"Well, certainly Strassburger's tough enough. Why didn't he take the job?"

Christoph got out of his chair and began to walk around the room.

"He told the Minister of Finance that Waldstein and Co. could not spare his services at this time of crisis, that the Barons had given him the opportunity to reach his present position and that he cannot leave them now because they need him to bring the firm through."

"That sounds sensible enough," I said.

"Very sensible." He had stopped to look out the window again.

"But not convincing to you?"

"No." He continued to stare out into the rain.

I said: "Be Rathenau all over again."

Christoph turned. "Of course. That's the real reason."

"You think he's afraid of getting shot?"

"Oh no, I don't think that's it. In any case, he would not court assassination the way Rathenau did. The reason is that if a Jewish partner in a Jewish banking firm becomes the Reichswährungscommissar, then to many, many people the whole program immediately becomes a Jewish plot, some scheme for the Jews to make more money, and they won't believe the thing will work, and as we've said if they don't believe it will work, then it *can't* work. And whatever happens the people who have been wiped out by the inflation will stay wiped out, most likely more people will be wiped out by these corrective measures — and then of course the whole mess becomes the fault of —"

The telephone rang.

"Yes? Yes, Bobby. . . . Aha. . . . Aha. . . ." The corners of Christoph's mouth pulled down into a kind of grimace as he listened. "Hmm. . . . Does the market know this yet? . . . Hmm. . . . What did Strassburger say? . . . Well, is he selling or is he buying, or what? . . . *Military advice?* How can I give anybody military advice on the basis of this kind of information? No, I will *not* call them! What would happen if every bank in town calls up . . . Yes, I agree with you, I'm coming over this minute." His face was flushed as he slammed the receiver into the cradle. "Disconto-Gesellschaft just heard from their man again. He says the S.A. and Oberland corps have disarmed the police on one of the bridges and they are marching toward the War Ministry to join up with Röhm. General Ludendorff is leading the march, with Hitler and Göring right beside him. The stock market is in turmoil and Strassburger wants me to call the Bendlerstrasse again. You'll please excuse me, Peter. . . ."

"Of course. I'll come back when you have time —"

"No, stay here, I won't be long." He stopped in the doorway. "Shall we sell your stocks?"

"Ask Strassburger."

Christoph nodded and was gone.

It was almost time for Lili to come home from school, so I could have gone to the Pariser Platz. Or I could have visited one of the museums and lost myself — as I often did — in work of men whose results I could never hope to equal. But I didn't. I sat there, watched the rain, wondered whether it was raining in Munich, wondered why it should matter so much to me whether Hans von Seeckt or Adolf Hitler governs Germany. I remembered Whitney

Wood accusing Miss Boatwright and me of "going native."
How do I cash in my chips and go home if Lili can't go
with me? I don't *want* to go home. I never felt very much
at home at home. I haven't had one letter since I've been
here. Written me off.

Suppose Hitler wins? Could he do anything to the
Waldsteins? What could he do to them? They're just buying Hitler's voice is the way Whitney Wood explained it.
"They": big industrialists, coal barons, steel barons . . .
need Hitler to crush the Communists and the Socialists, to
keep the workers in line. "They" are not going to let an
Austrian corporal run anything once the hated Republic
has been overthrown. . . .

That's what Whitney Wood's been told, and he believes
it.

Does Christoph Keith believe it?

Does Oberverwaltungsgerichtsrat Dr. von Winterfeldt
believe it?

Does Sigrid von Waldstein believe it?

Does Lieutenant Count Brühl believe it?

For that matter, do the partners of Waldstein & Co. believe it? Remembering the faces in the dining room just
now . . .

And yet, is anybody going to tell those gentlemen to
cash in *their* chips? The very idea made me smile — in
that silent room on Friday afternoon, the ninth of November, 1923, so I was smiling when the door burst open and
Helena — looking magnificent in a black beret and a
black glistening raincoat — shouted, "Oh, you've heard
the news!"

"No, what news?"

One of the footmen was carrying a wicker basket,
which he put on the floor in front of me.

"Get another glass," she told him. "I didn't know Mr.
Ellis was here. Where is my great banker?"

"He's with Dr. Strassburger," I said. "What news do
you have?"

"The Putsch is over. Herr Hitler ran away!"

"Are you sure? We just heard that General Ludendorff
was leading a march through the city, they overran the
police —"

"Well they didn't overrun them when they got to the
Odeonsplatz." She put her head out of the door. "Fräulein
Schmidt, will you be so good as to fetch my husband?"

"Oh Your Highness — pardon . . . Gnädige Frau — Herr Oberleutnant is with Geheimrat Dr. Strassburger —"

"Tell Dr. Strassburger he shall come too, and tell my uncles, and perhaps a few more glasses should be brought. . . ."

By the time I got the corks out of the champagne bottles the little room had filled with bankers, all silently listening to Helena, who sat with her legs crossed on the edge of Christoph's open desk and told them what she had heard.

Nobody asked her from whom she had heard of these events, less than an hour after they happened. They watched and they listened and they looked at her legs with various degrees of disapproval. The partners of Waldstein & Co. were not accustomed to wives on the premises — and certainly not as the center of attention — but of course in this as in everything else Helena was special. And they wanted to hear what she had to report.

"The reason they got across the bridge was that the police had been told to unload their rifles, so the S.A. and the Oberland just swarmed over them. Captured the police and marched into the town. They were singing. Crowds of people marched along. Ludendorff and Hitler and Göring and some others marched in the front. They marched toward the Odeonsplatz, because that's where Röhm was, holed up in the Wehrkreiskommando. The Odeonsplatz was blocked off, some entrances by Reichswehr, some entrances by Landespolizei. Ludendorff turned into the Residenzstrasse, which is so narrow that they could only march six abreast, but they had to follow Ludendorff, because no German soldier will shoot at Ludendorff, he is their talisman. So the Residenzstrasse comes into the Odeonsplatz at the Feldherrnhalle, a little war monument, sort of a pavilion there, you know, and this was guarded by a troop of Landespolizei, with rifles, and their lieutenant called upon the marchers to stop but they kept on marching, and somebody yelled, 'Don't shoot, it's Excellency Ludendorff!' but somebody did shoot, nobody knows who shot first, and then the police fired a volley and the marchers in the front rank dropped to the pavement — all except Ludendorff. He kept right on walking toward the police with his hands in his pockets, walking right through the police into the Odeonsplatz. And finally they decided to invite him to the police station, and when they got to the police station, the duty sergeant asked him what his name was!'

A burst of laughter broke the tension.

"But what happened to Hitler?" asked Bobby von Waldstein.

"He got up from the pile of people in the street and he ran, and there was a car parked at the corner, and Hitler jumped into the car and was driven away."

"Was he shot?" somebody asked.

"They don't know. But Göring was shot. He was seen leaning in a doorway. Blood all over his trousers. And then he disappeared too. But not with Hitler."

"Was anybody killed?" asked Baron Fritz.

"Yes, one man who was marching beside Hitler, and they think a dozen more in the rear ranks, and two policemen."

Silence. Then a voice in the back: "Donnerwetter!"

"Well, what is happening now?" asked Christoph.

"Just complete confusion, apparently. The Nazis are going home. Röhm has surrendered the War Ministry but nobody knows what to do about him. He had infantry cadets in there, and they've been ordered back to their school. Crowds of people ran into the Odeonsplatz after the shooting, but they are being cleared out with lancers. Mounted lancers."

"I wonder if His Excellency the Commissioner-General Ritter von Kahr finds it safe to return the government of Bavaria to Munich," said Baron Eduard. He sounded sarcastic.

Helena didn't know anything about von Kahr.

"Well, in any event," said Baron Eduard, "it seems that the March on Berlin did not make it beyond the Odeonsplatz in Munich."

"This time," said Dr. Strassburger, and then the telephone on Christoph's desk rang. Helena handed him the receiver.

"Keith here. . . . I see. . . . Good. Yes, I'll tell them. Thank you." He hung up. "Our switchboard reports that all of you have many telephone inquiries. Both Dr. Strassburger and Baron Fritz have calls from Munich so apparently the lines are open. . . ."

The room emptied quickly.

Dr. Strassburger said: "Your Highness . . . forgive me,

Frau Keith, we are all in your debt for so quickly providing this vital information —"

"Yes, my dear," said Baron Eduard. "Our house has always prided itself on being well informed, but this must be a new record."

Helena lowered her eyelashes demurely. "At any rate, it is a pleasure to bring good news." She held out her hand. When Baron Eduard and Dr. Strassburger had gone, she turned to me. "Peter, will you take me home now?"

Take her home now? I looked at Christoph, who seemed very busy with the papers on his desk, and then his telephone rang again.

"Keith here. . . . Yes, of course, put him through. . . . Afternoon. What's the word from the Front? . . . Really? . . . Ran away? Was he hurt . . . Bavarian Landespolizei? That's damned impressive, isn't it? And then what happened?" Christoph put his hand over the mouthpiece and looked at us. "Same story, essentially. Will you take Helena home, Peter? I'll be along as soon as I can." Then back into the telephone: "Are they just letting them go home or are they arresting them?"

In the taxi Helena was very quiet.

"Is something wrong?" I asked.

She expelled her breath. "I did a stupid thing." She turned toward me, and I saw that her eyes were brimming. "But I meant it so well, Peter! I was happy, I was relieved, I thought he would be proud of me for bringing such important news so quickly, so *very* quickly, it can make all the difference to them in their financial matters —"

(Had they sold my stocks?)

"He *is* proud of you, Helena. They were all enormously impressed, I could see it. . . ."

"What I could see is them thinking, 'She must have heard all this in bed' and 'Does he really go to bed with a woman at lunchtime in the middle of a national crisis?' *That's* what they were thinking!"

"Oh no, Helena, I'm sure that never entered anybody's mind!"

"Oh yes, it entered *everybody's* mind." She blew her nose vigorously. "So stupid! So unnecessary! I'm too old to make such an ass of myself. And of Christoph!"

We rode along in silence. I noticed for the first time that the city teemed with soldiers. Truckloads of Reichswehr infantry were parked in front of the main telephone exchange in the Leipziger Strasse. An armored car and a squad of infantry filled one whole sidewalk in the Potsdamer Platz — rifles and bandoliers and hard eyes under the dripping helmets. When our taxi driver tried to reach the canal by taking a shortcut through the Bendlerstrasse, traffic police waved him away. Behind the police was a barbed-wire barricade, and behind the barricade a helmeted machine-gun crew watched us over their gun barrel. Down at the other end of the street, in front of the Reichswehr Headquarters, another armored car glistened in the rain. It did not look to me as if the man in charge of this mobilization had spent his lunch hour in bed.

When we got to the Lützowufer the driver wanted 500,000,000,000 marks.

"Now wait a minute," I protested. "I came in all the way from Grunewald this morning for the equivalent of 400,000,000,000 marks —"

"But that was this morning, sir. The *Kurs* has changed three times since then, and we've had one revolution!"

Of course I had forgotten to get German money at the Bank and I didn't have any more American coins, so I was about to give him a dollar bill, but Helena grabbed my hand. "Are you crazy? Here, give him this." She opened her purse and peeled off five of the new 100,000,-000.000 mark notes. They were only printed on one side, and the ink, still damp, left stains on her gloves.

Helena told her maid to bring us a bottle of champagne.
"*More* champagne?"
"I'm afraid I need it. Will you drink with me?"
"All right. But why do you need it?"
"To finish the story."
"Finish the story? Why didn't you finish it at the Bank?"
"Because I don't want Christoph to hear this part. But I've got to tell somebody."

The maid carried in a silver tray with a bottle of German *Sekt* and two glasses. Helena stood by the french window and looked out into the darkening afternoon. "Never mind the fire, Clara. Mr. Ellis can light it."

The maid went out and closed the door. I popped the cork, poured the *Sekt* (Sekt? von Seeckt? My mind stupidly focused on the words for the first time) and brought Helena her glass.

"It's Kaspar, isn't it?"

She nodded, sipping her wine, still looking out at the streetlights and the rain falling into the Landwehr Canal.

"Is he dead?"

"You know something? I honestly hope so. Isn't that terrible? They have not identified the bodies at the Feldherrnhalle. I might get a call any moment."

"But you think he was there?"

"Yes." She finished her glass. "When the S.A. attacked the Bürgerbräukeller last night, a new formation made its debut, so to speak."

"What kind of formation?"

"Elite guards, personal bodyguards, *Stosstrupp Adolf Hitler*, if you please. Black ski caps to distinguish them. And what do you suppose they wear on the front of their ski caps?"

"A swastika."

"Swastika is on the armband. On the ski cap is a little silver death's head!"

I didn't say anything. I drank my wine, feeling it now, feeling also that the room seemed dark and clammy, so I put my glass back on the tray and busied myself lighting the fire. It caught quickly. The room looked warm and beautiful again.

I turned around. "Helena, that doesn't necessarily mean he was there —"

"He was there. The only question is whether he's dead or whether he's hiding someplace — possibly wounded, like Göring — burning up inside, choking on his rage. Still another defeat! They must have felt so close to victory. One minute they're marching through the streets singing their songs, flags are flying, people are cheering, they are marching on Berlin . . . and the next minute they are flat on the cobblestones, Adolf Hitler is running away, another coup is kaput, another march is over. Can you *imagine* how he feels this moment — if he's alive?"

"Helena, you've got to tell Christoph about this!"

She shook her head. "Can't."

"Why not? He'll hear about it anyway. He's talking to

the Bendlerstrasse right now, he'll be talking to others, there will be newspaper stories —"

She walked over to the tray, refilled both glasses, handed me mine, sat down on the sofa and stared into the flames.

"Helena, suppose I could arrange for a job in New York . . . suppose I could find Christoph a temporary job with a bank or an investment house in New York. . . . Would you like to live in New York for a year or two?"

She looked at me. "He won't run away. He will not believe his brother would do anything to him, and he will not run away."

I was drinking the champagne. I might not have said it if I had not drunk so much champagne. "Did he tell you about Göring?"

Her eyes narrowed. "Did he tell me what about Göring?"

"Göring warned him that Kaspar was making threats, that Kaspar is still seething about the Rathenau thing, that we kept him out of the Rathenau thing, he thinks we betrayed Kern and Fischer —"

"Hermann Göring told this to Christoph? When?"

"I don't know, last summer."

"Peter, I just can't believe that!"

"You think I invented it?" And to prove I had not invented it (Why? Why did I have to prove anything to Helena?) I told her the whole story.

She listened with her head thrown back against the pillows, her eyes closed. The fire crackled.

When I finished the story she opened her eyes again. "You know, that Hermann Göring is really a swine."

"Maybe so, but in this case —"

"In this case, he just wanted to get Christoph away from the Jews, that's what he wanted, so he tells him that Kaspar is out of control —"

I suppose I was a little out of control myself now. "It wasn't just Göring who has warned about Kaspar."

"What do you mean?"

"He's said the same things to Sigrid."

"Sigrid?" Helena's voice rose. "Are you telling me that Sigrid has been seeing Kaspar?"

"Just once, Helena, and it was an accident, a coincidence," and I told her more or less what Sigrid had told me, and Helena began to cry, she put her head in her hands and cried, and somewhere the telephone began to ring, and the maid knocked and opened the door and said, "Fräulein Elizabeth für Mister Ellis," and then her face dropped and she backed out of the room leaving the door ajar and Helena said: "You're being summoned to the Pariser Platz," and I started to say something but there was nothing left to say, so I went to answer the telephone.

36.

A PIG LOSES MONEY ALL THE TIME

The musicans paused for a moment, and when they began to play the second movement, Lili's father suddenly stood up. Immediately the fifty or sixty guests in the big salon stood up too, some of them looking as surprised as I was.

"We don't give many Hauskonzerte," Lili had said. "It would look as if we are competing with the Mendelssohns. But there is some reason we have to give this one, somebody asked my father to introduce this new group in Berlin . . . you have a tailcoat, don't you?"

I didn't have a set of tails, so I had to wear an old one of Bobby's, and it didn't fit. A whole evening of violin music is a lot of violin music. It had been a long day. I was thinking about other things, vaguely conscious that this was the last piece, watching the musicians sawing enthusiastically through the first movement, but when the Baron stood up I had to sneak a look at the program I was sharing with Lili. Joseph Haydn, Violin Quartet in C major, "Kaiserquartett." As they played the movement, very slowly, I watched the faces around me and as I wondered at the different ways that strong emotion shows itself, I suddenly recognized the theme: "Deutschland über Alles."

The Russian nightclub where Bobby took us was in a basement: brick floor, wine racks along the walls, thick cigarette smoke, a blackhaired woman who played the balalaika and sang sad songs. The headwaiter seemed delighted to see Bobby. The other customers glanced at our evening clothes. We had to pay, in American money, before they would bring us anything, but that was normal now; the prices rose between the time you ordered something and the time you finished it — even in the middle of the night.

They brought us black bread and caviar and cold vodka in crystal glasses.

We ate and drank and listened to the music, and when there was a pause I said: "May I ask a very personal question?"

"Bobby or me?"

"Both of you. Why did your father stand up this evening?"

Bobby began: "That theme, Haydn's theme from that quartet, it was made into the *Deutschlandlied* —"

"I know it. That's why I'm asking. Last night Adolf Hitler had all the people in that beer hall on their feet singing that song."

They looked at each other. "That's why Father stood up," said Lili. "I was so proud of him!"

Bobby said: "The Nationalists, the National Socialists, all those people on the far Right, they claim this is not our country. This *is* our country!"

"But why 'über Alles'? Why does Germany have to be *over* everybody else?"

"Oh, that's not what it means!" Lili exclaimed, and Bobby interrupted her. "It means, you know, to *us*, to the people, the people love their country above all else. "Über Alles.' That's what it means. You understand?"

When Lili went to the toilet, Bobby told me he was going to the United States.

"Does your family know?"

"Of course not."

"What will you do?"

"Join Kyra in Los Angeles. Will you sign the guarantee for me too?"

"Bobby, she's with the other man —"

"No. He has left her, married an American lady, the widow of a film producer."

"And Kyra has asked you to come?"

"Yes, she has. Will you help me?"

"What will you do out there?"

"No idea. Something will turn up. Or I will bring her back."

"Bobby . . . Don't do it."

"I can't help it. When you love somebody, you love them. You don't love them *because* of; you love them *despite*. People think I don't know the bad things about her. I know them. It makes no difference. I'm not happy without her, and if she needs me I must go."

"Bobby, I only signed that paper because I was told your parents wanted me to do it. Now if I help you . . . what will happen to me and Lili?"

"Why should my parents find out?"

"Bobby, have you checked whether you need that kind of a guarantee for a visitor's visa —"

"What is a visitor's visa?" asked Lili, as the Russian woman began to sing something that made all the other Russians join in.

The song ended in a roar of voices and loud applause, a small ensemble began to play an American foxtrot, and the woman who had led the singing came over to our table. Bobby and I rose as he made the introductions. I got the impression that she was surprised to see him, and us. Lili did not smile when she was introduced. Her face froze and she stood up. "Peter, I want to dance, please."

We danced. "That wasn't very polite," I said.

"I don't have to be polite to her."

"I thought a lady had to be polite to everyone."

"Perhaps in America."

"What are you so angry about?"

"We should not have come here."

"But you wanted to see it."

"Yes. Now I have seen it. Tell Bobby I am waiting in his car."

"Don't you like to dance with me?"

"Not here."

"What's wrong with this place? They're having such a good time —"

"And they all know Bobby. And we know *why* they all know Bobby! Tell him I will be in the car, Peter."

We almost got too close before we realized what was going on. All three of us were crowded into Bobby's open two-seater Bugatti, bundled up against the raw November dawn. Since Lili had a chance to be out tonight, she was making the most of it and had persuaded Bobby to take us to several other all-night places, and now I didn't know exactly where we were, heading for the Villa Keith in Grunewald, cutting through some very different neighborhoods where people were already going to work.

"Look at that," said Bobby, pointing. A large crowd had gathered in front of a bakery, men and women with gray faces and gray clothes who carried wicker baskets and metal buckets and shopping nets crammed full of paper money, so many people that they spilled over the sidewalk and filled most of the street.

Inside the bakery a light went on, the door opened, a white-dressed baker came out, averted his eyes from the crowd, hung up a sign, went back in again and closed the door. The light went out. A woman screamed. Men shouted.

"Don't try to drive by there," I said, suddenly conscious of how we looked: the glistening chrome radiator of the Bugatti, the gleaming blue paint, our white silk evening scarves, and Lili sitting on my lap with a little fox stole wrapped around her ears.

Bobby, shifting gears, began to turn the car around and Lili moved her body to look over my shoulder just as the plate glass window of the bakery crashed to the pavement.

"They're throwing things at *us!*" shouted Lili, amazed, but we were roaring out of range.

On Sunday, November 11, two trucks full of Bavarian Landespolizei arrived at the house of one Ernst Hanfstängl (Harvard '09) in Uffing, a little town near Munich, where they found Adolf Hitler, dressed in pajamas. They arrested Hitler and locked him into the Fortress of Landsberg-am-Lech to await trial for high treason.

On Monday, November 12, Dr. Horace Greeley Hjalmar Schacht was appointed Reich Currency Commissioner and President of the new Rentenbank.

"Why is he called Horace Greeley?" I asked Christoph on the telephone.

"His father was a German immigrant in New York and apparently admired this Mr. Greeley, whoever he was."

I explained who Horace Greeley was.

"He said, 'Go West, young man'? How curious. Herr Schacht Senior went east, came home to Germany. Hjalmar Schacht worked for the Dresdner Bank, then became one of the top men at the Darmstädter und National Bank — we call them 'Danatbank.' He's considered very clever and very conservative. Believes in gold and a balanced budget. The Barons don't like him, but they think he's the right man."

"Is he tough enough?"

"We shall see. They say he's a cold fish, but he will have to perform miracles: persuade people to accept these Rentenmarks that are coming on Thursday; persuade the government to balance its budget — which means discharging thousands of civil servants — persuade the Reichsbank to stop discounting every bank loan and every piece of private money that's been printed in this country, *and* persuade the Allies to reduce their reparation demands. I'm just glad that Strassburger's not in the job!"

"Christoph, what did Dr. Strassburger do about my stocks on Friday afternoon? When there was all the excitement about the Putsch."

"Nothing."

"Nothing?"

"You've still got them. Strassburger said in the first place we never sell in a panic, and in the second place, what would you do with the money? You would have received something like . . . let me see . . ." Pause while he was apparently making a calculation. "You would have received something over three *billiarde* marks, that is three thousand billions in English terms, three quadrillion in American terms. You understand what that means?"

"No. I'm lost."

"We are all a little lost, but write down three with fifteen zeros behind it."

"I did. I wrote it in my ledger: 3,000,000,000,000,000 marks. "What's that in dollars?"

"When? Friday afternoon? This morning? This afternoon? On Thursday, when the Rentenmark begins to circulate? Or at the end of the month when you would settle your account?"

"Well, what about this morning? If you sold my stocks this morning, how many dollars could I buy with three quadrillion marks or whatever they are?"

"That will take a few minutes to tell you, because we must get all the stock prices first and then the exact *Kurs* —"

"Christoph, I'm sorry to be so much trouble —"

"Nonsense, this is our job. I will telephone in a few minutes."

I drank my coffee and looked at newspaper photographs from Munich: six members of the Stosstrupp Adolf Hitler, festooned with rifles and sidearms and ammunition bandoliers, arresting one civilian, a Socialist city councilman; General Erich Ludendorff, with a moustache and three chins, glaring at embarrassed Bavarian police officers; Ernst Röhm with a swastika on his arm and a white scar across his dark cat's face, surrendering the War Ministry to a helmeted Reichswehr lieutenant . . .

Christoph called back: If I sold my stocks right now and paid my debt to Waldstein & Co. I should clear about four thousand dollars.

"Gosh, I felt a lot richer than that!"

He didn't say anything for a moment, and when he spoke there was a caustic tone in his voice. "I think most people in Germany would consider you quite rich. Four thousand dollars would buy half of Berlin this morning!"

"Christoph, you all have taken very good care of me! I'm not complaining, I'm asking for advice."

"Yes. Well, the problem is, my boy, we don't quite know what to do ourselves. We really don't. The thing is balanced on the knife's edge now. What can Schacht do? What will the Reischsbank do — because they are entirely independent of the cabinet and of Schacht and of his new Rentenbank, you know. The quotation I just gave you is based on the official Berlin *Kurs* this morning: 630 *milliards*, or billions in American terms — that is, 630 with nine zeros — 630 billion marks to one dollar, but many people think the mark will fall into the trillions —

American trillions, twelve zeros — by the end of the month —"

"Trillions of marks to the dollar? That would mean I would get much less than four thousand dollars?"

"Depends on what we can get for your stocks then — in marks. We certainly don't want to sell your stocks now, put you into marks, and then watch the mark keep dropping in relation to the dollar."

"Christoph, I just can't make up my mind about this. Could I come over and talk with Dr. Strassburger?"

I had to wait while Christoph called Strassburger's office on another line.

"No, I'm sorry, he's in meetings with the Disconto-Gesellschaft all day, then apparently Schacht wants to see him tomorrow, they think perhaps he can see you late tomorrow afternoon —"

"Well . . . Christoph, I think I'll sit tight until I can talk to Dr. Strassburger."

"Very well. Peter, there is another matter, much more pleasant."

"You know what we say on Wall Street?" asked Whitney Wood. "We say a Bull makes money some of the time, and a Bear makes money some of the time, but a Pig loses money all of the time!"

"Whitney!" Miss Boatwright turned so I had to stop painting. "You're not calling Peter a pig!"

"No, I'm not, my dear. I'm giving an allegorical answer to his request for investment advice."

"That's right, Miss Boatwright, I just asked his opinion as to what I should do and could you please turn toward the window again, because the light on your face —"

She did as I asked but her expression still wasn't right. The usual serenity wasn't there.

"I think it's bad enough that the Germans talk about money all the time, but at least they have an excuse. I really don't think the two of you have *any* excuse, and I'm frankly tired of the subject."

"Well, he's got a problem and he needs some advice and my advice is get into dollars and stay in dollars until this situation has clarified itself —"

"I can't get in to see Dr. Strassburger —"

"I'm not surprised to hear it. These fellows have their hands full this week."

Whitney Wood had not even taken off his overcoat. His suitcases were out in his taxi. He was on his way to London to attend another meeting with General Dawes. I had never heard of General Dawes, who was setting up still another commission to decide how much reparations the Germans were to pay and how they were to pay it, but Dawes was a friend of Whitney Wood's and had sent for him, again.

"Goodbye, Mr. Wood, and thank you for the advice. I think I'd better take it. I'll give them the instructions tomorrow."

"Yeah, I wouldn't wait much longer, boy. Things are moving fast, and nobody knows in what direction." He shook hands and turned toward Miss Boatwright, who stood up.

"I'll take you to the door," she said and went out into the hall with him.

When she returned to her chair by the window she looked so sad that I changed brushes and mixed some white paint and worked on the collar of her dress.

"He thinks he'll be back in two weeks," she said.

"Oh, that's good, Miss Boatwright."

"This summons from General Dawes was rather unexpected. We had tickets for the Philharmonie tonight. Furtwängler is conducting. Would thee care to be my escort, Peter?"

"Oh thank you, Miss Boatwright, I'd love to, but I can't. You know my friend Keith has a friend, a sculptor by the name of Kowalski, and this Kowalski has given us some tickets to the Artist's Ball at the Kunstgewerbeschule — whatever that is — apparently they wear costumes and masks —"

"Oh, what fun!" said Miss Boatwright. "I assume thee is taking Lili?"

"Yes, Helena persuaded her mother somehow, but I've got to have her home by midnight, like Cinderella, because I kept her out all night on Friday, even though Bobby was with us the whole time. Don't you think the Waldsteins are being a little — I mean she's eighteen, Miss Boatwright. . . ."

37.

THE ARTISTS' BALL

As we got out of the taxi at No. 4 Pariser Platz the church bells were ringing: "Just like Cinderella!" said Lili furiously. She had taken off her mask and folded up the huge white Spreewald bonnet because it was too hard to handle in the taxi, but she had refused to kiss me on the way home.

"Look, this isn't my fault, why are you taking it out on me?"

"You're going right back there, aren't you?"

"Well —"

"Well, the party just *begins* at midnight and I'm supposed to go to bed like a child?" Lili was crying with anger now. The taxi driver was waiting because I hadn't paid him.

"Don't you understand that I promised to have you back? If I didn't keep my promise they'd. . . . I don't know what they'd do. Are you trying to get me in trouble with your parents?"

"I think you are quite happy to go back there and dance with those other girls. Especially with Helena!"

"With Helena? I promised Christoph I'd dance with her because he really can't, you know all about —"

"Ach, what nonsense, she had more partners than any woman in the place, it's almost disgusting, at her age —"

"She looks good in that outfit."

"A woman in hussar uniform, to show her legs and her behind! That was considered erotic in 1912. Today it's just embarrassing, I think." She stood there beside the huge door, holding the white bonnet and the mask, a very angry girl.

She rang the bell.

"Lili, I'll pay the taxi and come in for a drink."

"No, they've gone upstairs but they are awake and they would not like it. Go back to the ball."

A footman opened the door. "Good evening, Fraülein."

"Evening, Joseph." She looked at me. "All right, one glass of wine in the library. Go pay the taxi."

Christoph and I had dressed at the Villa Keith. On such short notice there was no time for elaborate costumes. Frau Keith had gone out somewhere with her colonel. Frau Meier climbed up to the attic, groaning and talking to herself but actually enthusiastic about the project. Die Herren gehen auf Maskenball!

Meier served sausages and boiled potatoes and beer. Then we went upstairs to Christoph's room, where Frau Meier proudly displayed what she had found: for me, a dark green hunting costume — green hat with a peacock feather, green wool shooting jacket with antler bone buttons, green kneebreeches and gaiters; for Christoph, a leather flying suit just like the one he had worn at Verdun, and an aviator's cap complete with goggles.

When we came down the stairs, the Meiers stood in the hall and applauded.

"Oh Mister Ellis, it fits you perfectly!" exclaimed Frau Meier. "Herr Oberleutnant will not need a mask, but I found this for you." She handed me a children's false-face mask, a yellow Chinaman with Fu Manchu moustaches and a rubber band to hold it in place.

"Whose shooting outfit is this, Frau Meier?"

Her husband had opened the door. "Here is the taxi, gentlemen."

"That was made for Herr Kaspar years ago, Mister Ellis —"

"Just a moment," I said, "I forgot something. Get in the taxi, Christoph, I'll be right there," and I ran up the stairs into my room, took the little Smith & Wesson out of the drawer of my bedside table and dropped it into one of the deep pockets of the shooting jacket.

Why?

That was the first thought that struck me — struck me like a blow between the eyes — when she opened the door to her apartment, stuck out her chest and clicked her heels at us.

Why did she do that?

"My God!" was all that Christoph said at first and I glanced sideways to see if it meant anything special to him. Hadn't she told him about the Stosstrupp Adolf Hitler? Hadn't he heard about it some other way? What is she trying to say and to whom is she saying it?

She wore the dress uniform of the Death's Head Hussars: grinning white skull-and-crossbones on a black fur tschako beneath which some golden hair appeared; a black domino mask across her eyes; a short black jacket braided with silver, buttoned tightly across her breasts; skin-tight black trousers tucked into gleaming black riding boots; and spurs.

"The boots aren't quite right —" she began, sounding frightened, I thought. "I had to use my own because the real ones didn't fit —"

"My God, you look fantastic!" said Christoph. He didn't know.

"You like it? You don't think it's a little . . . old-fashioned?"

"I think it's absolutely splendid. Don't you think it's splendid, Peter?" He took her in his arms and kissed her. "I've never kissed a hussar before." The tschako fell off and her hair tumbled over the leather sleeve of his flying suit. "I've never made love to a hussar either."

"Give me my tickets, Christoph, I'll get Lili and we'll meet you at the ball."

The library smelled of cigars and oiled leather bindings. A few coals in the grate and a small reading lamp provided the only light. The atmosphere was romantic, but we had too much fuss.

First there had been a fuss about the wine. The wine was locked up and this footman didn't have the key. There was a little Cognac in Herr Baron's decanter in the dining room. . . .

"Well, bring that."

He brought it on a silver tray, with two glasses.

Then there was a fuss about who would lock the front door.

"Thank you, Joseph. You can go up now, I will let Mr. Ellis out."

"With respect, Fraülein Elizabeth, it is my job to lock the house —" but when he had retreated and closed the library doors, the real fuss began.

"Now wait a minute, Lili —"

"Don't talk, I don't want to talk!"

"You just told me your parents are awake upstairs."

"Those doors won't open from the outside."

"That's a line from Schnitzler."

"Will you not stop blabbering?"

We were on the leather sofa now, she on top of me. Her mouth, tasting of Cognac, covered mine. Her hair was in my eyes so I couldn't see anything, but I could feel her hands —

"Now wait a minute. . . ."

"You don't want to!"

"Of course I want to, but not this way. Can't you understand that? If we get caught like this, they'll never let me see you again —"

"We'll not get caught."

"And anyway, this isn't . . . You've never done it, have you?"

"Are you so cautious with all the girls?"

"I don't want to marry all the girls."

"Ah, quel sentiment!" She sat up, blew the hair out of her face and shook her head. "You really are incredible! You want to have a virgin bride. Is that some American tradition? Some religious requirement?"

"I thought most religions required it."

"I am not a student of religion and I think you better return to the ball."

"Darling, don't be mad at me, I love you, I'm a lot older, I don't want you to start this way —"

"How do you think anybody starts? I must be the only girl in Berlin in this position *and I do not like it!*" She was sweating. The Spreewald costume — she had shown me — required three petticoats, and they rustled as she jumped to her feet. "Back to the ball, Mr. Ellis. No virgins there!"

"Lili . . . let's get married. Let's just hire a car and drive out to some little town and get married at their Standesamt, the way Helena and Christoph did."

"Another American custom? You can't do that in Germany. You need all kinds of papers, you need birth certificates — and I need my father's permission. In writing."

"Are you sure?"

"You think I'm the only girl in my class who wants to

get married? Believe me, we have experts on this field of law."

"Then work on your parents. Why are they so concerned about your finishing school first? Why can't you marry me and then finish school?"

"Because I'm not allowed to finish school if I'm married. No married woman is allowed in school. My God, the girls in school are all virgins, you know. A married woman would tell them things. . . ." Suddenly she began to laugh and hurled herself back onto the sofa, a great blooming flower of lace petticoats, with two silk stems. "Oh, Peter, don't you see what an *ass* you are?"

> *Yes, we have no Bananas*
> *We have no Bananas today. . . .*

Twice as many people now, the huge hall is packed.

Black band playing.

Helena's face is flushed.

Top buttons of Helena's black-and-silver jacket are unbuttoned.

Helena is tipped back in her chair with her black riding boots crossed upon the adjoining chair.

Helena is surrounded by a clown, a Venetian gondolier, a Highlander wearing a kilt — all presumably artists.

Halli-hallo, our huntsman returns from the hunt! Didn't expect to see you again tonight. Somebody give him a drink.

They are drinking *Sekt*.

Who is paying for all this? I wonder.

Where is Christoph I ask.

Probably still at the police station.

What!

Oh yes, you missed the excitement. Adolf Hitler appeared.

What?

Turned out to be a woman, says the gondolier.

Somebody knocked her down before they knew it was a woman, says the Highlander.

There was a fight and the cops came and Christoph and Hans Kowalski and Bert Brecht all had to go as witnesses or something, says Helena.

Hand on my shoulder.

A shadow in white and back: white flying cap, black

mask, white silk scarf, long white driving coat, black
trousers showing under the coat.

Lady over there wishes to dance with you, says Bobby.

What lady? Where?

The odalisque in harem trousers, drinking beer with that
coal miner against the wall.

She turns away from the coal miner to watch: Black veil
and a golden brassiere and trousers of white gauze and
golden slippers and nothing else.

Achtung Achtung, shouts Helena as I stand up. *Wird
Scharf geschossen!* Making my way through dancers
packed so tight they barely have room to dance, I remember what that means. It means live ammunition.

I thought I recognized the Chinese huntsman, she whis-
pers into my ear.

She smells of beer and perfume and sweat.

Pressed hard against me she feels thinner. Ribs beneath
my fingers.

I don't have it anymore, she says. They gave me stuff
that made me sick as a dog but I'm all right now.

That's wonderful.

Won't you come back?

That would be hard.

We need you.

I told him I wasn't coming back if he beats you.

He can't really help it. He drinks so much that he can't
get it up anymore unless he can make a woman yell a
little.

Is he here?

He was, but they took him to the Alexanderplatz. Some
stupid bitch came dressed as Adolf Hitler, with a brown
shirt and a swastika and Fritz was so potted that he
didn't see it was a woman and he punched her in the
mouth and she went right down and the people with
her jumped on Fritz and somebody called the bulls and
they took him —

Aren't you going to get him out?

Shit no, let him get himself out.

I can't understand why you stay with him.

I can't either. Maybe I'm just lazy. But it was better when
you were there, Peter.

Is Baby here?

No, Fritz could only organize two tickets.

Is she home watching the boy?

Mutti's with the boy. Baby's in the Friedrichstrasse. The only reason I'm here is that Fritz thinks I'll find somebody. Like the Herr Baron I sent over to get you.

You know Bobby?

All the girls know Baron Bobby. He's always kind, he's always polite, he treats you like a princess. I'm not fancy enough for him, of course.

Is that coal miner an artist? He's been watching us the whole time.

He *owns* coal mines.

And of course he's got dollars.

He's got Dutch guilders.

And he wants you to go to his hotel?

Wrong. He wants to do it in the Tiergarten.

In the Tiergarten, this time of year?

He wants to do it in the back of his limousine with his chauffeur driving us through the Tiergarten.

Very romantic.

Listen, if you take me home tonight I'll tell him to find somebody else to play in his car.

Can't do it, Bärbel. I'd like to.

You took your rich girl home, didn't you?

I still can't do it.

They're sure to keep Fritz in the can overnight. No? If you really think I'm still sick, you can screw Baby. We sort of need you down there. . . . No use, eh? All right then, adieu, my gallant cavalier. I'll have to ride in the Tiergarten.

Very important people like Alfred von Waldstein don't bother with costumes. White tie and tails, and a black mask.

Sigrid wears a beautiful embroidered dress and a white apron and a white lace cap and her blond hair braided into pigtails, a peasant bride from the Mark Brandenburg —

And her eyes meet mine, her sky-blue eyes widen in horror, she lunges toward me and rips my Chinese falseface off and shouts: *Where did you get the Jäger outfit?*

I tell her.

Alfred asks: What is the matter with you tonight? Grabbing her arm.

Her face is red now, flushed with blood: I don't like it
here. I want to go home.

Alfred says: You went all the way out to Zeydlitz to get
your costume —

I don't like it here, and I want to go home. Biting her
lips.

Alfred asks: Was it that skull out there? Is that what has
upset you?

What skull? I ask.

Somebody in the crowd outside, there are hundreds of
people trying to get in, one fellow wore a death's-head
mask —

Where is Christoph? Sigrid asks.

I tell her where Christoph went, and just then I see him,
with his goggles pushed up over the flying cap, limping
back through the wildly dancing crowd with his cane in
one hand and a bottle of champagne in the other. Hans
Kowalski, wearing a tall white chef's hat, clears the
path, and coming up behind is Bertolt Brecht, no mask,
no costume, just a greasy leather jacket and dark trousers — and a guitar.

The black musicians walk off the bandstand, wiping their
faces.

A babble of voices fills the hall.

I am standing in the crowd with Sigrid.

What did he look like? That man with the death's-head?

He had his arm in a sling.

A tremendous pounding begins. People are banging
glasses and bottles on the tables.

> We want Brecht!
> We want Brecht!

Brecht climbs onto a table with his guitar. The hall is silent. He begins to strum. He begins to sing in his high
hoarse voice:

> Nicht so faul, sonst gibt es nicht Genuss!
> Was man will, sagt Baal, ist was man muss.
> Wenn ihr Kot macht, ist's, sagt Baal, geb' acht,
> Besser noch als wenn ihr garnichts macht!

Applause and whistles, some shouts of "Schweinerei!" but
more demands for more.

The German is too hard for me, or maybe I'm drunk. I
hear the words; I don't understand them.

> *Seid 'nur nicht so faul und so verweicht,*
> *Denn Geniessen is bei Gott nicht leicht!*
> *Starke Glieder braucht man und Erfahrung auch:*
> *Und mitunter stört ein dicker Bauch.*

More? All right, one more.
Sigrid von Waldstein is not listening to Brecht's "Choral
   vom Grossen Baal."
Sigrid von Waldstein's eyes are searching the crowd.

> *Man muss stark sein, den Genuss macht schwach.*
> *Geht es schief, sich freuen noch am Krach!*
> *Der bleibt ewig jung, wie er's auch treibt,*
> *Der sich jeden Abend selbst entleibt.*

Waves of applause, and up on the balcony two harlequins
   are dumping wicker baskets full of German marks.
Another band, not black this time, begins to play a waltz
   as falling banknotes fill the air like confetti. Like November leaves.
The waltz is an old song about the faithful hussar who
   loves his girl "ein ganzes Jahr," and I am dancing with
   the hussar now.
With her boots and her fur tschako she is taller than I
   am, red-faced, waltzing beautifully although she has
   been drinking steadily through the night.
Sorry I'm so wet, my dear, I'm sweating champagne.
   What the devil's wrong with Sigrid?
She saw somebody wearing a death's-head —
She saw a ghost. I've looked all over this menagerie, and
   the only death's-head is right up here on my cap . . .
   and he'll ward off the other ghost. . . . Smiling into
   my face: Will he not, Peter?

Another cold November dawn. The wind blows through
the open doors as people leave. The worthless paper
marks swirl around the emptying dance floor and out into
the street, bills of 100,000 marks and 500,000 marks and
1,000,000 marks and 100,000,000 marks fly about our
ankles and across the pavement and into the gutters as
we climb into a taxi.

Where shall we go for breakfast, I ask.

Phew, I'm tired of people, says Helena. Come along to the Lützowufer and I'll make us an omelette. Clara is out and you can sleep in her room.

Christoph is very quiet, looking out of the window. Does that mean he doesn't want me in the apartment? I don't feel like going back to the Villa Keith. I must find my own place this week.

Is something wrong with you? Helena asks him.

Christoph shakes his head but he continues to look out the window.

Has this got something to do with all the fuss that Sigrid was making? but now we are at the Lützowufer, and there is the usual negotiation about the taxi fare and then we walk upstairs and the moment Helena has unlocked the door of the apartment she shouts *There's somebody in here!* and dashes five steps down the hall and rips open the door to the living room and even before we hear the shot that deafens us we see her smashed back against the opposite wall, see her drop in a heap with everything pouring out through the golden hair.

And I can't stop Christoph! I have the Smith & Wesson in my right hand, I'm trying to hold him back with my left but I cannot hold him and that is how he gets in front of me coming around the door post to face the apparition slouched back into the big sofa: blond hair, white skull false-face pulled down just enough to reveal his forehead and his eyes, a Luger in his right hand with the longest barrel I've ever seen expertly cradled across his plaster-cast left elbow — and the bullet that takes out part of my lung has already passed through his brother's heart.

BOOK FOUR

STRIKE TWELVE ZEROS

38.

AMYTAL DREAMS

I still remember the dreams. I still dream them, sometimes. Schwester Anna, the night nurse, was the one who told me what they were giving me. Something new, she said, from Bayer-Leverkusen. For the pain, for the excitement, for sleep.

One dream I've dreamt so often is exciting and sad at the same time, because I'm making love, it is just unbearably good, but she is doing it all, she is on top and her breasts are in my face and I can't see her face and I don't know who she is. At first I don't. Too big to be Baby, too heavy. Too big to be Lili and I know she isn't Lili anyway. She might be Bärbel, but she isn't, she doesn't feel or move or smell like Bärbel and I keep trying to turn my head to see her face, and every time I think I *do* realize (remember?) who she is I feel the breath-stopping pain in my back and I'm face-down on the table in the white-tiled emergency room of the Charité again, a room full of bare-armed nurses in bloody rubber aprons and a green Schutzpolitzei officers and the smell of ether, and I'm dreaming again, dreaming that none of it really happened, falling backwards endlessly through clouds of yellow ether, dreaming that it was all a dream. . . .

I guess that's not the best way to begin this part. What is the best way to begin?

When I had to admit that it wasn't a dream?

When I saw in their eyes the same looks I had seen in France, after they dug me out from under all the people — parts of people — who had been blown out of Douglas Pratt's ambulance?

I don't know.

Maybe the place to start is with Miss Boatwright's quiet voice. "It's *all right* to cry. Remember? That was the problem then, thee couldn't cry."

So I cried.

That was after Miss Boatwright had moved me out of the huge icy disinfectant-reeking municipal hospital into Professor Jaffa's private clinic near the University, where I was in my own room with Schwester Gertrud in the daytime and Schwester Anna at night.

It is hard to tell about this period because I lost all sense of time. At first they kept the curtains closed. After a while I began to associate big fat Schwester Gertrud with morning sunshine on the ceiling and dark little Schwester Anna with the injections that were supposed to make me sleep, ease the pain, ease the excitement, give me nice dreams, but not addictive, *not* morphine, something new. (Schwester Anna and Schwester Gertrud had both served in France and wore medals on their starched blue uniforms. Miss Boatwright told them I had come through Verdun without a scratch. "Gnädiges Fräulein, *nobody* came through Verdun without a scratch!" was Schwester Anna's retort. "Some scratches are inside." "I stand corrected, Schwester Anna — and I'm happy you are on this case.")

Professor Jaffa was a chalk-white bald eagle with a shiny skull and a long white coat. He swept in just after every dawn and watched his assistants change the drain in my back and that always hurt, but gradually it hurt less when I breathed.

Miss Boatwright came every day. Sometimes she came twice a day. She brought a sketch pad and pencils and charcoal and pens and ink, and she made the nurses rig a table so that I could at least try to work even though I had to lie on my side because of the drain and even though it hurt when I moved my arm.

"It doesn't matter if it hurts. Thee must not let those muscles weaken. Thee must not let those fingers forget their skill!" and Professor Jaffa said she was right, so finally I did try a little pencil sketch of Schwester Gertrud sitting in the chair and knitting and it hurt, but I guess maybe I understood that the physical pain distracted a little from the other pain.

The Amytal did not help the other pain. Nothing helped, ever.

Miss Boatwright did her best. "Peter, it is simply too much for them. Even the most peripheral connection with one political murder was *almost* too much. We remember how that was, don't we? Now two more! A member of the family! An employee of the Bank! Suggestion of fratricide! They just can't face this kind of a scandal. And the newspapers have made a circus! Old photographs from the 1919 Revolution; *'Brothers! Don't Shoot!'*; pictures of Jacob Waldstein in the days of Napoleon; pictures of Helena when she married the Prince; pictures of Christoph with his fighter squadron. They even sent photographers in a boat to take pictures of Schloss Havelblick. That's why Lili can't come. They won't let her."

"She could write."

"Oh, she will write. I know she will. But when Bobby went off, right in the middle of this — well, it was the last straw, they are convinced thee helped him —"

"How could I help him lying here?"

"They're not quite rational about this, Peter."

"Nobody seems quite rational. Frau Keith hasn't replied to my letter."

"That's also understandable. She bitterly resents thy statements to the police."

"Miss Boatwright, I told them what happened."

"We cannot blame the woman if she refuses to believe that one of her sons has killed the other."

"But he did!"

"Dearest boy, thee knows that *I* believe it."

"The police don't, do they?"

"I have not spoken with the police, of course, but I understand that Dr. von Winterfeldt reports some skepticism, and so do the newspapers."

"Why? Why don't they believe me?"

"A skeleton stalking the Lützowufer? A bodyguard of Adolf Hitler puts on a false-face in order to ambush his own brother?"

"They think I made that up?"

Miss Boatwright shook her head. "My impression is they don't know what to think. I'm afraid thy role in the Rathenau case and now in this one has made thee something of a mystery man to the newspapers — and to the authorities. Why was an American art student carrying a revolver, for example?"

"Miss Boatwright, they don't think I —"

"No, of course not. The bullets . . . his bullets were of a different caliber."

"I don't remember firing —"

"The police report that the revolver was in thy hand, one bullet had been fired, and Helena's sofa was drenched with blood."

"I hit him after he'd put a bullet through me? Makes me look like Wyatt Earp, doesn't it?"

"Makes thee look . . . like something other than an art student."

"What should I do?"

"Get well," said Miss Boatwright.

We were sitting on the gunwale of the racing sloop and our feet were in the wet black sand and the sun was shining on Helena and Lili splashing toward us, pulling off their bathing caps and Christoph said, "Let's just forget about it. The corkscrew is at the bottom of the hamper," and Schwester Gertrud's body odor was beside me. "Mister Ellis? It is already ten o'clock and a gentleman from the American Embassy has been waiting half an hour. . . ." She gave me a calling card.

Langdon W. MacVeagh III, First Lieutenant, Infantry, Deputy to the Military Attaché to the Ambassador of the United States of America, was acutely uncomfortable. He wore a business suit and a vest and his hair was parted in the middle and apparently he had come to see me to find out whatever happened to various members of the Harvard football varsity whom he had encountered at the Point. I only knew what happened to one of them.

"He was driving an ambulance that took a direct hit from a German shell on the Chemin des Dames. April sixteenth, 1917."

"Oh, I'm sorry to hear that."

"Yeah, we were all sorry about it."

He tried politics. Stresemann had resigned as Chancellor, as I no doubt knew, but remained as Foreign Minister in the new coalition government of Wilhelm Marx, no relation, ha ha.

"But General von Seeckt is still running the country?"

"Well, not officially, of course —"

The Amytal from the night was wearing off and my back hurt. "What can I do for you, MacVeagh?"

"Well, as a matter of fact . . ."

Well, as a matter of fact the Ministry of the Interior

had just notified the Ambassador that my visa would be withdrawn as soon as I was well enough to travel.

They were throwing me out.

My first reaction was to ring for Schwester Gertrud, but I got hold of myself.

"Did they give any reason?"

"Not at first. Merely that you were what they call persona non grata. That's Latin. It means —"

"I know what it means. Did anybody ask them why I'm suddenly persona non grata?"

"Yes. The Ambassador is aware of your friendship with the Waldstein banking family and with Mr. Wood, and he asked Harrison of our Civil Affairs section to see if the Foreign Ministry would ask the Ministry of the Interior —"

"So what did they say?"

"You haven't heard the latest news, of course, because the police have only notified the papers this morning —"

"What latest news?"

"They found this man yesterday, this fellow you said shot Keith and his wife —"

"They found Kaspar Keith?"

"They found his body."

"His body? Look, lieutenant, would you be good enough to tell me this whole thing and not make me drag it out of you this way?"

"Okay, here's what they told us: The manager of some estate out in the Mark Brandenburg called the local constabulary out there, they found a dead man in one of their hay barns. Didn't know who he was or how he got there. So a policeman went out on a bicycle. By the time he got to the place, the old lady who owns it had identified the body as Keith —"

"The old lady being the Countess Brühl?"

"That's right! You know these people?"

"Tell me the rest, will you."

"The Prussian State Police took over, they brought him in and did an autopsy. The guy's left arm and elbow were smashed, his left arm was in a cast, but that's not what killed him. What killed him was a fresh wound in his chest. Loss of blood, infection —"

"— and my bullet still in him?"

"Right."

"How was he dressed?"

"Dressed as a farm worker."

"A farm worker. I see. Did the Prussian State Police talk to Lieutenant Count Brühl of the Reichswehr, do you know?"

"I wouldn't know anything about that."

"But in any event, now that the story I told the police turns out to be true, I'm suddenly declared persona non grata."

"I wouldn't put it that way."

"How would you put it? What did the Ministry of the Interior tell the Foreign Ministry?"

"Look, Ellis, I was sent over here as a courtesy to deliver the message, so you could make your plans. They could have written you a letter —"

"Come on, man, I've got the right to be given a reason, for God's sake!"

"Well, the fact is we don't think they have a specific reason. We think they think you might be in our intelligence —"

"That's right! That's exactly what they think. And you know I'm not."

"No *sir,* I don't know any such thing."

"What?"

"You could be working out of G-2 Washington, you could be in Naval Intelligence —"

"And your boss the Military Attaché wouldn't know it? The Ambassador wouldn't know it? And if for some reason I *were* in our intelligence, why on God's green earth would I involve myself in a mess of this kind? What sense would that make?"

Lieutenant MacVeagh folded his hands. "It doesn't make any sense, and that's what has the Krauts worried. Now they've got three deaths, they've got to make some kind of judicial determination about what happened, technically they have to dispose of two homicide charges and they don't quite know what may turn up. The newspapers have been printing rather juicy gossip —"

"What do you mean by juicy gossip?"

"I'm sure you can imagine —"

"No, I can't imagine!"

"Well, this lady who was killed, Frau Keith, before her marriage was a friend of General von Seeckt *and* of Walther Rathenau and now she's killed in a fight between two brothers — one a Nazi, the other an employee of Wald-

stein's bank — and an American who carries a revolver
. . . I guess some people in the German government think
they've got enough trouble already, they can do without
this. . . ."

"Mess?"

MacVeagh stood up. "Ellis, I guess I'd better go."

"Since everybody else is dead, if they get rid of me they
get rid of the mess. Is that the theory?"

"I hope your wound heals very quickly, old man. Don't
hesitate to get in touch with me if I can be of any help to
you." He was gone.

I rang the bell and Schwester Gertrud appeared.

"Give me a shot, please."

"But, Mr. Ellis! Only at night! Only for sleep! You cannot do the picture. What will Miss Boatwright say?"

"The Professor said I could have it if the pain is severe.
It *is* severe, Schwester Gertrud. *Please!*"

"Don't wake him, Schwester!"

"Baronin von Waldstein, Mr. Ellis! You don't want to
sleep all afternoon, and Frau Baronin has come to see
you, and I have made you some of Miss Boatwright's
tea —"

Sigrid's black lamb coat was flecked with snow.
Schwester Gertrud helped her take it off, hung it in the
closet, poured the tea. . . . "Frau Baronin, he's had light
medication several hours ago, he should drink a little tea,
we do not want him to sleep all day. . . ." She left the
room and closed the door.

Sigrid came to the bed and kissed my forehead. "Oh,
Peter, my God!"

"I've been dreaming . . . I'm not quite awake . . . I'm
so glad to see you —" I struggled out of the Amytal fog.
They hadn't given me much.

She took a blue envelope from her purse and put it on
my bedside table.

"From Lili."

"I'm glad to see that too."

We drank our tea and looked at each other for a minute.

"Peter . . . I don't know where to begin."

"Why don't you begin in the hay barn of Schloss
Zeydlitz?"

"You know about that? I came here to tell you —"

I explained about Lieutenant MacVeagh.

"Peter, I came in from the island the moment my brother telephoned. He didn't know anything about it until Mother called. He's been at the Bendlerstrasse and his apartment for weeks, he has not been to Zeydlitz, nobody knows how Kaspar got there, or what he wanted —"

"Well, I can imagine what he wanted. He wanted medical attention, he wanted a place to hide — and he wanted you."

"But we didn't know that, Peter. We had nothing to do with any of this!"

"You recognized him at the ball."

Sigrid shook her head slowly, looking out of the window. "I don't know. . . . I *didn't* really recognize him, I only had such a strange feeling, but then, just a moment later, there he was *again!* I mean his hunting suit. . . . Peter, I thought I was going mad!"

"They why didn't you tell us?"

"Tell Alfred? I didn't have the courage."

"In Munich they had a warrant for his arrest."

"Yes. So I should betray him? I already betrayed him once —"

"Betray him? He had a pistol in that sling!"

"How could I know that, Peter? I saw he was wounded."

"You thought he'd come to dance the Charleston?"

"No . . . I thought he had come to be the ghost at the party, with that horrible mask — His friends are shot or hiding or in jail, and here in Berlin we are having a costume ball!"

"Sigrid, you're the one who warned me against him."

"Yes."

Lying on my side, I stared out of the window. It was snowing again. I could only see the tops of bare trees along the river and the gray stucco wall of one of the University clinics. I couldn't see the river.

"Peter, I came here to explain. *Try* to explain. I just did not know what to do that night. I could not tell Alfred because Alfred would have called the police. You too, I think. But I did tell Christoph. You must believe that. I told him, 'I think your brother is in this crowd.' I told him, Peter! But Christoph was so — I don't know, so fatalistic, as if —" Sigrid shrugged her shoulders. "As if he didn't care: 'All right, so my brother is here, what can I do?' You understand me?"

. . . Christoph staring out of the taxi window. I turned to look at her, and my lung hurt. "You know that I killed Kaspar?"

"Of course. You had no choice. I only wish —"

"— That I'd shot first?"

Sigrid began to cry. She took a handkerchief from her purse and wiped her eyes. "My God, what has become of our country when a boy like that will shoot his brother, his brother's wife —"

"Sigrid, he wasn't a boy anymore — and he'd shot . . . many people."

Sigrid blew her nose, stood up, and walked over to the window. *"Ach Mensch*, the whole thing's my fault, he loved me, and just when his world collapsed, when the workers tore off his epaulets, tore off the symbol of his position, of his manhood — just then I left him for another man!"

She looked out at the snow falling into the river Spree.

"It wasn't your fault. You couldn't change your feelings. You couldn't compare Kaspar with Alfred."

She continued to look out of the window. "Did Miss Boatwright tell you about the funeral — all the fuss? No, perhaps she did not hear the details. Oh, it was dreadful, Peter. *Dreadful!* Frau Keith wanted Christoph buried with his father at Potsdam, in the military cemetery — with or without Helena. But Christoph wasn't in the army anymore, he did not die in service, the regulations don't permit this — so Frau Keith sends her colonel to get special permission from General von Seeckt — can you imagine? And in the meantime Helena's father insists his daughter will *not* be buried in the garrison at Potsdam, no matter what von Seeckt decides. And what about the funeral service? It turns out that Helena is Catholic, became a Catholic before the War, when she married the Prince, so what kind of funeral do we have? And where? Everybody talks to everybody else, everybody argues and is furious — and in the end of course Alfred must decide, so we have a simple memorial service in the big hall at the Pariser Platz, the string quartet plays Haydn, different people stand up and say things — very much like the Quaker Meeting except it is an enormous crowd of people — the whole family, theatre people, bank people,

Christoph's old army people . . . and then we drive them
out to the island and we carry them up the hillside to the
orchard beneath our Little House, the men have dug a
grave there, the Protestant chaplain says a little prayer
and then they throw the earth on the coffins. . . ."

Sigrid was crying again, still looking out of the window.

"And now they find Kaspar. In my mother's barn!
Your American bullet proves he shot his brother. Where
are they going to bury Kaspar? Is she going to ask von
Seeckt for special permission again?"

"Sigrid —"

She turned to face me. "And the newspapers! You cannot imagine! Every newspaper sees its own political opinions justified: the National Socialists see Jewish bankers
destroying a family of Prussian officers; the Centrists and
the Social Democrats see confirmed erosion of the solid
virtues of German society, failure of the business community to support the democratic principles of Weimar,
echoes of the Rathenau affair; the Communists see costume balls while millions are starving, debauchery among
the plutocrats, treachery among their hired mercenaries.
Even the *Vossische Zeitung,* conservative as they are,
wrote a crazy editorial about the March on Berlin being
physically halted at the Feldherrnhalle in Munich but
symbolically carried out by this what they call 'Cain-and-
Abel murder' in the apartment of a socially prominent
actress on the Lützowufer. And the *Berliner Illustrierte*
prints pictures, pictures, pictures!"

"And the Waldsteins don't like it."

"Don't like it? They are beside themselves! They don't
mind to be rich and important, they like to have money
and power and beautiful houses and the Chancellor at the
dinner table, but they don't like publicity. They don't like
to be conspicuous. And they certainly want nothing to do
with *Fememord* or anything of that sort."

"Which now includes me."

She nodded. "Not Alfred, of course. But his father and
his uncle and the others, and you must understand the
reason, Peter. On one hand they feel secure, they have
been here hundreds of years, they have their money, they
have their titles, they are accepted — but then they see
what happened to Walther Rathenau, they see the crowds
listening to Hitler when he screams terrible lies about the
Jews, they see Kaspar Keith shoot his own brother, they

see Kaspar Keith shoot Helena, they feel millions of eyes turning to look at them, they suddenly feel . . ." She paused, seeking the right word. "Not so secure? Exposed? Nothing to do really with you. You are only somehow . . . somehow a part of what has happened and that is why —" She stopped, looking down, compressing her lips.

"That's why they don't want to see me."

No answer. She looked at the floor.

"Or let me see Lili."

Still no answer.

"So there is no point asking them to help me, asking them to speak with Dr. Stresemann so that I can stay in Berlin?"

Sigrid's eyes came up. "Why do you want to stay in Berlin?"

Snaredrums beating march time. Massed bands moving in step. Thousands of boots crashing in step: two . . . four . . . six . . . eight . . . a hundred thousand voices:

> *Die Fahne hoch!*
> *Die Reihen dicht geschlossen!*
> *S.A. marschiert*
> *Mit ruhigfestem Schritt . . .*

And the banners are everywhere; huge, blood-red with fat black swastikas, fluttering above the marching columns, hanging motionless from every window. . . .

No matter how much Amytal they gave me, I couldn't have dreamed that dream in 1923.

Horst Wessel was a Neukölln pimp; Horst Wessel was a Neukölln S.A. commander; Horst Wessel didn't write that song until 1930.

We know that, don't we?

So I couldn't have dreamed that dream in 1923.

But I did.

39.

LETTERS

Dearest Peter:

What can I say to you?

Sigrid is bringing this and will explain why I have not come to see you. I am watched *every minute,* my father and even my mother have become a little crazy — that is the only way to describe it — over all the stories in the newspapers and even more over Bobby, who has run away to the Russian woman in America.

I try and try to explain that none of this is *your* fault, but I cannot convince them.

In the meantime Miss Boatwright brings reports that you have the best doctors and nurses and that you are out of danger. The whole thing seems like a terrible dream. To me. When I wake up in the morning I think, Oh it was just a nightmare, what an *awful* nightmare, and tonight we will go to another party with Helena and Christoph, and then I remember how the gardeners shoveled the earth, how the earth sounded when it fell on their coffins!

I feel so *terrible* about the mean and silly things I said to Helena sometimes — about all her men — but it was really only *envy!* I wished that I could be so *radiant,* so full of *joie de vivre!* I think men like that even more than beauty. You are just born beautiful or you are not, but this is something else, this comes from inside, and I just cannot imagine her in that box under the earth.

And Christoph, your best friend! You save his life and his brother takes it! The newspapers talk about Cain and Abel. The most horrible story in the Bible.

I do believe that is why Bobby ran away. I mean, perhaps he *planned* before, but Christoph's death decided him. Bobby was closer to Christoph than to Alfred. Christoph was really more the older brother than Alfred.

348

Now I must put this in the envelope because Sigrid is here and I must give her this when nobody sees it.

Please get well *quickly*, my dear, because I want to see you *so much!*

XXX LOVE XXX LOVE XXX LILI

WHITE ENVELOPE

WALDSTEIN & CO.
No. 4, Gendarmenmarkt
Berlin W

den 10. Dezember 1923

Mr. Peter Ellis
c/o Klinik Prof. Dr. Jaffa
No. 2, Artilleriestrasse (Ebertsbrücke)
Berlin N

Dear Ellis:

I write this first communication since the tragedies of November because my friend and client Prof. Dr. Sigismund JAFFA advises that your physical health has improved to the point where you may wish to hear about matters of the outside world.

Before turning to the affairs of commerce permit me to share with you our shock and sorrow upon the tragic loss of our colleague and your friend, and his wife, and also to offer a statement of my personal admiration for your soldierly conduct so to speak in battle which, while not preventing the terrible deed, at least put a deserved end to the life of its perpetrator!

The loss of Christoph Keith is not only the loss of a valued co-worker and friend. The loss of Christoph Keith is also a loss for the German Nation, which has already lost so many of its best young men, the men who would otherwise have led the next generation out of the present disorder into an age of peace, prosperity and brotherhood. It was my private hope that his military training, his inborn talent for leadership *plus* the financial experience he was acquiring with us would — some years hence — combine to produce a *business-statesman* without peer in this Nation. With "Die Schöne Helena" at his side, he could, in my opinion, have risen to the *highest positions* this Nation offers. But that was not to be. . . .

My dear young man, I must now turn, reluctantly, to matters of business. Since I assume that you have not been able to follow the financial news in the press, I will begin with the briefest summary of what has happened during the wildest weeks in my memory, the wildest weeks in the memory of any banker or businessman in this Nation:

In sum, the inflation seems to be ending. Dr. Schacht's Rentenmark is being accepted by the people. It is difficult to explain the reason for this, because the reason is based primarily upon *mass psychology* rather than economics. The idea that the Rentenmark is secured by a first mortgage upon *German earth* and *German industry* — while as a practical and legal matter quite meaningless — nevertheless seems to mean something to the *German people* and seems to be restoring their confidence in German paper money as a medium of exchange. The farmers, in particular, are now accepting Rentenmarks in payment for their crops and thus the 1923 harvest has been released, farm products are moving into the cities, the famine is ending and so therefore are the civil disturbances.

How did all this happen? While the Rentenmark notes were being printed, the old paper marks continued to fall in relation to the dollar. On 20. November the black market *Kurs* was 11,000,000,000,000 to the dollar! However, the official rate on the Berlin Stock Exchange that day was "only" 4,200,000,000,000 to the dollar. It seemed possible to some of us and to Dr. Schacht that we might be able to "hold" this rate long enough to fix it as the conversion rate for the Rentenmark, because that rate would make the numbers come out exactly even — although "even" is almost a bad joke in this sense! Consequently Dr. Schacht as Reich Currency Commissioner decreed that:

1,000,000,000,000 paper marks = 1 Rentenmark = 10/42 of 1 dollar.

To state this another way: the old paper mark was to be worth one million-millionth of one Rentenmark, and therefore to convert from paper marks to Rentenmarks it was only necessary to *strike off twelve zeros!*

So far, at least, this conversion rate has been maintained: the black market *Kurs*, and the *Kurs* on the Cologne Exchange (occupied as you know by the French army!) has fallen steadily from 11,000,000,000,000 to the dollar on 20. November until just this morning, when it reached the "official" Berlin Stock Exchange *Kurs* of 4,200,000,000,000 to the dollar. It would appear, therefore, that Dr. Schacht has succeeded in "stabilizing" the mark.

These stabilization operations were accompanied by a *catastrophic* and *entirely unexpected* fall in the market price of stocks on the Berlin Exchange. There are various theories for this; I will not trouble you with them. It is always easier to explain what *has* happened on the stock market than what *will* happen!

In any event, the value of the stocks in your account suddenly dropped *below* the value of your dollar notes to us. There was nothing for us to do, in the circumstances, but sell your securities for what we could get (as shown in the enclosed statement of I. XII. 23) which was considerably less than the amount of your notes.

It will not make you feel better to know that *millions* of people in this Nation have also been financially ruined — mostly not by the stock market fall, but by the utter devaluation of the mark, which has destroyed every savings account, every annuity, every pension, every life insurance policy in Germany! The mark has apparently been stabilized, but the middle class has been reduced to the level of the proletariat. Those who are employed may recover; those who were dependent upon pensions or capital or savings are reduced to selling their silverware and their furniture and, in some cases, themselves.

My illustrious partners, although suffering enormous losses of capital, consider the events of the last weeks to be a necessary and inevitable *purge*. They feel that if some reasonable agreement on reparations can be negotiated next year, then Germany may finally be able to achieve domestic peace and economic prosperity.

I pray that their optimism is justified. In the Jägerstrasse I see respectable old ladies sitting behind card tables attempting to sell knives and forks they were given as wedding presents. . . . To whom will these people turn?

But none of this applies to you. You are young, you have no financial responsibilities, when you recover your health you will continue your artistic endeavors anywhere you choose to do so, and *if you examine the postcard I*

have enclosed, you may find a suggestion of help to you
in the future.

This letter has become too long. If you have any questions about the bank statement, please direct them to
Herr Borgenicht of our accounting department, who will
be only too happy to answer them. On behalf of myself
and of the entire firm may I offer best wishes for the fast-
est possible recovery of your health.

> With highest respect!
> E. Strassburger

I couldn't make much out of the statement, several
pages of transactions typed on flimsy paper — a dizzy-
ing array of zeros after each number. My cash balance
at Waldstein & Co. as of December 1, 1923, appeared
to be about 21,000,000,000,000 marks. Strike twelve
zeros? Twenty-one Rentenmarks. About five dollars?
My debit position, however, was always stated in dollars.
I owed over $750. In other words, I was not only broke,
I was over my head in debt to Waldstein & Co.

The postcard was a view of the Brandenburg Gate and
the Pariser Platz. On the other side, written in ink, was
the following unsigned message:

$500 from Amsterdam affiliates transferred to account
of Miss Susan Boatwright, Morgan Harjes & Co. Paris
(affiliate of J. P. Morgan & Co. New York). As these
funds are outside control of Waldstein & Co. and outside jurisdiction of German courts, Waldstein & Co.
unable to comply with Reichsbank regulations as to
assertion of liens against trading accounts in debit positions.

Waldstein & Co. was saying goodbye. Miss Boatwright
was paying my bills.

40.

PROFESSOR JAFFA'S PROGNOSIS

"Again! Deep breath! . . . Hurt?"

"Yes."

"Good. . . . This hurt?"

"No, sir."

"Also good. Like the needlework?"

"I can't see back there, Doctor Jaffa."

"Schwester, the mirror please —"

"Wow!"

"What does that mean, 'wow'? Saw worse in France, didn't you?"

"Much worse. You've done a wonderful job."

"I have done a wonderful job and you had 'Schwein,' as we say in Berlin. You know what that means?"

"Good luck."

"Very *damned* good luck. Don't know why we call it that. Hole in the front won't show much. Clean entry, surprisingly. Three stitches. Hole in the back a different story. And the lung tissue. You won't become a marathon runner but the breathing should get easier now. Your father will approve, I believe."

"You know about my father?"

"Had a letter from him. Professor of Surgery, University of Pennsylvania. Wanted an exact description of the wound, diagram of bullet path, course of treatment. Write it in German, he said. Served under Hofmeister in Munich, he said. '95–'96."

"I have not heard from my father —"

"He seemed interested in your condition. I have told him you will live."

"But not in Germany, Doctor Jaffa."

"You're American. Why live in Germany? As a matter of fact, I have sent my son to do his residency in New York. With Dr. Walter Kuhn, Lenox Hill Hospital."

"Why, Doctor Jaffa?"

"If he prefers to live in America he will have to take your examinations —"

"Why would he prefer to live in America when he's German?"

"Schwester Gertrud, will you get us both some tea, please? . . . Does 'Jaffa' sound like a very German name to you? Do you think the gentleman who put that bullet through you would consider my son a *German?* He's our youngest, and the only doctor. One of his brothers fell on the Marne, the other at Verdun. But that doesn't matter, we're not German to the friends of Herr Kaspar Keith. And how many friends do you think he has out there? Did you see the photographs from Munich? Thousands marching, thousands wearing the swastika."

"But the army put them down. Hitler ran away, and now he's in jail."

"Yes, Hitler's in jail. You know how many they actually *arrested,* out of those thousands? A few dozen. You know how many they will put on trial? One dozen — maybe. You know what's going to happen to them? A few months in jail, at the most. Now if they had been Communists — you have heard what happened in Munich in 1919, what happened right here in Berlin?"

"Yes, I have. But you're not in favor of Communism?"

"No, young man, I'm certainly not in favor of Communism, but Communism is not the danger to this country. Did you read what Chancellor Wirth said after Rathenau was shot? The Enemy stands on the Right. And if the Republic doesn't destroy that Enemy, that Enemy is going to destroy the Republic."

"You think that's going to happen?"

"Am I a fortune-teller? I have mortgaged this building to Waldsteins' so that my son can study medicine in New York."

"You know, I don't think the Waldsteins feel that enthusiastic about the Republic, or that concerned about the Right."

"Correct. The Waldsteins rest their faith in Herr Generaloberst von Seeckt and his Reichswehr. The army will keep order in the country. Dr. Schacht and Dr. Strassburger will restore the economy, with some help from Herr Stinnes and Herr Thyssen and Herr Kirdorf and Herr Krupp von Bohlen and the rest of those gentlemen. Dr. Stresemann will persuade the Allies to reduce their demands for reparations and the French to get out of the Ruhr. The sun will shine again on Germany, and on Waldstein and Co."

"You don't believe that, Dr. Jaffa?"

"That the sun will shine again? My dear young man, I'm not only the Waldsteins' customer, I'm the Waldsteins' doctor. Known them all my life. Admire them. Perhaps I envy them. But I also worry about them, I get angry about them. Want to know why? I will tell you why. Because the Jewish people in Germany need leaders — need them desperately — and the Waldsteins ought to be those leaders, perhaps they were born to be those leaders. But are they? They are not! On the contrary: They have persuaded themselves that they are not Jews at all. With their titles, with their poet — and now their novelist — their friendships with three Kaisers, their relations with Bismarck, their mansion on the Pariser Platz, their palace on the Havel, their Huguenot and Junker wives, their Christmas trees . . . surely the Waldsteins are not Jews! But what did the man who shot his own brother think they were? What does that Austrian corporal in Fortress Landsberg think they are? . . . I'm sorry for this outburst, I can only permit myself such remarks to a man from another country. You will not repeat them. . . . Here is our tea."

41.

THE OTHER SUBJECT

The footman who opened the door said, "Good afternoon, Mr. Ellis" without expression, took my coat and hat, and led me through the great hall, past the enormous Christmas tree, through the salon and into the library. The house appeared to be empty. I knew that it wasn't; it was silently listening.

"A glass of sherry, sir?"

"No, thank you."

"Herr Baron has been advised of your arrival."

"Thank you."

He closed the door.

It was only a few blocks from my room in Miss Boatwright's apartment, but it was the longest walk I had attempted so far, and I felt shaky. There was a coal fire in the grate, and I warmed myself, watching the snow falling into the brick courtyard. I wondered again why this audience was being granted here instead of at the Gendarmenmarkt; perhaps they didn't want me seen at the Bank; perhaps this was just one of the days Baron von Waldstein went home for lunch and a nap.

Then he came in: polite smile, firm handshake, would I like a glass of sherry, please be seated — "Jaffa tells me you are still in bandages."

"Yes, but they're mostly to support the ribs, I'm pretty much healed."

"No trouble breathing?"

"Very little, sir. He took wonderful care of me. . . . Baron von Waldstein, I greatly appreciate this opportunity to see you in person."

"You wrote a good letter. Made me feel . . . discourteous."

"Every word in that letter is true, sir. I'm *not* an intelligence agent, I am *not* involved in *any* political activity of any kind, the things that happened — all of them — happened because I tried to help Christoph keep his brother away from the Rathenau plot —"

The Baron raised his hand. "Mr. Ellis, you need not repeat it all, and I see no reason to debate the matter. You know that we all like you, I told you last summer that in principle my wife and I had no objection" — he paused to think of a neutral word — "no objection to an alliance between you and our daughter. But circumstances changed. In the first place, we now feel a sense of actual physical danger for her. You have been in Berlin — what, not yet two years? and have involved yourself in three political murders!"

"But they all arose out of the same —"

"*Three political murders!* And in the second place, the German government has apparently decided that your presence in the Reich is not desirable for reasons of security. Now what is my response to *that,* Mr. Ellis?" The Baron was glaring at me now. "I am to entrust my daughter, eighteen years old, to a man my government expels from my country?"

"Baron . . ." I shook my head. "I just can't understand why they did that. Reasons of security? With your connections . . . It seems to me — and I say this with respect — that you must know more about that decision than I do."

"I know nothing about that decision. *Nothing!*"

"You could easily find out, sir."

No reply. He looked out of the window.

"You don't want to find out?"

"I must assume the authorities have their reasons. Matters of police administration and public security are not my business."

"Baron von Waldstein, you *know* I'm not a threat to public security."

"Three political murders! An avalanche of newspaper publicity! In politics, you know, appearances count as much as facts. Perhaps more."

Hopeless. I would have to raise the other subject, the subject I didn't even want to think about, the subject I had been brooding over, having nightmares about.

I haven't been afraid much. I was afraid at Verdun. I was afraid on the Chemin des Dames. I was not afraid those moments in Helena's apartment, because there wasn't time. Right now, sitting in a leather club chair in the library at No. 4, Pariser Platz, I was scared to death.

"Baron von Waldstein . . . I really don't know how to say this. . . . You tell me you have doubts about Lili's safety with me. I hope you will not consider it impertinent for me to say that I have doubts — terrible doubts — about Lili's safety with you — No, I don't mean with you, I mean here in Germany, I mean the safety of your whole family, your whole . . . people? . . . here in Germany. I don't want to say these things, I'm forcing myself to say them because I must say them, sir. . . ." And suddenly I did have trouble breathing, it hurt, I had to stop while the Baron took off his pince-nez and frowned at me.

Where should I begin this? And how?

"Baron, last summer . . . I don't know exactly when, not long before your birthday, Hermann Göring telephoned Christoph —"

"What?"

"Hermann Göring telephoned Christoph at your Bank

and then they met in some bar somewhere for a drink. . . ."

I told Baron von Waldstein the whole story of Göring's warnings to Christoph.

Impassive, he listened until I finished. Then he said: "I suppose I am disappointed that Christoph Keith did not tell me this himself. Otherwise, what does it mean? Are you surprised that Hitler's men propose to take action against the Jews? They have been shouting it for years."

"Göring was right about the Putsch, and he was right about Kaspar."

"He was right about Kaspar. He was wrong about the Putsch. The Putsch failed because the police and the army stood fast. Hitler ran away. Göring ran away. Hitler is in jail. Göring is hiding in Austria. All of them are completely discredited. A joke."

"Sir, I was in your Bank the day of the Putsch, when nobody could tell who was winning down in Munich. I didn't hear anybody laugh."

"What do you mean by that remark?"

"Sir, you saw the photographs from Munich! Thousands of people singing and marching and cheering the Nazis on! Swastikas everywhere! The police put a handful of people in jail, another handful ran away, and the rest just went home. Where are they going to be the next time this happens?"

"I have every hope that there will be no next time. The situation has changed while you were in the hospital. Drastically. We have every indication that the mark is stabilized, that inflation is ending very quickly, that the Allies will finally listen to reason on the matter of reparations. The expenses of the government are substantially reduced. The Ruhr has gone back to work. We have at last a strong government, firmly supported by the army. I personally look forward to 1923 with optimism, for German industry and for the German people —"

"But what about the people who are wiped out? What about your kitchen maid from the Spreewald? What about Frau Keith?"

The Baron ran his hand across his eyes. "What are you trying to say to me, young man?"

What was I trying to say, really?

"I feel rising hostility against the Jews in Germany, I

think the Nazis will continue to blame the Jews for the inflation —"

"I agree with you," said the Baron. "There is rising hostility, and Nationalist extremists will do their best to make it worse. What is it you want from *me?*" He began to drum his fingers on the wooden arm of his chair.

"Well, to begin with, I most respectfully ask you to permit me to marry Lili and take her to the United States with me."

"Because there is no hostility toward Jews in the United States?"

"Sir?"

"I understand that your father served for a year under Professor Hofmeister in Munich. Well, I served for a year with Jacob Schiff, Kuhn, Loeb and Co., New York, the biggest competition for J. P. Morgan."

"I didn't know that, Baron."

"Yes. Most interesting experience. I learned a great deal. One of the things I learned is that in America, people with Jewish names are not allowed in the best hotels. Another thing I learned is that every town has a golf club, and they do not accept Jewish members. Not even Jacob Schiff. And the beach places on Long Island, they do not permit Jews to buy houses there. Not even Jacob Schiff."

"I think Mr. Otto Kahn, who is in that same firm, has a palatial establishment at Cold Spring Harbor —"

"I am not an admirer of Otto Kahn. He was born in Mannheim and he spent the war making propaganda against Germany!"

By now the Baron was on his feet and this discussion was out of control.

"Baron von Waldstein, the last thing I want to do is make you angry —"

"You have, however! You mean well, but you are a very naïve young man and you don't know what you are talking about. Yes, there is anti-Semitism here in Germany, always has been, I assure you we are aware of it, but to a large extent we have . . . dealt with it. Jewish people — religious Jews and Christians of Jewish descent — have achieved a position here — particularly in what used to be the Kingdom of Prussia — that is unrivaled anywhere in the world. I include England in that statement, I include France, and I most certainly include your

360 *Arthur R. G. Solmssen*

country, although it was organized, as I understand, on the theory that all men are created equal!"

"Baron, these things you mention — hotels and country clubs —"

"Not just hotels and country clubs. Banks! The National City Bank! Jacob Schiff was so proud when they made him a director, in 1899. I understand they still have not one Jewish officer!"

"Baron, these things are perfectly true, I can't deny them, but they wouldn't have anything to do with Lili, they wouldn't apply to my wife —"

"Wouldn't apply to your wife. That's very reassuring to hear!"

"It's a different thing, sir. It is — sort of a *social* thing —"

"Yes, that was my observation: the Jews are placed in a social layer that is *above* the Negroes but *below* . . . what do you call them? The Whites?"

"Sir —"

"The House of Waldstein has been *inextricably* rooted in the culture and the commerce and the history of the Kingdom of Prussia and the German nation since the middle of the eighteenth century, and in recognition of that fact the first Kaiser Wilhelm raised my father to the nobility, and not just to the nobility but to the *Freiherrschaft*. You expect me to send a girl who was born a Baroness, with a name that is in every schoolbook, to a country where she may not be considered entirely *white?*" His voice was shaking.

"But you told me you had no objection, in principle —"

"That was *here*. Our assumption was that you could remain here, become a painter . . . you seem to have talent, people here are buying your pictures. . . . I assure you I had no intention of sending my daughter permanently to America. *None!*" He paused to take a breath. His face told me that the subject was closed. Silence. I could hear my heart.

"For that matter, have you sold any pictures in your own country?" His voice was steadier.

"No, I haven't, Baron. I've been away for several years, I had really just begun. . . ."

"Then may one ask how you propose to live, not to mention support a wife?" *On the five hundred dollars we let you keep?* He didn't say the words, but they hung there just the same.

"I think my family would help me get started again."

"Do you? Have you heard from your family recently?"

"No, sir."

"Why not?"

"Because they want me to come home and go to work . . . or to school . . . I mean to the university."

"They want you at the university, but you come home with an eighteen-year-old wife, an eighteen-year-old schoolgirl who has never so much as made her own bed, who does not know how to boil an egg — and you expect them to support you while you make a name as a painter?" He shook his head. "My dear young man, put yourself in my position. What would you do?"

I had nothing to say. I folded my hands and looked down at the carpet.

"Miss Boatwright reports you are sailing from Hamburg?"

"Yes, sir. New Year's Eve."

"What ship?"

"I think it's called *Albert Berlin.*"

"You think it's called *Albert Berlin,* eh?" The Baron shook his head and sat down again, heavily, expelling his breath. "Sic transit gloria mundi. The name is Albert B-a-l-l-i-n, but you have never heard it?"

"No, sir."

"So!" The Baron turned to look out of the window. "He was a friend of mine. As a matter of fact he was an example of what we were discussing a moment ago. Came from nowhere. Father was a little Jewish business man in Hamburg. Went bankrupt — the father. Albert Ballin joined the Hamburg-Amerika Line — we call it the HAPAG — as a young man. They had a few little ships. Carried emigrants to America. That was in the 'eighties. By the time the War began he had built the HAPAG into one of the most powerful lines in the world, and himself into one of the most powerful men in Germany. First citizen of Hamburg. Personal friend of the Kaiser. Hundreds of ships on every ocean. His triumph was the *Imperator,* 52,000 tons, 5,000 people, the biggest thing afloat. The Kaiser was there to launch it. Nineteen-twelve. Everybody was there. I was there; we helped to raise the money. Had a golden eagle on her bow, and Ballin's motto: 'Mein Feld ist die Welt.' "

The Baron looked at me again. "That motto isn't up there anymore, and neither is the name. Your British cousins took her as reparations. They call her *Berengaria*. People cried when they took her out of Hamburg for the last time. You have to get on in Southampton now, or Cherbourg. But Albert Ballin didn't live to see that."

"What happened to him?"

"Well, the war ruined the shipping business for Germany, he ruined his health worrying about it. Couldn't sleep at night. Terrible insomnia, sleeping pills . . . Tried and tried to convince our generals and our admirals that the U-boats would bring your country into the war, and that we couldn't win if the United States came in against us. You know what happened. Then he saw the revolution coming, the people simply had enough. He begged the Kaiser to make peace while we still had some bargaining power, but the Kaiser was too stubborn and the war lords were too strong. When the revolution *did* come, it came in the ports: Wilhelmshaven, Kiel, Bremen, Hamburg. . . . Ballin heard that the sailors were going to arrest him — the great shipowner, you see, the plutocrat, the friend of the Kaiser — He swallowed a bottle of Veronal."

Another long silence. I thought: General Ludendorff didn't commit suicide; Field Marshal von Hindenburg didn't commit suicide; Admiral von Tirpitz didn't commit suicide; the Kaiser didn't commit suicide. . . .

"But we are rebuilding the HAPAG!" The Baron slammed his fist onto the arm of his chair. "They've taken our *Imperator*, they've taken our *Bismarck*, they've taken our *Vaterland*, they've taken all our giants, and so far we've only been able to build a couple of smaller ships like the *Ballin* — she's only twenty thousand tons — but we're going to concentrate on faster ships, faster than anybody else's —"

"Baron von Waldstein, may I see Lili alone for a few minutes?"

"Oh, I'm sorry, that will not be possible. Lili is in Austria."

"In Austria?"

"Yes, my brother has a place in Tyrol, they usually go

there in the summer, but the skiing is becoming so popular with young people, they thought this year hey would open it in the Christmas holidays, so Alfred and Sigrid went down with the baby and the old Ma and they took Lili along too — Just a minute young man, I understand how you feel, and I have something for you —"

They didn't even say goodbye?

I was on my feet, moving toward the door.

"Baron von Waldstein —"

He was up too, tugging the bell pull.

"— I'd better go, sir."

"Yes, only not quite alone. One moment, please." He actually grabbed my elbow.

The same footman appeared at the door. His expression changed a little when he saw my face.

"Get the package for Mr. Ellis. I think they put it into the coatroom. . . ."

The footman disappeared again, and the Baron, his hand still on my elbow, guided me gently out of the library, through the salon and to the Christmas tree, to the exact spot where, a year before, he had given me the bottle containing the sailboat. *Where had I left that bottle?*

"We have another Christmas present for you," he said as the footman appeared with a large flat package, wrapped in brown paper. The footman didn't know what to do with it.

"Stand it on that sofa and unwrap it very carefully," said the Baron.

The footman untied the twine and folded back the heavy wrapping paper, to reveal Bärbel, entirely naked except for one black stocking, busily engaged in putting on the other stocking.

"That picture's not finished," I gasped. "I never finished it, he took it away and sold it —"

"Apparently Max Liebermann thinks it's finished."

"Sir?"

"He saw it in a gallery and he bought it. For me. And let me assure you that he doesn't buy paintings very often, he sells them. To tell the truth, he sold me this one, too. He says it demonstrates a developing style of your own. He says this is more striking than the one you did of Lili. Of course you were able to show much more of this lady, and Liebermann still has an eye for that. And maybe your title amused him."

"It doesn't have a title —"

"Certainly it has a title." We moved closer. The footman pulled the brown paper away from the bottom of the plain dark frame, and I saw a small white tag with prewar Art Nouveau letters: *Prinzessin in Berlin.*

42.

ROLLING HOME

Nun ade, du mein leib' Heimatland,
Lieb' Heimatland, ade.
Es geht nun fort zum fremden Strand
Lieb' Heimatland, ade!

The band was playing on the first-class promenade deck, but you could hear it all over the ship and all over the huge, teeming St. Pauli Landing Stages — great echoing hangars through which people and luggage moved slowly from buses and taxis and railroad cars, past the customs and ticket and passport control and over the two gangways; one led up to the glassed-in promenade, the other straight across through an open hatch in the black steel hull, into the lower depth of the S.S. *Albert Ballin.*

Can you be homesick going home? Can you be so homesick that you deliberately try to get drunk in the dining car between Berlin and Hamburg?

The answer is Yes, you can.

Miss Boatwright had taken me to the Lehrter Bahnhof that morning. I had shipped a small trunk with a few unfinished pictures. I carried one suitcase and the *Princess in Berlin,* still wrapped in brown paper.

We stood on the crowded platform and looked at each other.

The conductors began to close the doors. Whistles blew.

"I'd better get on, Miss Boatwright. I hope Mr. Wood likes the portrait."

"I'm sure he'll like it, although it flatters me outrageously."

"No, that's what you look like. . . . Miss Boatwright, I want to thank you so much —"

"Peter Ellis, there's nothing to thank me for. A severe crisis has made thee a stronger man. I can see it. I wish thee a safe journey home and a happy New Year. Give my love to everyone, and put this in thy pocket."

An envelope.

"Get on the train!"

"Is this money, Miss Boatwright?"

"Get on the train!"

They were shutting the doors, so I had to scramble into the car, but I pushed my way into the first compartment and put my head out the window. Other people were doing it too.

"Miss Boatwright, what is this money?"

"That's what they transferred to my account in Paris, plus a fee from Whitney Wood."

"Miss Boatwright, you paid Professor Jaffa! You paid for my steamship ticket!" The train was moving, and Miss Boatwright took a few steps along the platform.

"The Waldsteins paid Professor Jaffa," she called, and then there were too many other people in front of her, waving, and I couldn't see her anymore. The train gathered speed, left the station, and passed through miles of freight yards, my last view of Berlin.

> *Give my regards to Broadway*
> *Remember me to Herald Square . . .*

"First and Second Class this way, please!" They shouted it over and over again, in German and in English. They didn't shout it in Polish or in Russian. The people for Third Class were crowded behind a wooden fence: men with black hats and black beards and long black coats; women in black dresses and shawls; bundles, baskets, cardboard boxes; many children of all sizes.

"My God, just look at them," said a woman somewhere behind me. "At least they're going to America and not staying here."

"The Americans feel they have enough, too. They're

reducing the quotas again next year. That's why there's such a mob of them."

I turned around but couldn't see who was speaking.

"Passport please, sir?"

"I don't have my passport. You're supposed to return it to me here." I handed him my letter from the Polizei Präsidium Alexanderplatz, feeling a sudden silence behind me, feeling the eyes, feeling grateful for the Scotch I had consumed in the dining car.

"Will you step into our office, Mr. Ellis?"

There wasn't any trouble at all. The Grenzpolizei station was full of noise, shouting in unintelligible Eastern languages, crying, shouting in German about whatever was wrong with their papers — but when the officer with me presented my letter, the Germans behind the counter stopped shouting, looked me over coldly, extracted my passport from a drawer, made me sign a receipt, and handed it over. "Have a good voyage home, sir. And a happy New Year."

Gangplank. Sunshine and ice-cold air for a moment.

> *Muss i denn, muss i denn zum Städtele hinaus*
> *— Städtele hinaus —*
> *Und du, mein Schatz, bleibst hier?*

I was right beside the red-faced sweating musicians and the music was blasting in my ear. The promenade was jammed: passengers and people saying goodbye, kissing and crying, waiters passing trays of champagne, bellboys carrying flowers, porters carrying luggage. . . .

"My name is Ellis, I'm in the Second Class —

"Yes, sir, Mr. Ellis. You are in Cabin 242, C Deck, with Herr August Ansbach. The boy will take your suitcase."

> *Kann i gleich net allweil bei dir sein*
> *Han i doch mein Freud an dir. . . .*
> *Wenn i komm, wenn i komm,*
> *Wenn i wiederum komm*
> *— wiederum komm,*
> *Kehr i ein, mein Schatz, bei dir!*

Wiederum komm? Come back again? Not bloody likely! I followed the uniformed boy down the narrow steel companionway, but I could hardly see him.

Herr August Ansbach was not in the cabin but he had certainly established his presence. Blue silk pajamas and a blue bathrobe were carefully laid across the lower bunk, two large and expensive steamer trunks, two beautiful leather suitcases and a crocodile toilet case left very little room for my bag; the closet was almost filled with suits and the bureau drawers were almost filled with immaculate shirts, socks and underwear.

I tipped the boy and he left. I unwrapped the *Princess in Berlin* and propped her up on the upper bunk, leaning against the bulkhead.

The ship was throbbing now. I could hear the gongs that meant the visitors had to leave. I desperately wanted fresh air — and a drink.

> *Oh, say, does that star-spangled banner yet wa-ave,*
> *O'er the la-and of the free*
> *And the home of the brave!*

When I reached the open deck — the forecastle this time — the band was finishing the anthem and I glanced squinting up into the sunshine at the second mast, where an American flag was snapping in the wind. I had not heard that song for a long time. . . .

The gangplanks had been removed, the hawsers had been released, a couple of tugboats began to ease us away from the landing out of the basin, into the main stream of the Elbe. The tugs belched coal smoke. I was overwhelmed with a memory of Schloss Havelblick.

Foghorn. People shouting and waving.

> *Deutschland, Deutschland, über Alles,*
> *Über Alles in der Welt. . . .*

Quite a lot of people sang along. A handsome woman in a black fur coat stood alone, holding a handkerchief to her eyes.

Foghorn. The tugs fell back, S.S. *Albert Ballin* was under power, moving through the brilliant cloudless win-

ter afternoon, moving swiftly through the enormous maze
of the harbor — cranes and warehouses and landing
piers, shipyards and drydocks and grain elevators; ocean
liners and freighters and tankers and tugboats pulling
trains of barges, ferryboats, carrying railroad cars . . .
foghorns, coal smoke, seagulls, gray water with chunks
of ice bobbing. . . .

I wished the band would stop playing, but I had the
feeling that this band on this ship on this night would
never stop. I wished that somebody had not taught me
the words to all these songs:

> *Hamburg ist ein schönes Städtchen*
> *Siehst du wohl!*
> *Weil es an der Elbe liegt*
> *Siehst du wohl!*
>
> *Drinnen wohnen schöne Mädchen*
> *Aber keine Jungfer nicht,*
> *Siehst du wohl! . . .*
> *Denn es ist ja so schwer*
> *Aus der Heimat zu geh'n*
> *Wenn die Hoffnung nicht wär*
> *Auf ein Wieder-Wiederseh'n*
> *Lebe wohl,*
> *Lebe wohl,*
> *Auf Wiederseh'n!*

"It's four hours to the sea," somebody said. "Might as
well have lunch before it gets rough."

I wanted to speak to the woman who was crying but I
couldn't. I went to look for a bar.

I wasn't paying attention to them, at first. I was drinking another Scotch-and-water, feeling it burn, trying to
concentrate on that, trying not to hear two Americans on
my right topping each other's inflation anecdotes — "No,
but listen to *this:* we rented the whole Schloss — food,
servants, wine, *everything* — for twenty-five bucks,
and . . ." from my left came the words "verfluchte
Schande."

It wasn't the words themselves, which mean something
like "damned shame"; it was the tone — soft, almost a

whisper, but loaded with such fury that I turned to regard the two Germans on my left.

They were drinking beer, they were staring down into
their glasses, and the verfluchte Schande obviously had
nothing to do with the boasting on my right. They were
absorbed in something else. Both looked like ordinary
middle-aged business types: celluloid collars; slightly
threadbare black suits; vests; wedding rings. One had
long hair parted in the middle and a pince-nez; the other
had a crew-cut and a neck that bulged over his collar.
There was nothing special about them, nothing sinister;
neither had that face I had learned to recognize, that
"Offiziersgesicht" described by one witness to Rathenau's
murder, that cold-eyed, handsome, slightly demented
look of the Freikorps Epp, the Freikorps Rossbach, the
Marinebrigade Ehrhardt — and the Stosstrupp Adolf
Hitler. These were just two traveling salesmen, hoping to
make deals for German goods in New York and Chicago
and St. Louis. . . .

"It isn't much of a ship," said the crew-cut, very softly.
"But it's our first new liner since the War — and they
name it after a Jew!"

"*Na ja,*" said the pince-nez with something of a shrug.
"He built the HAPAG, you know. They must have been
under pressure —"

"Of course they were under pressure! From the bankers
who put up the money —"

"*Mr. Ellis, please? Mr. Peter Ellis?*" A bellboy stepped
into the compartment, shouting.

The boy stood aside to let me in, but there was hardly
room: Cabin 242 already contained two uniformed ship's
officers and a very tall very fat young man who was busily
trying to wrap my *Princess in Berlin* back into the brown
paper. He had a pink acne-pitted complexion and slicked-
down black hair; he wore an expensive blue pinstripe suit
with a white carnation.

"Simply unbelievable . . . ," he was saying when they
all turned to look at me.

"Mr. Peter Ellis?" asked the assistant purser.

"Right."

The deck officer began: "Herr Ansbach here has made
an accusation —"

"This picture within the last two weeks by the firm of Joseph Ansbach and Co. to Professor Max Liebermann was sold!" bellowed Herr Ansbach in English. He stopped trying to wrap the picture and now faced me, his hands on his hips. "You have heard of the art gallery Joseph Ansbach in Berlin, my dear sir? Potsdamer Strasse 101?"

Silence.

I guess I was a little drunk by now. Maybe I was still thinking about the voices in the bar. Maybe I was ashamed of myself for running off behind the bellboy instead of saying something to them. At any rate, I was in no mood to bother with this clown.

"You know my name is Peter Ellis," I said, in German.

More silence.

"I painted that picture, but it's not finished."

Young Herr Ansbach stooped to examine my Princess, who was now lying half-wrapped on the bureau. The assistant purser and the deck officer leaned forward too.

"Hmm. Ellis 'twenty-three.'" Ansbach still insisted on speaking English.

"That's not my signature because it isn't finished. Fritz Falke put my name on it and sold it to your gallery. And kept the money, I might add."

"Fritz Falke you know?" Ansbach thoughtfully picked his nose. "Ellis, *Ellis,* yes . . . the American friend, yes? Always the same girls . . . *So!* But *this* picture, all the same, was personally sold by my father to Professor Liebermann, who does not buy paintings every day, I can tell you, and therefore it is the . . . it is the ownership of Professor Liebermann —"

I told them what happened. In German.

"You have of this documentary proof?" demanded Ansbach.

"No, I do not have of this documentary proof, but I have the picture." I really had enough by now — or maybe too much — and it all came bursting out, in English, at these three startled men who thought they had caught a thief. "Are you accusing me of having stolen this picture — my own unfinished picture — from Professor Liebermann? From Baron von Waldstein? Because if you are, I'm going to a lawyer the day we land in New York, and I'm going to sue you for slander, and if the Hamburg-Amerika Line assists you in this matter I'm going to sue them too, and when my lawyer produces affidavits from

Baron von Waldstein and Professor Liebermann, you are going to look like a god-damned fool, Ansbach!"

Sometimes I think that Germans *like* to be yelled at. The atmosphere changed instantly.

"Herr Ansbach," said the assistant purser, "perhaps it would be advisable for you to consider Mr. Ellis's position during the voyage —"

"Perhaps you are right," said Ansbach, speaking German to them. "I will take the matter under advisement, I can send my father a telegram from Southampton. . . ."

The deck officer turned to the assistant purser. "In view of this . . . situation, perhaps some rearrangements of cabins . . . ?"

The assistant purser rolled his eyes. "Herr Müller, if you please! You know the ship is full! We would have to move somebody else in here —"

"Gentlemen," said Ansbach, who had been staring at me with an entirely new expression, "perhaps Mr. Ellis and I can discuss the matter alone for a few minutes? If we desire a change we will notify you before dinner. Thank you for your help."

Visibly relieved, they bowed, withdrew, and closed the door.

Ansbach was still staring at me. "Ellis? Baron von Waldstein? You are the fellow . . . in the newspapers . . . with your revolver you shot the Nazi brother Keith . . . the Cain and Abel murder?"

What could I say?

"Mensch!" bellowed Ansbach, moving forward and grabbing my hand. "You are a god-damned *hero*, you know that? I wish they would shoot every single one of those swine!"

"Well, there are a couple in the bar, if you want to begin."

"You have your revolver?" he asked, sotto voce, apparently in earnest.

"No, I don't have my revolver, and your government doesn't think I'm a hero. They threw me out of Germany."

"I say you are a hero, I say I am proud to know you, I say I will be proud to share this cabin with you, and I apologize for the fuss about this lady here. All right?"

"All right."

"All right. Let us have lunch."

Of course it was too late for lunch. They didn't want to serve us in the Second Class Dining Room, but after Ansbach slipped the headwaiter a dollar bill, they did.

"God-damned second class! With my father I never traveled in the Second Class, it is the god-damned inflation, what it has done to our liquid capital you would not believe. . . ."

I wasn't hungry. I ordered a ham sandwich and another Scotch-and-water. He ordered potato soup and smoked eel with cucumbers and Schweinsrippchen with red cabbage and half a bottle of Moselle, which he cut with seltzer water.

He talked as he ate and drank his way through. He was going to New York to establish a branch of his father's art gallery. He wanted to practice his English.

"I remember now your other paintings quite well. They are carefully done and pleasing to the public."

"Thank you."

"You mentioned Falke. I carry in my luggage six or ten of Falke's pen-and-ink drawings. You know them: fat naked whores, fat ugly businessmen, officers with the faces of pigs, beggars without legs —"

"Yes. I know them."

"You think I sell a lot of Falke's work in New York?"

"No."

"No, I think so, too. But in some future time, he may be recognized. You think? A picture of our time?"

"Yes."

"Yes, I too. We show them sometimes, and we wait. In the meantime, I have many other pictures, very beautiful pictures. . . . I could sell your Princess in five minutes."

"She's not finished."

"All right, finish her. You have other pictures? You have other pictures like those girls on the bed?" He looked up over my shoulder. "Yes, what is it?"

I turned to see a bellboy, the same one who had called me out of the bar. He was holding a small parcel, wrapped in brown paper and tied with black string.

"Mister Ellis, Cabin 242?"

"Yes."

He handed me the package. "From the purser's office, sir. Delivered by a bank messenger just before we sailed —"

Ansbach raised his voice: "And it's taken all this time —"

"That's all right, thank you." I gave the boy a coin and began to tear at the strings, because I recognized the handwriting. I was clumsy and it took me a moment to get the wrapping off.

"Oh, wonderful," said Ansbach. "Someone has sent you a bon voyage bottle. What's in it?"

"A sailboat," I said, handing him the bottle, then tearing open the blue envelope.

"That is Schleswig-Holstein on the right, the province of Hannover on the left . . . that next lighthouse I think is Brunsbüttel, where the Kiel Canal comes in. When we turn there we enter the estuary —"

August Ansbach, bundled in a long plaid greatcoat with a fur collar, was marching me around the deck, pointing out the sights as we steamed through the darkening winter afternoon, past mile after mile of snow-covered flatlands, past villages, past lighthouses. . . .

The band was playing again.

> *There's a long, long trail a-winding. . . .*
> *Into my Amytal dreams . . .*

What an odd song for them to be playing, I thought. I was not thinking very clearly anymore, which was the point, and I wasn't steady on my feet, either.

August Ansbach wanted me to take a nap.

"Look here, this is New Year's Eve, you know, Sylvesterabend. You have a tuxedo? I tell you what we do: we get some sleep now, then we put on our tuxedos and we — how do you say that? Steal? We steal into First Class, we meet a couple of nice girls, we dance, we drink champagne. . . ."

I told him that was about the last thing I wanted to do.

"Oh yes, is what you need, my friend. I will persuade you. Meeting ladies, is easier by two. . . . In any case, I want a little sleep now. Don't stay up here too long, or you freeze. Even with whisky inside!" He clapped me on the back and walked away.

We cleared the light at Brunsbüttel and moved across the wide estuary of the Elbe. The band on the promenade deck fell silent; passengers and musicians all had to rest before the exertions of Sylvesterabend.

"Warum denn weinen she had written *wenn man auseinandergeht,*
Wenn an der nächsten Ecke schon ein Andrer steht?"

"Why cry? Why not? There is no one else at the next corner — no one else I want so much — and there never will be, so is it all right to cry?"
No address, no date, no signature.

I walked as far forward as I could get and leaned against the railing, feeling the bottle hard in the outside pocket of my overcoat. I smelled coal smoke. I smelled the sea. I stood there for a long time as the sun sank, as the S.S. *Albert Ballin* passed Cuxhaven where the land ends and rounded the lightships marking the channel. We were out of the Elbe now. Turning west, turning toward the last gleam of sunlight, the ship began to roll a little in the North Sea swell, rolling me into a new year and a lonesome life, rolling me home.

———

On August 31, 1935, the Board of Directors of the Hamburg-Amerika Line announced that henceforth the S.S. *Albert Ballin* would carry the name S.S. *Hansa.*

The best
in modern fiction from
BALLANTINE